John Watson was ⌐⌐⌐⌐⌐⌐⌐⌐⌐⌐⌐⌐⌐⌐⌐ ⌐ndon and began his working life as a messenger boy in an advertising agency. He progressed slowly up the ladder as a copywriter for direct response advertising. He founded his first company in 1978 at the age of twenty-nine and his second three years later, which he sold with a turnover of £100 million.

He lives in Sussex with his wife and two childen.

Also by John Watson
THE IRON MAN

THE FINAL ACT

John Watson

WARNER BOOKS

A *Warner* Book

First published in Great Britain in 2000 by Warner Books

Copyright © John Robert Watson 2000

Extract from *War Beneath the Sea* reproduced by
kind permission of Peter Padfield and John Murray
(Publishers) Ltd.

A CIP catalogue record for this book
is available from the British Library.

ISBN 0 7515 2557 X

Typeset by Solidus (Bristol) Limited
Printed and bound in Great Britain by
Clays Ltd, St Ives plc

Warner Books
A Division of
Little, Brown and Company (UK)
Brettenham House
Lancaster Place
London WC2E 7EN

1942: ON BOARD U-333

Kapitänleutnant Peter Cremer arrived on the coast of Florida on 4 May, thankful to find the shipping channel marked out for him with buoys as in peacetime. As darkness fell he surfaced to an astonishing scene and allowed his men up to the bridge one at a time to share it while breathing in the scented air from the holiday paradise. After blacked-out Europe it seemed a different world. The buoys winked; powerful rays from the Jupiter Inlet Lighthouse circled repeatedly seawards; beams from car headlights followed one another along the coast roads past illuminated frontages and neon signs of hotels whose names could be read through glasses, and further down the coast Miami and its suburbs cast an incandescent glow on the underside of the night clouds. 'Before this sea of light, against this footlight glare of a carefree New World, were passing the silhouettes of ships recognisable in every detail and sharp as outlines in a sales catalogue.'

War Beneath The Sea, Peter Padfield

During the Second World War, almost every major city of Europe, Russia and Japan, and thousands of towns and villages in North Africa and the Far East, suffered damage ranging from almost complete devastation to a few burnt-out huts. The nations engaged in the bitter hostilities saw their economies wrecked and their countries reduced to, in some cases, near-medieval subsistence. For five years the destruction piled ruins on the ruins. Once-prosperous capitals were reduced to desolate smoking rubble-fields, stinking with unburied dead, where starving refugees scrabbled a twilight existence in a human disaster which makes any of today's African famines, or Balkan attempts at genocide, pale into insignificance.

Yet one participant – the biggest of them all – fared very differently from the others. Though its soldiers and sailors and airmen died in their hundreds of thousands, and many more thousands suffered the grief and sorrow that the rest of the peoples of the world shared, the vast majority of the civilian population of the United States of America not only saw little of the war; they saw nothing of the war at all.

From the outbreak of the conflict to its final day, not a single bomb, shell or bullet landed on the American mainland.

But it was not for want of trying...

The Main Characters

Otto Heine, born in Hamburg and now living in New York, an old man

Christian Bach, a young American of German descent, grandson of the *Hindenburg*'s Captain Erich Bach

Greenland, 2000:

Billy Tan, an American financier

Louise DeAngelis, a TV reporter

Wiltshire, 2000:

Bethe Fischer, Deputy State Prosecutor, German Government

Lillian Beasley, retired Royal Navy Intelligence clerk

Hamburg/Berlin 1945, and on the Hindenburg:

Kapitan sur See **Erich Bach**, commander of the *Hindenburg*, grandfather of Christian

Admiral **Sluys**, Bach's superior in Berlin

Korvettenkapitan **Schiller**, second-in-command to Bach

Oberleutnant sur See **Bruller**, navigation officer
Oberleutnant sur See **Ecke**, engineering officer
Oberleutnant sur See **Jensch**, communications officer
Kapitan leutnant **Kinzel**, artillery officer
Leutnant sur See **Moehle**, junior officer in charge of
    radar – Sluys's spy on the ship
Schnee, chief petty officer in charge of the young Otto
    Heine
Rois, ship's cook

On board HMS Trent, 1945:

Captain **Brocklehurst** ('Badger'), commander of HMS
    Trent
Lieutenant **Bill Burrows**, second-in-command

On board the deep-sea salvage tug Zuider, Greenland, 2000:

Captain **Jos De Wit**

PROLOGUE

NEW YORK CITY
19 JULY 2000

Otto Heine watched the news report on a vintage Zenith television, first with a sense of sheer disbelief and then with an increasing sense of excitement. For the only time since he had come to America all those years ago, his one great dream looked like coming true – even if somebody else was making it happen, even if he himself was not there, and even if he was too goddamn old for it to make a great deal of difference to his life anyway.

But the battleship *Hindenburg* and its strange story had played too big a part in the life of Otto Heine for him to do anything other than sit there watching, bemused, as a sleek, wealthy American Oriental, Billy Tan, spoke confidently from the hazy screen about his plan to drag the old hulk of the ship out of the Greenland ice and haul it home to America.

Heine lived on his own in a small apartment in the basement of a run-down block on New York's upper West Side which he had owned for twenty years, though how he came by such a property remained a mystery that even he would never talk about: the rumour was that it was the payment of a lucky gambling debt. Heine was convinced that one day a wealthy property developer would knock on his door and offer him millions of dollars for the dump, but so far nobody had. He had lived with such hopes all his life. He was seventy-four years old, but didn't look it. He was small, wiry, more active than most men ten, maybe twenty, years younger, and still had a full head of jet-black hair, even if the jet-black was not altogether as natural as it once had been.

That day, as usual, had been spent in Zauber's bar, where he could play cards with the small group of other Germans who still remembered the old days. Today, he had won $36 from them, a good day in Otto's book, and had left them grumbling as he made his way home. He locked and bolted the door behind him to settle down for the night.

There had never been a Frau Heine. Not that Otto didn't like women. In his younger days he had liked them too much, so much so that he had found it impossible to really settle down. There was always someone – and something – better, around the next corner, as far as Otto was concerned. In his younger days he had an alarming ability to attract women, which surprised other men because Otto was neither tall, nor unusually handsome, nor even rich. There was just something about him that women found impossible to resist; a charming mixture of rebel and little boy, a devilish streak, massive self-confidence – and, of course, his vivid blue eyes. Even now, at his age, he had not lost interest in women. It was just that the opportunities these days were much rarer than before. But being alone didn't worry him. Otto Heine had been a loner all his life.

He went to the oversized fridge in the small kitchen and took out a bottle of beer. He would only drink bottled Czech *Budvar*. He opened the cap with a hiss, sat down on the worn armchair and switched on the old TV. He had so many channels that he never watched one of them for more than a few minutes at a time. Most of them were rubbish. The sports channels were good, if there was anything other than baseball on them; he had lived in America since 1945, had learned English and even saluted the flag on odd occasions, but he could never understand baseball's attractions. He flicked through with the big remote control.

The same rubbish. Game shows with idiots. Chat shows with more idiots. Adverts for car showrooms and stores.

He flicked past one of the news channels. Another interview with someone he'd never heard of. And then a shiver ran down Otto's spine and he stopped dead.

There had been a caption on the screen. A single word that brought back a tidal wave of memories – or had he mis-read it?

He flicked back instantly. God in heaven! The caption was still there, run across the bottom of the screen, underneath the plump features of an Oriental with shiny black hair:

Live from the wreck of the Hindenburg

He stopped breathing for a second, perhaps a little longer. A flood of adrenalin coursed through his body, tightening his stomach. The bottle in his hand dribbled from the opened top. With his eyes fixed on the screen, he leaned slowly back in the old armchair.

The *Hindenburg*. All those years ago ... those bloody battles ... those idiots who tried to kill us all. And the gold, the gold, millions of dollars' worth of gold – still,

Otto Heine was sure, lying there after all this time. Did they know about the gold, all eight and three-quarter tons of it?

Otto Heine had spent his life since arriving in America dreaming about what was on that ship. It was worth a lot then; God knows what it would be worth today. Millions at least. Tens of millions. Hundreds of millions. He knew where it was, what it looked like, and he knew it was still sitting there, ice-cold and gleaming. Since he had fought his way across the icy sea, into Canada, and then quietly slipped across the border, that gold had haunted his waking hours and his dreaming ones too. He was rich, hugely rich – Otto Heine was undoubtedly one of the richest men in America. The only trouble was that his money was stuck on that evil old wreck which had so very nearly killed him. All he had to do was make his way to the wreck to rescue his money. But in the fifty-five years that he had dreamed about it, he had never found a way. Once – in the Seventies, when interest in the ship was high – he thought he had found someone to run an expedition. But they cried off – financial reasons, so they said – and he had to let them go because he would never reveal what the ship concealed deep inside its rusting guts.

And so Otto Heine sat alone in his small apartment, watching the Oriental talk confidently about his plan. He actually wanted to rescue the wreck, and as he listened Heine's heart thumped and his small, wrinkled hands clenched and unclenched quickly.

Did they know about the gold? Who was this Billy Tan anyway? And when would they get it out?

As he watched, and the cameraman zoomed in once more on that familiar, brooding shadow, Otto Heine slowly developed a plan in his mind, his last chance to avenge the years of poverty. That ship had nearly killed him. It had stolen him from Germany and forced him into America. It had offered him the chance to get rich and then taken it away, turning him against his will into some goddamned hero for all of five minutes, when all he wanted was either to escape or get his hands on the bullion hidden deep within the vessel.

No, they did not know about the gold, he could see that from Tan's face and from the way of him. If they knew about it, they would be more secretive. Only a fool would brag about the wreck on TV if he knew it contained such a treasure – bringing every rascal from a thousand miles around, most of them governments. All they wanted was to drag it out – it would take just three weeks – and turn it into some kind of show. Otto smiled: a tourist attraction, no less!

He carried on watching until the girl handed back to the studio and a groomed, sports-jacketed black man assured the viewers that they would stay with the story for the next few weeks.

Otto sat and thought for a full five minutes, oblivious to the TV. Then he slowly rose from his chair, his mind filling with plans. Could he do it? He walked over to his small kitchen table, took down the calendar that hung above, and sat down with it in front of him. Yes, he thought after a few moments; yes, it's possible. Within three weeks. And why not? He had done crazier things in his time. And for God's sake, this was his last chance anyway. Whenever would it happen again – at least, while Otto Heine was still alive and had breath in his body?

He hung the calendar back on the wall. He made some coffee, thick and strong, and kept on thinking. The only problem, my dear Otto, is how the fuck are you actually going to get there? How much money do I have? Maybe three or four hundred dollars at most until those bastards pay their next lot of rent, and half of them will be late.

The problem puzzled him for some time. Finally he climbed slowly into the sagging double bed and closed his eyes, but sleep was not going to come – as, these days, it seemed not to do. There was the ship. There was the gold. There was somebody, at long last, getting to the ship. But there was no Otto.

And then he quietly sat up and switched on the single dim light. He had a smile on his face. It was easy. Otto had the one thing that this Billy Tan wanted. Otto Heine knew the story of the ship. Why it had set sail from Hamburg. What its mission really was. Billy Tan would want to know all of these things, Otto was sure, totally sure. He would want to know the full story of why the *Hindenburg* came to be scuttled in the ice-pack.

He would love to hear the story from Otto Heine. Because, of course, it was Otto Heine who had scuttled the ship and left it rusting there in the first place.

1

OFF THE GREENLAND COAST
9 JULY 2000

The ship had lain there, growing streaks of rust like lichen over its monstrous hull and its jagged super-structure, for fifty-five silent years. The ice would creep up the shallow inlet every September and crawl over the hulk, shrouding it with a white crust for the long Arctic winter, and then would reluctantly retreat in May, leaving the ship exposed and naked. Only in the severest winters would the entire vessel disappear. Most of the time, the upperworks – the top of the huge funnel and the topmost sections of the mast – would remain visible, sticking through the ice-cap like temporary grave markers waiting for the marble headstone to arrive. These days, as the ice seemed to arrive later and disappear earlier, even more of the ship stayed above the ice; the last winter had left the top of one of the huge turrets clear of the snow for the first time.

The ship lay on the sea bed. But the bed of the inlet was only thirty feet down at the deepest, less at the landward end, and so the vessel rested with much of the hull and the entire superstructure above the cold, clear water. The sea bed was soft gravel. Over the years, the massive weight of the ship had pushed itself into the bottom, tilting gently to one side year after year, until now the top of the mast leaned over at twenty-four degrees.

In the worst winters, the ice sheet had crept over the whole vessel. It had squeezed and gripped the ship with all of its strength, but nothing could crush the monster. The sides of the hull were thick armour plate, Krupp's finest cemented steel, designed to withstand the massive power of several tons of high-explosive shell smashing into it at high velocity. The ice assaulted the ship year after year, but only the superstructure areas where armour plating was regarded as wasteful were affected – and even then, what damage was done had mostly happened before the ship was abandoned.

The vessel lay bow first in the inlet, so that its fore rose into the air, with the stern in the deeper water. At over 823 feet long, the stern was out into the sea, protruding from the inlet as though the berth was just a little too small. The forward part of the ship was therefore slightly better protected than the stern; the two big turrets forward of the bridge each still carried their two huge guns, although the hydraulics which moved them had long ago failed and they now drooped at their lowest elevations, resting like felled trees, those in the forward turret nearly touching the leaning deck.

The rust had gripped the old steelwork and turned the once-grey battleship into a dusty red. But the Arctic air, always so cold, could hold little moisture, and so the damage was not so severe as if the ship had come to its last resting-place further south. The more sheltered parts had survived the best. The big turrets, highest out of the water, were streaked and stained on the outside, but the inside was protected from the elements by turret doors which had remained closed for fifty-five years. Much of the machinery to drive the guns, crafted by Germany's best engineers from stainless steel and copper and brass, remained almost as good as the day when the ship was hastily scuttled.

The exterior, though, bore signs of damage that no ice-pack could inflict. There were several large holes on the deck; jagged sheets of steel gaped upwards, pulled back as though assaulted by a huge can opener. Parts of the superstructure were missing, and other parts were also holed. Underneath the rust stains almost all the forward part of the vessel around the bridge area was blackened and distorted from some great heat. Even the grey slabs of armour covering the sides of the hull were blemished: in some places, the hull walls had yard-wide flakes, almost circular, gouged out from them. The bow itself was mostly missing, as though it had been wrenched away from the body of the vessel. Ripped and shredded curls of steel were all that remained, other than the part of the bow that was once below water but now protruded up on to the shingle beach in the summers when the ice receded. Nearby a length of anchor chain, each link six feet across, hung down the side of the ship. But there was nothing on the end of it.

Even the parts of the ship that were unscathed had an unfinished look to them. Areas of the deck towards the stern had plates missing; there were signs that wooden planks had covered the holes, but these had long since rotted. And there were no turrets at the back of the vessel. The two big circular holes where the turrets would have sat were covered with badly welded thin steel plating which in places had rusted right through. Portholes were cut into the superstructure, but seemed never to have had any-thing in them. Once they had been covered with canvas against the elements, but like the wood, this too had long since vanished.

There was no name on the ship. No numbers, no flags, no obvious clue to its identity.

For the first ten years of its life in the ice it had lain unknown. The inlet was on the western Greenland coast, high inside the northerly latitudes where the ice crusted the ocean every year, and no ship or aircraft came anywhere near it until, one morning in August 1955, a US Navy survey vessel spotted a strange echo on its radar and tried to move in closer. Although the inlet itself was free of ice, the sea around it remained, as it usually did, almost solid with ice floes. The US ship was no icebreaker. It flew off a helicopter for a brief reconnaissance; they took a few pictures and showed them to the astonished captain and officers.

But the US Navy was less impressed. It was still just ten years after the war, and the waters of every ocean were littered with wrecks. The biggest ones were simply blown up if they represented a threat to navigation. Anything else was just not interesting. Thus the reports of the wreck of a big battleship in the ice pack were simply filed: it wasn't in anyone's way, so let it rust in peace like hundreds of similar wrecks around the world.

Spotted occasionally by over-flying aircraft and the odd ship, in 1968 the vessel was provisionally identified as a large German battleship: everyone else's war junk had been accounted for. There was some doubt as to which one it was: the mystery was finally solved four years later when an obscure British naval historian suggested that it was the wreck of the *Hindenburg*, the unfinished sister-ship of the *Bismarck* which, according to rumours, had sailed from Hamburg in the last days of the war on a mission that remained a mystery.

The ship began to attract more attention from then onwards. The National Geographic Society decided to mount an expedition there in 1973, complete with film crew. Interest in such war relics was beginning to grow. But the expedition was defeated, not by the ice but finally by finance: the cash was simply not available.

There were three separate expeditions between 1973 and 1982. The first managed to arrive in the middle of one of the worst summer storms that the region had ever known. They returned with some blurred footage of the top of the superstructure. The second expedition was put together by a shadowy, ill-organised group who were more interested in loot than anything else. They reached the ship, spent a day inside it, carried away what relics there were of obvious value, and retreated to sell their haul on the black market. The third expedition was run by the Russians. Although Greenland was regarded as clearly within the American sphere of influence, a Russian icebreaker broke through the ice one May day and put ashore a full crew who spent three days on the wreck until they opened a steel door and discovered that one of the magazines was still full of menacing grey shells, and beat a hasty retreat. But they finally managed to clarify the identity and the fate of the vessel. It was indeed the *Hindenburg*, and although the hull was intact the ship was full of water. The story slowly seeped through to the West.

The world had started to develop a greater interest in the relics of war. First, more expeditions were planned. Then, according to a government official in

Germany, the ship was a war grave and couldn't be touched. This was annulled a few months later when the Russians confirmed that the vessel was empty. No bodies, no war grave. Then the academics started to raise funds. The only ships of that era – German ones, at least – were on the bottom of the sea. The *Hindenburg* was therefore, they argued, unique in history, and should be rescued from the ice.

And then the conservationists got involved. They objected to sending in teams of salvage people with the associated mess. Worse, they proclaimed, the whole thing – still full of high-explosive shells – would blow itself sky-high and litter the ice-cap with rubbish. Next, the German government came back into the fray. The last thing it wanted to see was this relic of Nazi Germany put on public parade. The ship is still ours, it insisted. It wasn't wrecked but scuttled. We want it left alone.

But nobody took any notice of them, and expeditions were still being put together. One film crew managed to get enough footage to make a long documentary, and, shells or not, they ventured inside the hulk. But the producers realised that a rusting wreck lacked the drama to make more than ten minutes of it truly interesting. And there was no archive footage of the *Hindenburg* in its prime – the 'before and after' sequence that would bring it all to life. The short film sold well enough as a sensationalised account of an old ship, but it failed to add anything to what a few people already knew.

That, for a while, seemed to be as much interest as the old ship could muster. Everything started to go quiet. In the later 1980s and early 1990s, the world had other things on its mind, and *Hindenburg* listed a little more, rusted a little more, and looked as though it would end its days locked for ever in the ice, a distant curiosity.

Until the day Billy Tan and his expedition arrived.

*

It was supposed to be summer and the sun was shining over the rear deck of the MV *Zuider*, but Billy Tan still needed a thick coat and gloves as he waited for the TV crew to get themselves ready. The big Dutch salvage tug was anchored in a gentle swell five miles off the coast; this year, the ice was thinner than ever and the ice sheet between them and the distant wreck of the *Hindenburg* – clearly visible as a jagged black outline – had broken up like a sheet of floating crazy paving.

Billy Tan was no stranger to TV appearances, but he still couldn't work out why it always seemed to take half an hour for the cameraman and the sound-man to sort themselves out. If they worked for him he'd have fired them long before the cameraman finally shouted out 'stable' and the girl turned her bored face into a sudden, brilliant smile as she faced the camera. She came on with the lights, thought Billy, still waiting patiently as she went through her carefully rehearsed opening lines.

'You're joining me on board the salvage vessel *Zuider*, on one of the most extraordinary expeditions of modern times. We're in the far north, beyond the Arctic Circle, and behind me' – Billy could see the cameraman move the camera on his shoulder slightly and press a button which made the lens zoom in – 'lies the wreck of the *Hindenburg*, once the pride of Hitler's Navy. The old ship has been lying here, covered in ice, for over fifty years. But today, the *Hindenburg* faces a new future. Soon it is to be dragged from the ice and towed back to Washington, under an extraordinary new idea dreamed up by an extraordinary man, the well-known Billy Tan ...' and the camera moved back to focus on Billy's face. 'But before that, we'll take a quick break. Stay watching for one of the strangest stories you'll *ever* hear,' and the cameraman curtly nodded. The smile on the girl's face suddenly switched off, and without even talking to Billy she turned away to look at her notes.

'How long?' asked Billy of the cameraman, who was fiddling with the controls. The cold made the machine more delicate than usual.

'Three minutes. Gotta pay the wages. You want some powder? Your nose is shining.'

An assistant came over and dabbed something perfumed on Billy Tan's nose. The cameraman nodded and carried on fiddling.

'OK, you people. Thirty seconds,' commanded the reporter.

The cameraman heaved the big Sony on to his shoulder once more. The girl watched a small monitor on the floor for her cue from the New York control room. Suddenly the smile returned and she started talking again.

'Welcome back to Greenland and the wreck of the German battleship *Hindenburg*. With me this evening is Billy Tan, well-known Wall Street whizzkid and until recently the owner of Technology Park in California, which he has just sold for nearly one billion dollars. Billy, what's all this about?' The cameraman suddenly moved the camera to Billy Tan's face.

Her introduction left out more than it said. Billy Tan was born in San Francisco of Chinese parents in the early 1950s. He had gone to college, graduated by the skin of his teeth, then moved east to New York where his blunt regard for financial niceties soon had him earning large sums on Wall Street, as well as the interest of the SEC. He got out just before the great collapse in 1991, with something more than $5 million, which he then invested in a site near Paolo Alto to build a theme park based around computers. He managed to persuade IBM and Microsoft, amongst others, to donate various historical relics, which he combined with a sense of showmanship to turn it into an extraordinarily successful venture. By 1998 he already had several offers, and he had just pocketed nearly $100 million in cash from a large French company. The $1 billion the reporter was talking about represented the turnover of the business, for Christ's sake, not what he had got for it.

'Not quite a billion, Miss DeAngelis. Quite a bit less, I'm afraid.'

'I'm so sorry,' she gushed. 'But still a lot, I take it?'

But Billy Tan was not going to fall into that old trap. 'Enough, thank you, Miss DeAngelis,' he replied with a sunny smile.

She ignored him anyway. 'So, Mr Tan, you have a plan to rescue this old battleship and bring it back to America. Is that correct?'

'That's right. The *Hindenburg* was the unfinished sister-ship to the famous *Bismarck*. It left Hamburg one night at the end of the war and disappeared for a while, then was caught at sea but escaped, and finally ended up wrecked here in the ice, where it's been for the last fifty-five years. It's the only survivor of Germany's past naval might. I intend to bring it out of the ice, sail it across the Atlantic and bring it up to Chesapeake Bay where I will be opening the most amazing theme park ever seen.'

'That's quite a plan. But how on earth do you

propose to get the ship out of the ice?' The girl radiated a wide, toothy grin that made Tan, who had been interviewed too often, deeply suspicious.

'It's not all that difficult. I've hired the best salvage people in the world, the Dutch De Wit company, and they'll help me. The hull is in good shape, and should float well once we pump it out. There's a bit of damage to the bow, but the watertight compartments are fine. We wait for the year's highest tide, which is in three weeks' time, and haul it off with one of De Wit's deep-sea salvage tugs. Then we simply tow it home. I don't expect any real problems, or none that we can't deal with.'

'I see. So what do you say, Mr Tan, to those people who think the *Hindenburg* should be left alone in dignity?'

The question caught Tan on the hop, even though he was familiar with the interview technique of asking the nice questions first and then bowling a nasty one just as the interviewee began to relax. 'What people?' he asked, surprised, and then realised he'd fallen right in. But it was too late.

'Oh, Mr Tan, I'm surprised you don't know. There are many people who see this ship as a war relic, maybe even a war grave, that shouldn't be looted for commercial gain.'

Billy Tan gritted his teeth. Smile, smile, he told himself. 'Well, that's absolutely right. We aim to treat this ship as a real piece of history. What we want to do is rescue and restore it instead of leaving it here to rot away in the ice. We have too much respect for the ship to let that happen.'

But the girl, seeing that Billy was fighting back, changed tack suddenly. In truth, the story itself bored her rigid. Her job was only to provoke her subject so that she created a good interview, with some real sparks flying. She hoped someone big from one of the networks would be watching and, as far as she was concerned, this was a great chance. Working for this under-funded cable channel was not her idea of fame and glory.

'And what about the legal position, Mr Tan? Under American law it's illegal to tamper with Navy wrecks. And I think you've had a bit of trouble with the government in the past. It that true?'

Fuck the bitch. Billy gritted his teeth. 'No, not at all. Like almost everyone else on Wall Street, I was happy to discuss business matters with the authorities and give them my fullest co-operation. There was never any question of it being more than that, of course,' and Billy laughed. It was totally untrue, but she didn't know that.

'But what about the law on wrecks, Mr Tan?' She had now adopted a serious, concerned look to foil Tan's sudden laugh. You're not taking this seriously, she managed to say without a word.

Billy paused. 'Well, we've looked into that carefully. It's a German wreck on Greenland territory, and so of course it doesn't come under American law. Our advice is that the ship is basically owned by no one, as it *is* a wreck.'

'So just anyone can come and tear it apart?'

'No. It simply means that we're within our rights to come and try to rescue this great ship for everyone to see.'

'You have some good lawyers, then, Mr Tan?'

'No better than your network's lawyers, I daresay.'

She was running this one dry. Better go back to the story. 'So, how exactly do you plan to do all of this?' she asked, smiling once more.

Billy relaxed. He'd survived for now, at least. They spent the next three minutes discussing the technicalities of the rescue operation: how the ship would be sealed against the sea; how tow-lines would be attached; how big pumps would empty the *Hindenburg* of fifty-five years' worth of seepage, melted snow and rainwater; how the massive high-tech salvage tug they were standing on would haul the ship off the shingle and pull it back out through the ice cleared away by the huge Russian icebreaker on its way to the scene.

Then, into his stride, Billy Tan spoke eloquently about his plans for the theme park, a celebration of the Navy and of the war where the *Hindenburg*, moored off Annapolis in the Chesapeake Bay, would be the centre-piece, and how this would be the biggest attraction ever seen on the east coast.

The interviewer let him run and then, just to prove she was in charge, cut him off in mid-flow and turned to the camera. 'Thank you, Billy Tan. We'll be reporting from the scene of the *Hindenburg* wreck up here in the far north same time tomorrow evening. This is Louise DeAngelis on board the *Zuider*, and now back to New York.' Her smile got wider as she finished. She froze, grin in place, for ten seconds. Then the cameraman nodded.

The broadcast was over.

'Hey, Billy, nothing personal in those questions, you know,' said the interviewer as she buttoned up her coat, the smile gone and replaced by her hard professional frown.

'No, nothing personal, Miss DeAngelis. Next time I'll throw you off the fucking ship.'

'Oh, come on. It's just good TV, you know that.'

'Sure, no problem.'

'Great. Now, where can a girl get a drink round here?'

Billy Tan led her down the deck to the ship's warm, well-appointed lounge. She was the last person he could afford to upset; it was something of a coup to get her up here at all. Besides, he still rated his chances of getting her into bed at some point in the voyage.

In the lounge, they settled over drinks.

'OK, Billy, tell me for real. What're the chances?'

'Off the record?'

'Sure, off the record.'

'Technically, it's easy. Just fucking expensive. We need the icebreaker, we need a big crew, we need this tow ship and a few other things besides. We also need the weather to be on our side. The whole operation can't take any longer than three weeks. We need a high tide to float the fucker out and if we miss it we're screwed. If bad weather comes, we'll just have to sit it out. This part of the world is either dead calm like now or it blows a fucking storm, in which case we have to get out of here.'

'I heard there are explosives on board. Isn't that dangerous?'

'Maybe. One of the magazines is stuffed full of shells for the guns, big ones and small ones. We've already taken a look at them.'

'And?'

'Our guy thinks they're safe enough. The worst stuff is the cordite charges. High explosive to propel the shells. There's a room full of that, which we shall have to get rid of.'

'How?'

'Burn it.'

'You're joking.'

'No. The stuff burns if you're careful. Doesn't go

bang – so my man tells me. We'll burn it when we get back. Should be good for a story. As for the shells, they would have to have detonators in the noses to make them go off. They're all clean. We plan to leave everything where it is until we get the ship back to the States. They survived the original trip without much trouble, after all. Besides, it will make a good story when we tow the fucker up to Annapolis and park it outside the college where they train all those John Wayne Navy characters. You want an exclusive?'

She ignored the suggestion. 'You make it sound easy. So what's the big catch?'

'Like you suggested, it's the legal side. If it's really a wreck, we can just go in and salvage it. Belongs to no one. We claim salvage rights. Nobody can touch us. Washington can't do a thing because it's not a US ship so the laws don't work.'

'What do you mean, *if* it's a wreck? It looks like a wreck, for Christ's sake,' said the girl.

'Not necessarily. There's a legal point. A wreck is only a wreck if it was lost by accident or act of God or some such shit. The trouble is, it looks as though the ship might have been scuttled.'

'Billy, don't give me all this Captain Kirk sea shit, OK?'

'Sorry. *Scuttled* – means it was deliberately got rid of. Sunk or beached. Not an accident, in other words. In this particular case, it looks like somebody deliberately ran it aground and pissed off.'

'So?'

'In which case we have a teensy-weensy problem. Scuttled ships are not considered wrecks by some fucking law or other. Which means it still belongs to the fucking Germans.'

'How the hell does anybody know?'

'Search me. But the Germans won't like us going in there, whatever the truth is. My lawyers tell me they've got wind of the plan and they intend to try to prove it was scuttled. God knows how, unless they get someone up here.'

'Was it scuttled?'

Of course it was fucking scuttled. All the seacocks were wide open. Someone beached the bastard and let the sea in. Had a dive crew in there yesterday. By tonight they'll all be closed up again, swear to God. That way it becomes a wreck, and if the fucking Germans pass some law, we'll be away before they know it.

'Of course not.' Billy smiled, staring directly at Louise DeAngelis. He was wondering what she might be wearing underneath the tight jeans and the clinging polo-neck jumper.

'You'd stay within the law, I take it?'

'Do I look stupid? Listen, you want another drink?' Billy moved a little closer.

*

Christian Bach took as great an interest in the broadcast as Otto Heine had just done, but for very different reasons.

Younger than Otto by fifty years, Christian Bach lived on the edge of Muskego, twenty miles outside Milwaukee, above the small gun store that still belonged to his father, Hans.

Hans had arrived in America as a refugee in 1945 at the age of four with his penniless mother, Marthe. As he grew up, he failed significantly to fulfil the great American dream: he remained, usually, deep in debt, and over the years managed to develop a profound resentment of what America had done to him, fuelled by the stories told to him by his mother of how he had come from a wealthy and respectable family in Germany and how America had taken it all away from him. His mother had told him many stories, though, and it was sometimes difficult to tell if it was all just her overworked imagination.

When Marthe died she left a small sum of money, and Hans bought the gun store just outside the town centre where he planned to make his fortune. But his surly treatment of anybody who was not one of his own small circle of friends, and his habit of closing early most days to go off hunting in the vast woodlands just a few miles from the town, limited his store's income to just about covering its costs in a good month and significantly less than that in a bad one.

Two years earlier, Hans decided he had had enough and handed the store over to his son, Christian. Born in 1976, Christian had grown up as a pure American, unable even to speak what little German his father knew. He went though school easily enough, and was considered a good basketball player at one time: he had a height and a bearing that his grandmother, Marthe, used to tell him was the spitting image of grandfather Bach – the family's shadowy hero, Erich, the great sea captain who was really a rich man, who had been lost at sea in strange circumstances. Christian's father would tell him stories about grandfather Bach's life, but he never took much notice of what was said.

But Christian had something in him … a meanness of spirit and a quiet ability to commit acts of surprising violence … that kept him out of the team. At one practice match, one of his own side accidentally knocked Christian to the floor. Christian did nothing during the match but at the end, in the locker room, he took the young man and coolly administered a beating which very nearly had Christian arrested by the local police – had not his father Hans intervened with the Sheriff, who was one of his cronies.

Since then Christian had become more of a loner, like his father, with few friends. But in one respect, he showed a dramatic difference. The moment he took over the store – it becoming clear that he was not interested in working for anyone else – he started to turn it round, and within a year he had mounted enough cut-price promotions to build a respectable clientele as well as a respectable income.

Suddenly Christian Bach, although still young, had become a moderately well-off young man. But instead of turning him into a good citizen, this simply gave him the resources to indulge in the few things that really captured his interest. He had a profound love of weapons; he had an equally profound dislike of what he and his father saw as the betrayal of ordinary Americans by rich liberals in Washington; and he managed to combine the two dislikes with another trait inherited from Hans, the desire to live an outdoor life.

When not working in his gun store, Christian was a survivalist who liked to spend his weekends around a campfire, drinking beer, planning fantasy revolutions and who they would shoot first when they got to Washington.

He had already attracted the attentions of the FBI. The threats posed to public figures by people who were regarded as lunatics were real: Kennedy's killer, Lee Harvey Oswald, for all the conspiracy theories, was just a screwed-up little man who wanted to make a mark on the world. Since then there had been a long tradition of disillusioned, inadequate men who spent years uttering public threats to wipe out one politician or another, being ignored, and then finally committing the act. There had probably always been such people around, ever since the Declaration of Independence was signed, but modern weaponry had placed awesome power in the hands of men who chose to use it. When the right to bear arms was enshrined in the constitution, the worst that anyone could get hold of was a muzzle-loader of questionable accuracy. Now, any fool with a grudge could walk into a shop like Christian Bach's and, with minimum identification, walk out with a high-powered automatic machine gun powerful enough to bring down an aircraft.

Repeated attempts had been made to control the trade. Teenagers with a grudge had opened fire on their classmates on more than one occasion and wiped out half of them. High-velocity shells meant that your aim didn't need to be good: one would take off a hand or an arm and the victim would bleed to death or die of shock in minutes. But every time control was proposed, a wealthy and well-organised lobby would move into the attack and crush it.

Which was why the utterances of Christian Bach were constantly monitored and noted by a special division of the FBI, known internally as 'The Nut Squad'. Two years ago he had been hauled in, after having been heard making threats against the local Democrat Congressman. They had come for him early one morning and held him in a cell for eight hours before spending two days questioning him. He was secretly delighted. They were taking him seriously, and all of a sudden Bach began to feel important. Naturally he denied everything, hoping that he would be held for even longer and questioned by even more important people, maybe even from Washington.

But they let him go.

'Is that it?' he had asked of the surly agent who handed him back his keys and his possessions.

'Listen, sonny, we get a hundred nuts like you through here every week. Just fuck off and keep your mouth shut. Go play with your fucking guns.'

It was obvious that they didn't take him seriously after all, and this annoyed Christian Bach. He drove himself back home fuming, his sense of grievance growing. One day they will have to take me seriously, he told himself.

He continued to make ever more outlandish threats to his friends and people in bars. Now he knew he was being watched, he had an audience to play to. The FBI people made notes in the growing file, but they had to watch hundreds like him and there was nothing especially alarming about Bach to distinguish him from all the other crazies who wanted to shoot the President or blow up Congress.

That evening, Christian had left the store open and sneaked upstairs to get a beer. There was good business to be done up until nine. He flipped on the TV and zapped through the channels. Like Otto Heine he nearly flicked past the Billy Tan interview, but there was something about Tan that caught Christian's interest and he watched the interview unfold as he picked up and played with an old Russian Kalashnikov that someone had brought in for part-exchange.

The first mention of the *Hindenburg*, and the cameraman's dramatic zoom into the distant wreck, struck Christian Bach as forcibly as it struck Otto Heine.

The *Hindenburg* – the old wrecked ship that his father had told him the stories about: how grand-father Erich had been in command of the ship on a secret mission from Germany, how he had fought his way across the Atlantic, only to be betrayed by his own men who saved their own skins and left Erich to die somewhere in the wild North Atlantic wilderness – a tale told by the single survivor, a young man named Heinrich Schiller who had been second-in-command.

Christian knew of the ship. He knew the stories. It was part of his family history. He even had a picture of the vessel, taken from an old magazine article, framed and hung in the store downstairs with a caption underneath:

THE BACH FAMILY ARRIVE IN AMERICA

He had taken little real interest, assuming that even if the stories were true there was damn all in it for him. But now here was that fat Chink, Tan, proposing to pull the goddamned ship from the ice and turn the *Hindenburg* into a tourist attraction. Christian Bach put down the Kalashnikov and lit a Marlboro with an ancient Zippo lighter. Jesus! Through his mind ran a thousand possibilities. Christian had a brain for business. Here, he was sure, was some kind of deal, although he wasn't quite certain what. But he was sure as fuck not going to let that greasy Chinaman make a fortune from his grandfather's wreck, no fucking way.

2

LACOCK, WILTSHIRE, ENGLAND
21 JULY 2000

The cottage was at the end of a long, muddy track. Cow parsley and nettles grew thickly down the margins of the lane, which was shaded and kept damp by a line of overhanging, ragged oaks, and Bethe Fischer had to push her way through all of them, getting her Burberry soaked and her shoes coated in the thick Wiltshire mud. The taxi driver refused to drive up the track. He had taken one look and shrugged his shoulders. He promised to wait, but Bethe was not convinced.

When she arrived, via the train and a long taxi ride out from Chippenham, she had been enchanted by the village and the abbey, even in the English rain; the place was like the cover of a box of chocolates, all thatch and whitewash and roses over the door. But they carried on up a long hill and left the village behind.

The taxi driver had kept stopping to check the map that Bethe had given him.

'Don't know this bit at all, miss. Where'd you say it was?'

'I have no idea. There is the map.'

Bloody foreigner. He folded the map up and kept driving. Eventually, a mile along a minor road, he saw the sign:

Brinkwells Cottage. No Footpath.
Private. Keep Out.

That was where he decided he would wait, so Bethe had hesitantly got out of the car. A lazy drizzle was drifting down from a grey sky. This was supposed to be summer, she thought ruefully. What in the name of God am I doing here?

*

Early the previous morning in Bonn, on the banks of the Rhine, in a low glass-and-concrete building set in a well-tended garden, Bethe Fischer and her assistants had also watched Billy Tan's broadcast, recorded for her earlier the previous evening. The tape had arrived at the crack of dawn, as had a telephone call from the Interior Ministry for whom Bethe worked. It left her in no doubt that if she valued her future career she should watch the tape and ensure this man never succeeded by whatever means she found necessary. It was, the caller said, in the interests of the German government that this should happen. Particularly with an election looming. We do not want to see Germany's name dragged through the mud, as usual. Bethe Fischer understood.

The broadcast ended and one of the assistants snapped the remote control at the expensive Sony set with some violence. The TV died to silence. They said nothing, waiting for Bethe to speak as she sat back in the leather chair and tugged at the back of her blonde hair.

'So, Klaus, what do you think our position is?' she said finally.

Klaus, the maritime specialist, was delighted to be asked. 'Absolutely clear. German law, international law, every precedent you can think of. A wrecked ship is anyone's. Anyone can claim salvage if they can get hold of it. But if the ship was deliberately wrecked and then abandoned – the Navy people call it 'scuttled' – it's still ours and he can't touch it. If he does, we go through the American courts and sue the backside off him.'

'What about making it a war grave?'

'Only if there are bodies on board. No one has ever reported bodies.'

'So if we say it was scuttled, we have no problem?'

'Well, not quite that simple, of course. We can apply for an injunction if he touches it. We'll have to show cause, produce some evidence that will support us. He'll fight back, naturally, so our case needs to be provable.'

'And there lies the problem, eh, Klaus? Proof?'

'Quite so. We have the stories, of course. The only reliable testimony we have is from a man named Schiller who died a few days after being rescued by the British. According to that, there was the mutiny and then the ship just disappeared. Other than that, nothing. The files all went missing – in the war, I mean,' he added unnecessarily.

Bethe turned to another assistant. 'Which you've managed to sort out?'

'Well, sort of. The British have been very helpful, but they tell me there is very little in the files they hold. All the stuff they captured at the end of the war has been looked at, but they say there is very little reference to the ship.'

'You believe them?'

'Yes, I believe them. They're just as keen to stop this

happening as we are. One of their people has trawled through the old MI6 records and Naval Intelligence records, and they seem to have found someone who might be able to help.'

'Who?'

'One of their Intelligence people from the war. Still alive and living somewhere in the sticks. Might be able to put the story together.'

'Well, having seen that man getting ready to loot our ship, you'd better get over there and see him.'

'Her.'

'I beg your pardon?'

'Her. A woman. Lillian Alice Beasley, age 84. Single and never married. Worked for British Intelligence up until the Sixties when she retired. Supposed to know quite a lot about the *Hindenburg* story by all accounts.'

'She never said a thing?'

'No. Official Secrets Act. She was of the generation which took that sort of thing seriously.'

'She'll talk to us, though?'

'I'm told she will. She's being sent a letter, someone high up. All clear, go ahead.'

'Better get over there.'

'Not a good idea by all accounts. Not me, I mean. She's supposed to be a bit ... well, eccentric is how they described her. Suggest we send a woman. More likely to talk. Germans talking to her about the war, that sort of problem. Feels a bit funny about seeing a man.'

'Me, you mean?' asked Bethe Fischer with some amusement.

'Might as well. Who better?' added the official hastily.

And so it was that the Deputy State Prosecutor, one of the highest legal officials of the German government, found herself setting off to pay a nervous visit to an eccentric English pensioner to try to find out what might have happened to one of their own ships fifty-five years ago.

*

Bethe struggled down the track for a long quarter-mile before she finally caught sight of the cottage, almost hidden in a hollow and surrounded by huge trees that towered over the building. Even from a distance the place looked wild and deserted. It had once been thatched, but now sheets of green-painted corrugated iron covered the roof, stained with rust. The walls were a dull grey and dark windows glowered suspiciously under deep eaves. Bethe made her way along the track, which rapidly steepened as it led her down into the hollow. The surface got worse: deep ruts where tractors had passed in the rain made the centre of the track impassable unless she wanted mud up to her thighs, so she squeezed along beside a ramshackle barbed-wire fence, and then caught the belt of her raincoat. She swore richly as she unhooked it.

There was a gate at the end of the track, half off its hinges, and another sign: BEWARE OF THE DOG. Bethe had to assume that the old woman was expecting her, for God's sake. She prayed that whatever animal was on the loose was firmly tied up as she lifted and pushed open the gate.

The patch of land around the cottage was a garden of sorts. Most of it was rough, damp grass; a rusted roller occupied one corner, and a shed made of odd panels of wood leaned near it. Someone had dug out a patch of rich earth in the grass and the soft green leaves of potatoes, half of which had already been harvested, rambled like a small jungle across it. There was no sign of a dog.

The front door was faded green and peeling. No bell, no knocker. Bethe hugged her briefcase close to her and rapped on the wood with her bare knuckles. It seemed to make such an insignificant noise that she almost immediately slapped the door with her open hand.

'Hello? Miss Beasley?' she called at the same time. There was a long silence.

Bethe waited for a moment and then thumped on the door with her fist, several times. 'Miss Beasley? *Miss Beasley?*'

Without warning there was a sudden rapid barking ... almost a yelping ... of a dog, close behind the door. Bethe jumped back. The yelping stopped and silence returned. The thing sounded like a bloody great Alsatian. Maybe nobody was in, Bethe vaguely hoped, though her message had been clear enough. This day, this time. She looked back up the track. It was the middle of the afternoon but the sky had darkened and slow, fat drops of rain were scattering themselves across the grass. It was a long way back. Damn it. She left the door and made her way round to the back of the cottage past nettles and brambles, and piles of wood and rubbish. There was another door; this one was open.

Bethe nervously pushed it open a little more. 'Miss Beasley?' she called, in a softer voice for fear of the dog or something worse inside the gloomy interior.

'You! What do you want? Who are you?' called a voice behind her, from the garden. Bethe jumped and turned, but as she did so the door flew open and a monstrous black Labrador, fat but angry, leaped from inside and bared its teeth at her, growling and moaning. On one side was the dog and now, on the other, was the owner of the voice, a thin, crouched figure, peering at her through thick glasses, one lens of which was covered with a filthy plaster, a rusty garden fork held in both hands like a heavy sword.

'Who are you?' called the old woman once more.

'It's me, Fischer, Bethe Fischer, from Germany. I sent you a message. You told me to come today.'

'Fischer?' said the old woman, coming a little closer, still holding the garden fork.

'*Ja*. Yes. I am from Bonn. About the ship. You must remember?'

'Yes, yes. What are you doing there? Come inside. Don't mind Chuff. He's harmless. Just smells a lot.' Suddenly the old woman seemed much less aggressive. Bethe waited until she had gone inside and then followed her. She was still carrying the fork, but deposited it in the small, stone-floored kitchen which Bethe now found herself in.

She was right about the dog. Something smelled. It was the sticky, dense stink of animals and damp bedding and dirty clothes. She could almost touch it.

'Thank you for seeing me,' ventured Bethe, to open a conversation.

'Do you like dogs?'

'Well, yes, very much, thank you,' replied Bethe.

'Can't stand the bloody thing. Chuff lives up the road and is always hanging about. Can't get shot of the wretched animal. Prefer cats myself. Cleaner.'

'Yes, I see,' responded Bethe.

'Can't do you tealeaf tea, I'm sorry. Don't like that either. Peppermint tea any good?'

'No, thank you. Please don't trouble.'

'Suit yourself. Chuff, *sod off* before I bloody shoot you,' and the fat Labrador plumped himself down on the floor in front of Bethe, wagging his filthy tail. Bethe stood back a little.

The old woman ignored the animal and rooted through a pile of washing-up in a stained porcelain sink, rescuing a mug which she inspected critically before running it under the tap and then pouring water from a kettle on to a tea bag with a length of string on it. The smell of peppermint instantly filled the kitchen.

'Sit yourself down, then,' said Lil Beasley, settling herself into a small wooden chair next to the sink.

'Thank you. You have a very nice old house here,' started Bethe.

'Oh, no need to be polite. It's a bloody dump. Falling down. Some rich idiot from London will buy it and turn it into a right little tart's palace one day. Left me by a very poor aunt who must have felt guilty about something. What do you want?'

Bethe was taken aback by her abrupt question. 'You got my message?'

'Of course. And my letter from Sir bloody Stanley whatshisface, deputy under-something or other, OHMS and crests all over. I'm supposed to be nice to you. Tell everything I know. Orders.'

'I hope you don't mind?'

Lil laughed, but it was not from a sense of humour. 'Mind? Why should I mind? The war was a bloody long time ago. I don't suppose you remember it at all.'

'I am afraid not. I was not born until 1955. My mother, of course, remembered it very well.'

'Where?'

'Sorry?'

'Where were you born?'

'I see. I was born in München. Munich.'

'Munich. Don't know the place. And your family? In the war, I mean?'

Why was this old woman so interested? 'My father

was a prisoner of the Americans for four years. He was suspected of being a Nazi. Then he was released. He became a lawyer and died three years ago. My mother still lives, though she is very unwell.'

'Was he a Nazi?'

'Yes, I think he was. A very minor one, but he was a Party member. I do not believe he killed anyone. He worked in the local law office.'

'You're honest, I'll say that for you. After the war there was not a single Nazi, you know that? Miracle, I bloody call it. Vanished from the face of the earth. Just jolly good Germans left, wouldn't hurt a fly. Adolf Hitler? Never heard of him.'

'Of course it is something we prefer to forget.'

'Of course it is. Won't bloody let you, though, will we?'

Bethe shrugged her shoulders. The woman wanted to fight the war all over again, as so many English did. They seemed to forget their own dark deeds over the centuries. But she couldn't afford to upset this strange old woman.

'May we talk about the *Hindenburg*?'

'I suppose we may.'

'You worked for Intelligence in the war. I understand you recall the events surrounding the last voyage of the ship?'

'Some of them. But why do you want to know? What's so bloody important that I deserve visits from high officials of the German government and letters from Her Majesty's Secret Intelligence bunch of nasties? Goodness me! All of a sudden Lil Beasley is in demand. Never been so bloody popular.'

'This was not explained?'

'Do they ever?'

'I see. So. A few weeks ago a certain American

gentleman, very wealthy, decides to set sail to Greenland with a Dutch salvage crew. His plan is to pull the ship out of the ice and sail it back to America. There he will turn it into a tourist attraction. My government is not keen on the idea. We do not want one of our old ships treated in this way. It opens too many old wounds; it shows no respect. You must remember we have an election coming up. This sort of thing is not popular.'

'And what the hell am I supposed to do about it?'

'Under international law, the ship can only be moved if it is a genuine wreck. In other words, if it was lost by enemy action or by act of God, and was abandoned by its crew. On the other hand, if it was deliberately run aground, scuttled and abandoned, it is no longer considered a wreck. Then the ship still belongs to Germany, and we can get an injunction in the American courts to stop this happening.'

'And you think *I* know what happened?'

'We have been told that you were involved in the chase of the ship over the last days. Perhaps you recall something that will clarify the position?'

'You mean, do I know if it was scuttled or not?'

'Yes, if you wish. That is what I need to know.'

'And if I tell you it was a wreck?'

'Then it *is* a wreck. I am interested only in the truth. Then we have no case and we must let Mr Tan get on with his ...'

'Pillage? That's a good English word for it.'

'If you wish.'

'Who's Tan, then?' Lil Beasley got up and went to the filthy sink, washed out a glass and refilled it with water from the kettle.

'Billy Tan is a very rich American of Oriental origins. He has made a great deal of money on Wall Street by not altogether legal means, since when he has spent some time avoiding the attentions of the financial authorities. Now he has appeared on television to tell the world all about his plan, we suppose to build up publicity for the venture.'

'Which is?'

'We understand it is a theme park or some such arrangement.'

'So what you really object to is a load of grubby schoolkids dropping hamburger all over your precious ship? Is that the problem?'

Bethe started to grow angry, in spite of herself. 'I do not think that is the objection at all. The ship is a German ship, the product of a certain madness that afflicted us. It is wrecked in the ice. Many of my countrymen lost their lives on the ship. It should stay there until it rusts away. It is not a tourist attraction, least of all for Americans. And it is inconceivable that it should ever return to Germany. Miss Beasley, you perhaps do not understand the burden of – let us say "guilt" – that we feel about those days. It was something that belongs to a different generation but for which we are constantly paying the price. The ship should remain where it is. Untouched.'

'But only if you can prove that it was scuttled, not wrecked?'

'Correct.'

'You know about the ship?'

'A little.'

'We knew all about it, of course. You thought you were being bloody clever, hiding it. You thought we never knew. But we did. Pictures. Intelligence. We had someone in the Hamburg docks, you know that? They got caught in '43 and we never heard from them again. Shot, I imagine.'

'A lot of people were.'

'But we never got to it. I wanted them to. No point in having something like that hanging around unless it was going to be used. Kept telling them, but they wouldn't bloody well listen. As bloody usual.'

'It was imagined that the existence of the ship was secret?'

'Might as well have been. Unfinished. Useless hulk. That's what they all said. Not worth wasting the resources on. So it bloody well sat there, didn't it, until Moehle and his merry band took off up the Elbe. Caught our lot on the hop. Didn't bloody well believe it even then.' Lil Beasley sat back in her chair and smiled. But she stayed quiet.

Bethe Fischer looked up and waited. There was no point in pushing the woman. She was too old to care.

Lil suddenly got up. 'Chuff? *Chuff?* Get here, boy!'

The fat Labrador, who had gone to sleep, farted gently as it woke up and started wagging its tail. Bethe wrinkled her nose at the pungent smell. What did she feed this foul animal on – eggs? The dog heaved itself awkwardly to its feet, stumped across to where Lil was standing and stood expectantly in front of her. Now what?

The old woman leaned down and patted the dog's head. It plopped itself at her feet, spreading its hind legs apart so that its fat belly touched the floor between its outstretched legs, and it farted again. Bethe thought she might be sick. The irony of the situation was not lost on her. Bethe was the vanquished, begging for favours at the door of the victor. Bethe owned a handsome house in the suburbs, drove a large Mercedes sports car and took month-long holidays on the Italian Riviera every summer; she was begging for help from a woman who lived in a slum with a fat dog that stank to high heaven. Who won, who lost? Bethe saw only the sad Englishwoman, still reliving the war, still worried about winners and losers, fighting in her own mind the battles that to Bethe were just history. The English had become a sad, withdrawn, embittered race, not wanting to go forward, hiding in the dim corners of a history which only they seemed to care about.

'I wrote it all down, you know,' announced Lil Beasley, all of a sudden.

'I'm sorry?'

'Wrote it all down. The whole thing. A history. Couldn't do a thing with it, of course. Official Secrets Act. Sworn to secrecy for the rest of my natural. Still, now I'm allowed to show it, aren't I?'

'I believe that would be possible, yes.'

'Wait here.' Lil vanished into the room next door. The fat dog looked mournful, then pushed itself to its feet and limped over towards Bethe, and to her horror rested its head on her knee and licked her leg with a rusty-looking tongue. She could smell the animal's breath now. But she restrained the urge to push the foul thing away, for fear of offending the mad woman.

Bethe sat frozen for a full five or six minutes, unable to move. Then Lil came back into the room. She was carrying three large manila envelopes, wrinkled with age like her face. The fat dog abandoned its attentions and returned to Lil.

The old woman stood in front of Bethe, holding the three envelopes to her chest like a baby. 'This is it,' she announced, proudly.

'The story of the ship?'

'Quite a lot more other stuff, besides.'

'There is a lot.'

'Take a look.' Lil Beasley opened one of the

envelopes. Bethe was expecting a scribbled pile of notes; instead she saw a neatly bound manuscript of yellow paper. When Lil handed it over she saw it was typed, on an old machine, with big characters and wide double-spacing, and wide margins. Bethe recognised the style: civil service, draft documents for ministers to scribble on.

'Took me five bloody years, after I retired.'

'It is a remarkable work.' Bethe was genuinely impressed. The old woman had set down an entire secret history. She had scanned the first few lines and the manuscript was clearly well written and intelligent.

'Don't be bloody patronising. You haven't read it.'

'May I do so?'

'Suppose you may. Orders, really.'

'I will bring it back in, let me say, two days. May I copy it?'

'No, and no. No, you may not copy it. No, you may not bring it back. You want to read it, it stays here.'

'There is very much of it,' said Bethe doubtfully. 'I will need to make notes if I am not permitted to copy it.'

'Take your time. Stay the night. I might even make you a meal.'

The thought of staying the night here filled Bethe with horror. But this was a gold seam. She had not expected anything like it. It was an opportunity she could not, in all conscience, turn down. She looked at her Cartier watch. It was gone four in the afternoon. Although she was a fast reader, she had not a chance of getting through the manuscript in under – what? – four or five hours. And making notes too.

'Thank you. Perhaps. Where may I work?'

'Here. On the table.'

'Thank you.'

'Look, here's the second chapter,' said Lil, handing over the contents of one of the envelopes proudly.

Bethe's face fell. 'There's more?'

'Of course. It's a bloody history. Twenty-two chapters. Shall I get the others?'

The woman had brought only the first three. Bethe shrugged. She would be there for the night.

*

Lil had cooked a meal for both of them. A strange dish of boiled potatoes with fatty bacon and cheese melted on top, it was, surprisingly, virtually eatable. The old woman had kept quiet during the meal, encouraging Bethe to read the manuscript as she ate. It was difficult to read and eat at the same time, particularly with Lil watching her like a hawk.

Most of the manuscript was concerned with esoteric details of British Naval Intelligence during the war. It was well written, even Bethe could appreciate that, but it was of little real interest to anyone other than a historian. It was mostly concerned with personalities; and it painted many of them – all of them men, Bethe noted with some sympathy – as half-wits who nearly single-handedly lost the war. The story started in 1939 as war was declared, and it took Bethe an hour to pick through the first chapter.

Lil Beasley left her reading and took the fat dog out for a walk. As she closed the door Bethe seriously considered making a run for it, manuscript and all. But she thought better of it and kept reading.

Lil returned an hour later. Outside it was getting dark.

'I'll make up the spare bed for you. How's it going?'

'Yes, thank you. It is very good. Very good.'

Lil flushed slightly with pride. Nobody had ever read the book. Nobody ever would, of course, other than this German lawyer, of all people.

Another hour passed, and still no mention of the *Hindenburg*. But now Bethe was becoming absorbed in the clash of personalities which seemed to be the main subject of Lil Beasley's history, and she was taken aback when Lil suddenly spoke. 'Time for bed for me. You'll want to go up now?' It was more like a polite order than a question.

Bethe put the manuscript down. 'Yes, I think so. Where is the bathroom?'

'Bathroom? Goodness me, no bathrooms here. You want the lav? It's out the back. Take this torch, the bulb's gone and I can't reach the bloody thing.'

Bethe returned after a perilous expedition to the small hut outside the house; she had thought she would be physically sick. Lil led her up the narrow, steep stairs to a small bedroom, little bigger than a large cupboard. It contained a small single bed, one table, one light, one washstand, and a pile of more brown manila envelopes.

The room was musty. Bethe noticed a large spider in the corner, and assumed there must be a colony of others. The place hadn't been used for years, by the look of it. She turned down the sheet suspiciously. The bed at least looked clean. She took off her skirt and shirt but left everything else on, and carefully got into the bed with the pile of manuscripts on the bare floorboards next to her.

She propped herself up on the pillows and, her notebook on the bed in front of her, started flipping quickly through the pages. Still there was the same fascinating but useless account of internal politics. Having flipped through chapters 4, 5, then 6, 7 and 8, she was getting tired. She slipped the manuscript of chapter 8 back into the creased manila envelope and picked up the envelope marked '9' in a neat, tiny script written in a curious dark red ink. Bethe yawned hugely and looked at her Cartier. It was gone midnight. The spider had crawled across the ceiling above her and she watched it for a moment, wondering if it might fall on her. She returned to the manuscript, and started flicking through the pages once again. It wasn't until she had reached the last few pages that she realised with a start that the *Hindenburg* story was being told. She flipped back again. There was the start:

I first knew that the Hindenburg *had left its home port when I discovered two apparently unconnected intelligence reports sitting on a desk that no one else had managed to see the significance of . . .*

Bethe started to read carefully now. The story slowly became clear. Lil's initial suspicions about the vessel, rejected by the foolish – male – authorities at the British Admiralty; how she always suspected that the sister ship to *Bismarck* had never really been broken up. Then the story of how Lil herself – she was always the hero of the narrative – pieced together the movements of the ship from when it finally left Hamburg. Page by page, an increasingly incredulous Bethe Fischer read one of the most curious tales she had ever come across, told in Lil Beasley's totally assured style as though she herself had been on the ship when it set out from the Elbe estuary one dark night in April as the Russian divisions closed in on one side and the British closed in on the other.

3

HAMBURG, GERMANY
19 APRIL 1945

Otto Heine flinched as a shell, probably Russian, landed three streets away and sent a fierce rumble across the grubby ruins which were once the proud and ancient port of Hamburg. Klompe, the fat postmaster, threw himself to the ground, much to Heine's amusement, but when Heine held out a hand to help the old man up all he got for his troubles was a filthy curse and the ancient Luger pistol waved with real enthusiasm in his face. Klompe brushed the brick dust from the trousers of the ill-fitting *Volkssturm* uniform he had managed to lay his hands on and tried to reassert his authority.

'Stand back! Stand back!' he shouted in what was meant to be a loud voice but ended up as no more than a croak.

Heine shrugged his shoulders. 'Look, grandpa, I'm standing back. No trouble, see?' he said as reasonably as he could. The fact was, ever since fat Klompe had strutted up to attempt to conscript him forcibly into the last-ditch fight to save the fatherland, Heine had difficulty taking him seriously. He had known Klompe when he was just a city postmaster, serving one of the districts near the docks. He was a nice enough old fellow – pompous, official, proud of his uniform, but then postmasters all over Germany were the same. Now here was fat Klompe, sixty years old if he was a day, suddenly appearing in the uniform of a *Volkssturm* colonel, complete with a Luger pistol that for all Heine knew was a toy, attempting to turn Otto Heine, of all people, into a member of Adolf Hitler's mighty Navy. The fact that the mighty Navy was finished – as was Hamburg, and indeed the rest of Germany – seemed to be lost on the old fool. He had his orders. He had been promoted. It was his task to round up every able-bodied man and boy over the age of ten and send them into the fight. In particular, he was to round up twenty youths and get them to the Naval Yard by that afternoon.

And Klompe knew Otto Heine, too. It was a particular pleasure to arrest this young thug and get him into the forces where they would kick some discipline into the lad's grinning face. Heine was one of those kids who had managed to avoid everything and yet always seemed to have cigarettes and chocolate and always wore an insolent smile on his face. He had no respect for authority, none at all; Klompe had even seen him laughing when the Fuhrer himself was talking on the radio. Heine was still young, but he was already a street-wise thug, and Klompe had made a special point of hunting him down the moment he had been handed the second-hand uniform.

'Get in the truck, now!' barked Klompe.

'Sure, old man. No problem. This truck here?'

'Do you see another one, idiot?'

'This truck here, then. On the back, you say? Or up front?'

Klompe was getting angrier, but Heine's insolence

had a threatening edge to it. From underneath the ragged canvas on the back of the truck, three frightened faces had appeared and were now looking at the scene between fat Klompe in his uniform and wiry Otto Heine dressed in a military greatcoat with the insignia removed. The faces were young, just schoolkids: they were part of Klompe's haul of twenty urchins whom he had tempted on to the back of his truck with promises of a good meal and warm clothes. None of them had needed a threat of force, which relieved Klompe greatly. He was not cut out for this sort of thing and Heine's reaction was upsetting him. The rest had come without trouble. Heine was just trying to spite him.

And, indeed, Heine couldn't but help enjoy winding Klompe up, gun or not. 'Perhaps you would like me to drive? Look, I can do that for you,' and he started walking to the front of the truck.

Klompe was going red in the face as he awkwardly shuffled towards the truck to put himself between Heine and the door. 'No, no. Get in the back ...' and the old man reached out to grab Heine by the sleeve to stop his confident progress towards the cab.

Heine stopped suddenly and looked down at Klompe's podgy hand. 'Oh, I see. It's a fight you want, then?' asked Heine, suddenly looking Klompe straight in the eye. The old man released Heine's sleeve and stood back.

'Fool! I am an officer in the *Volkssturm* and I have been given my instructions. You must do exactly what I say.'

'I don't give a fuck if you're Adolf Hitler himself. Anyway, you're just a postman. Where did you steal that uniform? Listen, Klompe, if I were you, I'd get out of here. The Reds are twenty miles away over *there* and the British twenty miles away over *there*, and basically, Klompe, my good old friend, the whole place is fucked. Put down that gun and go home before you get hurt.'

The kids' faces were looking around the corner now from the back of the truck. They were starting to smile.

But Klompe had his orders. 'You cannot speak to me like this, Heine. You cannot say these things. The Fuhrer fights on, you heard the radio the other night. You are one of these traitors, aren't you? One of the Reds who wants to hand us all over to Moscow when the bastards get here? I know your type, Heine. Now, get on the truck before I lose my temper – now!' Klompe started to look distinctly dangerous.

Heine raised his hands in mock surrender. 'OK, OK. You win, Klompe. I'm going. Just drive carefully, OK? There's a lot of shooting going on. And you mind that uniform, hear? You'll have to hand it back soon.'

Klompe spat on the loose cobbles of the road and watched in silence as Otto Heine finally jumped into the back of the truck. Even the way the kid just casually sprang over the high tailgate seemed an insult to Klompe's authority.

Klompe straightened himself up, looking around to make sure that nobody had seen the humiliation. There were no other people on the street. It was cold and overcast, and the ruins of the ancient buildings around them stood like trees stripped of their leaves, naked and dead in the deserted morning light. In the distance, through the gaping ruins, columns of smoke drifted upwards from countless fires ignited by the remorseless shelling of the Soviet forward divisions as they slaughtered their way westwards, the final nightmare of every German now coming true.

But Klompe had heard, with his own ears, Josef Goebbels himself order every man to fight to the last. Salvation was coming. The southern Army Group, fresh and superbly equipped, was even now fighting its way towards Berlin where they would throw back the Mongol hordes and raise Germany once more to greatness. The Fuhrer himself was in good spirits: it is his birthday tomorrow and he sends greetings to his brave fighters on all fronts. So, rescue was at hand. He knew it all along. Klompe started up the engine and drove off, looking out for more deserters and cowards to collect along the way, to fulfil the orders given to him last night. It was urgent. We depend on you. Klompe proudly drove down another ruined street. Behind him another shell landed and brought down a warehouse, crashing across the road in a cascade of masonry and a rolling cloud of black dust, obliterating the spot where Klompe and Heine had been arguing. Heine saw the explosion from the back of the truck, but as usual kept his thoughts to himself.

*

Kapitan sur See Erich Bach could also hear the explosions of Russian shells, but deep in the bunker under the wreckage of the Reich Chancellery in Berlin they sounded distant and muffled. Bach was sitting stiffly in what he presumed was a waiting room, a small, bare cubicle with damp concrete walls. A picture of Adolf Hitler gazing into the distance was fixed to the concrete with four large screws. Was this to stop it being stolen or to keep it on the wall every time the place shuddered under the impact of another Russian shell?

Bach had not been to Berlin for over a year, and his journey to the bunker had been both dangerous and depressing. Clearly the war was going badly, but even to Bach the true extent of the devastation was a surprise. He had received the summons at his office in Wilhelmshaven, just as he was getting ready to move his command – what little was left of it – further west. He had got Willi, his staff driver, to find an unmarked Mercedes, and they had set off south to Berlin the day before. The endless North German plain seemed as bleak and cold as ever, and untouched by the war. The same dull cows grazed slowly in the fields, the same small farmhouses, with their high-pitched roofs, remained as they had always been. Yet the road down which he was driving was the centre of a corridor that narrowed every day, the Russians twenty miles or less to the east, and the British and the Americans the same distance to the west, an isolated strip of land that was just about all that was left of an empire which only four years earlier stretched from the Atlantic to the Urals.

Willi avoided the towns and as the light was starting to fade they entered the suburbs of Berlin. Here the shocks awaited Bach; first there was an eerie emptiness. The streets, more or less undamaged at the edge of the city, were empty. No people. But no troops. No police. No defences. It wasn't what Bach was expecting as the last stand which that idiot Goebbels had promised. Where was the 'ring of steel' that the American criminals were supposed to break and founder against? It was another mile into the city that the destruction started. First, just individual buildings were missing, like gaps in teeth. But soon whole streets had disappeared. Little effort had been made to clear away the rubble. In some places, weak fountains of water burbled upwards from broken mains, the pressure now too low from a thousand breaks to create any further damage.

Willi threaded the Mercedes carefully down the streets, making for the centre. Bach saw a group of men in uniform in the distance. He ordered Willi to stop and walked from the car to talk to them. He wanted to know what was happening. But as he drew closer, he had another shock. There were six of them, all wearing *Wehrmacht* uniforms. But the uniforms were filthy and torn. And the men ... they were old, older than his father by the look of them. Sixty, seventy? None of them was shaved. They had grey, pinched faces and wide, staring eyes. They watched Bach with suspicion as he approached in his black *Kriegsmarine* uniform. So, thought Bach, here was Goebbels' ring of steel.

'Where is your officer? Don't you salute?' asked Bach of the sullen group. But he got no answer. All six simply stared at him, unmoving. He couldn't tell if they were mad, frightened, or had just given up. He fumbled in his breast pocket and unbuttoned it, produced a pack of Navy cigarettes and offered them to the nearest ancient soldier. The old man looked at the pack and then slowly took it from Bach, his hand shaking violently. Still the group remained rooted to the spot. Bach turned and walked quickly back to Willi, and they resumed their journey.

The explosions were very near now. The Brandenburg Gate, forbidding and black, was wreathed in smoke, and the leaden sky was streaked with clouds that were not natural. Several times Willi had to stop and back up to find a way around a pile of rubble. The worst problem was the overhead tram wires that had collapsed across most of the street, leaving a tangle like string that in places was impossible to get through, even when the road was otherwise clear. And in places, in small corners, Bach could see bodies. Nobody could be bothered to bury the dead any more.

They came to the bunker. Here the ring of steel was more in evidence: concrete blocks and tank traps blocked off the streets leading towards the bunker, and nervous-looking youths in SS uniforms watched every movement with suspicion. Bach had to clear five barriers, and at each one officers inspected his papers carefully and made phone calls before allowing them to pass. Ever since the assassination attempt even high-ranking staff were suspected; Navy men, with their reputation for independence, even more so. He finally reached the entrance to the bunker where he reported his presence to an effeminate orderly who returned after keeping him waiting for half an hour, and showed him to a small room with two bunks in it. He was to stay here overnight, and would be seen in the morning. Bach let Willi know and retired to the room where he fell into a fitful sleep, disturbed by distant explosions and somebody climbing into – and then a few hours later, climbing out of – the bunk above him. He never found out who his room-mate was.

He rose at six the next morning to get ready for his appointment at eight; but once he had reported to the same effeminate orderly he was told that the Admiral would not be available until later. He had no option but to wait.

Erich Bach sat on the steel and canvas chair, his back straight, his hands resting on his knees. He was a tall, thin man, built like a stork, with a great hooked nose and enormous ears that protruded like handles from the sides of his head. He habitually wore a Prussian crew-cut which took away all the hair from the sides and the back of his head and left just a fur of grey in a small circle on top. His eyes were deep blue;

his weathered cheeks needed long scars down each one of them to turn him into the very image of a Prussian officer, but he had no time for that sort of nonsense. Bach was a dedicated Navy man, having joined at sixteen, and the Navy to him was the whole point of life. He saw his first action at Jutland twenty-eight years ago, in the Kaiser's Navy, and on the whole he had accounted well for himself. When, in 1918, he heard that the fleet was sailing to Scapa Flow to surrender to the Royal Navy, he could scarcely believe it. The Grand Fleet was intact; the Army was still capable of fighting. Why surrender? But he followed orders and watched as the ships, in a final act of defiance, were scuttled by their captains.

Then Bach watched the rise of the Austrian corporal, Adolf Hitler – with some amusement at first. He was a coarse little man, a street thug. He seemed to have a political following, of course, and so – like most middle-class Germans who were proud of their country – Bach assumed he could be easily manipulated if he gained power. And anyway, Bach was doing well in the Navy. When Hitler became Chancellor, he assumed things would work out. And soon plans to start rebuilding the Navy were announced, and Bach was content to play his part. The Navy remained the most important thing. It was bigger than Austrian corporals. Much bigger.

As he sat deep below ground while Berlin was being reduced to rubble above him, Bach was conscious of the irony that had him sitting there awaiting the orders from the Austrian corporal at this final moment. The Navy was all but destroyed; surrender could not be far away. But even now, Bach felt the same sense of duty. He knew all was lost. But Germany would outlive this little dictator, in one form or

another; and Bach could never, *ever*, think of sur-
rendering, not after the humiliation of Scapa Flow. If
Bach was the last Navy man on the last Navy lifeboat
still afloat, he would still never give up: not because of
that little shit Hitler or the rest of the Nazi thugs, but
for the Navy and for himself. Somewhere in the
appalling mess there had to be some honour, some
pride.

The Navy had never wholly bent to Hitler's will. The
Nazi salute was never used: even now an officer
would return the outflung arm of a Nazi with a crisp
and proper Navy salute, and it irritated the hell out of
them. Even Raeder – and now Donitz – would not
return the Fuhrer's Nazi salute in like kind.

He had no idea what his orders would be. But Erich
Bach sat there, knowing full well that pride alone
would make him carry them out: in fact, the worse it
got the more inclined he was to do his job with
perfection, just to prove to these madmen how strong
Navy traditions were.

More than an hour passed. The bunker rumbled,
almost constantly, with distant explosions. He had
heard that advance parties of Bolsheviks were already
in the eastern suburbs. At one point there was a huge
explosion directly above them, and dust and debris
were shaken down from the ceiling, covering Bach's
uniform in a pale grey dust that he calmly brushed
off. There was a slight tremor in his hand, and he
licked his lips now and then, but it was not from fear.
What Bach needed, right now, was ... without warning
the effeminate orderly leaned his head around the
door. 'Bach? You are to come with me.'

Bach looked at the youngster. He was SS, of course,
but his rank was a lowly one. The captain raised his
eyebrows. 'Are you speaking to me?'

The orderly went red. 'If you would be so kind. This way, *Herr Kapitan*. We're in a bit of hurry this morning. My apologies.'

Bach stood and followed the lad down a long corridor lined with pipes and wires. The temperature must have been 90 degrees, and he began to perspire. They stopped at a huge steel door that was halfway open. The orderly showed Bach inside and a group of four Navy officers stood up suddenly as he entered. They had been sitting at a small trestle table drinking coffee.

'Erich, good morning. A pleasure to see you, in the circumstances,' started the shortest of the four, Admiral Sluys, one of Naval Staff High Command and an acquaintance of Bach's, if not a friend.

'Good morning, Admiral,' replied Bach stiffly. He was wondering what on earth this illustrious group wanted with him. Apart from Sluys, there was Krancke, from Northern Command, to whom he had once reported; Werner, the newly appointed Naval Intelligence head, whom he knew from pictures; and Puttkamer, Chief of Naval Construction. They all looked serious, and clearly had something in mind.

'Sit down, please, Erich. Have some coffee. You must have had a dreadful journey.'

Bach took a cup of coffee. It was real. He hadn't tasted real coffee for a year if not longer. 'You know what it's like out there, of course,' he replied. He was not going to pass comment.

'Oh, yes, we know how bad it is, Captain,' said Werner, the Naval Intelligence chief, a balding man who acted younger than he looked. Excited and nervous, he obviously wanted to talk, and he plunged straight in even though Bach offered no reply. Did Sluys look slightly uncomfortable, or was it Bach's imagination?

'Look,' continued Werner, pointing to a map of Germany. 'The Bolsheviks are days away from overrunning Berlin. The British are here, in the north, and the Americans are here ... and here ... in the south and the west. Soon we will have to evacuate Berlin.'

Bach was not surprised, but what on earth did they want with him if the whole thing was finished? Werner stayed silent, desperate for Bach to answer. He prolonged the pause but then, more out of politeness than curiosity, gave the eager Werner a reply. 'Berlin?' he asked. 'That's bad, of course.'

'But, Captain, the Fuhrer has laid his plans carefully,' continued Werner, with some relish. The man was unhinged, thought Bach to himself, but the others seemed to follow him with enthusiasm. 'It looks bad, but we fight on. The Fuhrer has ordered us south, to the National Redoubt around Berchtesgarten. We can hold out for months, even years.' He looked at Bach with a strange light of triumph in his eyes.

'Good, good,' nodded Bach slowly. The man was worse than mad, he thought.

Sluys, the Admiral, intervened. 'And then, when the Americans realise we cannot be defeated, they will give up and want to negotiate. Especially when they see the Russians all over Europe. They will beg us to return and help them run the country. Isn't that right, Werner?' The Admiral was stony-faced and to Bach he seemed to be deadly serious. Was Sluys mad too?

Werner remained enthusiastic. 'Certainly, Admiral. That's the Fuhrer's plan. Anyway, Captain, that's not what we called you here for. Admiral, will you introduce our idea to the good captain?'

The others sat down again, leaving Sluys standing; he looked at his watch as though he had a pressing appointment somewhere else.

'Erich, we have a special job for you. Something a little out of the ordinary, a little hazardous. You may not want to take it, especially in the circumstances. I shall understand, of course. It's up to you.'

Bach shrugged. 'I am a captain in the German Navy, Admiral. While that Navy still exists, I am here to receive my orders. It's nothing to do with choice, is it?'

'Perhaps not, Erich. But listen to our plan first, then decide. How about that?'

'You give me orders, Admiral, I carry them out.' Bach was not going to let them shuffle off their responsibilities. They still had to take the decisions, even if they were all mad.

'Very well. I shall explain. The Fuhrer himself has ordered this plan. You understand it comes from the very top, Erich? The Fuhrer is determined that the Americans should understand what war is about. He believes that the American people have been spared the bombing and the destruction that has been visited upon Germany. Not a single bomb, not a single shell, has fallen upon the American mainland. While they have been trying to crush Germany, Erich, they have been left alone. Did you know that they do not even have a blackout?'

'I had heard the stories, Admiral. From the U-boat people.'

'They are true, Erich, all true. While we suffer, the Americans drive around with headlights blazing and their neon lights flashing. As far as the ordinary American is concerned, the war is so far away as to make no difference. This is a situation that the Fuhrer has decided to change. He has ordered us, Erich, to visit upon Washington and the White House the same devastation that is being meted out to us here in Berlin, on the Reichschancellery itself. What do you

think of that?' asked the Admiral, but instead of looking at Bach he was looking sideways at Werner.

'An interesting idea. A little late, perhaps?'

Werner missed the sarcasm and jumped straight in.
'My dear Captain, exactly. That is the whole point. They
will never expect such a blow. Surprise is the Fuhrer's
great talent. It will show the Americans that Germany
remains a force to be reckoned with. Consider the way
our Ardennes offensive took them by surprise. Even
at this late stage, the Americans will be shocked. We
will take the war to their heartland. Of course the
Fuhrer does not expect to achieve a great military
victory. It is propaganda, Captain. A blow to morale.
Just think of the White House itself, a smoking ruin!
Then the Americans will be forced to negotiate. They
will know we cannot be beaten, even if Berlin falls.'
Werner's eyes were shining.

'And how does the Fuhrer propose that this is done,
exactly?' Bach hoped that this time the sarcasm in his
comment was sufficiently obvious.

If it was, it was Admiral Sluys who ignored it this
time. 'Of course, the Luftwaffe cannot reach America.
It is beyond the range of our bombers. Our secret
rocket weapons also cannot cross the Atlantic just yet.
We have to rely, in the final days, on the Navy. The
Fuhrer has ordered us to sail to Washington, in one of
our battleships, where we are to shell the White
House. And we would like you, Erich, to lead the
mission.'

There was a long silence. Bach remained sitting
stiffly in his seat, astounded. The foetid atmosphere of
the bunker was unreal, like the final act of some mad
Wagner opera. Now these men had been driven crazy
too, even Sluys. This was a fantasy. There was no
Luftwaffe left. No rockets. And the last battleships had

been bombed to smoking wreckage by the RAF months ago.

Here they were, sitting in a concrete bunker, rocked by explosions, surrounded by their enemies, days if not hours from an ignominious defeat, and these people were seriously talking about shelling the White House.

'So, Erich?' asked Sluys eventually, watching Bach's face. 'You think we are mad?'

'Admiral, it is, let us say, a very strange request. I cannot immediately see how such a mission is possible.'

'You are being very polite, Erich. You still think we are mad. But never mind. If we could prove that such a mission *was* possible, even now, how would you feel about it? You said earlier that you would obey orders.'

'If such a mission could be carried out, then of course. If you give me the orders and the means to carry it out, I will do it. Frankly, gentlemen, I cannot think how such a mission could take place, or what kind of vessel could do this. If there is even any ship to start with, of course.'

'Erich, there is such a ship,' said Sluys quietly.

It was Krancke's turn to speak, the Northern Command *Konteadmiral*. 'Captain, we have a battleship ready to sail, tomorrow ideally. We are crewing it as we speak. It is a ship that we have held in reserve. You will recall the *Bismarck*?'

Bach shrugged. The *Bismarck* was once the pride of the German Navy, a huge battleship of 50,000 tons, capable of nearly thirty knots. In 1941 she had escaped the British blockade and made her way into the Atlantic. But she was eventually cornered and, after taking a furious battering, she finally sank with the loss of over 1,000 lives. Since then, the Fuhrer had ordered his remaining capital ships more or less confined to port. No Navy man could ever forget *Bismarck*: it was branded on his heart.

'Of course I know the *Bismarck*,' replied Bach shortly.

'And you know about the other two ships? *Friedrich der Grosse* and *Hindenburg*?'

Bismarck was launched in 1939; the other two ships were the same class and were in various stages of completion when the *Bismarck* was destroyed. Following the disaster, Hitler turned against the battleship as a weapon and ordered them broken up on the stocks, their steel and equipment used for something he regarded as more useful. Or so Bach had always believed.

'*Friedrich der Grosse* was broken up,' continued Krancke. 'That you will know about. But the *Hindenburg* ... well, Captain, I can now let you into a well-kept secret. The *Hindenburg* was not broken up. Far from it. We carried on building it. At Hamburg. The Fuhrer ordered its task changed, of course. In 1941 he conceived of this plan to bombard Washington or New York, and for the last four years we have been trying to complete the ship.'

It was Puttkamer who spoke next, the softly spoken bespectacled engineer who had found himself in charge of Naval Construction. 'We had many starts and stops, Captain. The Fuhrer himself sometimes had great enthusiasm for the idea, and sometimes not. And we had the bombing to contend with, naturally. But finally the ship was finished a year ago, just awaiting the right time to use it. Now, I suppose, is as good a time as any.'

Bach could not keep the surprise from his voice. 'The *Hindenburg*? Good God, Puttkamer! How on earth could you build a battleship and keep it secret?'

Puttkamer smiled. 'Not easy, Captain. Not easy. But it's not really a battleship any more. We modified the design considerably, given the rather single-minded task it was to have. The vessel has no boilers or turbines. Needs too much crew. We stripped out the two outer shafts as well; we left just the one shaft and we managed to lay our hands on two large diesels, so your engineering complement will be a lot easier to manage. It will only do around twelve knots rather than the design speed of thirty, but we think that's sufficient. Saves on fuel, too, of course. We reduced the armament, naturally. It's now got two turrets instead of four, just the forward ones, with two 15-inch guns in each. The other guns were stripped off, apart from the 37-millimetre anti-aircraft stuff. No torpedoes, no aircraft, just a stripped-down ship for the job.'

'And how is this ship supposed to get there?'

'We don't think there will be any real opposition right now, frankly, Captain. The Allied Navies have other things on their minds. Most of the American Navy is now in the Pacific; the British are also occupied elsewhere. Donitz is keeping the remains of them busy with his U-boats, even now. You should be able to slip through unnoticed. You will take the northern route, of course. You will have complete surprise on your side and you should make the American seaboard with little trouble. But we armoured your ship heavily just in case. The side belts are 14.2 inches and the decks are 12.6 inches, thicker over magazines and engine rooms. This is more even than *Bismarck* had. She should stay afloat even after some heavy bombing, Captain. Oh, and we piled on some extra below the waterline. Torpedoes, you know. That's why she's a bit slow.'

'And no one knew about it? The Allies didn't bomb it?'

'We built the thing undercover, Captain. Huge camouflage nets, high screens. No one could see it. Frankly, no one was even looking for it after we put out the story that it was being broken up.'

'What about the people who built it? All the shipyard workers?'

Puttkamer looked embarrassed. 'Well, Captain, we were not allowed to use them. For security reasons. We had, let us say, some help provided to us.'

'You mean prisoners? Slave labour?'

'It was the decision at the time, Erich,' intervened Sluys. Even Bach knew what would have happened to the workers once they had finished the task. It was a fact of life, albeit one that Bach preferred not to face.

'And what sort of job did they do?' he asked finally.

'Well, not exactly up to our normal standards, Captain. But enough to do the job,' said Puttkamer defensively.

Sluys intervened again. 'The idea, Erich, is that you take the ship and complete the task. Remember, it is propaganda. Political. Once you have shelled the White House, your orders are to retreat immediately and scuttle the ship. We will have a U-boat waiting where you and your men will be taken off. The ship may not be the best in the world, but it only has to complete a one-way voyage. For the same reason, you need only a skeleton crew. One hundred men will be sufficient.'

'And I'm supposed to sail this thing quietly across the Atlantic? What if I'm seen?'

'The opposition, Erich, will be minimal. We're convinced of that. But our U-boats are still active. The Norwegian bases are still ours, and Donitz has ordered them to fight to the last. You know they are having some successes. Donitz is aware of our plan. He will ensure that U-boats concentrate their attacks well away from your course to divert the enemy. And he can provide U-boat escorts for the first few days.'

Bach looked sceptical. The U-boats were few now, with their range limited by lack of fuel. Such cover as they might give was going to be poor.

'And if I get there, what about Norfolk?' At the entrance to the Chesapeake Bay lay the biggest US naval yard in the country. Bach would have to sail under their noses.

'Surprise, Erich. You know they don't worry about a blackout. Their coastal defences, such as they are, will be asleep or on holiday. The last thing they will expect is a German battleship sailing past them, especially now they think the war is won. Do it at night, Erich, and they won't even see you until it's too late. You'll only be in there a few hours; they'll hardly have time to get steam up. A few aircraft perhaps. But Puttkamer's armour should keep you safe enough, until you get out. If you do this, it will be a huge success,' said Sluys, but Bach thought his voice was uncertain.

'For the Fuhrer, Captain. For the Fatherland. For National Socialism,' intoned Werner, a fanatical light gleaming in his eyes.

'For Germany, Erich,' repeated Sluys softly, looking directly at the captain.

Bach looked at the faces of all four men. Werner, still excited and eager with anticipation; Krancke, matter of fact, a job to be done. Puttkamer, more interested in building his ship than anything else; and Sluys, who seemed to be going along with everything. The rumble of explosions still growled through the thick concrete of the bunker walls.

'When? When am I supposed to do this?' asked Bach.

It was Werner who jumped in, eager as ever. 'Your ship is being prepared as we speak. You are to set sail tomorrow, Captain. The twentieth. The Fuhrer's fifty-sixth birthday. It will be a fitting tribute.'

'If you accept the task, Erich, that is,' said Sluys.

'It is not my place to accept or reject. Are you giving me an order?'

'Of course. You sail tomorrow,' exclaimed Werner.

Bach ignored the excited Nazi and looked directly at Sluys. 'An order, Herr Admiral?'

'Very well, Captain,' replied Sluys, formally. 'You are to take the ship and complete the task outlined. Krancke here has detailed orders for you. You will sail tomorrow. Eighteen-thirty hours. In the dark. Is that clear?'

'Perfectly, Herr Admiral. And where will I find the *Hindenburg*?'

'Oh, Erich, you won't find it anywhere – will he, Werner?'

'The *Hindenburg*, Captain, was renamed just last week. You will find it in Hamburg. And your ship is now called *Der Fuhrer*, Captain Bach. Good luck,' and Werner threw out his arm in the Nazi salute.

Bach ignored him. Krancke had already pushed a brown envelope into Bach's hands, the precise orders that he was to follow. Sluys, Krancke and Puttkamer, all Navy men, stood and gave Bach the conventional salute. He returned it crisply and left the room.

*

Sluys hurried down one of the dim, damp corridors. It had taken him ten minutes to shake off that eager fool Werner, whom he didn't trust further than he could throw him. Now he was running late; meeting in the bunker was hazardous, and they had to keep to careful schedules to avoid suspicions. Finally he arrived at the small office that they used for their meetings. It was well off the beaten track. And in these final days, internal security was strong near the Fuhrer's suite but almost forgotten elsewhere. They had met three times already and not a soul had even noticed they were missing.

He pushed the door open. The six officers and a single nervous-looking civilian inside went suddenly quiet until they recognised Sluys.

'You're late. Any problems?' asked one of them, an Army General, anxiously.

'No, just that idiot Werner. He wanted to carry on talking. He knows nothing. Don't worry.'

'So, how did it go? Are we on or off?'

'Bach is a good man. I feel badly for leading him into this. But he's fine. He's accepted the task and he's on his way up to Hamburg now. I only hope he actually gets there.'

'When does he sail?' continued the General.

'Tomorrow, as agreed. There's a high tide at nine-teen-hundred hours. He'll leave half an hour before then and pass Cuxhaven just as the tide is coming back up. He'll be out and into the North Sea under cover of darkness.'

'And he suspects nothing?'

'Of course not. He'll never find out, knowing Bach. He's a real-life hero, dedicated to the Navy. Give him an order and he'll follow it wherever it gets him. Just make sure the cargo is loaded without any fuss. Where is it now?'

'Don't worry, Admiral. They left yesterday. Two trucks. They'll be at Hamburg tonight or tomorrow. There won't be a problem.'

'And they look good? Real, I mean? Nothing suspicious?'

'Of course they look real. They *are* real. It's just the insides that are not quite what Bach would expect. We have twenty 15-inch shells to carry the bulk of the stuff, and a dozen small ones which are a damn sight easier to handle. If something goes wrong the big shells are impossible for one person to move. The small ones are, let us say, somewhat more negotiable. Everything's been thought of, Sluys, so don't worry. No one will find out.'

'I hope not, General. And I hope we're right about Bach getting there without opposition.'

'You shouldn't worry so much, Admiral. The American Navy has disappeared to the Pacific. There's hardly a ship left in the Atlantic, apart from some destroyers and a few Coastguard cutters near the coast. The British are already talking about paying off crews. Their air recon is spending all its time over this bloody place or chasing Donitz's last remaining U-boats. No, Admiral, the last thing anyone will expect is a battleship they don't even know about heading for Washington. They all assume the war is over. Bach should have a clear run. And then when he's near the coast, our message will alert the Americans and the good captain will be forced to deliver our cargo safely to its destination. If Bach is as good you say, Admiral, our plan should be complete just as the Russians take charge of this dump. Besides, we can trust our other man on board, can't we? You seemed confident enough about him.'

'Moehle? He's a good man, a bit young and naïve, but he's reliable enough,' answered Sluys. The Admiral knew Bach well; the captain was too honourable, too straightforward, if he had a fault. He needed someone to watch over the captain who would act as his eyes and his ears, and his fist if necessary. He had chosen a young technical officer, Moehle, and briefed him carefully: he was to stay in the background and keep Bach under constant watch as the voyage progressed.

'But this Moehle, Captain. He will watch? Keep an eye on things? I have your assurance?' The questions came from the single civilian in the dim room, a short, nervous-looking man. He was sitting on a chair with his legs together and his hands laid neatly on each knee. His name was Dr Heinrich Thy, and he had a very specific job in the Reichsbank as supervisor of the gold reserves of Hitler's central bank which even now, in the very last days, remained substantial.

Sluys looked coldly at the civilian. 'Nothing is certain. You take the same risk as the rest of us. He's the best we can do in the circumstances. There is no other choice.'

The doctor remained silent and shifted uncomfortably in his chair.

Sluys was right. There was no other choice.

All that now remained was to discuss the final escape from the bunker, towards the west, where Sluys and the others planned to meet the approaching American forces. They would slip quietly away, one by one, so that their conspiracy would remain unnoticed. None of them felt that it was treason; all of them were honourable men, not afraid to die. But they would not see Germany destroyed like this. It was their duty to get to the Americans.

Of course, the Americans would simply try to imprison them.

But once Bach arrived with his cargo of eight and three-quarter tons of the Reichsbank's gold reserves, worth $10,976,000 at the official fixed US Treasury price of $35 per ounce – more on the unofficial market* –

---

*Author's note: this amount of gold would be worth $89,629,600 at 1999 prices of $286 per ounce.

hidden inside the dummy shells, they felt their
chances of negotiating something ... anything ... out
of the collapsing Reich would be greatly improved.

*

Bach had found Willi, his driver. The man had managed,
God only knew how, to find not only three jerrycans
of precious petrol but another carton of cigarettes –
neither man smoked, but cigarettes were better than
currency. And now they set off, back through the
ruins of Berlin, to pick up the road north to Hamburg
where his new and strange ship would, according to
his orders, be waiting, covered still in camouflage
netting which they were supposed to be removing
even now. He read through his detailed orders twice.
Like all Naval Staff orders they were highly detailed,
right down to provisioning requirements. Everything
seemed to be taken care of.

But as Bach drove past the smoking ruins and the
small groups of shabby civilians picking through the
rubble – what were they looking for? – more than a
few doubts were crossing his mind. He had his orders.
He remained a Navy captain; he would never repeat
the disasters of Scapa Flow. But this? Bach was no fool.
Germany was finished; the only battle left to fight was
to decide who would own the corpse. Would it be the
Bolsheviks or the Americans? He disliked the idea of
either; the Bolsheviks were worse than sub-human, of
course, and they would want to extract an awesome
price for what Germany had done to them. But, as far
as Bach was concerned, the Americans were little
better. A future Europe as a colony of Washington had
few attractions. Best to let the lot of them fight it out.
Germany would still be Germany at the end of it;
not much more than a smoking ruin, perhaps, but

Germany nevertheless. He had heard that the British wanted to bulldoze every German town and village and turn the whole country into a rural backwater, and turn the people into a nation of dull peasants who never again caused trouble. Perhaps this was the best solution. One day Germany would recover, and it remained Bach's overriding duty to do the best for the country, no matter who was running the place.

Duty was everything. Once duty went, everything that Bach knew collapsed. As he sat in the back of the car, his thoughts turned to his family. Like most Navy men, he managed to compartmentalise his family into what was almost a different world. At sea, when he was on duty, they rarely intruded into his thoughts, and only became real when he was on home leave. It was impossible to survive otherwise. Navy wives knew this and had to accept it. But now the images of his wife, Marthe, and his four-year-old son Hans, kept pushing their way into his mind. He hadn't seen them for a month; he had already warned her to take special care. Now, something inside him knew that he would probably not see either of them again. But somehow this just hardened Bach's resolve; it was the price to be paid. The sacrifice on the altar of duty had to be great, to appease the gods. There was no greater sacrifice that Bach could have made.

Willi had cleared the outer suburbs and was on the *autobahn* to Hamburg, now just 250 kilometres away. The road was deserted other than for the occasional Army truck. Willi floored the accelerator and the big Mercedes reached 110 kilometres per hour. If the road stayed clear they would make Hamburg by nightfall.

And now Captain Erich Bach, hero of the Navy, unseen by Willi, unscrewed the top of a small silver hip flask and pressed it to his lips. He had not dared take it into the bunker with him, and had left it hidden in his greatcoat pocket. He trusted Willi not to look for it. Now he was alone he could finally get to it. At times, in the bunker, he had had to bite his lip to keep himself under some control. The burning brandy flooded a sudden warmth through him. He paused and closed his eyes, then took another long, slow mouthful. The tremor in his hand – which had been worsening since yesterday – suddenly stopped. He looked out of the window of the car and voiced a silent farewell to Marthe, to Hans and to Germany.

Across the fields to the north and the east, distant columns of smoke, bent by the wind, drifted into the cold April sky.

4

Otto Heine buttoned his greatcoat up to his throat as a sharp, cold wind gusted in from across the estuary. He was standing next to a thin gangway angled up to a grey steel monster of a ship. The camouflage netting high above them, slung like a vast green cobweb over the masts and the single squat smokestack, was being cut away by small groups of men, and drifts of it would flutter down like outsized leaves.

Heine was surprised by the activity. He knew the yards well: he had spent much of the war doing profitable deals with most of the people who worked in them. But this corner was always guarded, always out of bounds, even for the Navy people he knew. Screened off and netted over, everyone knew something was going on, but no one knew what. Slave labour would come and go, trucks full of dull-eyed, pinched-cheeked Russians or Poles, and the stories were that a great secret weapon was being constructed. In the last few months the yard, pounded by the British at night and the Americans by day, had become a wasteland. Most of it was deserted now; the ships that were left had been sunk where they were tied up.

And now here was what looked like a brand-new ship, guarded and crewed, getting ready to sail in the middle of all this shit.

'You – what's your name?' shouted a dark-haired, stocky man wearing the uniform of a *Stabsfeldwebel*, a chief petty officer. Klompe's haul of kids had been thrown off the back of the truck and told to stand to attention on the quay. Heine had wandered off to the edge of the quay to get a better view of the ship.

'Me? Otto. What's your name?' replied Heine.

'Don't take the piss, sonny. Get back in that line and stay there until I tell you to move. Now, what's your full fucking name?'

The man looked as if he wasn't in a mood to joke. Heine did as he was told and shuffled back into the line with ill-concealed disdain.

'Otto Heine.'

But the man ignored him now. Heine and the rest of the lads – some, he thought, were no older than twelve – stood in a ragged line, while the stocky man started scribbling on a clipboard.

'Listen. My name is Schnee, but you can call me Chief Petty Officer Schnee. You are hereby conscripted into the German Navy. As of now, Otto Heine and the rest of you, you are under my orders. I am a busy man and, if you keep quiet and do what you're told, you won't see much of me. Keep your heads down, that's my advice. But if you want to see a lot of me, Heine, then just take the piss. No problem. I'll fucking tear your bollocks off, one by one, and feed them to the fucking fish.' Schnee walked down the line of frightened kids, stopped opposite Heine and put his face into his until their noses almost touched. 'So, you understand me, Otto Heine?' said Schnee quietly.

Otto didn't even blink. He returned the stare with his eyebrows slightly raised. He wasn't going to get into a fight with this man, but he didn't intend to submit to him either.

Schnee saw the look in Heine's eyes. He had no time for this sort of thing. His job was to take this rubbish from the street and turn them into something approaching sailors by the time the ship sailed, God knows why or how. So, some kid wanted to show how tough he was? Schnee had been doing this job for years and had seen them come and go. Now, with the war lost and this strange ship getting ready to sail, he really wondered what the point of it all was. Still, he had his orders. He carried on staring at Heine, then shook his head sadly and turned to the rest of them.

'Right, you follow me on to the ship and I'll show you your quarters. You're lucky. There's plenty of room. You'll find uniforms on board; get cleaned up and get into them.' He looked at his watch. 'You've got an hour until I want to see you on parade. Now, follow me.'

Schnee turned and led the way on to the huge grey ship. With Heine at the rear, the line of kids dutifully followed Schnee along the teak deck until they reached a steel door; Schnee went through it and they descended a series of ladders, down three deck levels, and then along a dark companionway lit by dim yellow lamps. The companionway seemed endless. Finally Schnee stopped and pushed open a wooden door. He motioned the boys into the room, a featureless box with two ranks of steel poles supporting the deckhead. Two long wooden tables that looked as though they had come from a workshop, and a few unmatched chairs, were the only furnishings; and there was a heap of fabric dumped in one corner. On the table was a pile of clothing in Navy black.

'Hammocks,' said Schnee, pointing to the fabric heap on the floor. 'You sort one out and tie it to the poles. Uniforms. Find one that fits. The heads are down the companionway. That's what we call toilets in the Navy. It's your job to keep them clean. You've got one hour,' and Schnee slammed the door behind him.

There was a silence in the cabin as the lads stood and looked at their new surroundings. One or two were close to tears. Klompe had taken anybody he found. Several of the boys were starving, literally, and were grateful to have a roof over their heads. But some had been simply unlucky enough to be out on the streets, with families at home. And now nobody seemed to know what to do.

Heine watched them. He pitied them. They were just kids, most of them with no sense. But he would let them sort themselves out. What were they to do with him, after all? He had to look after himself; that was his motto. Otto Heine's only responsibility is Otto Heine. End of story.

'Do you know what's going to happen?' one of the boys asked Heine, breaking the silence. All the faces turned to him. There was something about Otto that made them assume that he knew the score.

'Me? Listen, kid, I don't know a thing.' Heine felt awkward but he still wasn't going to get sucked into this mess. Leave me alone. Worry about yourselves. Well, that idiot Schnee would be back soon. Better keep him quiet. Get a uniform on, let him get us up on deck. Then I'll figure out what to do. I'm not staying on this fucking thing, for a start. Heine went to the table and sorted through the uniforms. They were thick and scratchy; pants and tunic with the sailor's neck-flap. They were far from clean, he noted with distaste. He found one that looked as though it fitted and dressed himself in it as the other kids stood and watched. He felt their eyes boring into him, watching his every move.

Once he had his uniform on, the rest suddenly gathered round and started to dress as well. Heine stood back in amusement and watched them. Once they were all kitted out, he untangled a hammock, found the quietest part of the cabin and strung it up between the poles. He'd done this before; sometimes his father had allowed him on the ships when he was younger. Once it was tied, he jumped into it and stretched out. Let the others do *that*, he thought to himself with some amusement.

They followed his example, but none of them tried to actually get into the hammock. It was as though Heine had a special right to lie there, relaxing, while they stood around awaiting orders.

True to his word, Schnee arrived exactly one hour later. They all stood to what they thought was attention as he walked into the room. Heine lazily swung off the hammock, last of all, and leaned against one of the posts that supported it, arms folded. Schnee looked at him but decided to save him for later.

'Right, look sharp. Follow me,' and he led the way back down the long companionway and up the three flights of ladders. But he didn't take them out on deck, much to Heine's irritation. Instead he led them down another series of companionways into a large hall lined with rows of tables. Small groups of other ratings were scattered around the hall, eating from tin plates and drinking from tin mugs. All that could be heard was the clatter of the plates and mugs. No one was talking.

'This is your mess. Where you eat. Breakfast is at seven. You get a midday meal at twelve, and an evening meal at six if you're not on duty. Eat now. I'll be back in half an hour,' and he left them to their own devices.

Once more Heine was left to make the running. He was hungry. At the end of the hall was a long hatchway where two sullen men in whites were chatting idly to each other. As he walked towards them, he could feel the others following. He wanted to tell them to get lost; they were starting to get on his nerves. But he ignored them and approached the hatch. There was a pile of metal plates and mugs at one side. The two men watched him as he took up one, replaced it and picked up another which was just as dirty. It would have to do.

'What have you got? Anything good today?' he asked cheerily.

The men looked at him with sour expressions. 'Just hold your fucking plate out, sonny. You get what you're given.'

Heine held out his plate. A lump of grey, grittylooking bread was thrown on to it, and a dollop of something that had been cooked hours ago. 'Thanks. Looks excellent. What exactly is it?'

'Lunch.'

'Listen, old man, do me a favour. Tell me what the fuck is in this shit before I ram it up your arse. How about it?' said Heine quietly but with deadly seriousness.

The man saw the look in Heine's eyes. 'Meat of some kind. I don't know. It comes in big tins. We just heat the stuff up. That's all there is.'

'See? That didn't hurt a bit. It looks wonderful. It's so good I'll have a bit more. So will my friends here. And some extra bread.'

'Suit yourself,' said one of the men, and Heine's small group of followers got extra rations. He could do no wrong in their eyes. He realised that it would make them stick to him all the more but, what the hell, these Navy people should learn to be civilised. The lads followed Heine to a table, where they all sat down with him. He spooned some of the mess into his mouth and grimaced. It tasted like shit, whatever that tasted like. This was not what Heine was used to. And he did not like this lot following him around like sheep. He could feel them looking at him as he tried to eat.

He finished two more spoonfuls, then suddenly stood up. 'Listen, nothing personal. It's just that I prefer to eat alone, if that's all right.' He moved to another table, empty, and quietly resumed his meal. But he could still feel their eyes glancing at him.

*

They reached Hamburg by eight, just as the sky was darkening. The journey had taken nearly six hours.

A few kilometres after they had left Berlin they ran into a long line of civilians heading north, refugees making for the sea, hoping to escape the wrath of the Bolsheviks. Willi decided to leave the *autobahn* and take to the side roads, which had slowed them down. And then there was an attack from the air; they had run into an Army convoy, going God knows where, and seconds later a flight of American aircraft had screamed overhead, returning for a strafing run. Bach and Willi had dashed from the car and thrown themselves into a ditch. The whole road ahead of them erupted into a small storm of dust and flying metal as the pilots gunned the line of vehicles. The trucks rocked on their springs as bullets ripped into them. The run was over in seconds; not a single truck had caught fire, but the leading ones were in shreds. Their drivers slowly emerged from the same ditch, scanning the horizon. But the Americans had flown off.

The Mercedes had a cracked windscreen from the flying debris, but was otherwise undamaged. Bach ordered Willi to drive on. The soldiers were milling about aimlessly, unsure which way to go. Bach could not help them.

Now Willi slowly approached the yard. The outer perimeter, as Heine had already discovered, was deserted. The grey Elbe was littered with the torn wreckage of ships, and the massive cranes that once towered over the huge Blohm and Voss yard were now toppled, collapsed like a pile of sticks. Half the city was in ruins. The dull thud of distant artillery seemed to Bach to have moved closer.

The Luftwaffe had long since deserted the skies, and Allied aircraft made routine bombing runs almost every hour, but for the last two or three days things had been quieter than normal. Once inside the yard, Bach ordered Willi to stop the car and get out.

The two men stood opposite each other on the cobbles. 'Willi, it's time for you to go,' started Bach, quietly and awkwardly. 'I am sailing tonight and I doubt I shall be back. I have a letter to Marthe and my son Hans. Will you please see that they get it? I have also written a letter for you; if you are captured, it will exonerate you from any dealings with the Nazis. Do what you can for my wife, Willi. I have a little money. Marthe knows where. Use it as you please. Take good care of them, Willi. Tell them – well, I don't know what. Go west. As soon as you can. It's finished here.'

'Captain, take care of yourself. Thanks for looking after me. They'd have sent me to the Russian front otherwise, I should think.'

'Not you, Willi. You'd be a lousy soldier. You're too fat.'

'Not now, Captain. Not now,' laughed Willi. Both men looked at each other. Bach was a cold, reserved man, not given to displays of emotion. This was as much as Willi had heard in the three years he had been driving him. When Willi held out his hand, Bach looked at it for a moment and then gripped it with surprising warmth, clasping his other hand over Willi's. No more words were spoken. Willi got back in the car and slowly reversed, then drove gently out of the yard, past the ruined gates and into the failing light. Bach turned and walked quickly down the quay.

So, where was *Der Fuhrer*? Krancke's instructions were clear enough, but Bach had spent little time in the yard and knew it less well than Heine did. Berth 18, said the orders. He walked past a wrecked frigate lying still tied to the quay, its stern settled on the bottom and the bow high in the air.

There was a number carved into the granite edge of the quayside: 14. He carried on walking. Gulls screamed in the evening light, trying to find food. Ahead of him was a vast shed, the walls made of corrugated iron, and the quay seemed to disappear underneath it. The structure looked temporary. Krancke had said the ship was shielded.

As he got nearer the structure, he could make out a small door. Near it was a guard post and, unlike any-where else in the yard, it was manned. There were four SS men in black uniforms and helmets. He approached it.

'Papers?' barked one of the men, half Bach's age. Krancke had warned him. Bach handed over the letter signed by Sluys. The boy read it but looked unimpressed. 'Very well, Captain. I have orders to escort you on board.'

'Thank you.'

The SS man took Bach through the small door in the corrugated iron. What he saw inside took his

breath away. Undamaged, freshly painted, lights glittering, here lay the ship that had started life identical to
Bismarck as the *Hindenburg,* and which now was to
be called *Der Fuhrer* – supposedly scrapped in 1941
but now finished. The size of the vessel was awesome,
even to Bach. From stem to stern it measured 823 feet,
quite the longest ship that he had ever seen. The
armoured sides towered high above him; and stretching even further was the central conning tower, over
100 feet above the deck, draped with the camouflage
netting that was being slowly removed. But, as
Puttkamer had told him, the ship had been stripped
down. The after end looked empty: the two turrets
that should have been there were missing. And the
side armaments – there should have been six small
turrets holding the 5.9-inch guns, and eight smaller
ones with 4.1-inch guns – had never been fitted. There
were just eight blister turrets containing the 37-mm
anti-aircraft guns. But *Der Fuhrer* remained awesome
nevertheless. The four 15-inch guns she carried in her
two forward turrets were ample to do the job that
Werner was so enthusiastic about.

Bach could see the thickened armour-plate belt
running along the sides of the hull; no scuttles –
portholes – weakened the structure. The ship must be
as dark as Hades inside, he thought.

Bach followed his escort down the side of the ship.
When he reached the gangway he was escorted up.
Someone must have called ahead; there was a small
reception committee standing to attention on the
deck. From his written orders he already knew the
names of the small group of officers who were to
accompany him on this voyage of madness. Along
with the reduced crew he had just six officers to
help him run the ship. His escort introduced him

to the first of them, Bach's new second-in-command,
Korvettenkapitan Schiller, a young man with a repu-
tation for being bright and ambitious – or so said
Krancke's notes. Schiller took over the introductions.

'Captain, welcome to *Der Fuhrer*. May I introduce
Kapitanleutnant Kinzel, artillery …' and Bach shook
his hand '… *Oberleutnant sur See* Bruller, navigation
… *Oberleutnant sur See* Ecke, engineering …
Oberleutnant sur See Jensch, communications … and
Leutnant sur See Moehle, our radar specialist.'

One by one the officers saluted Bach. They all
seemed so terribly young; Moehle, the most junior,
didn't look more than twenty. Was this all they had
left? Had any of them been to sea before? None of
them knew the mission – Krancke had told him to
brief them when they were under way; 'just in case', as
his note had so carefully put it. Bach returned the
salute and shook each man by the hand. Schiller, the
introductions over, led Bach to the officers' mess in the
forward part of the ship.

As they walked, Bach now noticed how crudely
the vessel was finished. Puttkamer was right. The job
had not been done to the standards he would have
expected. Piping was held in place by rope; glass was
missing from some of the windows, weatherproofed
with board instead. The paintwork, on closer inspection,
was patchy, and splashes of grey littered the decks and
spattered the windows that did have glass. Already
streaks of rust showed through.

Ecke, his new engineering officer, was next to him.
'You've looked at the engines, Ecke?' asked Bach.

'Of course. Just two MAN diesels, Captain, driving
one shaft. A strange arrangement.'

'I understand. I just hope they're better than the rest
of the ship looks.'

'No problems, Captain. The engineering is first class. There's just not a great deal of it.'

They reached the officers' mess, which was as badly finished as the rest of the ship. On one bulkhead, taking pride of place, was the obligatory portrait of Adolf Hitler. Bach assembled his small complement of officers in front of it.

'Thank you for your welcome, gentlemen. None of you have sailed with me before, so let me introduce myself as a rather old-fashioned captain. I believe in duty, above all, and so long as you believe the same, we'll get on splendidly. I also believe in tradition, gentlemen. To me, it is bad luck to change a ship's name. I have never sailed on a vessel that did not bear its original name, and I do not intend to start now. As of today, this ship returns to its proper name of *Hindenburg*, and with all due respect to the Fuhrer I would like this picture behind me replaced with our ship's namesake. Schiller, ensure this is done before we dine tonight. Next, our orders are to sail with the tide tomorrow at eighteen-thirty hours, under cover of darkness. I want this ship ready to cast off on the stroke of half-past the hour. Lastly, none of you know what our operational orders are. I am afraid I cannot brief you in any detail until we have cleared Cuxhaven tomorrow. However, I think it is only fair to warn you now that a perilous and difficult task lies ahead. The situation here in Germany is, let us say, due for change. None of you should accompany me unless you have complete enthusiasm for any orders I will give you. You each have the option, right now, of resigning your commissions and leaving the ship. I will sign your papers in the proper manner. But if you do not resign, you will remain German Navy officers. That means we will never surrender, we will never give up, no matter what our orders are. The choice is yours. I will leave you to think about it. We dine at nine. And, gentlemen, no alcohol. I like a dry ship. Good evening.'

Bach abruptly turned and left the mess, making for the cabin that Schiller had pointed out to him on their way through the ship, leaving his bemused and worried officers behind him.

*

A few minutes before nine that evening, on the quay, two battered 6.3-ton Tatra III six-wheel trucks carefully backed up to position their loads, side by side, directly underneath a crane. The rear ends of each truck were sagging on their axles under the heavy weight inside.

The drivers climbed slowly out and went up to the guard on the quay.

'Last load of shells. Twenty fifteen-inch, a dozen six-inch. You want to sign for them?' asked one of the drivers.

'Who? Me?' replied the guard, a boy of eighteen, looking mystified. But then a voice from above rang out. It was Moehle, leaning over the guard rail, on his way to the officers'mess.

'You down there! What's the problem?'

'Sir, two loads of shells. They want them signed for. Sir.'

'Wait there. I'll come down,' shouted Moehle, and disappeared. He arrived at the two trucks minutes later, emerging from the darkness that lay beyond the yellow pool of light from the overhead lamp.

He inspected the drivers' manifests. 'These were supposed to have been here hours ago. What happened?'

'Happened? You're joking. The place is falling apart. Had to take so many detours we bloody nearly ran out of fuel. Don't complain. They're here now. You want the damn things or not?' The drivers, curiously, were *Wehrmacht,* and were openly contemptuous of Moehle's rank.

Moehle ignored the insult and signed the papers, then curtly told the drivers to get something to eat, if they could find anything. Then he ordered the young guard to get a loading crew sorted at the double, while Moehle himself went to find a crane-driver. Fifteen minutes later the twenty big shells were being lifted by the eyes screwed into their noses – where later a detonator would be fitted when they were ready to fire – high over the deck, and then down a deep hatchway where they were carefully fitted into the ready-made racking that would hold them securely throughout the voyage. As each shell was lifted, the truck groaned on its springs and rose an inch or more, relieved of the weight.

'I want them on the bottom. Make sure of that,' called Moehle, standing above the hatch and shouting down to the loading crews. The crews shrugged their shoulders and carefully placed the shells on the bottom row of racks, where spaces had conveniently been left vacant.

The twelve smaller shells were simply carried down to the magazine by hand, in wooden boxes that held two at a time. Moehle again insisted that the boxes were placed at the very bottom of the racking, where, once more, spaces had been left for them.

The two men who carried the six boxes were sweating after their effort, even though the wind had become icy cold.

The loading of the shells took just over an hour. Finally both trucks were empty, the armoured doors to the magazine closed, the hatch shut and Moehle and the loading crews dispersed.

'Peculiar shells, those,' remarked Fritsch, the crane-driver who had helped move them, wrapping a woollen scarf around his neck to keep out the cold.

'Why?' asked his companion.

'Heavy. Very heavy. Poor old girl was struggling to lift them.'

'The crane's knackered, Otfried. Like this bloody place.'

'Probably. Very probably,' commented the crane-driver as they made their way home through the deserted, ruined streets, thinking no more about the strangely heavy shells.

*

Schnee had the boys lined up inside the empty aircraft hanger just behind the squat, single funnel. A single powerful yellow light illuminated the whole area. It was already late, but Schnee had his orders from Schiller to get everyone ready by tomorrow evening. Schnee was one of four chief petty officers who had charge of the eighty or so ratings scattered around the ship. He didn't know it, and neither did the others, but Schiller had chosen them because they were the oldest CPOs he knew of. In Schiller's book, older meant experienced and less likely to fuss; getting a bunch of raw recruits – most of them, frankly, press-ganged into service as few other experienced ratings were available in the devastated port – ready within the forty-eight hours he had been given was not going to be an easy task.

He hoped that by using four chiefs, with all their experience, they would make an effective command structure in the absence of a normal one. He still didn't know what the hell all this was about, but like Bach he had his orders and he was going to carry them out, come what may.

Schnee was equally bemused by the orders Schiller had given him. He had dealt with some rough crews before, but never a bunch of frightened schoolkids who didn't know one end of a ship from the other. Apart from that cocky little shit Heine. He'd have him when the moment was right. Take him down a peg or two. In the meantime, he had to try to get some semblance of order out of this lot.

'Name?' he barked for the twelfth time. He was filling in the forms – in fact, no one had given him any paperwork at all, so he decided to make it up. He felt this was more correct. The lad, a skinny sandy-haired youth of sixteen, whispered his name in a shy mumble. 'Address?' The address was written down. 'Education?' The details of his schooling were recorded in Schnee's slow and neat handwriting.

One by one he worked his way down the line. He knew Heine was at the end of the row, just waiting to be cocky. Let him wait.

For his part, Heine was thinking very carefully through the problems of getting off the ship. There was no point in trying right now. The fucking thing was surrounded by guards; it must be the only thing left in Germany that was so well guarded. And sneaking off at night would make him all the more conspicuous. No, thought Heine, bide your time. His best plan was to wait until morning, but early. He had enough experience of the art of thieving to know that in the early morning, in daylight, people don't expect things to happen. At night-time, they're suspicious. In the morning, they feel safe. Which was why, whenever Otto had had a job to do, he had always chosen the hour or two after dawn. So walking off the ship, confident, in uniform, with a cheery greeting to the guards, a box under his arm as a prop for the errand he would say he was running if asked, would appear to be the most natural thing in the world. In the meantime, he'd spend a night in the dry and warmth of the ship. Things were not so bad.

Schnee had finally reached him. 'So, Otto Heine …' started Schnee.

'That's me.'

'I don't suppose you have an address? The Hamburg doss-house, perhaps?' The kids sniggered.

'No. I usually stay at the Alster.' The lads now laughed out loud; the Alster had been – it lay in ruins now – one of the best hotels in Hamburg.

'And education? What would you like me to put down?'

'Oh, just the local gymnasium. Would you like me to spell it?'

'Thank you, Heine. That won't be necessary. Now, that completes the list. I have everyone down here. So I will tell you what your jobs are.' Schnee went back through the list and assigned each lad to various tasks that Schiller needed done. Most of them were deckhands for the departure of the ship; other duties would be given to them during the voyage. Schnee finished the list off.

'You left me out. What do I do?' asked Heine, put out at being ignored.

'Heine? Oh, sorry, Heine. Let me see – here we are. Galley, Heine. Galleyhand. You'll like it down there. You've already met the cook, I believe. He asked for you personally. Report right now, Heine. He's looking forward to seeing you again.'

*

Dinner was stiff and awkward. Bach had never been one for the social niceties and the lack of alcohol – not even a beer – didn't help matters along. He spoke to each man in turn and asked about his career, even though Krancke's notes had explained everything. The officers found Bach polite but not really interested, as though he was just going through the form. The food was evil, as well. Tinned sardines formed the main course, and they tasted as though they'd been preserved in engine oil. Bach didn't notice it.

On the bulkhead, the picture of Adolf Hitler was missing. In the storerooms, Schiller had found the framed oil painting of Hindenburg, which had been originally intended for the ship. The thickset man glowered through his huge walrus moustache, looking down on them like a stern father.

Just as they were finishing, Moehle, the young radar officer, slipped in.

'Good evening. We started at nine,' commented Bach dryly.

'Yes, sir. I'm sorry, sir. Problem. Had to deal with it.'

'Don't be late again, Moehle. I expect my officers to be better organised than that.'

'Yes, sir. Sorry, sir,' and Moehle slipped into his seat, reddening in the face.

A steward in a fraying white jacket cleared away the plates. There was a long silence. Bach wiped his mouth carefully and looked at his officers.

'Well, gentlemen?'

Schiller spoke for the rest of them. 'Captain, we would like to thank you for giving us the opportunity to leave. We understand the situation. None of us care to resign our commissions. We remain officers in the German Navy. All of us.'

'Even when you don't know what is about to happen?'

'We know that Germany is finished. What could be

worse than staying? Whatever you have in mind for us has to be better. We await our orders, Captain.'

Bach paused. He was starting to speak when the steward suddenly burst back into the room.

'Air raid – sir,' he shouted, and ran out again.

Bach smiled. 'The timing is remarkable, gentlemen. It will save me having to thank you. I suggest we go below.' He calmly led his officers from the wardroom – located on the upper deck and therefore only lightly armoured – down several ladders to where the thick plating of the deck would protect them.

The sound of the RAF Lancasters droning above them was like the moaning of a great herd of animals, rising and falling as the beats of the engines synchronised and then unsynchronised with each other. There were forty aircraft, flying in low, unhindered by the Luftwaffe and now not even by any ground fire, sent on a mission to destroy the U-boats on the northern coast from where they continued their deadly activities under Donitz's orders. That night it was not just Hamburg; Kiel was due for a pasting as well.

The Pathfinders had already been and gone. The Elbe formed a perfect aiming point, visible even in the light of an intermittent moon. The flight of the Pathfinders, and the sudden eruption of red flares, served as the only air-raid warning available to those on the ground.

One by one, following each other like well-behaved schoolchildren, the bombers grumbled slowly overhead, the engine note suddenly increasing as the load of bombs left the bomb-bays and the aircraft became several tons lighter. The first few aircraft dropped the heavy stuff, 500-lb blockbusters. The practice was to use these to blow apart installations and buildings, exposing the innards to the second wave of aircraft carrying incendiary bombs to complete the devastation by burning them out.

Bach and his officers felt rather than heard the first of the heavy bombs marching, one after the other, towards them. It felt like a giant hand slapping the ship slowly. The bombs came in groups, as each aircraft deposited its load.

Schiller and Bach looked at each other. They were definitely getting nearer.

Was the ship itself a target?

There was a pause, and then – clearly audible now – another line of heavy bombs exploded, each one louder than the last. Another pause. Bach and Schiller thought they could feel the dull grey bombs whistling gently through the night air above Hamburg, twisting and yawing in the slipstreams, until they finally nosed down towards ... there was a massive blast, from what felt to be directly above them. The noise was so intense that it was more than a blast – it was a scream of sound, crackling and bouncing off the bulkheads. The lights went out immediately. The ship was physically rocking. A second later there was another huge blast, but this time it seemed further away. Then another – and another – marching away across the quay. There was a silence, but their ears were ringing and they couldn't see a thing.

'Is there no bloody emergency lighting on this thing?' yelled a voice, but nobody knew whose it was.

'Stay where you are,' ordered Bach calmly. He had used the darkness to take a quick drink from his hip flask, and he was feeling calmer. 'Incendiaries are next. Wait for a minute and then we'll go up and see what's happened. There should be plenty of light by then.'

They waited in a tense silence, each man with his

own thoughts. There were more explosions but they were distant now, and getting further and further away.

*

Heine had made his way reluctantly down towards the mess hall and the galley to report for duty when the first bombs fell. He was on the main deck when half a dozen small aircraft whined low overhead, and then bright red flares erupted across the river in a silent display. He knew exactly what was coming.

He disappeared down the nearest hatchway and closed it softly behind him. This was his chance. In the confusion of an air raid all the officers, all the guards, would be hiding. Heine could make his escape unseen. Perfect. He just needed to wait until all hell was breaking loose around them, as it would do in a few moments' time now that the Pathfinders had lit up the target.

Air raids no longer worried Otto Heine. He'd been through too many of them. If they got you, they got you. If they didn't, take advantage of the situation. In a few moments the bombers would be flying in. He'd wait until the last of them went over and then get off this pile of shit while everyone else was pissing themselves. He hoped Schnee would be standing right underneath one when it went off.

The first blasts were distant but approaching. He crouched down behind the steel door.

Like Bach and his officers further forward, Heine heard the bombs marching steadily towards them. Not good, he thought to himself. And then there was the blast from the bomb that fell into the water and exploded twenty feet from the forward section of the ship, rocking the whole vessel and bringing down part of the corrugated iron wall. He held his breath.

Any more? No – the bombs carried on away from them. Now was the time. He pushed open the door. There was an acrid smell; something was burning nearby. Over the top of the remains of the huge corrugated iron barrier, he could see the glow from the burning incendiaries. He hurried out on to the deck and made his way aft, where there was a gangway. It was still there, deserted of course. He ran quickly along the deck, keeping close in to the superstructure. There was an eerie silence now that the bombs had moved off into the distance, and Heine could hear his footsteps ringing on the deck. He had almost reached the gangway when a voice stopped him.

'Who's there?' it asked. But it was a young voice, pleading, not challenging.

Heine stopped. In the distant glow he saw one of the kids who just a few hours before had been on the truck with him, press-ganged by the idiot Klompe.

'It's me, Heine. You all right?'

'I don't think so. Something hit me. It hurts.'

'You'll be all right. Stay under cover. I'm off.'

'No, don't go!'

'Listen, kid, don't worry, someone will come.'

'Help me. It hurts.'

Heine swore. Little bastard. What concern was it of his? The gangway was still empty. He could spare a second. Heine knelt down; the kid was crouched in a corner, his arms held tightly across his stomach.

'Where's it hurt? Let me take a look.'

'Here. My stomach. Something hit me.'

'Take your fucking hands away, kid. I can't see a thing.'

The boy did as Heine instructed him and something shiny flopped down on to the deck. In the dim light Heine couldn't see what it was. When he touched it, it was warm, plump, sticky. Like an animal, alive and pulsing. With a sudden shock he realised it was the lad's innards, spilling out through a wound where a bomb splinter had neatly sliced across his abdomen, opening a long gash as cleanly as a surgeon's knife.

Heine was hard, hard as nails. Nothing ever worried Otto Heine. Now he felt himself go clammy and cold, instantly. His breath shallowed and he was feeling dizzy. Oh, shit. I can't fucking keel over here, he thought.

'Listen, kid, you're all right. Just a second.' He stripped off his own scratchy tunic and laid it quickly over the bulging object that lay on the boy's lap; neither of them wanted to see it.

But the youngster had gone silent, although he was still breathing. Heine looked around. There was no one, his escape was still open. Then the boy moaned again, reached out a hand and gripped Heine's arm tightly.

'Fuck you, kid, fuck you,' said Heine gently.

'Don't go. Don't go.'

'Take it easy. I'm here.'

The boy's grip tightened even more. A full minute passed. Then Heine heard the sounds of voices and running feet. The ship was coming back to life. He glanced at the gangway; it was still clear.

But he couldn't release the boy's grip.

It was Schnee who a minute later ran past and found them. By then, the lights were coming on again and the guards had re-emerged on the quay. Heine swore again. He didn't say a word to Schnee; he just gently loosened the boy's grip. The hand was already starting to go cold. He turned and walked back towards the stern.

*

'Are we in any state to go?' demanded Bach of Schiller and the others. He had asked the question a moment before, but no one seemed to understand him.

'You mean now?' asked Schiller, dubiously.

'Now. We nearly took a hit there. I don't want to hang around. If the ship is ready, we'll go right now. How's the tide, Bruller?'

'Er, don't know, sir. I'll find out.'

'Ecke, how long to get the engines running?'

The two big marine diesel engines would need, ideally, two hours of warming through before firing up. But Ecke reckoned he could get them running after about an hour if he took a few short cuts. 'I'll start on them. Give me an hour,' and Ecke disappeared in the direction of his engine room.

'Schiller, we'll need tugs. Go and organise the lazy dogs.'

'Sir, tide is up but on the ebb,' called Bruller.

'Can we clear the river?'

'Only if we go within the hour. Otherwise we'll ground at Cuxhaven.'

'Very well. We cast off in one hour exactly. Twenty-three-hundred hours. Get the ship ready, gentlemen.' His tone brooked no argument, no discussion. He took Ecke's promise literally. This was the first time that any of them had seen Bach as a ship's commander, and he was clearly a man who knew his own mind.

The ship started to come to life. Schiller found his tugs and their masters and instructed them to get ready to move the ponderous battleship from its berth. Ecke had begun warming up his engines; a thin skein of black smoke from the pre-heaters, set to maximum, drifted from the stack as the two big diesels were warmed. Bruller, the navigation officer, was calculating his tidal curves; the draught of the ship was thirty-two feet. It was sixty-two miles from Hamburg to Cuxhaven at the mouth of the Elbe. At seven knots, which was what Schiller had told him they could achieve down the river, it would take them nine hours to run the distance; less with an outgoing tide to help them. At the Medem Sand, the lowest sounding was around five fathoms, just thirty feet. But by then the tide would be rising again, according to Bruller's calculations. It was a spring tide that evening; the rise was a little over ten feet. In any event, the soundings on the chart were always the lowest theoretical figure that the water would drop to; he reckoned he would have at least six clear feet of water under his keel at the shallowest point.

Exactly one hour passed. 'Stand by fore, stand by aft!' ordered Bach, looking at his watch. The tugs had already come up and were taking the strain on their lines. Their lights were on – it wouldn't make a lot of difference now, as what looked like half the dock area was ablaze from the incendiaries. The corrugated iron screen around the bow had been partially demolished by the earlier bomb and the way was almost clear out into the water. They would push the rest of the screening aside as they came out.

Schnee had his recruits standing by the lines, ready to cast off and haul in. He watched them, praying they wouldn't completely mess up the operation.

'Let go forward,' ordered Bach.

The shore hands lifted the thick hawsers off the bollards; on Schnee's orders the deck crews wrestled the lines on to the slowly rotating capstans.

'Bring the bow out, please,' ordered Bach. Schiller spoke to the tug masters who slowly pulled the bow away from the quay. As they did so, the aft lines were let go. The tugs strained at the lines until the bow of the ship was in the middle of the dock. Then the aft tug started the same process. Smoothly and without fuss, the 60,000-ton ship moved away from the quay and, partially under its own power and partially helped by the tugs, nosed slowly out of the dock and into the estuary.

The maiden voyage of *Der Fuhrer*, now renamed by Captain Erich Bach with its original name of *Hindenburg*, was at last under way.

5

There were no lights in the estuary. Those which hadn't been bombed or shelled had been turned off in an attempt to limit the damage from Allied air strikes. The glow from the burning city was behind them now and their eyes had become used to the dark. The tugs, besides, had been told to use searchlights if they needed.

A pilot was mandatory according to the strict port regulations. But no pilot was to be found. Schiller had navigated the Elbe many times and would have to do the job himself.

The biggest problem was not the lack of lights or, indeed, the twists and turns of the main channel. The danger was the mass of wrecks, half-sunk, littering the estuary for miles. Most of them had been sunk where they were moored, near the quays that lined the estuary for several miles. The main channel was passable, but only just – several hulks lay directly across Bach's path.

'Captain, the tug-master says there's half a freighter right across our course.'

Bach had thought about this eventuality as Willi had driven him over the river on the way to the ship – the wrecks were clear to see.

'Tell the tugs to stand away. We're going to ram the thing, Schiller. Ecke?'

'Yes, sir?' responded the engineer eagerly. It was like going into action.

'Maximum speed, please.'

Ecke spoke to his engine-room crew. The distant thud of the two slow diesels gathered pace.

The stem of the *Hindenburg* was armoured around the waterline, mainly as protection for ramming, a surprisingly common tactic for captains who were chasing down submarines. The bottom of the ship was also massively reinforced with Krupp cemented armour plate, alternating layers of high-grade steels welded on to over-sized frames in large seamless sheets. Puttkamer had been testing the resistance of armour plate – designed to withstand the sudden kinetic energy of a half-ton shell impacting on it – against the more diffuse but generally more powerful blast of a torpedo warhead. The problem was not the armour plate itself – the plating withstood the blast with little effect – but with the seams. The blast, spread over a wide area, tended to push the seams of the armour apart, thus holing the ship anyway. For the kind of punishment he expected this ship would have to take, Puttkamer got Krupp to develop much larger sheets. And instead of bolting the armour to the framing, he used the then-new technique of electric arc welding to melt the sheets into each other, a long and difficult job that had added a full year to the construction of the ship. But he ended up with a hull of immense strength.

After *Titanic* and *Bismarck*, Puttkamer was not stupid enough to announce that he had built an unsinkable ship; but he knew it would take more than a few torpedoes to sink the vessel. German engineering not only survived to the end of the war but

outlived it – Puttkamer would be arrested by the
Americans, taken to the States, and there he would
spend a happy career building advanced warships for
the American Navy well into the 1970s.

And now Bach was about to give Puttkamer's
engineering its first real test.

The freighter, or half of it, lay slewed directly across
the channel that Bach needed to take to avoid ground-
ing on either side. The stern of the old ship was buried
in the silt, the jagged mid-section pointing upwards
into the air. The fore part of the ship was nowhere to
be seen.

'Lights, please,' Bach ordered.

Two brilliant searchlights sent long pale fingers of
yellow light across the black water. The jagged stump
of the freighter was found and the lights converged
on the wreck.

'Helm, come to starboard,' ordered Bach. The
helmsman turned the wheel slightly to the right.

'Speed?' asked Bach.

'Coming up to ten knots,' replied Ecke.

Even at ten knots, the huge ship represented a massive force bearing down on the remains of the freighter.
There was silence on the bridge now. The officers were
holding grab-rails to brace themselves for the impact.
At the stem, a clean bow-wave had formed as the vessel
picked up speed. At the stern, the huge single screw
beat through the shallow water and churned up a mass
of black silt. The four tug-masters stood off, watching
the huge, shadowy walls of steel gather speed.

From the bridge, the wreck came nearer and
nearer. Then the searchlights reached the limits of
their depression and could no longer track it; the
wreck vanished into the darkness, directly in line with
the bow.

Schiller left the enclosed bridge and went outside, on to the wing, where he hoped to get a better view. He gripped the railing tightly and flexed his knees to absorb the sudden impact.

There was a slight rocking motion. No one heard a sound. The ship carried on gathering speed, now eleven knots. The armoured giant, all 60,000 tons of it, had carved though the rusting plating of the freighter like wire going through cheese. The armoured bottom then neatly flattened the remains as it passed over them, pushing them deep into the silt. By the time the huge screw passed over, what little remained was pushed deep into the bottom, yards clear of the manganese-bronze blades.

They waited on the bridge, surprised by the lack of impact. Had they missed it? A minute passed, and Schiller ordered lights to sweep the stern. There was no trace of the wreck.

'Reduce revolutions, please. Ask the tugs to pick us up. Get one of them to take a look at the stem, see what the damage is,' ordered an unconvinced Bach.

The tug-master reported back. A scratch in the paintwork. Would they like him to touch it up? The bridge crew laughed. This ship was beginning to impress them.

The tugs took the lines once more and escorted the ship up the narrow channel in the darkness, working their way up the Elbe towards Cuxhaven and the North Sea. The banks on each side were dark, but the silence was still punctuated by distant rumbles, and to the east the sky flashed as though a distant thunderstorm was raging.

Bach and Schiller stood in the darkness of the bridge, with only the dull red light of the compass binnacle glowing dimly.

'Well, Schiller, that's Germany. Not much left of it now.'

'No, sir.'

'Any family?'

'Only my parents. In Cologne.'

'Have you heard from them?'

'No, Captain. Not for the last few months.'

'I hope they're all right. The Allies will be there now.' Bach paused. 'Do you think we should have surrendered?'

'Surrendered? I didn't think such a word existed in the Navy, sir.'

Bach laughed. 'It doesn't. I was at Jutland, you know, Schiller. We took on the Royal Navy and they didn't defeat us. Then, one morning, we were ordered to set sail. No one said where. We raised our flags and set off – the whole damned fleet sailing in line, stretched for miles. We were headed for Scapa, where their ships were bottled up. This was the big one, we thought. Then, a day away, they told us that the Kaiser had abdicated, that we were sailing the ships to hand them over. Surrender, Schiller, and not a shot had been fired.'

'I know the story, Captain.'

'But have you any idea what it felt like? By God, man, you should have been there. Like lambs we were, naughty boys handing over our toys. We anchored in the sound as instructed; then we opened the seacocks and sent the whole lot of them to the bottom. The British were furious, but they couldn't do a thing. You should have seen their faces, Schiller.' The anger was clear in Bach's voice, but there was huge sadness.

'Not this time, then, Captain?'

'No, Schiller, not this time. Germany is a smoking wasteland, the Bolsheviks are raping their way to Berlin, that Austrian barbarian is probably on his way south

as we speak, and the Americans and British are bombing anything that's still upright. In a month, there
won't be a stone left standing. But no, Schiller, no
surrender. Not for the German Navy. Not again. Even if
we're the last ship left afloat, we carry on. I mean, it's
not that we've got anything to lose, is it?' But Bach
didn't sound wholly convinced.

'No. I suppose not.'

'Best to agree with your captain, Schiller. Makes him
happy. I hope your parents are safe. Anyway, back to
work now.'

'Yes, Captain,' and Schiller, still surprised by Bach's
sudden speech, lifted his Zeiss glasses to see what he
could of the channel ahead of them.

*

Moehle, still inside on the dark bridge, watched the
captain and first officer talking quietly outside. The
bridge was otherwise silent but busy, each man concentrating on navigating the ship up the channel.

The radio room was located two decks down, in the
armoured citadel that formed the fighting command
centre of the ship. He soundlessly left the bridge and
slipped down the ladders. There was a young rating in
the room, smoking against Bach's orders, his feet on
the desk.

'Attention!' said Moehle, suddenly. The lad nearly fell
over as he tried to get his feet off the desk and flick
the cigarette away.

'OK, OK, take it easy – I'm not the captain. Anyway,
you shouldn't be smoking, should you?'

'No, sir, sorry, sir,' replied the rating nervously.

'Never mind. I need to send a message to Berlin. You
have today's settings? I'll code it myself while you slip
out and finish your cigarette. I won't be long.'

The rating looked more uncomfortable. 'I'm not supposed ...'

But Moehle interrupted him. The rating was under strict orders to allow no one other than the captain and first officer near the Enigma code machine and settings. The Naval High Command had grown increasingly paranoid over security. Over the last few years the interception of U-boats and surface ships by the British seemed too easy, as though someone was reading the coded signals reporting positions – which, at Bletchley Park, they were doing on a daily basis. But the Germans simply could not conceive that the codes had been broken. It was a mathematical impossibility, the High Command was assured. But the rate of sinking of U-boats seemed inexplicable, and attention was turned on what was assumed to be a group of disaffected officers who might be passing on information. It was the only possible explanation. 'Don't get so upset, son. I won't report you. Take a break. It's the only chance you'll get, believe me.'

The boy looked relieved. 'You know how to use this stuff?'

'Technical Corps. Look ...' and Moehle showed him the gold cogwheel with lightning flash on his sleeve above the single stripe.

The lad was now convinced. 'That's fine, sir. Here are the keys. The settings are in the book. You take the date page and then move the code one day along. It's a new arrangement. Stops unauthorised people using the machine.'

'Thanks, son. I'll be five minutes.'

The boy left the room and closed the door behind him. Moehle opened the mahogany cover to the Enigma coding machine. It was the latest five-rotor type, totally secure and completely unbreakable according to Naval

High Command. He found the settings book and turned to 19 April 1945, then looked to the next page. There were rows of figures and letters. Moehle set each rotor to the required setting given by the book. It took three minutes to set up. Then he keyed in his message on the keyboard. Every time he pressed a key the rotors turned, and the numbers displayed on the code panel showed a different value.

The message was short:

> *Personal for Sluys. Your driver has left, 23.00 hours. Car running well. Luggage on board. Moehle.*

Moehle then used the Morse key to transmit the numbers of the coded message, where a coding clerk in the Berlin bunker eventually translated it to plain German. 'Well,' he remarked to a comrade, 'Sluys is getting ready to run as well.' Most of the traffic now was similar, as the officers made their own private arrangements to escape.

The message sent, Moehle left the room. The rating he had sent out was sitting on a locker, smoking his cigarette.

'That's fine, thanks. What's your name?' asked Moehle.

'Lemp, sir.'

'Lemp, you're a good sailor. Let me know if you need anything. Good sailors should be encouraged. Well done.'

'Thank you, sir,' replied Lemp, feeling pleased. Having a friend on the bridge was a handy thing for a rating, a very handy thing indeed.

Moehle pulled himself quickly up the ladders to the bridge, which was still silent with concentration. Schiller was watching the flashing light of the depth sounder as they moved slowly over a shallow part of the channel. No one saw Moehle come back.

*

At Bletchley Park, an old country house north of London, the rambling collection of huts that had sprung up around the house itself was mostly quiet that night. The intensity of the war in Europe was waning; only Donitz's fanatical U-boats were causing real problems, but even then the traffic was light and so easy to read that it took just four de-crypters to keep up with it. The Enigma codes had long since been broken, and Donitz's messages of exhortation to his few remaining commanders at sea were read in Whitehall often at the same time as the commanders themselves saw them.

Moehle's signal was captured from the ether by one of the monitoring stations set up by Montgomery's advancing Army group on the North German plain, and was being keyed into the de-coding machines within ten minutes of being sent. But it wouldn't de-code. Edna Phipps, the de-crypt clerk on duty that night, was shown the gibberish and the original message. She looked at it, puzzled for a moment, then smiled.

'It's *Kriegsmarine* code, not Donitz's lot. They advance the settings by a day. Donitz trusts his commanders, but the rest of them don't. Use tomorrow's settings.'

The girl did as she was told and the message translated clearly. Phipps took another look at it. So, Sluys was getting ready, too. But why use this code? Surely only warships were meant to use it? And there were no bloody warships left. Oh well, it wasn't important. The U-boat messages had total priority. The bastards were fighting to the bitter end, and every bit of intelligence was useful against them. She'd mention Moehle's strange message to someone when she got the chance.

*

Heine watched the dim banks of the Elbe slip slowly behind him. The view through the narrow scuttle was all he could now see of the outside world. The galley surrounded him. Sweat dripped from his face, not from any exertion but from the steam that filled the place, keeping the temperature at some ungodly level. And as if that wasn't bad enough, the smell of disinfectant made his eyes water. The bastard Schnee had managed to find him the worst job on the ship; and Rois, the cook – although he was barely able to open a tin – had enjoyed taking his revenge on Heine for the insults he had received earlier. Rois was a thick, sweaty, arrogant and grubby man, built like a battleship. He picked at his nose almost constantly.

'Ever washed up?'

'Never.'

'Good. You'll enjoy learning. First scrape the shit off. Then wash the fucking things. Got it? I'll check every plate, Heine, so fucking watch it.'

Heine shrugged and started on the pile. The mush of something-or-other was still slimy on the plates. He had to scrape hard to get it off into the stinking bin, already overflowing with a disgusting swill of fat and gristle. Then he plunged the plates into a huge steel sink, where the hot water came up to his elbows. He used a wooden scraper to get the rest of the filth off, and deposited the cleaned plates on the long draining board. He had already been at it for half an hour and the pile had barely changed.

Rois came up. 'Getting on well, then, Heine?'

'Fine, thank you.'

'Enjoying it, eh?'

'Best job I've had.'

Rois picked up a clean plate. 'Goodness me, Heine. It seems that you've missed a bit. These plates are filthy.'

'No, they're not,' replied Heine, holding his temper down.

Rois leaned down, lifted the swill bin up in one heave and tipped the contents over the draining board where Heine's pile of washed tin plates was sitting. He shook the bin and gobs of fat and grease dripped slowly on to the plates in a stinking pile. Then he set the bin down. 'They are now, Heine. Look at them! Quite disgusting. Wash them all again. And clean this shit up while you're about it.'

Heine leaned against the sink, his hands dripping. He looked at Rois squarely in the eye. The man wanted a fight, that was clear; but Heine knew what would happen; that bastard Schnee would get him. Heine was not so stupid; he'd save Rois for another day, when Schnee wasn't around.

He leaned over and pulled the whole pile of dirtied plates back into the sink with a huge crash. Rois was taken aback; he opened the big brass tap and scalding-hot water gushed into the sink, splashing grease all around. Heine was splattered with the stuff, but he was too dirty to care.

'Careful, Heine, careful,' warned Rois.

But Heine ignored him and set to work re-cleaning the plates. Seeing that Heine wasn't going to play, Rois backed off and left him to it. Snotty little bastard. I'll get him.

*

The sky was light in the east, but the weather had freshened and a steady twenty-knot wind was coming out of the north-west, bringing squalls of sleet and rain across the vast open plains and sand-dunes, and delaying the onset of the morning in the heavy, overcast sky. It was gone seven in the morning, but at least nothing would be flying in this weather and their passage would pass unnoticed. They were passing the Medem Sand now, one of the banks that littered this part of the coast for miles. Cuxhaven was on the port bank, the town and the yards silent, calmly awaiting the approaching Allied armies.

The navigation here was tricky; the channel was narrow and in places shallowed to within a few feet of the ship's keel. But Bruller's calculations were precise and the tide, rising now, was keeping them clear.

Past Cuxhaven and the channel started to widen, although the sands on each side still posed a danger. The wind was finding them now, whipping up small, steep wavelets which battered against the towering steel sides of the vessel, breaking against it like a massive cliff. The ship didn't move a millimetre; it could have been rooted to the sea bed. But the wind was beginning to move the bow around, and the helmsman was starting to wind the wheel to keep the course.

'Schiller, we need more way. Are we clear enough?' Bach knew that, at their present slow speed, the ship had not enough forward motion to provide good steerage against the gusting wind. He was suggesting they drop the slow tugs and make their own way out.

Schiller went to the back of the bridge, to the big chart table. He looked at the winding channel – another two or three miles between the sands before they started to get into open water. But the tide was rising; and in any event, like Bach, Schiller wanted to get the ship well out to sea if the weather improved enough to allow the Allied aircraft to fly.

'I think we can, Captain.'

'Go ahead, Schiller. Full speed once the tugs are

clear. Get the hands to make ready for sea.'

The two remaining tugs hauled in their lines, released by the *Hindenburg*'s deck crews, and turned back for Hamburg and their own fates. The engines once again started to beat more frequently, and the deck crews came back inside, shutting scuttles and companion-ways behind them.

The small village of Dose was on the spit of low land that was the furthest promontory of the main-land; they passed it by quickly, on the port side, and now they were clear of land and into the North Sea itself. The Steil Sand still protected them from the seas, but the wind was whipping across them now. The better speed kept them cleanly on course and soon, as the sands were left behind, the rolling grey waves of the sea began to march towards them. Even now the ship hardly moved. With its massive tonnage, and par-ticularly the heavy armoured bottom, the *Hindenburg*, like its sister-ship *Bismarck*, was a handy vessel, good in a seaway and designed to provide a stable platform for the big guns. It would take a lot more than twenty knots of North Sea wind to move the ship.

And for Bach, it was a refreshing blast of fresh air. This was his element, far from the politics, the mess and the defeat and pressures of land. He loved the sea, he always had. Even as a child he would demand that his father's servants took him out to sea, not on the family's steam yacht but in a small dinghy, where he could feel the wind and taste the lashing spray. His father would go mad if he found out, but he was usually too busy in his Hamburg bank to even notice. He wondered if his own son, Hans, would ever experience the same feeling; he wondered where they were now – had Willi got the letter to them? He had told them to go west, find the American or British lines. It was better than waiting for the Bolsheviks. With the little money he had saved for them they might be able to make a new life somewhere. He would join them soon, he promised. He stood on the wing-bridge with the wind and rain stinging his face, looking ahead, the flat coast behind him now starting to fade in the squalls.

'Clear, Captain. Ten fathoms and dropping,' called Schiller from the open door after another half-hour.

'Thank you, Schiller.'

'Course, Captain? We have no orders, you see.'

'Steer 340 degrees.' The course was a touch west of north, taking them past Heligoland and towards the northern tip of Scotland. It was a familiar bearing to the officers on the bridge; every major ship heading for the Atlantic steered the same course if they wanted to avoid running the English Channel. Schiller chalked '340' on the board in front of the helmsman, who turned his wheel gently to starboard to bring the bow to the new heading. The waves were getting bigger now and occasional flurries of spray, mixed with sleet, blew across the foredeck.

'Schiller, call the galley. Get some coffee up here. Then call Ecke from the engine room. I want to see you all in ten minutes,' ordered the Captain.

So. The old man was going to reveal all. Schiller spoke to each of the officers and then called the galley.

*

Heine had been up all night, washing the plates. Rois had watched him suspiciously from a distance but had left the kid alone. He enjoyed watching him, hour after hour, with his arms in the filthy water. Let him do it till he drops, thought Rois. But Heine would give him no such pleasure. As soon as the pile had diminished, another load would arrive. Heine simply kept going. He enjoyed feeling Rois stare at him.

And then came Schiller's order. Coffee. At the double. It was a long walk to the bridge. On deck, Rois knew it was blowing, and wet. He'd send Heine. The little shit would be soaked by the time he got there, and the coffee would be cold, and then Schiller would probably send him back for some fresh with a cuff around the ear into the bargain.

'Heine, that's enough. You can stop now,' ordered Rois.

'I'm fine. Just getting into the swing of it.'

'I said stop. Bridge wants coffee. You take it.'

Heine wondered why Rois was being nice to him all of a sudden. But why argue? He wiped his hands, now wrinkled and bright red, on the filthy cloth he had been using, and rolled down his sleeves. Heine poured a big pot of coffee into a large can with a handle and screwed a lid on to it.

'Take that. And once you've done it, go and get some sleep. Back on duty right after lunch, Heine. No slacking. Now fuck off.'

Heine took the can, which was heavy and too hot to hold by itself; he had to use the thin wire handle, which cut into his hands that were sore from the disinfected water. He left the stinking galley and made his way to the deck. Rois had directed him to the port side, the weather side, of the ship. He had to force the door open against the gusting wind, and a faceful of hail hit him immediately. He pushed his way out and made his way forward. The decks were empty, slippery in the rain. He hugged the superstructure as much as possible, but it offered no shelter.

A big wave struck the bow and broke against it, sending a plume of spray up into the air. The wind gusted at just that moment and caught the plume, flinging it down the weather side of the ship. Heine got drenched.

'Fuck!' he yelled as loudly as he could, making himself feel only slightly better. The salt water stung bitterly on his hands, now cracking as they had started to dry out. The pot was soaked with icy water, too; the fucking stuff would be cold by the time he got it there. So that's what that bastard was up to. Rois, you really are going to regret this at some point. Heine was not the kind of man to forget.

Crouching in a small angle of the superstructure that offered a little shelter, he stripped off his uniform tunic; the back of it was still dry and he wrapped the can in it, the dry part facing inwards. Heine didn't give a stuff about the coffee – he just wanted to prove Rois wrong. Naked from the waist up, he leaned into the wind and pushed his way forward until finally he reached the bridge ladder. He took the tunic from around the can and put it on again – it had warmed up against the hot metal and even though wet it felt like a warm blanket. He took a deep breath to stop himself shivering, then ran up the ladder to the bridge and knocked on the door. Moehle was inside, and opened it for him.

'From the galley, coffee – sir.'

'Good God, boy, you're soaking. Where's your oilskins?'

'Sorry, sir, new to the ship.'

'Idiot. Make sure you get them. Here, stay inside for a few minutes and dry off. Pour the coffee out. Keep quiet.'

'Yes, sir.' As quietly as he could, Heine unscrewed the lid of the can and started to pour out the still-hot liquid. The powerful aroma suddenly filled the bridge.

Heine looked around. Bach – the captain, judging by the uniform – was speaking to the rest of the officers. He was a tall, thin man, but the most striking feature was the ears – great big flapping things with long lobes that stuck out almost at right-angles to Bach's head. With his short hair – or was he just balding? – Heine thought he looked faintly menacing.

As he poured the coffee, Heine listened carefully. He was only a rating, which for the officers on the bridge turned him into just a part of the background. Heine was always amused by the fact that people would talk to each other in complete confidence when the only people listening were menials: they vanished into the wallpaper. One of his best sources of information in Hamburg was once a waiter at the Alster. Over lunch, bankers and their customers would discuss their most private arrangements, even when his friend was leaning above them. He used to be worth a lot of money to Heine.

Bach was speaking, and holding a thin sheaf of yellow papers in his hand. 'Gentlemen, I have orders here directly from Berlin. From Sluys and the Naval Staff. Please feel free to read them afterwards. We are to sail into the Atlantic as secretly as possible and approach the coast of America. There we are to carry out what I can only describe as an extraordinary and audacious attack on the American mainland. The Fuhrer himself has ordered this mission, gentlemen. We are to sail into the Chesapeake Bay where we will commence a bombardment of Washington, and in particular the White House. It is to be a massive propaganda exercise, to force the Americans to see that Germany is not defeated and can still strike at the very heart of America. It will show them that we are very much alive and, so to speak, kicking. It will provide Berlin with a valuable negotiating position with which they hope to extricate themselves. By the time we reach our position, the Fuhrer will have regrouped at the National Redoubt in the south. The fight goes on, and we have an historic part to play in it. Once we have completed our mission, we are to scuttle the ship. Two large U-boats will be standing by to pick us up and bring us home, heroes, to Germany. Those, gentlemen, are my orders.'

The officers looked blankly at Bach. They were trying to work out what he had just said – or more precisely, whether they really understood what they thought he had just said. It took some moments for the idea to sink in. Surely this was some kind of bad joke?

Bach folded his arms. He waited while the officers looked at the captain, wondering if he was mad, too embarrassed to say anything about a plan that was clearly unhinged. Heine took advantage of the silence to hand out small tin mugs of the hot coffee as inconspicuously as possible. Each officer took a mug, ignoring Heine. He simply wasn't there.

It was Schiller who finally broke the awkward silence.

'How exactly are we to carry out this order, Captain? It seems a little . . .' he paused.

'Mad?' asked the captain. 'That's what I thought. But these are our orders, gentlemen. I gave you the opportunity to resign last night and all of you chose to stay. Mad or not, it is a task that Germany needs us to carry out. And in truth, I believe it is difficult but by no means impossible.'

Bach continued to explain how the mission would work. In fascinated silence Schiller and the others listened as he went through his orders: how the Allied Navies were distracted; how the American coast defences were almost non-existent; how they would run the gauntlet of the Norfolk Naval Base and how they would escape.

As Bach went through the details and answered

questions, the whole thing started to sound increasingly plausible. Somebody, somewhere, had planned this mission remarkably well.

Heine listened carefully as well. Having handed out the coffee, he took up a stance he had seen countless waiters adopt – statue-like, hands clasped behind his back, standing silently at the end of the bridge near the door, looking out of the window at the foam-spattered sea as it rolled slowly under the bow. Awaiting orders. Not thinking. Not there at all.

'Course?' asked Bruller, the navigation officer, once Bach had explained every final detail.

'We take the northern route. North of Iceland, through the Denmark Strait, follow the ice shelf. The fog and ice will conceal us for much of the route. Then due south about two hundred miles off the coast until we reach thirty-seven degrees north, then we run straight in, at night. At twelve knots, we'll be approaching Chesapeake Bay in fifteen days' time if all goes well.'

Schiller asked the one question that was then on everyone's mind. 'And, Captain, what happens if Berlin throws in the towel before then?'

Bach looked at his first officer. 'Don't worry, Schiller. There are no plans to surrender. The Fuhrer fights on, and we do too. It doesn't matter what happens in the north. Berlin will probably be overrun in the next few weeks anyway. But our mission continues, no matter what. We are, gentlemen, officers of the *Kriegsmarine*. We no longer accept surrender as an option. Remember Scapa Flow, Schiller.' Bach spoke quietly but with real force.

'Yes, sir. Thank you.'

'Very well. Remember, we do this for Germany. Carry on,' and Bach left the bridge to let the news sink in.

Once Bach had gone, there was a string of expletives from the officers.

'Fucking mad,' commented Kinzel, the gunnery officer. The others agreed. But Heine listened carefully, and instead of hearing serious doubts about the mission all he heard was a group of unenthusiastic sailors bitching about it, the way sailors do at the start of a voyage. These men would not stop this lunacy.

'You, boy,' called Schiller to Heine, as the bridge settled back to its routine.

'Sir?'

'Take this stuff back to the galley.'

Heine started to gather up the tin mugs. He'd collected all of them into the empty coffee can and was opening the bridge door to venture back towards the stern of the ship, this time on the leeward side, which would be sheltered from the wind.

'Are you with Rois?' asked Schiller.

'Yes, sir,' replied Heine.

'That old bastard, huh? Listen, son, tell him from me – Schiller – that you're on bridge duties. Coffee every hour. At least it's hot when you bring it. Tell him that. What's your name?'

'Heine, sir.'

'Good lad, Heine. Back in an hour.'

'Yes, sir,' replied Heine. He managed to get down the ladder to the slippery deck without dropping anything. Patronising fool, he thought as he hurried back towards the galley.

Heine was now horrified by what was happening. He had missed his chance to get off the ship due to the stupid kid back in Hamburg. Now the thing had set sail with him on board; he had assumed that the *Hindenberg* was just being moved to somewhere like Norway, safe from the Allies. There he would have made his escape. Instead, here he was, a prisoner on board a ship whose captain and officers were clearly mad, mad as dogs, heading for America where they would certainly be blown out of the water if the British didn't sink them first, which they almost certainly would. Heine could cope with most things, take them in his stride. But now, for the first time in his life, Otto Heine – who never let anything worry him – was seriously contemplating the thought of death at sea and he did not like the idea, not one little bit, and was getting – well, might as well face it, Otto – scared as shit.

He arrived back at the galley where Rois was waiting for him. By this time, Heine had had enough. He didn't wait for Rois to say anything; he walked straight up to him and crashed the empty coffee can and the mugs down on the wooden work surface that separated them.

'Coffee, Rois, on the bridge, every hour. Schiller's orders. I'm to take it. That's my new duty, Rois. You don't like it, tell Schiller. Now, I'm going to get half an hour's sleep, and if you disturb me, Rois, I swear to God I'll kill you. I'll be back for the coffee.' And with that, Heine simply went to a corner of the mess, put two chairs together and stretched out on them. He was snoring gently within a minute.

Rois grumbled to himself. He watched Heine for a few minutes, and then picked up the coffee can and mugs and started to wash them out.

6

Lil Beasley was still technically a civilian, even though she worked for the Admiralty on the Intelligence side. And nobody liked her. She was a woman; she was obviously very intelligent; she was upper class; and she was about as unattractive as it was possible for a youngish female to be, even in this war. Lil Beasley didn't give a damn. In fact, she probably didn't even know what people thought about her because that sort of thing simply didn't intrude into her own private world.

She had been recruited by Naval Intelligence early in the war because 'Daddy' was a Vice-Admiral, even if only in the engineering branch, and she could therefore be trusted. She also had a memory like a machine and a sharp, enquiring mind – not that these were as important as the family connections. This combination of talents had enabled her to sail through Cambridge. But just as she had graduated in Physics with a first, the war started and she spent the rest of the time in London, either in the ugly bunker off Whitehall which served as the War Room, or lately in the elegant Admiralty building nearby.

Her job was hard to define. Given her lowly status because she was a woman, and because she was not attractive enough for anyone to want her as a personal assistant, she ended up with 'Odds and Sods', a kind of intelligence rubbish heap. Each day, items of intelligence that fitted no known classification would be dumped in her rusting wire in-tray. Anything significant, anything rated interesting, would immediately be sent to the department chief. It was the leftovers that were given to Lil Beasley to handle.

But as was often the case in this war, Lil had found her true calling in life. She had a knack for making connections. From signals and intelligence reports sometimes months old, she was able to connect items of apparently irrelevant information and make a story out of them. Sometimes she was wrong. Quite a bit of the time she was right. So the Naval Intelligence people kept her going, fed and watered her, and left her quietly ploughing her own furrow, and now and then she would quietly uncover some priceless information. She received little credit for these rare successes, of course. But then she really didn't care about that either. Nobody knew what she cared about. She just got on and did the job.

But just as the *Hindenburg* was setting sail, Lil Beasley contracted a bad cold, more like flu, and she was forced to spend the next few days in bed, alone in the small flat behind the Tottenham Court Road that Daddy had bought for her before the war. As she lay wrapped in a thick blanket drinking thin soup, the basket on her desk slowly began to fill.

*

The great ship worked its way steadily northwards, and the weather began to worsen. On the morning of the third day since they left Hamburg, they were leaving the Faeroe Islands fifty miles to port, and the temperature had already dropped to near freezing. The squalls that had kept running over them as they headed north, and which had hidden their progress from any prying eyes, had now joined together into one unremitting wind that was screaming incessantly through the high masts. At thirty-five to forty knots, it was enough to churn the grey waters into a rolling mass of steadily marching seas that came upon the ship from the south-west. With the vessel keeping to the north by north-west course, each sea would approach from the stern quarter, lifting the huge mass of steel, twisting it, and then running down the length of the *Hindenburg* where it shook the ship off – lifting the bow first and then dropping it into the receding trough so that a mountain of icy spray would lift slowly into the air, where the howling wind would suddenly seize it and throw it forward into the back of the departing sea.

It meant that the ship was dry, but even the massive bulk of the *Hindenburg* was now rolling, albeit with a stately slowness. It was the kind of motion that would induce sea-sickness in even the most hardened sailors; and now, at the start of the voyage, nearly three-quarters of the ship's crew were in various states of distress.

Even Bach felt queasy. He was always like this right at the start of the voyage – most sailors were. After a few days had passed there was no problem, but for now he stood close to the bridge window and stared at the horizon, the only fixed point of reference on the whole rolling scene. This gave his brain the chance to establish a position for itself; it would then stop the endless process of trying to figure out the vertical, which was what caused the sickness in the first place. His knees unconsciously flexed as the decks lifted and fell and rolled beneath him, keeping his body upright using the distant horizon as the fixed frame, and this too alleviated the symptoms. The trouble was, if he moved from that position for more than a few minutes the sickness would overtake him and it would take hours to get back to normal.

He would have liked a drink. It was the only thing that really cured him. Ever since he had joined the Navy, he had hated the sickness and always strove to hide it. That was when he discovered the cure – brandy, and plenty of it. And he also found that brandy helped him to talk to people. And brandy helped him face the shells and the guns and the bodies covered in blood. But he had always taken the greatest care to conceal the habit. It would not do, as far as Erich Bach was concerned, to show such weakness. He would never drink on the bridge. Whenever it got bad, he would retire to his cabin and take a few calming mouthfuls before returning to duty.

The rest of the officers were looking pale as well. And the radar set, located at the rear of the bridge, although still switched on, was faced with just an empty chair; three operators had been tried, but within minutes of sitting down to watch the glowing tube of the display they had given up. The last one had thrown up over the deck and the acid smell of the vomit still hung in the bridge.

The set was one of the latest of the shipborne radars, using a fixed antenna high above the main director atop the mainmast. The useful range of the set was about twelve miles, which was within visible range anyway; it came into its own when the weather was so bad that visibility was affected or, of course, at night.

Had anyone been sitting at the screen they would have observed, right on the very edge of the set, the little, fuzzy blip of another ship gaining on them from the south-west. The blip was small and indistinct and was closing the distance between them very, very slowly.

*

Commander Dick Spofforth didn't enjoy the luxury of an enclosed, heated bridge. There was such a bridge on *R41*, the destroyer *Volage*, but he found it almost impossible to use in this weather because it gave him such limited visibility. Wrapped in dripping oilskins, complete with a bright yellow sou'wester, he and his two officers looked more like trawler crew than Royal Navy.

The 1,700-ton ship was capable of thirty-four knots on a calm day, but Spofforth ordered the speed down to fifteen knots in the heaving sea. Even then the *Volage* rolled and staggered beneath them, making it difficult to keep visual track of the distant ship they had spotted two hours ago as it made slow progress to the north. With the other ship partially below the horizon, and with the weather and the motion of their own vessel, they could see very little other than a glimpse of a far-off stack and superstructure.

R41 was supposed to be returning from a patrol off the Norwegian coast, hoping to catch another U-boat to add to its tally of four, when it picked up the other ship on its new centimetric, high-definition radar. But just as they were getting a good echo, the new set decided to pack up, so Spofforth opted to follow the thing to see what it was. It had the single funnel and high superstructure of a warship, that was certain, from what he could see. But whose it was – that was another question. Years of combat made him reluctant to attract its attention by calling it up on the radio, even though every German vessel was supposed to be accounted for. No point in taking chances, he thought – not this late in the war, anyway.

He thought he would close it and find out its identity from a safe distance, but the weather was, if anything, getting worse and it slowed him down. To add to his nervousness, his fuel was low too.

He had sent a routine coded message to Fleet, telling them about the sighting and asking if they knew of anything in the area; but, as usual with low-priority signals, he was still waiting for a reply.

'Harry,' he shouted over the wind to his No. 2, 'find out what those buggers have done with that signal. If this is just a wild-goose chase then I'm going to call it off.'

'Right-ho,' shouted back Harry Frazer, and hand-over-hand went below to chase the reply to the signal. Just as Frazer disappeared, the handset screeched. It was ASDIC, down below, reporting a clear contact to the west, crossing, maybe half a mile. A U-boat.

Spofforth had no hesitation. He ordered full speed and a new course. The engine beat increased and the ship, just two years old, started to gather speed. The course quickly changed to the west; now the seas were coming at them beam-on. It meant that he could get his speed up, but the destroyer rolled alarmingly, listing to forty degrees and sometimes more. Spofforth didn't give a damn. If it was a U-boat, he wanted it. The last few months had been a turkey shoot for the destroyer commanders who had spent years struggling against the hidden menace of Donitz's fanatics. Lurking silently beneath the water, U-boats brought a terror to surface ships that the men had never known before. On calm nights, ships next to Spofforth's would suddenly erupt and sink, victims of another of the hidden terrorists. He and his crew had spent years living in nerve-stretching fear; now it was their turn, and they wanted total revenge before the expected surrender was announced.

Beneath the heaving sea, in the calm and the quiet, the commander of *U-199*, a new Type XXI, swore loudly against the luck that had brought a destroyer across the path he had chosen out into the Atlantic. His own sonar had picked up the sound of the ship and the sudden increase in revolutions. He knew it was a destroyer; nothing else had the same high-pitched whine. The U-boat increased depth and turned back on itself, hoping to outwit Spofforth. But Spofforth heard his turn and, now crashing bow-first into the sea, continued the chase. He would follow *U-199* for the next two days, twisting and turning southwards, sometimes losing it, until his fuel finally gave out and he had to hand over the chase, with ill-concealed irritation, to Coastal Command, who promptly sank the submarine with all hands while Spofforth was being towed back in.

Spofforth's original signal to the Admiralty eventually got an answer, about four hours after it was sent, but it was ignored in the excitement of the hunt for the U-boat:

To Volage *from Fleet. Your C334. No information on your sighting at that position. No large Allied vessels in area. Will ask Coastal Command to keep eyes open.*

That signal, together with Spofforth's original signal, was just one of the items that was now overflowing from Lil Beasley's 'Odd and Sods' pile at the Admiralty. Further down the pile – because it had arrived earlier – was Bletchley Park's report on Moehle's strange signal, noting the fact that it had been sent in an unusual code. It ended up on Lil's desk because nobody else could see anything important in it, but no one wanted to throw it away either:

> We have reports that Admiral Sluys in Berlin is getting ready to flee. Message was noted in code normally reserved for surface ships on passage. No German ships known to be at sea. Message signed by a 'Moehle'. Any interest?

But Lil was still at home. Her cold had turned into a racking, chesty cough and she felt as though someone had been kicking her in the ribs. She'd get in to the office the next day, maybe the day after. She took her job seriously. There was a war on, after all. Maybe she'd better ring in to get someone else to go through the pile. But she'd have to go downstairs, into the street, to the phone box opposite the hospital and, in any event, who would look at the stuff? No. The next day would be fine. She was sure she would be feeling better soon. So Lil's pile continued to grow.

*

The *Hindenburg* made its way northwards, unaware of the drama being played out behind it. Now they were well into the Norwegian Sea, Bruller had altered his course more to the north-west, taking them north of Iceland. The weather eased. The depression that had roared over them during the last few days was now past, and an area of high pressure calmed the sea and brought out the sun. But it was icy cold. Soon they began to see the first ice floes: small ones at first, with miles between them. But then they became more frequent, and soon the floes started to become bergs, one or two of them looking impressive.

Bach didn't like this weather. It was too clear. Air visibility was limitless. He could be spotted by any aircraft within a 100-mile radius of his ship. So he worked steadily northwards into the ice fields, which would take him well off the shipping lanes where any aircraft were likely to be. The danger was now from the bigger bergs. Even with the thick armour around and under him, Bach was not going to tempt fate by running into one of the bigger ones, although the smaller ones simply disappeared under his keel without a change to the ship's motion. He ordered a slower speed, posted lookouts on the bow and on the mainmast, and ordered the helmsman to steer an avoiding course if necessary. He posted more lookouts on the bridge and kept a close watch himself.

With so many eyes watching, it was inevitable that the aircraft would be spotted. Flying way to the south, it was seen by at least three crew members, all of whom called the bridge at the same time. Bach went out on to the wing-bridge to look for himself. It was barely visible, even through glasses, but it was there – a tiny silvery spot in the blue sky. In the cold air it wasn't leaving a contrail, which showed it was flying low, and that meant it was almost certainly a patrol rather than an aircraft on passage. It was the moment that every battleship's captain dreaded. Suddenly the cloak of invisibility was torn away from them.

'Get a range,' ordered Bach.

They used the main gunnery director, a huge optical instrument that worked exactly like an old-fashioned camera rangefinder: two separated lenses were focused through mirrors on the distant object and the two images made to coincide by the viewer. The angle of the mirrors relative to each other indicated the distance. The separation between the lenses was critical to accuracy, and on the *Hindenburg* the rangefinder had lenses sixty feet apart.

The operator brought the distant aircraft into focus and read off the angles to the fire computer, an electro-mechanical machine that converted angles and elevations into gun settings, but which this time was used to simply calculate the distance.

Within ten seconds, Bach had his answer.

'Thirty-two point four kilometres,' came the reply. Bach knew his ship could be seen, but the distance was so great that the aircraft had no hope of identifying his vessel. He had only one choice.

'Make smoke. Reverse course. Maximum speed,' Bach commanded.

The *Hindenburg* started to lean as the helmsman spun the wheel around, turning the ship from its westerly course to a southerly one and then to the east. Thick black smoke billowed from the single funnel, boiling out and over the ship in the still, calm air and quickly hiding it from view.

Bach had no option but to hide his ship and confuse the spotters by taking a new course, even if the dense black fog he was now producing made him all the more visible. He had to assume that the plane crew had already spotted him and would report what they were seeing.

In fact, the two-man crew on the Coastal Command Catalina, both Canadian, had been flying a routine ice patrol from their base in Iceland and they hadn't seen his ship until he started making smoke.

'What the hell is that?' asked the pilot, shading his eyes and peering into the distance. Sun-glint off the surface of the sea made it difficult to see.

'Smoke, looks to me,' responded the navigator.

'Ship on fire?'

'Maybe. Let's go down and take a look.'

The pilot thought about it for a moment. It was near the end of the patrol and they were on their way home. It was also their last tour of duty; for them, the war was now over. 'Maybe it's that big warship we were asked to look out for. I'd hate to get shot down in the last fucking week of this war. Get a heading for it and we'll report in later.'

The trail of smoke, still hanging over the sea and obscuring the ship, seemed to be moving slowly south-west by the time the navigator got his glasses on it. The vibration of the aircraft and the extreme range made it difficult to see anything very clearly.

The crew watched the steadily moving smoke trail for five minutes and then curled away, starting to climb for the return journey to Iceland. They would file their report on their return. There didn't seem to be any great urgency about the original request. Just keep your eyes open, it said. No need to make a big deal of it, it seemed to say.

The flight back to base would take them another three hours.

*

Bach was sure the aircraft had gone, and he brought the ship round from its false course to resume the voyage. But now he wanted to get even closer to the ice-cap. He was hoping for a change in the weather. The high-pressure area had brought down clear, cold air from the Arctic, and now he wanted a depression to come up, with a westerly wind, bringing moist warm air that would generate a rolling fog in which he could hide. He assumed he had been spotted, and he needed to remain as invisible as he could.

Bach had no weather reports to guide him. The

German weather ships that had been stationed in the
Atlantic approaches had long since been sunk or
captured. Now it was only U-boats that could supply
the information, but he hadn't picked up a broadcast
since they had set out. He assumed they must have
other things on their minds, if indeed there were any
of them left. All he had to rely on was his own experience and knowledge of the likely track of the endless
Atlantic weather fronts.

The distant ice-cap was drawing steadily closer. The
sky remained as clear and blue as ever, and the sea had
taken a slow, smooth, heaving swell as though it had
thickened like treacle. Ice now littered the surface in
small lumps and sheets which the big ship easily
pushed to one side. For now they seemed clear of the
large bergs.

Bach left the comfort of the bridge and walked
forward on to the wide foredeck beneath the shadows
of the two forward turrets, known as 'Anton' and
'Bruno'. The deck in front of the guns was a wide-
open space, empty other than the two massive anchor
capstans and the chains snaking down to the anchor
wells on each side. The deck would normally have had
a huge swastika painted on it, a warning to friendly
aircraft.

There were no friendly aircraft to warn off now –
there hadn't been for over a year – so the swastika had
never been painted on. The deck itself should have
been teak, narrow boards to cover the steel plating.
Further aft, they had got around to fitting the planking; but on the forward deck they had never bothered
with it, being up against time and supply problems.
The dull grey armour-plating was exposed to the sea
and the air, and had already taken on a coat of rust. It
wasn't even thought worth painting.

A lonely, solitary figure, Bach stood on the starboard side, hands clasped firmly behind his back, his captain's cap and long coat protecting him from the chill air. Schiller, standing on the bridge, was watching him. He looked like the noble captain in command of his vessel, standing proudly at the prow. In truth, Bach felt no such nobility. The doubts were beginning to overwhelm him. The aircraft in the distance, had it seen them or not? It had flown off quickly and hadn't come in to take a look, so maybe they were clear. Certainly there had been no further visits. But Bach knew you couldn't be sure. He had to assume they had been seen.

And he had heard nothing from Sluys, no signals, not a word. What was happening back in Berlin? Was the war over or were they fighting on? Here he was, stuck out in the middle of the Atlantic – endangering his ship on the ice, probably being followed – on a mission that to him remained questionable at best. But, he told himself, these were his orders. Germany depended on him. But deep down, Erich Bach knew that he was taking his ship and crew to their deaths, and he wasn't enjoying it. He needed another drink, but he had managed to bring just two bottles with him in his case and already he was halfway through the second one. He had convinced himself that it would be enough, but now he knew he would run out soon. Never mind. He didn't *really* need it, he told himself. When it went, it went. No problem. But it was starting to prey on his mind.

'Captain?' It was Moehle, the young Lieutenant, who had walked up across the bow plating to join Bach.

Bach remained standing, looking out to sea. He nodded, almost imperceptibly, to acknowledge Moehle's presence.

'Sorry to disturb you, Captain.'

'That's all right, Moehle. What can I do for you?'

What Moehle wanted was to find out what was in Bach's mind. The man was looking worried. This was not the hard-bitten captain that Sluys had told him about. Moehle had his orders to keep an eye on Bach anyway. Report what's happening, said Sluys.

'The aircraft, sir. Wondered if we should be doing anything about it?' lied Moehle, trying to think of something.

'It's gone, Moehle. Nothing we can do except make sure we stay hidden.'

'Yes, sir. Hope you don't mind me saying, Captain, but you look worried,' ventured Moehle, hoping that Bach wouldn't tear his head off.

Bach laughed. 'Worried, Moehle? Thank you for your concern. No, I'm fine. Look at that. It's a beautiful sight, the ice-cap. I always wondered what it would be like to explore up here. I've passed it many times but never set foot on it. It's a different world, Moehle.'

'Yes, Captain.'

'And you, Moehle? How are you feeling? Here you are, a young man, with your career barely begun and defeat staring us in the face. Strange times we live in.'

'Not really, Captain. We still have a chance. The Fuhrer fights on, I hear. The Americans and the Russians hate each other. The alliance must give out, especially as they start fighting each other when they meet in the middle of Germany. We have a great responsibility.'

Bach turned now to look at the younger man. 'You believe all that?'

'Of course. Don't you?' Moehle looked serious enough; but he looked intelligent too. Only a fool would swallow the nonsense about fighting on, and to Bach Moehle didn't look like a fool.

'Perhaps, Moehle, perhaps. Maybe you're right. And the rest of the officers?'

'Oh, absolutely behind you, sir. One hundred per cent.'

'Thank you, Moehle. I'll return to the bridge, I think. See you at dinner.'

'Yes, Captain,' and Moehle watched Bach turn crisply and walk quickly back down the plating, stepping over the high breakwater, under the massive gun turrets, and eventually disappearing up the ladder that led to the bridge. Moehle stayed at the guard rail. Now it was his turn to think. So, was Bach giving up the ghost? Sluys and the others had told him that Bach was dedicated to following orders, no matter what: the most loyal captain in the entire *Kriegsmarine*. Whatever happened, Bach would do the job. That's why he had been chosen. Down in the magazine below Bruno, the second of the turrets, lay the cargo of shells which was the whole point of this stupid mission. And was their beloved Erich Bach going to screw the whole thing up? Well, thought Moehle, he would have to keep watching the good captain.

*

Lil Beasley was still running a temperature and her nose was streaming, but she had had enough of sitting in the tiny, cold flat. She wrapped herself against the cold April wind and took the Underground to Trafalgar Square, where she walked through the doors of the Admiralty building just after lunchtime.

'Hello, Lil. How you feeling?' called one of the Wrens on duty in the dark lobby. Lil Beasley was notorious, and the enquiry was purely sarcastic.

'Terrible,' Lil growled, barely halting. She had no friends here and was in no mood to stop and talk. She walked past the Wren; as Lil disappeared down the dark concrete steps the girl waved two fingers silently at her back.

Lil got to the basement, where her small desk stood against a painted brick wall. Even on the brightest summer day she had to turn the light on. The temperature inside was little better than outside. It was April, after all: spring had officially arrived and therefore the heating was turned off, and sod what the thermometer said.

She unwrapped the big scarf and shuffled off the coat, dumping them over the back of her chair. She blew her nose again on her handkerchief and stuffed it back up the sleeve of the thick cardigan she wore as she pulled the heap of papers towards her. They had overflowed from her in-tray and she shuffled them into a neat pile. Then she started carefully reading each one. She was feeling better already. This was familiar territory, almost like home.

It took her two hours before she came to the signal from the Catalina:

> *Large ship near ice cap, 150 miles NW Iceland, making smoke, heading SE. Not identified.*

She read it again. And then once more, her brow furrowing. Her legendary memory was slower than usual, the cold no doubt, but a loud bell started ringing when she read the signal. '*Large ship*'? She went back through the pile she had already glanced at. Where was that bloody Bletchley signal she had read an hour ago? She found it, smoothed the flimsy paper out on her desk and read it carefully. It was Moehle's decoded message about Sluys getting ready to leave; appended to it were Bletchley's comments about it being in a code normally reserved for surface ships. *Any interest?* it finished. It was days old, near the bottom of the pile.

She paused for a moment. Something was happening here, she could feel it in her bones. But she didn't know what. The last piece of the jigsaw came ten minutes later when she resumed reading through the pile. It was Spofforth's signal from *Volage*. She paused again, placed that one neatly beside the Bletchley report and then put the signal from the Catalina next to the two of them. One, two, three, in a neat line.

Lil Beasley looked carefully at the messages. They were telling her something, loud and clear. It was bloody obvious, she thought. A German ship – a big one, at that – had set sail up the North Sea a few days ago. It had made its way north, to the ice-cap, and then had decided to turn around and make smoke. Why? What was it up to?

She went over to the large North Atlantic chart pinned on a wall and traced off in her mind the positions and course of the ship. It was slow, that was for sure, if the times between the signals were anything to go on. And then, why did it make smoke like that – and change the heading so dramatically? It was clear to Lil that the captain of the ship was trying to confuse the aircraft. He must have seen it – otherwise why the smoke? – and then reversed course to put them off the scent. And what on earth was the fool doing so close to the ice-cap, anyway? The more she thought about it, the more suspicious she became. The original message, signed by *Moehle* – what was all that about? Why would a trivial message concerning Sluys's travel arrangements originate from the ship, for heaven's sake? Didn't they have enough to worry about? To Lil's mind, it looked suspiciously like a word code – it must mean something completely different.

Then the bugger goes and hugs the ice-cap. Obviously wants to avoid detection. He's hiding something, he's on some kind of mission. Must be. Doesn't want to be seen. Where's he really heading? Nothing to the north. Must be America, north or south. And at best the thing was doing twelve knots, she had calculated, so what in the name of heaven was it?

And now another part of Lil's memory was starting to shout at her. *You know what ship it is, it's bloody obvious!* But she was not going to listen. The idea was impossible. And then the voice shouted again, and again, until finally she had to admit that there was a remote possibility – nothing more, mind you – that she knew exactly who this bugger really was.

Three years ago, after all the palaver over the sinking of the *Bismarck*, Lil's knack of making connections had come up with an extraordinary theory. When the *Bismarck* was laid down before the war, they had also laid the keels of two other sister-ships: the *Friederich der Grosse* and the *Hindenburg*. But Hitler's nerve for naval warfare, following the *Bismarck* fiasco, had failed, and orders went out to break up both the new ships. The Admiralty congratulated itself on destroying two huge battleships without even firing a shot directly at them.

But Lil didn't share the enthusiasm. The *Friederich*, that was certainly broken up. But the other one, she was not as convinced as everyone else was. She always found it difficult to understand why the Germans would simply throw such assets away. Hitler had too much of a taste for the grandiose to consign two huge battleships to the scrap heap. It just felt wrong. For some time, she had nothing to base her feelings on but then Lil's suspicions had been raised by several unconnected reports over the following year. Large numbers of Polish welders and shipworkers, slave labour from the yards in Danzig, had suddenly been taken, supposedly in secret, to Hamburg. Why? A big shipment of unusually thick armour plate had left Krupp's Essen works, again for Hamburg. Why? She asked for air photos, and managed to get three prints after six months of badgering. There was still something big in one corner of the yard, and someone had gone to great trouble to disguise it; it looked as though camouflage netting had been draped over it. She heard rumours, from various unnamed sources, that something big was being built. She saw one report that specifically stated that the *Hindenburg* was the ship under the camouflage and it was being converted, but the report came at third and maybe fourth hand – it had started with the Russians, and who trusted them anyway? – and sounded like a hundred different scare stories that regularly did the rounds of all of the Allied Intelligence networks.

But, taken all together, it was enough to make Lil think that something was happening. Maybe it really was the battleship. So she went to see her immediate superior, a not very pleasant individual named Wooley.

Wooley and Beasley didn't get on. Wooley thought she was an interfering busybody who was only there because she was a Vice-Admiral's daughter. Beasley thought Wooley was a brainless twerp, and she made her feelings plain whenever she had the misfortune to have to talk to him.

She told him that, in her opinion, one of the *Bismarck*-class battleships, very probably the *Hindenburg*, had never been broken up and was still in the yards, maybe nearing completion. Wooley listened, fidgeting, looked at her with pity and then promised to take it 'up the line' to get rid of her. He sent her a terse minute a whole week later.

*I mentioned your idea to Vice-Admiral Herdman. He
said, I have to report, that the existence of such a ship has
been known about for some time. The ship you imagined
you saw was in fact another large vessel, originally an
aircraft carrier, which has been used as spare parts
supply for other ships. Your other comments about slave
labour and armour plate are best explained by work on
other small ships which is known about. The
Vice-Admiral suggests you do not waste any more time
on this issue, and I have to say that I agree with
Herdman's views.*

To which Lil Beasley's only comment was 'bollocks', in
a loud voice.

And now, here the story was coming to the surface
once again. There was something big on the high seas.
Something that looked as though it had sailed from
Hamburg – or one of the northern ports, at any rate –
a few days back. Something that somebody was going to
some trouble to keep secret, God knows why, thought
Lil, when the bastards are already beaten.

Could it be the *Hindenburg*?

The idea slowly grew in her mind. She re-examined
the messages once again. Was this some last-ditch
attempt to break out? One thing was for sure, she told
herself: it certainly wasn't Scotch bloody mist.

She picked up the phone to Wooley's idiot of an
assistant and in a thick, croaking voice demanded to
see the Commander. She said she had something for
him; she didn't know quite what, but she knew it was
important. Lil insisted, she said, on a meeting as soon
as possible.

*

Dinner was at eight sharp, in the officers' mess. Bach

had insisted on proper uniforms and a proper meal. It was traditionally the place where the officers could discuss the day just ended and their plans for the next. It was therefore supposed to be relaxed, but Bach was incapable of creating an atmosphere that was anything other than stiff and formal. It would have helped, thought Schiller, if they could have had a drink.

Heine had now been given by Schiller not only bridge duty but mess duty as well. To Rois's obvious disgust, Heine would put on a white coat and stand at the hatch, waiting for the cook to deliver the food. At first Rois tried to make him late by keeping him waiting, but Heine simply went to a telephone and asked for Schiller; Rois produced the food before Schiller answered and Heine left it at that.

Now Schiller had asked for wine. Heine had told Rois, and Rois had managed to produce a pair of bottles of Rheingau which Heine had taken up to the mess. Only Schiller was there, and he uncorked both bottles. Once again Heine was left in the background as the others drifted in. They all noticed the two bottles on the table, but nobody said a word.

On the stroke of eight, Bach entered the room. He went straight to the head of the table, sat down and motioned to Heine to serve him. Heine carefully ladled some thin soup into Bach's bowl, and then worked his way down the table. Bach seemed to him to be deeply preoccupied, and the captain said nothing, but this was normal. Heine finished serving and resumed his position at the back of the mess.

Schiller, Kinzel, Bruller, Ecke, Jensch and Moehle all drank their soup in silence, waiting for the captain to speak the first word. But he remained obstinately quiet, which even for Bach was unusual. Half an hour earlier, Bach had all but finished the last bottle of brandy. He had enough left to refill his hip flask and that was it. Added to everything else, it left him feeling more nervous than he had since the voyage started. Not that he was going to show anyone, of course.

Heine cleared away the soup plates and laid out the plates for the main course. The silence continued. Once he had laid the plates, he started serving the fishy-smelling stew that Rois had concocted. Again, he stood at the back of the mess.

It was Schiller who broke the silence. 'Captain, I managed to find some wine – some Rheingau. Would you care for some?'

Bach looked up at Schiller. 'You know I forbid wine on my ships, Schiller. Get rid of it,' and he resumed eating. He didn't even glance at the two bottles.

'It's Rheingau, Captain. Haven't tasted it for years,' Schiller persisted.

'Nevertheless, you know my orders, Schiller. Please have it removed. Now.'

Bach had stopped eating. He had sensed the challenge.

'If it's all the same to you, Captain, I'll have it saved for later.'

'I don't think you will,' said Bach ominously. The others had stopped eating and were watching the developing scene.

'Captain?'

'I gave you an order, Schiller. I expect it to be obeyed without question.'

'Captain, I really don't see ...'

'*Schiller!*' shouted Bach suddenly, rising to his feet, his face now going red. 'For God's sake, man, when I give an order, I give an order. You do not question it. Do you understand?'

'Yes, Captain. I understand,' replied an angry

Schiller, unused to being shouted at even by a captain.

But Bach's temper was up. 'You think this is easy, Schiller? Sailing this bloody death trap on some ridiculous mission? I have my orders, even if Berlin is ruined and every last bloody German is dead, which by now they probably are, and I still obey those orders. I expect you to do the same, Schiller, whether you like them or not. Just as I have to do. If we're going to sacrifice this ship and all of you, then at least have the courtesy to keep quiet and do your job while we're about it.'

Bach was leaning over the table, his hands splayed on the cloth, his knuckles white and his face red. His large ears were even redder. The others had their heads bowed, except Schiller who was bristling with anger. Schiller had never seen Bach in this mood and he certainly was not going to accept this public humiliation. Not from anyone. He rose to his feet, fuming with indignation.

'Captain, how dare you question my loyalty? I have served you well so far and I do not see ...'

But Bach suddenly laughed, a bitter laugh. It was unnerving for the rest of them. 'Schiller, sit down, man, and don't make a fool of yourself. Do as you are told. You don't understand, do you? None of you understand. You should have been at Scapa Flow. The whole bloody fleet, given up without a shot. You know what that was like? And now, look at us ...' and he smiled at the officers gathered around the table '... here we are, the pride of the *Kriegsmarine*, never ever to surrender, and they've sent us on a mission where frankly, gentlemen, we do not stand a chance. If we had any sense, Schiller, we'd sail this thing straight down to Scotland and scuttle it.'

Schiller had resumed his seat. He looked at Bach. 'Well, Captain, why the hell don't we?' he asked quietly.

'Why, Schiller? I'll tell you why. Orders. The Navy. Germany. Pride. Stupidity, if you prefer. You tell me. But we're not going to sail down to Scotland, are we? We are good German officers. We will complete our mission as instructed. Now, gentlemen, if you will excuse me,' and Bach silently left the mess, closing the door behind him. They watched him go in amazement. Moehle looked less amazed and more worried. Was Bach going to break?

'The captain seems under some strain,' commented Bruller eventually.

They all quietly nodded. But the wine was left on the table, and Schiller started to pour it out. They each savoured it. 'And what do the rest of you think?' Schiller asked.

Each man there had had his own thoughts about the mission, ever since Bach had announced it. But none of them had spoken those thoughts out loud. Moehle listened carefully as one by one they began to talk.

'For me, it's a complete waste of time,' said Bruller. 'The whole thing is finished. But orders are orders, I suppose. I suppose we just carry on until we get sunk.'

'What choice is there anyway, Schiller?' asked Kinzel, the artillery officer. 'If we stay, we get bombed to shit. Germany is finished. We might as well get as far away as we can and do as much damage as we can. I don't see what else we could do.'

'Like you say, Kinzel, we don't have much choice,' said Jensch, the communications officer. 'Pass the wine, Schiller, and stop worrying about it. If our good captain gives us orders, I'll go with them.'

'And what if we don't stand a chance? What if Germany collapses? What if Germany has already collapsed?'

'What the hell, Schiller? We carry on. Unless you have some other plan?'

But Schiller just passed the second bottle of Rheingau. No, he had no plan. Up until then he was just obeying orders. But now he was starting to understand Bach's doubts. Was this worth it? But the others remained steadfast and unswerving. As far as they were concerned, orders remained orders.

Moehle just listened carefully and didn't join in. Clearly, Bach was under some strain. That he could understand. Now, maybe, was Schiller going the same way? The others were fine. Perhaps the time had come to find a way to make Bach a little more enthusiastic? Put a bit of iron in his soul. Sluys had warned him that this might be necessary.

Heine, too, had listened carefully, invisible and unseen. He had more or less given up all hope and was wondering idly about stealing a lifeboat to get away, but the idea was too far-fetched. But now here was a glimmer of a hope. Would these characters see some sense and get the fuck out of it? The captain seemed less than keen. Now Schiller appeared to be going the same way. The others – well, the others were no better than dogs, wagging their tails when instructed, who would happily walk unquestioningly to their deaths if somebody in a uniform ordered them to do so. These were the kind of idiots who had got Germany to where it was now. Why didn't they ever show any sense?

Heine started to clear away the remains of the dinner. They had eaten very little of Rois's fish stew. He scraped the disgusting remains, now cold, on to a single plate, he stacked that on top of the others and took them back to the galley. He was tired. He dumped the remains in front of Rois, who looked at the pile with disgust, then he threw off the white jacket and went back to the crew quarters.

The other kids were there, some reading, some writing letters. Who the fuck to? wondered Heine. He rolled himself skilfully into his hammock and closed his eyes.

'Otto?' It was Vogele, one of the youngsters who had been on the truck with him in Hamburg.

Heine tried to ignore the voice.

'Otto,' repeated Vogele, insistently.

'Leave me alone. I'm asleep.'

'Listen, Otto, we've heard a story. About where this ship is going. Is it true?'

Heine opened his eyes. 'What story?'

'We're going to America. To blow up Washington. Is it true?'

Heine smiled. 'Yes, Vogele, it's true. We sail to Washington, drop our anchor, and blow up the fucking White House. It's all true.'

'But we'll get killed, Otto. They're mad. They have to be stopped.'

'Oh, they're mad all right. Mad as dogs, every one of them. They don't stand a hope in hell.'

'And what happens to us, Otto? What happens to *you*?'

Heine pushed himself upright. 'What happens to us? What do you think happens? We all get blown to shit is what happens.'

'Stop them, Otto. You've got to stop them.' Vogele sounded desperate.

'Me? You're crazy. How am I going to stop them?'

'You can, if you wanted to. We're behind you, Otto. All of us. All the crew. There's a lot more of us than them. We'll follow you. Just lead us. We'll take over the ship if you show us what to do.'

'That's called mutiny.'

'Who cares? You want to die? Do you, Otto? We don't.'

And Otto Heine had to admit that no, he didn't want to die. But leading this bunch of kids? Let them sort themselves out. The last thing he wanted was to have the responsibility for this lot. Leave me be. I'll make my own arrangements, thank you very much. And you make yours.

'Vogele, you're crazy. Now fuck off and let me sleep.' Heine rolled over and shut his eyes again. Stupid idea.

7

Room 245 was a dingy, ill-lit meeting room on the second floor of the Admiralty building. The walls, once cream, now were yellow, and the floor was covered in a fraying dull green linoleum that had worn through into small holes. What little light came through the narrow window was reduced by the paper tape, now peeling away, stuck across the panes at the start of the war to prevent glass from flying around if a bomb went off outside.

Lil Beasley sat, upright and unconcerned, while Wooley, her boss, sat opposite her. He was reading and re-reading the report she had personally, and neatly, typed up for him on the yellow flimsy paper with the wide margins and double spacing that they had been taught to use in case someone higher up wanted to makes notes on the draft.

He had nothing else to do while they waited for Herdman, and Lil certainly wasn't going to engage in small talk. So Wooley, once again, started reading the two pages of flimsy.

Beasley didn't even watch him. She still felt unwell, and besides it was a matter of principle for her to ignore Wooley as much as possible. The feeling was mutual; Wooley had to live with her because she was old Navy establishment. Wooley was not. He had been an accountant before the war, and he disliked the old Admiralty families who still seemed to rule the roost. Herdman, the Vice-Admiral who was Wooley's boss, was establishment too, just like Beasley. But at least Herdman was a proper serving officer . . . and a man.

The door suddenly flew open and Herdman, pink-cheeked and round, breezed into the room, grabbed a chair and settled himself into it.

'Wooley, Lil, how are you both? Got something for me, then?'

Wooley was always mildly annoyed at the first-name familiarity between the two of them. 'Hello, sir,' he jumped in quickly, just to assert his authority. 'Miss Beasley here thinks she's found a German surface raider. One we don't know about. Heading out into the Atlantic.'

'German ships, eh, Lil? And what leads you to that particular conclusion?'

'It's all in my report, Peter.' Not being actually in the Navy, she still felt she could use his first name.

''Course it is, Lil. Just remind me, would you?'

He hadn't read it. Wooley had never known his boss read anything longer than a menu. He always preferred to hear it.

'First, Bletchley picked up a message to Sluys from a certain Moehle telling him his car was ready,' said Lil in her schoolmistress voice.

'Sluys is on the run, eh? Wouldn't mind getting hold of him.'

'Peter, that's not the point. It was sent in naval code but advanced a day; so far only surface ships have used that trick. Donitz trusts his submarine crews but Hitler doesn't trust the rest of the Navy. He thinks that advancing the code a day will fool any traitors who are passing on secrets. Stupid, of course, but there you are.'

'So why was a surface ship sending a message to Sluys about his car?'

'Precisely, Peter. Of course, it was some kind of word code. Telling Sluys something is happening. Moehle – the chap who signed the signal – wants to hide something from that nosy lot in Berlin.'

'Or knows we've cracked Enigma?'

'No, Peter. He'd have just used a different code,' she said, impatient with the man's slowness.

'So who's Moehle, anyway?'

'No idea.'

'Anything else?'

'Sighting by destroyer, on the horizon. Halfway out into the Atlantic, Peter, perfect course for a traditional breakout.'

'No confirmation?'

'They found a U-boat and hared off after it. Couldn't make the ship out, but thought it was biggish.'

'Biggish? *Biggish*? What the hell's *biggish* mean when it's at home, eh, Wooley?' He smiled, man to man. These women.

'That was what they said, Peter. Big bugger. Then a sighting by Coastal Command, north of Iceland, just off the ice shelf. Heading south-east and making smoke,' continued Lil, ignoring Herdman's insinuation.

'South-east?'

'To confuse the plane, Peter. Like the smoke. Must have seen them.' Lil Beasley sometimes wondered why men were so obtuse. It was obvious that the ship was trying to deceive them, which meant that it had something to hide.

'That's all?'

'That's all.'

'Miss Beasley has a view, sir. A theory.'

'Come on, Lil. Give it up.'

'Peter, it's not a theory. What you have here is a large German warship out of Hamburg heading out into the Atlantic, doing what it can to hide itself. The bloody thing stinks, Peter. Why would he risk the ice shelf? Why the word code? Why the deception? Where's he going?'

'Good story, Lil. Trouble is, old girl, the Germans haven't got anything big left. Nothing sailable. I mean, what sort of ship is this?'

'It's the bloody *Hindenburg*, Peter. That's what sort of ship it is. As you know perfectly bloody well.'

'Lil, dearest, not that again. *Please*. You know what my lords and masters think about that idea. Come on, Wooley. Any thoughts?'

Wooley didn't look at Lil Beasley. 'Difficult to tell, sir. I mean, Moehle's signal could be genuine. Maybe they've switched codes. Times are tricky for them at the moment. If Sluys wanted to make his escape secret, then perhaps he would use that sort of deception.'

'Good point, Wooley. Good point.'

Warming to his subject, Wooley carried on. 'Then the two sightings. There's nothing to connect them. Nothing to say that the destroyer didn't see one of our own ships.'

'Lil?'

'Nothing in the area, Peter. I did bloody well check, you know.'

Wooley jumped in, eager to demonstrate his superiority. 'Who can tell, sir? Things are getting a bit chaotic right now. Weather was bad. I mean, could have been one of ours, off course.'

'And the business up north?'

Wooley shrugged. 'Don't know. But it was heading south-east, sir, after all. Could have been anything. Maybe a U-boat on fire?'

'Too bloody big.'

Wooley ignored Lil's comment. 'And the speed, sir. Around twelve knots if it's the same ship, judging by the positions. Couldn't be a warship. Not that slow.'

'Lil?' asked Herdman, again.

'No idea. Even more suspicious. Why should a German warship be trolling along at twelve knots, Peter?'

'If it *is* a warship, Lil. Like I said, they ain't got any of the buggers left. Unless of course, your idea about the *Hindenburg* was right after all. Which of course it isn't, is it, Lil?'

'Of course not, Peter. Scotch bloody mist sailing around up there, I expect.' Lil Beasley had done her job. Now it was up to them. If these idiots wanted to ignore her, that was their business.

'Thanks, Lil. Thanks, Wooley. Interesting tale. Interesting. Tell you what. I'll get a proper recon done, how about that? Sounds funny, like you say, Lil. We'll go take a dekko at whatever this thing is and then we'll know. Where d'you think it might be now?'

Lil had worked out a position and gave it instantly. Wooley looked furious.

'Good work, Wooley. Right to let me know.'

'Thank you, sir.'

Herdman was already out of the door and closing it noisily behind him. Wooley stood up and left Lil Beasley to it. Bloody establishment. Thick as thieves.

*

An hour later Herdman was speaking on the phone to his superior.

'I'm sorry, sir, but Lil Beasley is no one's fool. She's convinced it's the *Hindenburg*.'

'She can't possibly know that, Herdman. She was getting on the same hobbyhorse a couple of years back, wasn't she?'

'She was. I managed to keep her quiet, but she knows full well it exists.'

The truth was, the Admiralty had known about the existence of the *Hindenburg* ever since the *Bismarck* was sunk. They had a spy in the Hamburg yards, someone very high up, a silent opponent of the Nazi regime who had supplied information on naval movements since 1939. And it was a source they were desperate to protect. The order had gone out: we know nothing about the *Hindenburg*. Air raids to destroy the ship were forbidden. It did not exist. It was so well camouflaged that any attempts to bomb it could only be interpreted as being based on inside information, giving away the source that continued to provide useful information about ships coming and leaving the yards. And anyway, the ship *was* unfinished, even if not broken up. For most of the war, no work was done on it. It posed no threat. If it ever sailed, then things might be different.

And then, just as work was starting to get the unfinished ship ready for sea – as noticed by Lil Beasley – the source woke one morning, glanced out from behind the curtains to check the road outside, as was his custom, and saw the nightmare that had haunted him for years suddenly about to come true: two truckloads of Waffen SS were quietly waiting in the street, one at the top, the other at the end, blocking it, and heading towards the door of his apartment block a man wearing a long coat and a trilby was purposefully walking, flanked by four armed soldiers.

He offered a short prayer to his God, and swallowed the blue pill that he had been sent a year ago ...

'She might know it exists, Herdman, but dammit, the thing's just a hulk.'

'Perhaps they finished it, sir.'

'Herdman, for God's sake, don't talk nonsense. You're getting like this woman. Why would they finish it? You know full well that Hitler abandoned his battleships after *Bismarck*. Fell in love with the U-boats. Believe me, the ship is still there and it's still a half-finished hulk, as we'll shortly prove. We'll be in Hamburg within the week, so I'm told. Now, tell this woman to calm down. Carry out your recon to see what's going on up there, and forget about this story.'

Herdman persisted. 'But Lil is convinced something is happening. She's not often wrong, you know.'

'This time Lil is wrong, Herdman. She's getting old, she's getting de-mob happy. I don't know why, but she's way out of line. The chances of a German battleship running around in the Atlantic are zero, Herdman, zero. Don't waste any more time on it.'

And *Titanic* and *Bismarck* were unsinkable as well, said Herdman to himself. 'Yes, sir,' he replied out loud, and replaced the phone quietly in the cradle. Frankly, if it was a choice between believing one of the Sea Lords or Lil Beasley, Vice-Admiral Peter Herdman knew without hesitation which way his vote would go. Even if he was utterly wrong.

*

Bach was back on the bridge the next morning. Neither he nor Schiller said a word about the events of the previous night. It was business as usual, but Schiller noticed that he was clearly very edgy.

They continued to cruise as close to the ice-cap as

they dared. The day had dawned with the same clear blue sky and oily swell, but now the barometer was starting to fall. Bach was still desperate to get some weather to hide in, but the morning wore on with no change to the sky. The captain would have prayed for a weather report if he had been religious.

Noon came and went. Eventually Bach had had enough.

'Schiller? Bruller? Come over to the chart table,' he ordered.

Both men joined the captain at the large oak table at the back of the bridge. A North Atlantic chart marked off their slow progress.

'This weather is no good. We're sitting ducks. The longer we stay here, the more likely we are to get spotted. I've decided to go south. We should find a depression further down. We're too far north here and we're getting stuck under this bloody high. We're missing the bad weather. Anyway, if they are looking for us, they'll look at the ice shelf. What do you think?'

Bruller and Schiller nodded. The Atlantic depressions would be marching, one after the other, eastwards, following the track of the Gulf Stream where the warm water brought the moisture-laden storms to the British Isles and Ireland. Bach was right. Up here, they were missing them. The high pressure seemed stuck obstinately over Greenland and was showing little sign of moving.

'Very well. Bruller, set a course due south until we get out into some weather.'

'Yes, sir,' and Bruller gave Schiller the new course, 195 degrees, slightly offset from an exact due south to make up for the gentle drift eastwards, which Schiller chalked up on the board in front of the helmsman.

The helmsman turned the wheel to port, and the

plate-sized card floating inside the brass compass
binnacle slowly began to move to the right as it maintained its position relative to magnetic north while the
ship moved around beneath it. The helmsman maintained the gentle turn until the line levelled up with
195 degrees, set the helm to amidships, corrected a few
times, and the *Hindenburg* settled to its new course.

Now Bach called another conference of his officers.
Time for some artillery practice, he told them. They
had a raw crew, untrained and unskilled. He wanted
the main 15-inch guns fired first, and then the 37-mm
anti-aircraft. Let's show these kids what this ship was
all about, he said. Schiller suspected that Bach was
really trying to prove that he was just as keen, just as
serious about the mission as he was meant to be.

Kinzel, the artillery officer, had already selected his
gun crews and given them some rudimentary training, especially in the process of bringing the shells up
from the magazines below the turrets and man-
handling them into the breeches of the big guns. But
nothing could compare with the experience of actually
firing the massive guns.

Indeed, the whole crew had to know what to do
when the ship was about to commence firing. The
noise was the least of the problems. The flash of the
exploding cordite when the guns went off, followed
by the blast wave, would easily kill or burn anyone
standing on the deck when the guns were fired. All
the hatches, all the scuttles – every opening of the ship
– had to be sealed off. Kinzel sometimes wondered,
with these big guns, whether they did more damage to
themselves than to an enemy.

They were designed to fire explosive shells
weighing over 2500 lb, and powered with nearly 500 lb
of propellant – the explosive power of a good-sized

bomb – they could lob the shells with surprising accuracy at targets up to 40,000 yards away, nearly 23 miles. The shells would strike the targets with massive kinetic energy; only the thickest armour plate was proof against a strike of such magnitude. And if the shell managed to penetrate a ship's armour, it would then explode within the vessel and wreck it from the inside.

In 1941, chased by the pride of the Royal Navy, the mighty *Hood*, the *Bismarck* had turned its guns on its pursuers and fired. A single shell arched high into the air, miles up, then turned over and plunged back towards the *Hood*. Having struck the weakly armoured deck plating and pierced it cleanly, it cut down through the bowels of the ship until, several decks below, the fuse ignited the shell and it erupted. The shell had reached one of the artillery magazines at that precise moment. A split second later, a massive explosion tore out the huge ship's bottom and split the vessel in two. In less than ten minutes, *Hood* sank beneath the stormy Atlantic, taking over 2,000 young sailors to a lonely and terrifying death.

Battleships like *Bismarck* and *Hindenburg* were the high-technology weapons in a pre-atomic arms race, which the great powers, between the wars, worked hard to try to limit; in military threat terms, building massive battleships was equivalent to building bigger and bigger nuclear weapons, and they were costly monsters, a massive drain on military budgets. In an attempt to keep expenditures under control, the Washington Conference of 1921/22 limited the size of guns used on warships between America, Britain and Japan. But Germany, defeated several years earlier and forbidden by the Treaty of Versailles from doing anything other than replace its fleet – and even then, having to wait twenty years since the previous ship was launched and limiting them to 10,000 tons anyway – wasn't included. In June 1935 the Anglo-German Naval Agreement was Britain's belated recognition of Germany's rearmament, allowing the Germans to build the 35,000-ton *Gneisenau* and *Scharnhorst*. But under Admiral Raeder, Hitler continued building bigger and bigger ships until in April 1939 the agreement was finally torn up, one of the first preludes to war.

Kinzel had just two turrets on his stripped-down ship instead of the four that it was meant to have. The forward turret, 'A', was known as Anton, and then – behind it and raised so that it could fire over the top of the forward turret – was 'B', Bruno. Already he had his crews – dressed in white flash-hoods and gloves – rotating the turrets and elevating the guns. Beneath them, each turret had its own magazine where the big shells were stored – and shells for the other guns – held upright in huge circular racks; and a deck down the propellants, contained in silk bags shaped like drums.

The whole area was massively armoured to protect the ship against the sort of shell strike that had done for *Hood*. The magazines and propellant stores were separated from each other by thick double doors; in action, they acted like air-locks, ensuring flash could not penetrate. More than one warship at Jutland had sent itself to the bottom by igniting its own magazine when its guns were fired.

Electric lifts whirred into action, first lifting shells upwards to the turrets, to be followed by the silk bags of propellant. The gun crews used gleaming hydraulic rams to push the enormous shells from the lifts into the breeches of the guns; then rammed bags of

propellant behind them before more hydraulics swung
the thick breech doors shut and turned them through
twenty degrees to engage the latching mechanism that
would hold them shut against the force the explosion.
The loading crew signalled the process complete and
the doors locked. The guns had to be loaded in level
position; once ready, they were immediately elevated
to the required setting to give the range. Inside the
foretop fire control position, high up on the forward
superstructure, Kinzel watched the indicators rise to
thirty degrees and the green 'ready' lamps come on.
Both guns in turret Anton were now ready to fire.

Bach, Schiller and the others had taken their positions
lower down inside the armoured conning tower, safe
from the blast effects that would rock the Admiral's
bridge they had been using for normal navigation,
positioned above them.

'Turret Anton ready for firing, Captain,' came
Kinzel's voice over the telephone.

'Crew stand by, stand by. Main guns firing in ten
seconds. Take cover, take cover.' Schiller's voice boomed
around the decks and the mess halls, echoing from the
loudspeaker system.

Ten seconds clicked steadily past. Kinzel pressed the
switch that sent a sudden surge of electric current
into the propellants of both guns, one a fraction of a
second before the other to stagger the impact of explosions against the ship. The cordite charges ignited,
literally like bombs, and the shells were hurled against
the rifling of the inside of the barrel to give them spin
before exiting in two huge bursts of flame and smoke.
They accelerated to over 2,000 mph, arching up into
the clear blue sky where they reached an altitude of
four miles before returning on their entry trajectories
where they impacted with the smooth, cold sea, twelve

miles away, and sent two geysers of white water leaping about a hundred feet into the air, one a second after the other.

Few of the younger crewmen had any idea of what to expect. Even Heine, cool as ever, was shocked by the impact of the firing on the ship itself. The whole vessel jumped – twice – as the shots went off. He was in the galley: plates threw themselves to the floor, the heavy wooden tables jumped and crashed back, one of them splitting. One bank of lights went out, the cable torn from the sockets by the force.

'Next time, Heine, I'll make sure you're outside when they go off. How about that?' giggled Rois as Heine crouched against another blast which never came.

'Fuck off,' whispered Heine, but Rois was on his feet to get to the door to see the fall of shot. It was the kind of thing that Rois would enjoy, thought Heine.

Bach was impressed. He had only served on ships with smaller-calibre weapons. These guns were an altogether different proposition. Was this mission such madness after all? Perhaps it really could be done.

Bach allowed Kinzel three more shots before ordering him to test out the 37-mm anti-aircraft guns. His crews took up position on three of the small guns and started blasting away into the clear sky, sending streams of tracer into the air. They would be enough, thought Bach, to frighten off a couple of small raiders; but if he was subjected to a major air attack, they would be useless. In Krancke's original orders, he had said that the best way to cope with an air attack would be to just sit it out; that Puttkamer had armoured the thing so heavily that he could survive even the most determined onslaught. Bach didn't want to test the theory.

The test firings were complete. Kinzel pronounced himself satisfied. Schiller had ordered the crew to stand down, and they were struggling out of the thick canvas flash-hoods when Moehle, who had been testing out his crude radar to see if the delicate antenna would stand up to the blasts from the big guns, noticed two distinct blips on the small screen. He watched them carefully for a few moments and then called the bridge from his room a deck below.

'Captain, I've picked up a signal on the radar.'

'What sort of signal?' replied Bach.

'Hard to say, Captain. Could be aircraft. Probably two or three of them. Approaching quite fast.'

'Range?'

'Right at the edge of screen, Captain. More than twenty-five miles.' It was the best he could do with the technology available to him. Twelve miles was the best range that the set was reliable for. All he could see was a smeared, indistinct blob that was moving closer to them. It could have been a flock of geese. But Bach knew already that what Moehle saw was no flock of geese. It was the news that Bach had been dreading but half-expecting. He knew they were aircraft, and he knew they were out there searching for him. Damn it, he thought to himself. Another couple of hours steaming and I'd be into some murk. The southern sky was already darkening and the barometer was dropping fast. But in truth, he was only surprised that his luck had held out for so long.

'Schiller, aircraft. Action stations. We have to bring them down.' It was less of an order and more a statement of fact.

The crew, still in chaos after being ordered to stand down, groaned as the alarms went off. It took a full minute before the word spread that no, this was not another practice: the enemy was on its way. The faces of the kids, a moment ago filled with excitement at the fun of playing with the guns, suddenly began to pale and tense. They looked at each other. This was real. This was war.

*

There were two Catalinas this time, flown by RAF Coastal Command pilots out of Iceland. They had been in the air for four hours, droning across the featureless sea, further and further north, to where the station commander had ordered them. Look for a big ship, identify it, radio your report, said the commander. The position he gave was very exact. But a good hour before they reached that position, there was a smudge on the distant horizon. The visibility was as clear as a bell, and the on-board radar was giving a good echo even at this extreme range.

'Bill? You see that? Bearing 300 degrees?' called Hiscocks, co-pilot of the first Catalina.

Bill Morrisey, the pilot of the second, looked in the direction Hiscocks had given him. Yes. There was a smudge on the quivering horizon. As he watched it, it gave out two tiny flashes, like sunglint on a distant mirror.

'Percy, did you see that?' called Morrisey back again.

'I did. Now what the hell is going on?' But he didn't wait for a reply to his question. 'Bill, take it down to 1,000 feet and we'll go in low. You go left, I'll take the right-hand side. Watch out. The bugger might shoot.'

In the lead plane, Percy Hiscocks eased back on the throttles and let the small flying-boat drift gently down towards the sea. They were about thirty miles off. The altimeter unwound gently until they reached 1,000 feet. The sea rushed along underneath them,

looking nearer than it was. Bill Morrisey in the second
Catalina followed him down and took position on his
left side, slightly behind.

The smudge grew quickly larger.

*

Bach knew he could do very little, but he intended to
try anyway. He felt in his bones that this was not going
to be an attack; they wouldn't have sent just two aircraft. This was a recon flight, two aircraft sent to see
what he was and where he was going. The real attack
would come later.

The trick now was to buy time by making life hell
for the two pilots heading for him, to drive them off
long before they could make a positive identification.
And if that failed, then he knew he had to down them,
if possible before they got their report off. Shorn of
his long-range anti-aircraft weapons, all he had were
the 37-mm guns, twin quick-firing cannon that were
effective at up to two miles.

He ordered every gun mount manned and ready to
fire, and then instructed the helmsman to take up a
course pointing directly at the oncoming aircraft.

He would offer them the minimum profile; his ship
would be difficult to identify bow-on. He would have
made smoke into the bargain, but the breeze which
had sprung up in the last hour was enough to blow
the smoke away.

Bach and his bridge crew had made their way up
from the armoured conning tower to the open bridge
where the view was much clearer.

'Schiller, can you see them?' asked Bach. He
desperately wanted a drink.

Schiller was peering at the two approaching dots
through his old Zeiss binoculars. 'They've gone low, sir.

But the wings are high on the fuselage; must be Catalinas.'

So, thought Bach, definitely recon then. Catalinas were slow, too. He stood a good chance of bringing them down. He lifted the heavy microphone of the PA system and spoke to the crew.

'This is the captain. The approaching aircraft are spotters, probably unarmed. They will try to identify us and then radio their reports back. They must fly close to see who we are with any certainty. This will be your opportunity to down them before they can get their reports off. This is vital. All gun crews will hold their fire until I order you to commence. Good shooting!' As he replaced the handset, he hoped no one noticed the slight shake of his hand.

The gun crews were supervised by the petty officers. Now the older officers turned to their crews – you heard the captain, don't let us down. Wait for the order and make every shot count.

The young crews, nervous at first, now began to feel more confident. The captain sounded as though he had a plan. And so they all settled to their posts, dressed in flash-hoods with steel helmets perched on top, watching the two aircraft growing slowly larger.

*

'The bugger's turned towards us,' called Hiscocks. 'I can see a big superstructure and what looks like a turret or maybe two.'

'Warship. Must be,' replied Morrisey.

'One of ours, Bill? Way out of the position I was given. Anyway, better take a look.'

Neither pilot was worried; the briefing did not suggest anything sinister. Neither man knew of any enemy warships in this part of the Atlantic. After all, the war was as good as won in Germany. There was no threat.

Hiscocks led them lower, down to 600 feet. The sea was calm and the breeze barely affected the aircraft. The narrow profile of the ship they were now quickly closing on was not giving away a great deal, and so the vessel was impossible to identify. The ship recognition books only gave side-on views. You had to count the number of smokestacks and turrets to be sure. Hiscocks wanted to fly down the side of the ship to get a good visual, as well as maybe seeing some positive identification.

The range closed.

'Seems quiet enough,' said Hiscocks at five miles. If the ship was an enemy vessel, it would have been putting up a barrage of flak by now to confuse them and drive them away.

Four miles. Three miles. Still no reaction from the ship bearing down on them.

'Big bugger, Bill. What the hell is it?' It was clear to Hiscocks that they were looking at a substantial warship, something unusually large. It couldn't be German; they'd lost their big stuff months ago. Couldn't be British; they'd have known about it. Yanks? It wouldn't be the first time they hadn't told anyone what they were up to. Could even be some big Russian ship that no one knew about.

Two miles. Still nothing.

*

Bach watched them. They were clear now; the dark shapes low over the water with the characteristic high wings and floats hanging down, and two big observation bubbles on each side. American-built Catalinas, the workhorses of Coastal Command with their huge range and endurance and ability to land on the water to pick up Allied crews.

They were now about two miles out. Moehle's man

on the radar was calling out the range as they closed.

Bach stood impassively on the bridge. The rest of the officers stood there too, waiting in silence for the order to come.

On the guns, each man had selected the aircraft he was aiming at and was even now steadily tracking it in his sights. The magazine crews stood by, ready with fresh ammunition. There was now an almost total silence on the ship, other than the steady rumble of the two big diesels pounding away at maximum revolutions to give the vessel maximum speed and manoeuvring ability.

'Three kilometres!' called radar. A mile and a half. Well within the range of the guns.

'Two kilometres,' called radar a moment later. That was Bach's signal for action.

'FIRE!' commanded Bach over the PA.

Suddenly each one of the ten 37-mm guns crackled into action, firing one shell every second from the twin barrels, the recoils flinging the spent brass cartridge cases into the air to land on the deck plating where they rang like church bells. Tracer ignited to make the trajectories clear even in the bright sunshine; five glittering lines converged on each aircraft.

*

There was a second or two of puzzlement as both pilots saw the sparkles flicker along the sides of the ship; then realisation dawned.

'Oh, fuck! Break off, break off!' yelled Hiscocks. The pilots had separated and started to fly down opposite sides of the ship when the *Hindenburg* opened up. Hiscocks and Morrisey rammed the throttles forward and the steady beat of the Wright engines turned into a screaming whine as though they were taking off.

Both pilots banked away, keeping the nose low to increase speed in an attempt to escape the sudden barrage. But banking away presented a much bigger target to the inexperienced crews. The 37-mm shells spattered into Morrisey's plane, ripping through the flimsy skin, killing his co-pilot instantly and puncturing both wing-tanks. Fuel began to spray from the tanks, to be ignited a moment later by a burning tracer shell. Morrisey fought to keep his aircraft level as the shells rammed home; he had no time to think now. He knew he was hit and that his co-pilot had probably bought it. Now he had to ditch: take the plane down in a controlled, level descent to land on the calm sea. It was his only hope. He pushed back on the throttles to bring the aircraft down; he could see the blazing wing above and to one side, but ignored it. Maybe he just had time ...

More shells arched out towards the stricken aircraft and took off the top half of the tail. Morrisey found his rudder suddenly loose. He took his feet off the pedal and braced himself for the landing. The nose wasn't high enough; he pulled back on the stick, but the controls didn't respond. The nose pointed down and then the aircraft hit the sea with a thump. It ploughed into the water, sending up plumes of spray from each side. But Morrisey was still alive. The plane slowed quickly in the water and he was breathing a sigh of relief when another cascade of shells tore into the aircraft. Morrisey never knew what happened. A huge fireball ignited the fuel that was spilling over the water and enveloped the Catalina. Once it had cleared away, there was nothing left except a scatter of debris on the sea and a cloud of ash that floated gently downwards.

Hiscocks saw nothing of this; he too was fighting for his life. Shells had taken out one of his engines and,

although he had managed to turn away from the ship,
he found the aircraft wasn't responding to the stick; he
presumed some control lines had been blown away. And
with just one engine left, the effect was now that it was
turning him slowly around, towards the ship itself. He
managed to keep one wing slightly high in an effort to
defeat the turn. The rate of turn slowed but didn't stop.

But now, at least he could see the ship clearly.
Hiscocks had been flying recon for two years; he
rarely needed his ship recognition books. The silhouettes of most major vessels were etched into his
brain. The tracer was flying past him now; he knew
it was just a matter of time before they would hit him
again. The internal communications system was
buggered and the holes in the skin made a whistling
sound that was difficult to speak over. He yelled at the
top of his voice, hoping his navigator and radio-man
could hear him.

'Dougie! Quick. One word on the radio. Get it off
now!' he yelled and gave the word. The navigator was
a young lad, fresh from training, and was sitting
terrified in his seat as the shells popped around him.
But he obeyed his order; he tapped out the single word
on the long-range Morse set. Then a shell first of all
tore out his radio set, and a fraction of a second later
ripped out his brains from below.

There was nothing Hiscocks could do; the aircraft
was slowly turning back towards the ship. He couldn't
even ditch the fucker. The last things Percy Hiscocks saw
were several lines of tracer converging on him from the
ship. He didn't even know if the message had gone.

*

Bach watched the second aircraft explode in mid-air
about 500 yards away. The gun crews were cheering,

leaping up and down, waving their grey steel helmets. A few seconds ago they had been more scared than ever in their lives, and now they were enjoying the exultation, the blood-lust, of victory. Not a man on board felt a thing for the downed aviators; there were no human beings on the aircraft – that was the way it felt – just mute machines trying to kill them, which had now been torn from the skies and hurled into the water.

Bach didn't feel quite the same. He was pleased his plan had worked and they had managed to get both Catalinas. But he had no idea if they had got a message off. The very fact that both of them were downed and would in a few hours be reported missing, would raise suspicions. Whatever happened, he knew that he was still under threat.

He ordered the gun crews to stand down after congratulating them. Eat, he told them. Relax for a few hours. What he didn't tell them was this was the start, not the finish, of their fight for survival. Now he knew his mission was in danger.

Moehle was watching him carefully. 'Congratulations, sir. No problem at all,' he ventured. How was the captain feeling?

Bach shook his head. 'Sorry, Moehle. Don't think it's always that easy. That was just the start. We've tweaked the tail and now somebody is going to get very, very angry.'

'But we can stand it, sir. Can't we?'

'Stand it, Moehle? It's not a question of standing it. We're out here on our own and we're sailing right into the enemy's teeth. Frankly, I have no idea how far we can stand anything.'

'You seemed confident enough a while back, sir. Orders are orders, you said,' replied Moehle quietly.

'You're right, Moehle. Orders are orders. Even if we have to kill everyone on board and send the ship to the bottom of the Atlantic. Orders are still orders, even when they are stupid. That's what we're here for.'

'You don't sound convinced, sir.'

'For God's sake, Moehle! Don't you understand? We haven't got a prayer. Now they've found us, all we can hope for is a bit of time and bad weather. Then we all die. Now get on with your duties,' Bach snapped.

Moehle turned away and left the captain. Once again he wondered how far Bach would go. He seemed stressed, on edge. Should he do something to get the man back on track? Something that would convince him to carry on? There was one thing that Moehle knew – which Bach didn't – that would drive the captain to complete the mission, no matter what. But he knew he could only use it in the gravest circumstances.

Bach scanned the horizon to the south. There was a line of cloud slowly growing, creeping up on them. It was about thirty miles off. Perhaps it was a friendly storm; anything would be preferable to this clear blue sky. The breeze was picking up as well, he thought. A gentle south-westerly, perhaps the first signs of an approaching front. The blue sea remained resolutely calm as the *Hindenburg* ploughed steadily southwards.

*

Vice-Admiral Peter Herdman found himself mightily puzzled. The signal had arrived from Coastal Command, but it made no sense. He was waiting for Lil to come in; she would have an idea, that was for sure. But she was at home right now, so he'd sent his car round to collect her.

There was a knock at the door, but before he could say anything Lil Beasley, still with her big mackintosh on and her face half covered in a scarf, stumped into the room, pulled out a chair, produced a filthy, crusted handkerchief and blew her nose loudly.

'Thanks for coming over, Lil. Sorry to drag you out. Here, look at this.' He pushed the yellow flimsy over his desk, where she picked it up and read it, her handkerchief still over her nose.

The signal was from Coastal Command:

Message from our recon party. Word 'Bismarck'
sent in Morse. No position but sent at 12.30 GMT.
Contact now lost.

'What time did they take off?' asked Lil.

'Quick as ever, eh, Lil? Worked that one out already. Whatever they saw, it's about two hundred miles south of where you thought it was. But, Lil old girl, what the fuck does "*Bismarck*" mean?'

Lil was not even puzzled. 'Sorry, Peter. Haven't got the foggiest.'

'No ideas, Lil? You're the one with the ideas.'

'Sorry, Peter. The only logical explanation is that they saw the *Bismarck* out there. That, or else it was some other ship that happens to look exactly like the *Bismarck*. And I'm not allowed to talk about that, am I? Any further contact?'

'Nothing. Which is why Coastal Command is upset. They'll be overdue soon.'

'Well, Peter?'

'Well, Lil. Sounds like something nasty out there. I think we'd better sort it out, don't you?'

'You do that, Peter. I tell you now, it stinks to hell. Something very strange is going on, and you can bet your life that the Hun has still got a trick or two up his sleeve. I don't give a fig what you or those fatheads upstairs say, it's the bloody *Hindenburg* or my name's not Lil bloody Beasley. You just listen to me, Peter Herdman. Watch out, that's my advice. Now can I go home?'

Herdman let her go. She was right. Something very strange was happening. The problem was, even if it was the old battleship, his orders were clear: it could not possibly be there.

8

—

Heine didn't share the general enthusiasm over the success of the action. He heard the cheering and the laughter after the guns went quiet, and he didn't like it at all. This was becoming serious and, as far as Heine was concerned, deadly. What if they were American planes? The Americans wouldn't stand for having their aircraft shot down. They'd be on them like a ton of bricks. All it would do was make Bach and the rest of the crazies even more unbearable. Heine shook his head. Bloody madness! Berlin by now was almost certainly in the hands of the Bolsheviks and Hitler a prisoner. Why carry on trying to commit suicide like this?

He brewed up some more coffee, poured it into a can – a heavy, insulated one he'd found in the stores – and set out for the bridge.

Rois and Schnee were waiting in one of the corners of the main deck. They were smoking hand-rolled cigarettes and laughing. Unlike Heine, the destruction of the two aircraft had greatly cheered the fat cook and the chief petty officer. This was more like it. Real war and the enemy getting completely fucked. Let's see how the bastards like that!

Rois and Schnee were of a similar age and background; working-class lads brought up in Danzig, hating the Poles, overjoyed at the German renaissance and seeing Hitler as the man who could save Germany from the Jews, the Communists, the gypsies and everyone else they hated. Rois had been in the Hitler Youth as a young man, but his endless petty crimes had forced even them to get rid of him. Schnee remained a good Navy man, but never advanced beyond the rank of chief. The *Kriegsmarine* still preserved the old German class hierarchy, and the chances of somebody of Schnee's background gaining promotion were about nil.

Both of them had watched the collapse of the Reich with increasing dismay. Like so many other Germans of their class and generation, neither man had really come to terms with it, no matter how obvious that collapse was becoming. When they learned of Bach's mission they felt only the pleasure of pure revenge, the twisted, secret delight in paying back the enemy for what they had done. They did not worry about the consequences. The probability of failure, that they would die a slow death at sea, did not cross their minds. They were *volk*, the people of the mighty Reich, and they would triumph in the end. All they could do now was laugh and joke about the way the planes had been shot to pieces.

They watched Heine walk down the deck, holding the heavy coffee can in both hands. He saw them at the same time. Something in their faces made his heart start to beat faster. He gripped the thin wire handle of the can.

'Well, now, it's my old friend … what's your name again, sonny? I forgot,' asked Schnee loudly, winking at his companion.

Heine really didn't want the trouble. He kept on walking past them.

'Hey, you – Heine. I asked you a fucking question.

Stand to attention. What's your name?' shouted Schnee as Heine passed him by. Heine hesitated for a moment, then stopped, put the can on the deck and stood to attention.

'You know my name, sir. Otto Heine. Was there anything you wanted? I'm on my way to the bridge, you see. Captain Bach's orders.' He said it as a challenge – he suddenly couldn't help himself.

'Oh, Otto Heine. Captain Bach's orders, if you please. Well, it's very good of you to stop and pass the time of day with us, isn't it, Rois?'

Rois was itching to have a go at Heine. On his own he would never dare; but now Schnee was here, it felt a lot easier. 'Chief, young Otto here is a very important man, very important indeed. Takes the captain's coffee up, good as gold. Captain Bach whistles, Otto comes running. Isn't that true?'

Heine stared at the ground, refusing to get drawn into eye contact. He was wishing now that he had been less cocky. But the damage was done. Besides, these idiots would get him killed.

'No answer, Otto Heine?' joined in Schnee. 'A superior officer is talking to you, lad. Where's your salute? And who said you could put the captain's coffee on the deck? Stand up straight or by God, lad, I'll kick your teeth out.' Schnee was starting to shout now. Rois was watching him and he had to reinforce his authority with this snotty little kid.

Heine sighed. He looked Schnee in the face and gave a perfunctory salute, then leaned down to pick up the coffee can. But Schnee put his foot on top of the can, slowly and deliberately, and stood there, watching Heine who straightened again and shrugged.

'Come on, come on. Don't be late with the captain's coffee,' chortled Rois.

'Wouldn't do, wouldn't do at all,' said Schnee softly, still looking directly at Heine.

Heine leaned down again and gripped the handle. 'Excuse me, sir,' he said quietly.

'Oh, sorry. Here you are,' smiled Schnee and took his foot off the can. Heine lifted the can, but had barely got it an inch off the deck when Schnee delivered a massive, swinging kick to it. The lid flew off, hot coffee sprayed across Heine's tunic and the can itself looped into the air, crashing back to the deck before rolling towards the steelwork of the bulwark where it came to a halt.

Something inside Heine was starting to give. Never lose your temper. Never let other people dictate what you do or feel. Always remain in control. That was what Otto Heine had learned over the years, and it had kept him out of trouble, out of jail, probably out of hospital on a few occasions. But deep inside he knew that these fools wanted more than just some sport with him; they were part of a process that was trying to dominate him, to break him. If they could do that, then he would lose all control over his destiny. And these people were cheerfully sailing on a mission that would see all of them dead. Now he had to get his life back under control while he had a chance, before these idiots did for him and the rest of the poor bastards on the ship. Otto, he told himself, it's now or never. Time to go forward or let them drag you down. And he had spent too long fighting his way up from the gutters of the Hamburg slums to let that happen.

He knew Rois and Schnee well enough, recognised them within seconds of first meeting them. They were small men, bullies, used to getting their own way because of their rank. He'd already scared the life out of Rois; he knew the fat cook would never dare do this on his own. Schnee was the dangerous one. But now he had no choice. It wasn't anger that made him do what he did; Heine would never let anger get the better of him. But now a decision was being forced on him, too early, by these fat fools who didn't have a brain between them. He would rather have chosen his own time, but Heine could see that he was not going to be able to walk past these two.

Heine calmly walked over to the can, which was now rolling gently with the slight motion of the ship, and picked it up. There was a small puddle of coffee left in the bottom. He retrieved the lid which had fallen close by.

'Now the captain will be *very* upset,' he remarked to Rois.

'Better get him some more fucking coffee then, lad,' laughed Schnee.

Heine had a good grip on the thin wire handle. Looking Schnee in the eyes, he calmly swung the can with as much force as he could into the other's face. Schnee saw it coming but didn't even try to duck. Perhaps it was the outrageousness of the action itself, or just the cold, calculating violence behind the strength of the swing that so amazed him. The can, insulated and therefore of some weight, connected with the front of Schnee's face, slightly to one side. A red mist puffed softly into the air and hung there for a moment. Schnee's face snapped to one side, like a boxer taking the full force of a sudden punch. The man staggered, then his knees gave way beneath him so that he collapsed in a limp straggle of arms and legs on the floor. His whole face was a sudden mass of blood from crushed and torn veins in his nose.

Rois was stepping quickly backwards. He had his arms out in front of him and his hands raised, fingers spread, either to ward off an attack from Heine or else to keep Schnee off him. He was staring at the chief, who was now rolling himself up to one knee, one hand pushing on the deck and the other softly touching the bloody mass of his nose. He was making a gurgling sound as though he was under water; bubbles of snot and blood came from his mouth and then burst, spattering on to the deck.

Heine stood for a moment and watched. He had crossed his line. At least, now, he was his own man, even if for just a moment or two. Of course they'd come for him; it was just a matter of time. But Heine was back on top, and that made him feel a hell of a lot better. The choices were back in his hands. He wasn't entirely sure what he was going to do, but he knew that he had set in place a train of events that would at least give him some chance of living rather than letting himself be taken against all sense to a certain and very bloody death.

Schnee was getting to his feet. An experienced fighter, he had been in more brawls in Hamburg and Kiel bars than he cared to remember, usually when he was drunk. He had never taken a blow quite like that before, and it had left him dazed. But that wouldn't stop him getting back at this little shit. Now he pushed himself upright and lunged in the direction of Heine, trying to grab his throat. But Heine was ready for him; he clasped both hands together and swung them like a hammer at Schnee's stomach, pushing inwards and upwards. Schnee managed to grab Heine's tunic at the shoulder when the blow connected, shoving the air from his lungs. His grip on Heine tightened, but it was for support now. Heine grabbed the man's thick wrist and pushed it upwards to break the hold, but Schnee wasn't going to let go. Heine shoved his knee into the man's groin, trying for his balls, but Schnee was bending over almost double now, fighting for breath, and Heine's knee just pushed into the fat of his stomach. Heine grabbed the man's hair from the top of his head and jerked his head upwards; then he swung his fist into the bloody face. It felt warm and soft, almost as if no bone was there, and when it connected it made a splashing sound.

Schnee finally sank slowly to the deck, on his knees, supporting himself with one hand, his head dropped low, fighting for breath, while drops of crimson blood dripped on to the plating.

Heine paused for a moment. Schnee was not going to move again for a while. Now he had to deal with the cook. Rois had pressed himself back into a corner; there was no way out. There was a look of mortal fear in the man's face as Heine reached up, took his ear between his fingers and started twisting. The man flinched and closed his eyes, expecting Heine to punch him. When the blow didn't arrive he opened his eyes.

'Listen, you fat shit. Are you listening to me?' demanded Heine.

Rois just nodded. Heine maintained a firm grip on the man's ear.

'I don't give a fuck for people like Schnee or people like you. You understand? You're all mad bastards and you're all going to die. You know that? You know what this ship is doing? It's going to shell the fucking White House, Rois, and guess what? The Americans are going to blow this thing out of the water long before you maniacs get anywhere near the place. You know *that*?'

Rois could say nothing.

'You're a spineless creep, Rois. You'd let these people kill us all, wouldn't you? So you take very good care, because I do not intend to let that happen. Not one word about this from you, otherwise I'll break every finger in your hands and pull your fucking eyeballs out. You know I'll do it, don't you?' Heine twisted Rois's ear with real pressure and the cook cried out.

'You know that, don't you?' demanded Heine again.

Rois nodded vigorously. Heine let him go. There was no point in beating the man, he thought, much as he wanted to.

And now what? Schnee was still kneeling on the deck, red blood still splashing from his face on to the deck plating. Should he get rid of the man? Roll him to the edge of the deck, shove him overboard – that would be easiest. Nobody would miss him for a while, not in all the excitement. And when he was missed, well, lost in action would be the likeliest explanation. He didn't think Rois would give the game away. The man was too scared.

But something stopped Heine. He didn't know himself why he didn't follow his natural instinct to get rid of Schnee. It wasn't that he was squeamish: he'd killed once before – an underworld figure who was going to kill him – and he'd disposed of the body easily enough. It wasn't even that he felt sympathy for Schnee. But for the first time in his life Heine had a vague stirring, deep down in his soul, of an unfamiliar feeling of responsibility. No longer could he just dump the evidence overboard. Heine looked at Schnee. It was what he deserved. But what next?

Heine had no time to wonder. A party of three was walking slowly down the deck towards them, one of them an officer – it looked like Schiller from a distance. They were not hurrying. None of them had seen anything.

Heine took an instant decision. There was no point in hiding. He had crossed his line and now he just wanted to drive the confrontation forward. Resolve the issue now, Otto, he told himself. The sooner the better, before the bastards got any further with the madness. He started waving at the approaching party.

'Here, over here!' he shouted.

Schiller and the two others paused for a moment and then broke into a run.

'God in heaven, what happened here?' asked Schiller, kneeling down to look at Schnee. Rois stood back, staying in the background.

Heine stayed silent.

'What happened, I asked?' repeated Schiller, looking first at Rois and then at Heine.

Rois kept quiet, still standing as far as away as he could with his back to the steel bulkhead.

'Never mind. You, Heine, give this man a hand. Rois, get the medic,' ordered Schiller.

Rois almost ran, grateful for the chance to escape. Schiller had produced a handkerchief from his pocket and was dabbing at Schnee's still dripping face, but the handkerchief was soaked in blood within a few seconds.

'Get the man's shirt off, Heine. Help me.' Schiller took hold of the back of Schnee's shirt and tried to rip it apart, but the seams were too strong to tear through.

Heine supported Schnee from the back, holding him upright while Schiller kept pulling at the shirt. Schnee groaned, gave a rattling cough, then vomited a gush of bloody sick over the kneeling Schiller.

'For fuck's sake ...' protested Schiller, jumping up with his hands spread wide, looking down in horror and disgust at the stinking mess that covered the front of his jacket and his trousers.

Heine stood up to help the officer. Schnee, unsupported, sank slowly back to the deck.

Schiller was just standing there, wondering what to do, when the medic arrived, minus Rois who wanted no more to do with the situation. The medic was carrying a small black bag which he immediately opened and produced a thick pad of gauze. He uncapped a small bottle, the contents of which he sprinkled on to the gauze, turning it bright purple; he then quickly applied the pad to Schnee's swelling face. Schnee grunted; the stuff was stinging him back into life.

'Heine, you come with me while I clean this shit off. You –' Schiller said to the medic '– get this man down to sickbay and report back to me. Jesus, what a mess.' Heine followed the angry Schiller to the officers' quarters in the forward part of the ship. Several sailors looked at the bloody, vomit-stained officer with astonishment as he stormed past.

'Wait,' ordered Schiller, and disappeared into his cabin. Heine stood outside. He didn't feel nervous. There was a certain inevitability in what was happening to him and he was content, for now, to let events unfold and take him where they would. He had made his move and now wanted to see the outcome, even though he had no real idea where it would lead. When he attacked Schnee, he knew he was going forward, even if he didn't know where. There was only one thing he was completely certain of: Otto Heine was not going to let these madmen kill him, no matter what he had to do to prevent the situation.

Schiller emerged from his cabin dressed in a fresh uniform. How many did these people own? wondered Heine. 'Come with me,' muttered Schiller.

Heine patiently followed the officer down long companionways and up ladders until finally they arrived outside Captain Bach's cabin. Schiller knocked loudly on the door.

There was a moment of silence and then a shuffling noise from within. A loud cough. Then Bach's voice. 'Come,' the Captain called. Schiller opened the door and stood aside. Heine had to go first.

Inside the sparse room – decorated only with a portrait of *Grosseadmiral* Raeder and not Adolf Hitler, noted Heine quickly – Bach was standing, hatless, with his hands clasped behind his back. Rois was also standing, stiffly to attention, at the side of the cabin. Heine was not really surprised to see him there. Schiller closed the door behind them.

'Name?' asked Bach in an offhand way.

'Heine. Otto. Sir.'

'Heine. How long have you been in the Navy?'

'Since the day before you sailed off with me. I was conscripted in Hamburg.'

'You didn't volunteer?' asked Bach, looking puzzled. He had been told that all the ratings had volunteered for this mission, out of their love for the Fatherland.

'I was forced at gunpoint on to this thing.'

Bach didn't pursue that matter. 'Never mind. You're the lad who brings the coffee, aren't you?'

'Yes, sir.'

'So what's all this nonsense about, then, Heine? I'm a busy man. I'm told Schnee is badly injured and you and Rois here were at the scene. So?'

Heine looked carefully at Rois. The cook just looked down at the floor. It was difficult to see if he had any sign of guilt on his face.

Bach stood stock-still, his blue eyes staring at Heine but with disinterest. As far as Bach was concerned, this was just a minor disciplinary matter, only involving him because it involved violence on the ship, which Naval Regulations required should be brought to the attention of the captain. Heine was a nobody, a coffee boy. Find out what happened, read out the punishment, and then get on with the serious business of getting the ship out of harm's way. Bach still clasped his hands behind his back, but his fingers drummed against each other with impatience.

'Well?' asked Bach again, before Heine had a chance to say a word. It was, perhaps, Bach's impatience that annoyed him most; or it could have been his authoritarian attitude, something which Heine never could get on with; but in truth, even though Heine himself didn't admit it, it was the way Bach simply didn't see him as a human being but just another rating to be told off like a naughty schoolboy. It reduced him to one of the crowd, and as Otto Heine had spent years fighting his way out of the mass, it was the one thing that made him deeply, deeply angry.

He had already crossed his line. Now there seemed no point in holding back. Let the story unfold. Fuck the lot of them. There's no way they could treat him like this.

'What happened was that Schnee was trying to get me. Him and Rois here. They started to attack me, so I fought back. It was self-defence. Schnee is some kind of homicidal maniac and frankly, Captain, I have no intention whatsoever of getting killed on this ship. The rest of you can go to hell if you want, but I would prefer to be left out of it.'

Bach raised his eyebrows. Who was this arrogant kid to talk to him like this? 'Heine, you will show some respect when you speak to me. I am the captain of this ship.'

'I know who you are. I know what your plans are as well, Captain.' Heine was getting angry now.

'You dare to talk to me like this?' asked Bach, now genuinely surprised. Nobody had spoken to him like this. *Ever.*

But Heine had no intention of stopping. Things had gone too far. 'Of course I dare talk to you like this. You're all crazy, you know that? Germany is defeated, Captain. You all realise that, yet you still want to sail this thing into the teeth of the Americans who will do for all of us, you and Schiller here included. I don't see the point, Captain, I really don't see the point. For God's sake, why do you want to kill us all?'

Bach was taken aback by Heine's outburst. It wasn't just what he said, but the way he said it: Heine was right – as far as Bach was concerned, he was just a snotty-nosed rating. Bach didn't expect the lucid, articulate objection he had just heard. It was like a pet dog suddenly standing up on its hind legs and talking.

Surprisingly, Bach then smiled. 'Goodness me, Schiller. What have you got yourself here? A street beggar from Hamburg who's suddenly become a leader amongst men?' Bach walked up to Heine, now looking at him as though he was a real person. He kept his hands clasped firmly behind his back. Heine tensed. Bach had a certain presence, something that made people edgy whenever he was near, something quietly threatening.

'You have opinions, then, young Heine? You have thoughts about the war? You disagree, perhaps, with some of our plans, some of our orders? Schiller, get young Heine here a chair. Sit yourself down. Perhaps we should have a chat about your views?' Schiller, a wry look on his face, pulled out a chair and motioned to Heine that he should sit on it.

Heine was not going to fall for Bach's easy sarcasm. 'Thank you. I'll stand.'

'You'll stand? Very well. Perhaps that's right. So, Schiller, what shall we do with our reluctant sailor here? Doesn't want to go to sea. Doesn't want to go to

war. Doesn't like our mission at all. Thinks we're trying to kill him into the bargain. Then goes and beats
up Schnee, one of our finest officers. What do you
think of that?'

Schiller found Bach's sarcasm difficult to take as
well. There was something unsettling about it. 'Sounds
as if Heine here has assaulted an officer. He admits it.
Standing orders give you absolute power, sir. Death if
you think the situation warrants it.'

'You hear that, Heine? Death if I think the situation
warrants it? Attacking an officer, even a non-
commissioned one ... that's insubordination, even
mutiny. I can have you shot right now. You understand?'

'Yes, Captain. I understand,' replied Heine, but he
wasn't going to be put off by Bach's threats.

'So. But of course, you know I won't have you shot,
don't you? You're a clever young man, Otto Heine.
You're right, of course. This war is a sad waste for
people like you. But there have been thousands like
you, who have already gone to their deaths – most of
them honourably, and some like thieves in the night.
Most of them a damn sight more useful than you, as
well. What makes you so special? Why should you be
the one to die a nice clean death and have a polite
burial at sea? Sorry, Heine, but you're going to die
along with the rest of us, torn into bloody mincemeat,
screaming and drowning. If that's the way we're going,
then you're coming too.'

'You're mad, Captain. There's no need for this. Why
condemn all these people to death? What have they
ever done to you?'

'Why, Heine? Good God, everyone wants to know
why. Even Schiller here wants to know why. I owe you
no explanation. You do as you're told.'

'Sorry, Captain, that's not good enough.'

Bach looked at Heine with what seemed to Schiller like sympathy. 'Of course it's not good enough. This is bloody war. What do you expect? Sanity? Don't kid yourself. Reason flew out of the window in 1939 when that little Austrian pig decided he would rule Europe. It's not good enough, Heine, but it's all you'll damn well get.'

'And the rest of the crew? What if they think it's not good enough, either?'

'Come on, young man, don't be stupid. You think they'll follow you in some mutiny? You've never been on a ship before, have you? Listen, put that idea right out of your head. The crew need to respect their captain. They're alone on the high seas, chased by the enemy. They're young, they're frightened, and what they want, Otto Heine, is not a mutiny led by your very good self but certainty and authority. They want real leadership, not fun and games. You saw what they were like when we downed those planes. Forget it, Heine. You're going to your death with the rest of us.'

'And you'll take us there, Captain. You don't give a fuck, do you?'

Bach coloured and moved closer to Heine, who still didn't shift an inch. They were face to face now. The tall, imperious face of Erich Bach, the old Germany, conservative, loyal, patriotic, utterly devoted to duty; and Otto Heine, barely out of his teens, his life torn apart by war, loyal to no one but himself, caring for nothing but his own skin. Schiller watched: there seemed to be a mutual respect between the two of them, a curious stand-off where Bach appeared to understand Heine's anger but would not change, and where Heine seemed to understand Bach's sense of duty but would not let him get away with it. Now Heine, deliberately it seemed to Schiller, had challenged that sense of duty. The comment went to Bach's very soul.

'Understand this, Heine. I care very, very deeply. More than you will ever understand.' Bach paused for a moment. 'You are the one who does not give, as you say, a fuck. You are concerned with saving a few lives. Your own, mainly. And for what? So you can return to a Germany overrun by Bolsheviks? Or worse, by the fat Americans who care for nothing except money? And where is Germany in all this? I have spent my life fighting to give Germany some soul, some respect. And yes, I have now been defeated twice. And you know what? This makes me even more determined to show the world what Germany is made of. Even in these last days, Heine – when all appears to be lost, and very probably is – we do our duty.'

'You hate that little Austrian madman. You said so yourself.'

'It's not for him,' Bach almost shouted. 'He had nothing to do with it, nothing at all. It's Germany, Heine. We have nothing left now. No country. But we still have pride, a faith in being German. Once we give that up, then we have nothing. No future. Pride is the last thing we have. That's why we do our duty. We are the last warriors, Heine, the final act. We go on to the end.' Bach suddenly turned away and returned to his desk. He flicked a few papers on it, his back to Heine, Rois and Schiller.

There was an awkward silence as some moments passed, very slowly. It felt like a minute or more, but was just a few seconds. Bach suddenly turned back to face Heine.

'You assaulted an officer. You admit it?'

'Yes.'

'Very well. Twenty-four hours in the brig. Solitary.

No food. Then back to work, under Rois here. Get out,' and now Bach almost snarled. He was angry, upset.

Schiller ordered Heine to attention, a pose that he reluctantly took, and marched him out of the cabin.

*

The brig on the *Hindenburg* was in the foremost part of the ship, virtually the bow itself. It was deep, too, on the sixth deck down. Heine led, with Schiller marching behind him shouting orders to turn left, or turn right, or go down yet another set of ladders. He was sweating by the time they reached the end of a long, dimly lit companionway. This part of the ship was skeletal; just steel frames and steel bulkheads, unpainted, unfinished and now rusting. The door to the brig was solid. Schiller had no key – there were only bolts, but all of them on the outside – and he struggled to free the four of them, rusting into their sockets. The door opened with a shriek. It was completely dark on the inside.

'In,' ordered Schiller.

Heine walked slowly into the cell. It was not only dark, it was small too, no more than two metres square but oddly high, at least five or six metres. The deckhead was almost invisible, lit only by the dim light from the single bulb in the companionway outside. There was nothing inside: no bed, no bench. It was a plain, small, dark, airless steel room, covered in rust. It was cold, too – there was only the unarmoured skin of the forward hull between the brig and the sea, and the splashing and sloshing as the ship ploughed through the water could be clearly heard.

There was barely room to sit, let alone lie down.

'You've got twenty-four hours in this place, Heine. I'll be back same time tomorrow.'

'Where do I piss, for Christ's sake?' asked Heine. He knew what the answer was going to be.

Schiller laughed out loud. 'In the corner, Heine, in the corner. Enjoy your stay.' He tried to slam shut the steel door but the hinges were too rusty, so he had to lean on it to heave it shut instead. The same shriek came from the steelwork. Schiller drove the bolts home one after the other, leaving the topmost bolt to last. There was no point in even putting a guard on Heine.

Schiller looked at his watch. Half-past four. He turned and walked quickly back down the long, dim companionway.

Inside the cell, Heine was breathing quickly. The darkness and the smallness of the cell were already closing in on him. He had never liked confined spaces. He reached out his right hand and could feel the damp steel bulkhead. Keeping that hand in place, he reached out his left hand and easily touched the other side of the cell. He closed his eyes tightly but now he could see the lights of total darkness, the whirling patterns and the sparkles manufactured by a brain suddenly deprived of any light whatsoever. He could feel his heart now, thumping in his stomach, faster and faster. Even though the cell was cold, he was starting to sweat.

Take it easy, Otto, take it easy. He deepened his breathing, trying to control the rising panic. Suddenly he wanted to scream. But he would not give any of them the pleasure. He forced himself to breathe slowly and deeply and the panic began to subside. One-two, one-two, he carefully timed his breath in, and then out. In, and then out. In, and then out

He started to relax. It took a full five minutes before he began to calm down. He had no means of knowing the time. It felt as if an hour had passed. The only contact with reality was the splashing, hissing noises from the bow as the ship moved steadily through the water. It sounded as though he was under water; in truth, the cell itself was almost exactly at the waterline.

Heine decided to sit down. He lowered himself to the damp, cold deck and settled himself on it. He just had the room to stretch his legs out, but he couldn't lie down flat. It didn't matter; he didn't want to.

The deck was colder than the bulkhead. Then his backside began to ache with the cold, so he stood up again. Had another hour passed? But Heine had been in the cell for a full twenty minutes. Another panic attack started to grip him. He had to fight to keep the scream from rising, but instead he beat the door with his fist five or six times, hard, but with the soft part of the end of his fist. It made him feel better; the hard steel was somehow reassuring, some reality in the dark, sightless world that he had been plunged into. He beat it again, but this time with less violence. Was this what it was like to be blind? He held his hands out in front of him, opened his eyes wide. There was no difference. Opened or closed, it was exactly the same. Pretend you're blind, then, Otto. Look at your world by feel. He ran his hands gently around the door first. He could feel the line where the door joined the frame; it fitted badly, and there was a slight gap in it, but no light came through. That bastard Schiller must have turned out the lights in the companionway. Then he could feel the hinges, two large ones, maybe six inches deep. The rust could be felt now; a scrubbiness on the metal, like an unshaven chin. He scraped with his fingernail and got down to the bare metal underneath. He could feel it shining, glimmering in the dimness with a steely sheen, even though he could not see it.

He ran his hands from the door across the

bulkhead to where it met the adjacent steelwork in a sharp corner. Here he could feel the roughness of the cut metal where it joined. Then he could feel some lumps – rivets? Heine continued to explore his cell by feel, square inch by square inch, slowly starting to visualise the bulkheads and the deck and even the colours of the rust.

Heine was no intellectual. For him, thinking was a process that he was unconscious of. But now he suddenly realised the power of his own imagination. With a shock he understood that he could see the cell almost as clearly in his mind's eye as in his real eye. Well, thought Otto, where shall we go?

He settled himself back down on the cold, damp deck. Then he started to walk through Hamburg, at night. It was before the war started. The streets were lit, the trams were rattling along, the shops were full. Perhaps it was Christmas; it was cold, of course, he could feel *that*.

Heine relaxed uneasily into his fantasy. Even though it was still only the afternoon, the fantasy soon began to turn into a dream. Otto Heine fell into a sleep that was his only possible escape.

9

As night fell, the western sky was coloured blood-red with ribbons of torn cloud slowly spreading towards the *Hindenburg* as it made its way steadily southwards over the dark sea. Bach's instincts for the weather were not letting him down. In the far north, beyond the ice shelf, the high pressure had stabilised somewhere over Greenland and the Atlantic depressions were being driven further south than was normal for that time of the year. If Bach wanted to hide from prying eyes for the rest of his voyage under the cover of a gale, he guessed he would find the weather he was looking for much further south in the ocean than his original plan.

The deep red of the sky convinced him. Bad weather was coming his way. He still had no weather reports; the German meteorological frequencies were silent. Once, he reflected, he could have sailed from the Arctic ice shelf to the Antarctic ice shelf down the whole length of the Atlantic, and he would have always been in contact with the deep-ocean weatherships, holding their stations for months at a time, broadcasting coded reports and forecasts. One by one the network had been broken up – some ships sunk, some captured. Now there was nothing to go on other than his own seaman's instincts. The bloody sky, the spreading cloud, the slow but noticeable rise in temperature as warm, moisture-laden air from the west started to move in. A storm front was building.

Bach took a last turn on the open bridge. The air was moving; he could feel a clear breeze from starboard that owed nothing to the steady motion of the vessel. The dark sea was still at ease, a long, slow, rolling swell that barely moved the ship in its course.

Bach went back inside and shut the evening air away. The bridge was in near darkness. There was a dim red light illuminating the compass binnacle so that the helmsman could see his course, but other than that not a single light was permitted, enabling the bridge officer's eyes to accustom to the dark. The ship was running without lights to avoid detection. Even Moehle's radar set was turned off: radar was seen as an aid for close-in navigation or for spotting – the idea of keeping a round-the-clock radar watch was not one that would gain acceptance for some years to come.

There was a small barograph at the back of the bridge, a slowly rotating drum holding a sheet of graph paper. A tiny pen would leave a trace of the rise or fall of barometric pressure as the drum turned. It was not an instrument that Bach, or the others, had much faith in. It was fine at anchor or in dock; but out on the open seas that delicate mechanism was usually upset by the motion of the ship, and so it was rarely given any attention. On this voyage, the sensitivity of the instrument was, as ever, affected: each drum took seven days to fully rotate, and over the last few days the traced line had wandered up and down with sudden spikes and troughs as the device suffered from the vibration of the ship. In rough weather the thing was hopeless.

But had Bach stopped to look at the barograph – his only source of information about the weather – he would have seen a change in the pressure that not even the erratic behaviour of the machine could disguise. Over the past three hours, the pressure had started to fall off a cliff – a sudden, dramatic depression was building just to his south. Bach was right – the weather was changing. But had he known by how much, perhaps he would have acted differently that night.

Bach checked the course, looked at the chart. All was well.

'Schiller, I'll miss dinner tonight. Carry on without me.'

'Yes, sir.'

'I'll be in my cabin. The weather's starting to close in a bit. Keep an eye on it, would you?'

'Yes, sir.'

'Good night, Schiller.'

'Good night, sir.'

Bach left the bridge to his first officer and retired to his cabin. He would eat there; he no longer found the company of his officers pleasant. He missed having his secret charge of brandy before dinner, which made it bearable for him to try to talk to them. He was down to his last few mouthfuls and it was preying on him.

And that incident earlier on today – that arrogant Otto Heine – had annoyed and depressed him too. He could tell that it had upset Schiller as well. Once again he was forced to confront the truth – that he was sailing with a crew of dead men. He didn't want to spend an hour enduring a guilty silence with men he was taking to their deaths. The atmosphere was starting to turn into something resembling a condemned cell, thought Bach.

Was there a way out? He didn't think so. Abject surrender was not something he would contemplate. A battle, a defeat in a fair fight – that would be a different story. At least it would be honourable. But now Bach had to confront the truth that it would not even be a fight. The moment his presence was known, the awesome might of the American Navy would simply annihilate his vessel. The mighty *Bismarck*, twice the ship this one was in terms of speed and armament and fighting crew, was ripped to pieces like a fox caught by the pack; the odds were now even more stacked against him if his secrecy was lost.

He could see the same thoughts running through the minds of his officers. Probably the rest of the crew as well, if Heine had got to them. Perhaps they would start a mutiny after all; at least that would get him off the hook. But as Bach entered his cabin and closed the door behind him, he knew that would not be possible – as he had explained to Heine, crews of warships were not like that. They wanted leadership, clear, firm orders. They would never take responsibility into their own hands. Such things simply did not happen.

He opened his locked briefcase. Both of the empty brandy bottles were still inside it. Something stopped him throwing them away. He found his hip flask in the bottom, unscrewed the top and sniffed the stinging alcohol that rose from the flask. How much was left? Lifting it carefully, he had to hold the flask nearly horizontal before the liquid touched his lips. He moistened them and licked the spirit off. He needed a drink, but he wanted to hoard it as well. He knew he would need it soon, once things started to get bad. As he licked the top of the flask, his hand was quivering again with the tremor. Damn it! He replaced the lid of the flask, screwing it down tightly, and threw it into his case.

A dark corner of his mind could see the two bottles of wine that Schiller had so insultingly placed on the table at dinner. Where were they? But he quickly pushed the thought away. Erich Bach would not – could not – beg drinks off the men. *Never.*

He sat down and started writing up the diary he had kept during all the war years. Suddenly, like a gunshot, the thought of what was happening in Germany crashed into his mind. Where were his wife and son? What had happened to Hamburg, to Berlin? At sea, Bach never permitted himself to think like this. He had trained himself to completely ignore what was happening at home – his job would have been impossible otherwise. Savagely he crushed another unwelcome thought out of existence; this was the real world, this was all that was important, he told himself. What was happening elsewhere was not his business. He crashed his fist down on the desk. The flimsy wood bent under the impact and bounced back – his diary flew up and dropped on the floor along with a heap of other papers.

There was a knock at the door. It was one of Rois's lads, with his dinner. Bach opened the door, but only slightly.

'No, no. I don't want any now. Sorry,' and he slammed the door closed in the boy's face.

The lad returned to the galley to tell the tale that the captain was unwell and was throwing papers around the room.

*

The storm built quickly. The centre was a fierce

depression 300 miles south and west of *Hindenburg*'s position that evening. Born in the Caribbean, it gained energy from the warm Gulf Stream waters and deepened rapidly, rotating with a stately, ominous energy. The gradient – the difference in air pressure between the centre of the depression and the surrounding higher-pressure air – was steep, forcing the air to spin faster and faster into the low-pressure centre. In time, it would spend its energy and arrive over England, several days later, to lash the seafronts of Weston-Super-Mare and Blackpool with a day of wind and rain, nothing out of the ordinary for an April weekend. But now the storm was gathering its full power. With hundreds of miles of open ocean to work on, the waves began to build, gathering in size and weight.

In the empty, storm-whipped wastes, the seas started to pile into each other, one on top of the next. Already ten feet from crest to trough, they grew in size as they merged, heaping up into steadily marching mountains of grey water. Now, in the troughs, the wind was silent, shielded by the massive bulk of the wave; thirty, sometimes forty feet higher; at the crest, the wind was screaming at fifty knots, ripping off the top of the sea into a flying sheet of white spray.

At first the seas were widely spaced. Although high and getting higher, the distance between them – as much as a quarter-mile between one crest and the next – hid their true height. But as the wind gathered strength, it pushed the seas together, speeding them up. The higher the waves became, the more windage they offered and the faster they were driven. Within an hour the waves were less than 100 yards apart, dramatically steepening the leading faces so that they now resembled moving cliffs. These were the waves that any mariner dreaded; even a small ship could take massive seas in its stride so long as they were not steep. But once the distance between them – the fetch – closed, then the sheer angle of the water could be enough to capsize even a big ship unless the skipper was careful. The bigger the vessel; the greater the danger. Smaller boats – deep-sea fishing craft – could often survive the worst storms because they tended simply to bob up and down. Big vessels lay like logs in such water; sometimes foundering simply as the result of their sheer size and bulk.

Bach and the *Hindenburg* were still some hours away from the storm. As Bach finally retired, the waves were already getting up. Hunched in his narrow bunk, he felt only the gentlest motion.

In the bow of the ship, Otto Heine was shivering in the darkness of his tiny cell. He woke briefly from strange dreams when the sloshing of the water around the bow began to increase, as did the motion of the ship. But he drifted quickly back to sleep. He was so cold that his feet and his hands were completely numb. His body was settling into a mild hypothermia that allowed him to mercifully wallow in semi-consciousness.

*

The storm was a more immediate problem for the captain of HMS *Trent*, a light cruiser that had spent the past year at Norfolk Naval Base being re-equipped by the Americans. Just as the refit programme was nearing completion, it became clear that the war was about to end. The refit was stopped and *Trent* had been ordered home. A scratch crew was shipped out, and still with work left to do she had quietly slipped her lines one morning to set off on what everyone on board assumed would be a peaceful cruise back across the Atlantic.

But Herdman had decided that Lil Beasley was right. In spite of what his lords and masters told him, something was clearly going on, and he wanted to know exactly what. Coastal Command in Iceland had finally reported their aircraft long overdue, presumed lost; and no report other than that curious single word '*Bismarck*', and that made no sense at all.

He needed someone to get out there and take a look. He had asked for the dispositions of ships in the area, but the cupboard was almost bare. Every major (and most minor) ships were either tied up and demobilising, or were running supplies across the Channel to feed Montgomery's rapid advance. There were some destroyers still operating around home waters, clearing up the last fanatical U-boats. But in the deep Atlantic, Herdman could find nothing on the active list. It was only by chance that one of the staff officers mentioned *Trent*.

'Nothing at all, I'm afraid. Unless you count *Trent*. But she's only on a delivery trip back from Norfolk. Half-ready and a scratch crew, definitely not on active service.' Herdman demanded to know who was commanding the ship. Ralph Brocklehurst. Herdman knew him well.

Herdman sent a coded signal within the hour, and a surprised Captain Brocklehurst, known inevitably as 'Badger' even to his men, suddenly had to get his ship ready for a mission a great deal more serious than the delivery cruise he had envisaged. Herdman's signal ordered him north. The only problem was that, according to US Navy weather reports, this would take Badger right through the middle of a bloody big storm that he'd spent the last couple of days doing his best to avoid.

And what the hell was he looking for? Herdman's

signal was puzzling. '*Large German warship, possibly battleship*' said the de-crypt. He'd ordered signals to get it repeated in case it was a mistake, but the message was real enough. What German battleships could there possibly be? They'd all been put out of action, surely? Brocklehurst shrugged his shoulders and got on with plotting a course. If Herdman ordered him to steam to the moon, then that was his bloody business.

Brocklehurst was looking at the proposed course against a sketch of the weather situation. The depression, small but clear, looked like a wood-knot on the paper – the isobars tightly packed, particularly around the southern edge through which Brocklehurst would have to sail: this was where the winds would be at their howling worst.

He couldn't sail ahead of it. According to the US met people, it was travelling too fast for him to outrun it from his present position. He could sail behind it, but unless he waited at least 24 hours the seas would be almost as bad. He didn't think Herdman would go for a delay, but it was worth a try.

'Bill, signal Herdman. would you? See if we can wait for a day or so. Tell him there's a bastard of a storm going through and we'll only end up spilling our gins tonight.'

Bill Burrows, Brocklehurst's first officer, grinned and went off to send the signal. He knew what the reply was going to be. When it came back within five minutes, *en clair* to boot, he grinned again and took it back to the bridge

Badger, deepest regrets re your drinks party. Matter in my last to you rather pressing. If you could possibly spare the time, First Lord would be awfully grateful. And I won't kick your arse from here to Pompey. Enjoy the trip.

'In other words, pull your bloody finger out, eh, Bill?'

'Looks like it.'

'Right. Warn the crew to rig for bad weather. Steer zero-two-zero degrees, best speed. Get on with it!'

'Zero-two-zero, aye aye, sir,' called the petty officer on the helm, winding the wheel to port to bring the ship's head round from its easterly course towards the north and the storm. The huge brass engine-room telegraphs were swung round to 'Full Ahead' and as the telegraphs rang back their answers, they could already feel the heel of the vessel as it took the turn, soon followed by a steady increase in the distant vibrations from the engines as the revolutions slowly built up. It took just ten minutes for *Trent* to settle to its new course and build its speed up to the twenty knots that was the comfortable top speed for the ship, without draining the oil bunkers too quickly. The crew, alerted by Burrows's orders over the tannoy, were unpleasantly shaken from their card games and their letter-writing. Suddenly, like the young crew of the *Hindenburg*, they found themselves plunged back into the reality of being sailors at war. Now they had to find oilskins, hidden in forgotten corners; now they had to work through the ship, securing hatches and scuttles, closing watertight doors, shifting the movable stuff into lockers and boxes, getting the ship ready to face bad weather. There was a lot of grumbling, but most of it hid a deeper anxiety. What was happening? Why the sudden change of course? Burrows had said nothing, other than 'new orders'. That, somehow, sounded even more ominous.

*

Heine's head crashed against the wet bulkhead with a sudden jolt, snapping him back to an unwelcome consciousness. His numb body was barely capable of moving; but the cell was doing the moving for him. Sometime during the past few hours – night or day, Heine no longer had any idea which – the ship had started to move in the increasing storm. At the bow the vessel's movement was at its most extreme. As the *Hindenburg* began to plough into bigger and bigger seas the bow rose and fell, crashing into the waves, heaving aside tons of green water in great clouds of spray, burying itself deeply into each sea so that the wave rose above the bow itself and then, shaking the water off, heaved itself upwards as the wave receded and it rose triumphantly into the air as though it had won the battle – only to find itself plunged once more downwards to confront the next advancing wall of water. Heine had stayed more or less asleep as the seas built; but now they had become massive, and the bow was moving through twenty and thirty feet vertically.

The pain from the blow to his head didn't reach through to his fogged brain. All he was suddenly aware of was the violent movement of the cell. It took him a few moments to work out what was going on. Then his brain started to function and he began to realise what was happening.

The motion became even more violent. He could hear the crashing as the bow struck the wave, followed by a sudden silence as it disappeared beneath the water; then a distant gurgling as it rose again. Instinctively he reached out for something to hold on to, but his hands grasped only the naked bulkheads and the wet deck. The ship gave another sudden lurch upwards, paused, and then plunged down again. Heine's body left the deck for a second, then he crashed against the bulkhead again, this time taking the blow on his shoulder and arm. He yelled with the sudden pain.

Heine was being thrown around like a child's doll. He was lucky that the brig was no bigger – at least he didn't have far to be flung. Eventually he worked out a solution and lay on the deck, stretched out flat. His feet touched the bulkhead, keeping his knees bent, while his outstretched arms pressed against the opposite rusting steel wall. This braced him on the floor. His back still left the deck as the ship started to fall, but nothing else moved and he managed to hold that position. The numbness in his legs and feet, induced by the cold, made the position less painful.

Heine settled, safe enough now from being pulped. But within seconds, the seasickness started to take hold of him. It began in the head: a tight headache, followed by a piercing pain in each eyeball. Then the growing pit in the stomach and the dizziness. Even though half-frozen, he began to sweat.

God in heaven, he thought, as he started retching; what are they going to do to me next?

*

Schiller was meant to go off watch at midnight, but the rising wind and sea worried him and he stayed on the bridge. Judging by the way the weather had turned so suddenly, he didn't think he'd be able to get much sleep anyway. He decided not to call Bach. The weather was not really dangerous. And the story from the lad who took him his meal had already reached his ears. The captain was behaving oddly, that was for sure. The man was under a lot of stress. But then, thought Schiller, if he abandoned this ridiculous mission, all would be well. Maybe Otto Heine was right after all. But Schiller didn't give much time to these thoughts. He rarely thought very much at all. He had a job to do and he assumed that the best

thing to do was to get on with it. Things would sort
themselves out.

The *Hindenburg* was taking the seas well. Schiller,
like most German naval officers, had a deep-seated
dislike of big warships at sea. The general feeling
amongst the Naval Staff was that the big ships looked
good but were terrible sea boats in anything like a
blow. Almost all the big German vessels suffered from
being both wet and unstable; indeed, some were
incapable of training their guns even in virtually
normal Atlantic conditions. During the 1930s it was
the cause of much internal debate. When the *Bismarck*
and her sister-ships were being laid down, almost the
entire Naval Staff demanded that they should be good
sea vessels or they would refuse to take delivery of
them. The designers had clearly listened. Although the
bow was plunging into the head seas, it was coming
up again easily enough. And the water sluicing across
the foredeck was cleared away by the big breakwater
erected across the ship, a V-shaped screen nearly a
metre tall. The forward turrets had been rotated to
face as far as possible towards the stern of the ship,
protecting them from the spray, but hardly any water
reached turret Anton, the forward of the two.

At bridge level, it would even have been possible to
stand on the exposed bridge had it not been for the
wind. Schiller opted to stay inside in any event; it was a
damn sight warmer and he had no intention of
freezing to death.

The *Hindenburg* gave a slight shudder as it crashed
into an unusually large sea, momentarily slowing its
progress. Two plumes of white spray flew silently into
the air, almost glowing in the darkness, before disappearing like ghosts. What sort of speed was he
making? Even though the log was showing twelve

knots, Schiller doubted that his speed over the ground was much better than five or six; he had the big seas and the head-wind against him.

'Getting a bit rough, isn't it?' It was Moehle, the young radar officer.

Schiller turned, surprised to see him. 'Bit late for you, Moehle. I thought you'd be in bed.'

'In this? You've got to be joking.'

'It's certainly blown up a bit. Getting worse, too.'

'Can't we get out of it?' asked Moehle.

Schiller laughed. 'The opposite, I'm afraid. The good captain wants the bad weather. The rougher it gets, the better he'll like it.'

Although an officer, Moehle was considered too young, and too technical, to talk to about navigational matters. He was in the dark as far as Bach's plans were concerned. 'For God's sake, why?' Moehle asked.

'Because of those planes. Bach reckons they'll be out looking for us, and wants to hide in the storm. This muck will ground anything. He's quite right, of course.'

Moehle thought about this. It would certainly hide them, but the problem was time. How much would this slow them? He'd already seen the chalked instructions for the course for the helmsman to steer – it was almost due south. Not only was the storm making the going difficult, but the course was far from direct to boot. 'Won't this slow us down?' he asked eventually, watching the rise and fall of the bow in the darkness ahead of them and bracing himself for the movement.

'At least a day. Maybe more. Still, the captain doesn't seem too worried about the timing. He's more concerned about being caught.'

'How is he? He seemed a bit strained the other night.'

'Bach? He's going crazy, if you ask me. Went to his cabin earlier, won't eat and is throwing stuff around.'

'That sounds terrible.'

'Probably not. But it's hard to tell. Between you and me, Moehle, I don't think Bach's heart is in this at all. That's his real problem. He thinks this is a crazy stunt, trying to shell the fucking White House. He's not wrong, if you ask me.'

'Is he going to call it off?'

Schiller laughed. 'Call it off? You must to be joking. Orders are orders. You heard the old man the other night. Surrender is the last thing he's going to do. Trouble is, Moehle, he's fighting a battle in his own head at the same time. I know he's stiff as a poker, but I think he really does care about this lot on board. He knows he's sending them all to their death – us included. He's tearing himself up about it. Bach's not going to surrender, but he might go round the bend first. It's hard to tell with him.'

'Why does he think we're all going to be killed?'

'Come on, Moehle. We're not going to get away with it, are we?'

'Of course not. You know it, so do I. But what's the worst that can happen? We fire a few shells, then they take us prisoner. I can think of a worse place to end up in at the end of the war.'

'Moehle, you're a trusting soul, aren't you? You really think that we shall be allowed to even fire a shot? Once the Americans get wind of us, we'll be blown to hell and back. Particularly with Bach in charge. Sorry, Moehle. Bach's right. We're dead men. Good God, you really thought we'd get away with it, didn't you?'

Moehle couldn't answer. He knew they would get away with it, knew that the moment they were within

reach the Americans would be told the real purpose
of the mission. But would Bach survive long enough to
get them there? Or would he do something stupid
before Moehle's carefully laid plan could take effect?
Bach was supposed to be the toughest officer in the
Navy, which was why Sluys and the other conspirators
back in Berlin had chosen him. Reliable. Unflappable.
And now here he was throwing tantrums in private.

'Then there's that Heine business, of course. I think
that's what got to him,' said Schiller after another big
sea shuddered the whole ship.

'Who's Heine?'

'One of the kids. Beat up that dreadful Schnee.
Deserved it, I should think. I hauled him up in front of
the old man and he had a real go at him – Heine, I
mean, had a go at Bach. He's a bright kid. God knows
what he's doing on this thing. Told Bach he was going
to kill us all and the crew wouldn't stand for it.
Threatened mutiny.'

'You believe him?'

'Good God no. That rabble couldn't organise a thing.
But Bach got quite rattled. Struck a nerve.'

'And this Heine. He's no threat?'

Schiller laughed again. Moehle was sounding like a
worried little rabbit to him. 'I don't think so, Moehle.
He's down there, right now. In the brig, up in the bow.
Must be getting quite uncomfortable.'

'Oh,' said Moehle. He watched another plume of
spray shimmer upwards in the darkness. 'I'll try and
get some sleep, I think. Thanks, Schiller.'

'Moehle, you worry too much. You're in the
Kriegsmarine. Follow orders and keep quiet – isn't
that what they say?'

Moehle smiled but didn't reply. He left the bridge
and, clinging to the handrails against the rise and fall

of the ship, made his way down towards the officers' quarters in the middle of the vessel, where the movement was less violent.

Walking unsteadily down the companionway, he passed Bach's cabin. The light was still on inside, showing a dim yellow line from beneath the thick wooden door across the bare steel deck. Moehle paused. Behind the door was the man who was supposed to make this whole thing happen, and who now was jeopardising the mission – if what Schiller was saying was true.

Sluys had been clear. Bach was too straight, too honourable to feel anything other than deceived and used once he found out the real reason for the journey. It was vital, according to Sluys, to leave it until the last possible moment. Then Bach would have no option – he'd have to surrender quietly once he realised he had been totally betrayed. But telling him before that was forbidden. The man would be so offended that he'd ... well, Sluys didn't know what he would do. But Moehle was now worried that Bach wouldn't even get that far. Schiller's story frightened the life out of him. What would happen if he suddenly gave up, right now? And was this Heine and the crew really a threat?

There was music coming from inside Bach's cabin and Moehle moved closer to the door. He knew the music well; Beethoven's Third, the *Eroica*. He had seen Furtwängler conduct it in Vienna last Christmas.

Moehle could sympathise with Bach, but he could not see him fail. Sluys had trusted Moehle, and Moehle felt his own sense of compelling duty. The Nazis had ruined Germany. It was up to him to start the long and painful process of climbing back up out of the ruin. One way or another, Bach's mission had to succeed.

Listening to the music, Moehle now knew what he must do. Bach was being tossed around on the seas of fate, with no idea where he was going any more. He, Moehle, would have to give him a renewed sense of direction, a fresh cause, a new mission. It was, surely, the only way. Moehle would speak to Bach; he would sit him down and quietly explain the real purpose of the mission. The shells down in the magazine. The new life in America. A chance for Germany to rebuild herself. Bach was an intelligent man. Sluys might have been right – not to reveal the real purpose of the mission until it was too late for Bach to be able to do anything about the situation. But now the situation had changed. Sluys would have agreed, Moehle told himself, that something had to be done. Otherwise the whole voyage would be in danger.

Bach would listen, protest perhaps, but then would come to understand what had to be done. He would recognise at last where his true duty lay. He and Moehle would then complete the final stage of the voyage according to Sluys's plan. They would sail in safety across the Atlantic until they reached Chesapeake Bay, and there they would gently surrender their ship, perhaps to cheers from the crew and even applause from the Americans at their cunning and bravery, handing over the treasure and helping to establish a new world of peace and harmony.

Moehle could almost hear the cheering. Should he knock on Bach's door now and start the conversation? He raised his hand, but something made him pause. Bach was clearly awake, but was three in the morning really the best time to start this off? He walked quickly away from the door, down the long, dim companion-way towards the small cabin that was his own private sanctuary.

Moehle could still hear the music in the distance. Then the ship plunged at the bow and started to roll suddenly. A rogue wave had caught them from a different angle and upset the helmsman's careful juggling of the wheel. Moehle was thrown against the raw steel bulkhead that formed the sides of the long companionway. He heard Bach's gramophone jump and the music in the distance became a ripping noise, and then suddenly stopped. The ship quickly heeled back again, and he carried on back to his cabin. But the distant music stayed silent. Moehle listened for a moment, heard no more, and closed his cabin door behind him.

*

Brocklehurst was closing on *Hindenburg* from the south, although neither he nor Bach knew it. At three that morning, the distance between the two ships was down to 180 nautical miles. *Trent*'s nearly northerly course would intersect *Hindenburg*'s south-westerly track about two hours after the German ship had passed. The distance would be less than twenty miles, but in this weather both ships could easily pass within two miles of each other and remain hidden. Apart from the mountainous seas that effectively limited the horizon, the low cloud and the lashing rain brought the visibility down to little more than a mile or two.

Both vessels were struggling to make way. *Hindenburg*'s effective speed over the ground was down to seven knots; *Trent*, with a sea coming at her from the port stern quarter, was less buffeted by the waves, but still she had to run carefully with the rolling seas to avoid broaching – turning beam-on to the following sea and capsizing – and so Brocklehurst had ordered fourteen knots, fast enough to keep the ship safe. Even so, the helmsman had his work cut out to keep the stern in just the right place as the seas rolled in underneath them and tried to corkscrew them around. On the courses and the speeds they were holding, the *Trent* would intersect in around twelve or thirteen hours' time, during the afternoon of 30 April, eleven days after the *Hindenburg* had set sail from Hamburg.

By seven that morning, the invisible sun had risen and the grey gloom was steadily lightening as Brocklehurst came up to the bridge.

'How's it looking, number one?' he asked, yawning as he buttoned up his thick woollen duffel coat.

'Good morning, sir. Glass is still dropping. Met boys' latest signal says no let-up for at least twenty-four hours. We're holding course and keeping fourteen knots. Half the crew are sick as dogs. Other than that, sir, it's a bloody wonderful morning.'

'Thank you, Bill. No sign of anything, I take it?'

'Not much, sir. Saw a seagull an hour ago but it was only stopping to have a shit on the foredeck.'

The helmsman, who was feeling distinctly green himself, couldn't help but snigger. Brocklehurst snorted as well.

Brocklehurst's problem was that Herdman's original signal gave absolutely no idea where this so-called German battleship was likely to be. He had sent another follow-up asking for more details, but had received no further information. It could be an hour away or half an ocean away. '*Assumed your general vicinity*' was all he got. Typical Admiralty, thought Brocklehurst. They made it sound as if he was out for a day's rowing on the Serpentine. In this weather, it would be hard enough to find America, let alone another ship.

'Bill, this new Yankee radar. What's the score with the thing?' asked Brocklehurst in a lower voice so that they could not be overheard.

'It's good, Badger. Centimetric stuff. Short wave-length, long range, bloody good definition.'

'Is it working?'

'It can be. I'll have to be nice to McConnell.' McConnell was the American civilian supplied courtesy of the US Navy, the only man on board who was conversant with the new Hughes set, supposedly a gift to the Royal Navy but in reality just a free sample to get their lordships' tongues hanging out. Although the British had more or less invented radar, and even named it – '*R*Adio *D*irection finding *A*nd *R*anging' – the huge American industrial establishment had the time, the money and the unbombed factories to develop it far faster than the bureaucrat-riddled British could manage. As the war came to an end, it was American systems that were making the running. This was the latest from Hughes, vastly increasing the effective range of ship-borne radar from the usual ten or eleven miles to thirty and forty miles; and also providing a high-definition picture free from wave clutter, which in conditions like these would render most radars of the time useless. That, at any rate, was what the manu-facturers claimed. Perhaps now was the time to put the set to the test.

'Have a word with him, Bill. If that thing's as good as they say, I should think it could prove useful.'

Burrows left the bridge to find the eminent Mr McConnell, a large, plump man with a shiny face and round glasses that made him look like an owl, who right now was very probably still in his cabin fast asleep, immune from the Navy discipline that regulated the lives of everyone else on the ship.

*

The collapse of the Reich had one last act to play. As

the Allies took Milan, the dictator Benito Mussolini, captured earlier by left-wing partisans, was hastily executed. His bloated body was left to hang upside-down like a side of meat in the Piazza Loretto, with his mistress Clara Petacci strung up next to him. The news reached the bunker quickly. Already most of the senior staff had fled. Sluys and his team had left two days earlier, just as the news of Mussolini's death reached them. Hitler, pale and ill, had reacted curiously: he married his long-time partner Eva Braun the following day in a ceremony that reminded the few who were there to witness it of a final settlement, a kind of payback for the years of unquestioning devotion.

Now the atmosphere in the bunker had become even more detached from reality. The Russian T-52s were just streets away, controlling more than a third of the city. Russian aircraft roamed the skies above, machine-gunning anything that moved. Bodies, swelling and stiff, lay where they fell. But still Hitler would not surrender. That morning, as the huge *Hindenburg* steadily pushed through the stormy Atlantic, the time in Berlin was just after midday. Hitler had retired to his private quarters with Eva Braun. An hour passed, then a muffled shot rang out. Aides ran to the room; the dictator's wife lay on the floor, motionless, her lips pale blue from the cyanide she had swallowed. On the sofa lay the collapsed body of Hitler, still dribbling blood from the torn mouth, his pistol on the floor. Hitler was dead. In less than seven days, the last German forces would finally surrender. The code word ordering the final capitulation had already been agreed: *Regenbogen*, 'rainbow', broadcast on Navy frequencies, would be the signal to either surrender or scuttle.

The last days were near.

10

Moehle had barely slept. Although the motion of the ship didn't upset him as much as it seemed to affect a lot of the others, it was a nagging anxiety that had woken him after three hours of restless sleep. Shortly after dawn he was up and dressed, pacing his small cabin. The clarity of his thinking a few hours earlier had suddenly vanished. He had thought he would take Bach to one side and talk to him, man to man. Now, in the light of day, he felt once again a desperate need to seek Sluys's view, back in Berlin. His confidence had evaporated. But to do that, he needed to get to the radio again. And Bach had imposed radio silence and had taken his key. Moehle was too junior an officer to hold keys to the sensitive parts of his ship, like the armoury. He was trying to think of a way of getting Bach to give it up. There was no point in trying the others; they would ask too many questions.

He looked at his watch. It was time to do *something*; he made his way up to the bridge. Bach was there, standing silently at the back, swaying gently to keep upright as the ship moved beneath him. He looked as though he hadn't slept at all.

Bach had arrived on the bridge an hour earlier and

relieved Schiller, dismissing him with just a cursory nod of the head. Whatever private torture he had endured alone in his cabin during the night was forgotten now; the weather had come up as he had forecast, worse if anything, and he was enjoying the primal fear of seeing the great seas rolling down towards the ship. Like Schiller, he shared the generally held views about the fleet's seaworthiness, but this ship was in a different class altogether. Like Bach, it enjoyed the storm, relishing each approaching mountain of water and plunging into it like a dog in the sea. Let the weather do its worst – it would delay him but a day, and he would arrive in three or four days' time at the outside.

'Captain?' Moehle had invented what sounded to him, at any rate, like a sufficiently good excuse.

Bach seemed not to hear. He stood, still swaying, staring ahead at the bow of the ship as plumes of white spray were flung into the air.

Moehle repeated his question and Bach suddenly stirred as though waking from a dream. He looked at Moehle, his eyes tinged red, but still did not speak.

'Captain, I need to get into the radio room. There are some tests I want to run on the radar. I think you have the keys?' He tried to sound as casual as he could, but his heart was thumping.

Bach looked away, out of the bridge windows at the heaving sea. 'Radio silence, Moehle.'

'Yes, sir. But I presume you want the radar working? This sort of weather plays havoc with the electrics. I can leave it like that if you'd prefer.'

'Why the radio room? Your machine is up here.'

'Only the display unit, Captain. The main electrical chassis is in the radio room.' Bach was no technician and Moehle knew it. There was nothing in the radio room that affected the radar, but the captain would have no idea.

Bach didn't seem to care a great deal. He gave a slight nod. Without taking his eyes off the sea outside, he unbuttoned the top breast pocket of his tunic and produced a small key. 'Bring it right back, Moehle, understand?'

'Of course, Captain. Ten minutes. No more.'

Moehle took a deep breath and pocketed the key. He made his way down to the radio room. Once inside, he carefully locked the door. He was sweating; he took a few moments to calm himself and then turned on the main power switch.

The vacuum tubes took two minutes to warm up and stabilise. While he waited for them he pulled out the codebooks and the coding machine, and hastily scribbled his message to Sluys before coding it with the day's settings, advanced one day. He worked quickly and kept his message short, jotting down the encoded series of letters and numbers, and then turned the big tuning dial to the Navy frequency that Sluys had allocated to him. He hoped the radio had stabilised. He pulled out the Morse key and tapped out the code.

Urgent for Sluys. The captain is not well.
May abandon. Should I talk? Difficult situation.
Reply one hour exactly. Moehle.

There wasn't time to try and figure out a word code; it would have to do. If anyone back in the bunker read it, it wouldn't mean much. He added a time and date, turned off the radio, tore his coding notes into shreds and stuffed them into his pocket, unlocked the door and returned to the bridge. Bach was still standing there.

'Finished?' asked the captain.

'Not sure, sir. The stuff is very delicate. I'll need to go back and check stability in about an hour. I've set up the cavity magnetron to see if it stays stable. Here's the key.' It was pure technical nonsense, but Moehle knew that Bach would have only the haziest understanding of the complexities of modern electrical engineering.

'Very well, Moehle. Hang on to it. Bring it back when you've finished.'

'Yes sir,' and Moehle heaved a silent sigh of relief.

*

Lil Beasley knew something would happen. Her bones told her. Ever since she had seen Herdman she had been on to Bletchley every morning, pestering them.

'Anything, anything at all, Naval code, advanced one day. Watch for it.' She knew something was out there on the high seas, trying to conceal itself. She knew that at some point it would try to contact Berlin, or wherever what was left of the German Naval High Command was hiding that day. German, British or American – high commands constantly wanted to interfere with what their captains were doing, and the bloody captains now couldn't change course without wanting to chatter back to their officers sitting in their comfortable chairs on dry land. For Lil, it was a godsend. The endless toing and froing of operational details over the airwaves could give a precise picture of what was going on.

That was why she knew this particular ship, whatever it was, was up to no good. It sent very few messages – which, for a German surface ship, was verging on the extraordinary. To want to stay so secret meant that something very big was in the air. But she also knew that it would be impossible for them to remain silent for ever. As time passed she became more and more importunate with the Bletchley people, calling every few hours. Lil was convinced that the German ship would have to break cover soon.

And then, that same afternoon, the airwaves started going mad.

The news of Hitler's death was spreading like wildfire, and everyone was yelling for information, for confirmation or denial. Only Lil Beasley ignored the sudden excitement. It was two hours since she had last called Bletchley. She dialled the number again and got through, as usual, to Frank Usher.

'Frank, anything?'

'Lil, you know what's just happened, don't you? We can't move for stuff coming in.'

'Frank, my love, don't be an ass. Not a word of it is in code, now, is it?'

'Maybe not.'

'So. Anything at all, however teensy? In code, of course, not all these rumours. Something interesting, Frank. Hand it over.'

'You're a bloody clairvoyant, Lil. Came in from decode ten minutes back.'

'Bingo! Knew it would, Frank. And?'

Frank Usher read out Moehle's brief message. '*Reply in one hour exactly*' it said. Lil looked at her watch. The message, according to the time the sender had added, was now forty-three minutes old.

'That's it? Did you get a fix? Any clues, Frank?'

'Sorry, Lil. Picked it up at Rugby, short wave. Could have been almost anywhere.'

'Can we pick up the reply? They're supposed to come back to our friend in seventeen minutes' time.'

'But who, Lil? Who's replying?'

'Berlin, of course, ninny.'

'Doubt it, old girl. Shouldn't think there's anyone left, not if the stories are true.'

And another light went on in Lil Beasley's head. Here was this Moehle, whoever he was, clearly getting in a panic. He yells to Berlin, Sluys in person. Call me back. But what if there's no one to call back? More panic. Moehle gets anxious. Calls again.

'Now tell me, Frank, if we knew something was coming, could we get a fix? DF and all that?' Radio signals were directional. One receiver would be able to plot a direction that the signal came from, but wouldn't know where along that line the transmission originated. But another receiver, preferably situated on the other side of the source signal, would be able to plot a second direction line. Draw both lines, and where they intersected would provide an approximate position of the transmitter. A third plot, intersecting with the other two, would confirm it.

'In theory, Lil. You're going to bloody well ask me to do it, aren't you? Look, I'll try, but in a quarter of an hour you've got as much chance of becoming First Sea Lord. If it works, I'll call.'

'Frank, it's important, you know that. Otherwise I wouldn't ask. I'll be waiting.'

Lil gently hung up the big black handset. I'll get you, Moehle, wherever you are, she told herself. She took out a cardigan she had been knitting and started working the needles furiously; she hadn't touched it for a month.

*

The hour was nearly up. Moehle had already shut himself inside the radio room, and the set was warm. It gave off a steady hum and there was the sharp smell of ozone and warm rubber. The big dial was already tuned to the Naval frequency. Moehle had his pencil and a sheet of yellow paper, ready to note down the code to be translated by the machine. He looked at his watch: one minute to go.

The minute came and he looked at the Morse key expectantly. 'One hour exactly' meant just that in the German Navy. The minute passed and there was no sound. Two minutes. Three, then four. At five minutes past the time, Moehle knew there was a problem.

Should he re-send the message? What had happened? Was Sluys still alive? Perhaps just a technical problem? He looked at the radio set and checked the frequency. It *looked* fine.

Just as he was thinking of re-coding to send it all over again, the Morse key blipped. At last! He grabbed the pencil and waited. A second later the key started blipping again, quickly now, chattering out a message. Moehle began noting down the code. It didn't take more than a moment for him to realise the message was being sent *en clair*, in uncoded German. Moehle had never seen this in his life; even the weather reports were coded. He wrote down each letter as the Morse key chattered.

All ships. Repeat of message. Please relay. The German Naval High Command confirms that the father of the German People passed away at 15.30 Berlin time. Grand Admiral Donitz has been named to succeed. Long live the Reich! This message will be repeated every half-hour on this frequency. Stand by for further orders.

The key fell suddenly silent. Moehle read and re-read the message. His heart thumped in his chest.

The news destroyed his plans. He was totally lost.

Where the hell was Sluys? Had he packed his bags and gone already? That was the plan – Sluys and the others would surely have left the bunker by now and were probably already out of Berlin. His mood changed quickly to anger. How dare they leave him here without an order, without an idea of what to bloody well do? In frustration he grabbed the Morse key and rattled off a message, also *en clair*:

> *Urgent for Sluys. Highest priority. I await your*
> *instructions. Contact me urgently. Situation now*
> *becoming desperate. Cannot maintain radio*
> *watch. Will stand by every hour, on hour. Moehle.*

Moehle stared at the key. He knew it was a hopeless message, but it made him feel better. Then he stood up, switched off the set and left the room. He was starting to sweat again, and he left a damp handprint on the brass handle of the door as he closed it behind him.

*

The big listening station at Rugby, briefed by Usher, had managed to switch in a directional aerial for short wave just in time to pick up the message; but Usher had said it was in code, which this one clearly wasn't. The operator shrugged, plotted the angle anyway, and phoned Bletchley as ordered. In Newfoundland, a similar arrangement had been set up at one of the remote listening stations that Bletchley maintained. Moehle's angry message was received and the angle duly plotted.

Ten minutes after Moehle had gone out of the room, Usher got through to Lil Beasley, who was waiting for the call.

'I reckon you're a German bloody spy, Lil. How do you know these things?' asked Usher.

'Did you get the bearings?' responded Lil with an uncharacteristic urgency.

'Steady the buffs! Here they are. Rugby is two-sixty-five degrees. Newfoundland is one-forty-five degrees. Give or take five degrees each side, so they tell me. Don't you want the message?'

'I didn't think you'd have decoded it yet.'

'No need, Lil. Clear text. Your man's in a panic by the sound of things.' He read Moehle's desperate call for help to her.

But now Lil Beasley was less interested in what the message said than in where it originated. She'd already got a North Atlantic chart ready. She laid off the Rugby bearing, drawing the line from a compass rose using a parallel ruler. Then she laid off the Newfoundland line. Both lines crossed in a position way to the south of where she would have expected, even allowing for the wide margin of error. She drew a circle around the position. She had no idea which way the German was heading, of course, but one or two more transmissions would give her a good idea, allowing her to plot the new position of the mystery vessel and thus its direction of travel.

She called Herdman.

'Peter, your German ship. Tell your people to look around fifty-two degrees north, twenty-eight degrees west. I might be able to give you a course in a few hours.'

Herdman trusted Lil Beasley totally. He signalled Brocklehurst on *Trent* with the position and told him to make best speed. And as an afterthought, he told him to be careful, without explaining exactly why. Brocklehurst, in turn, went to his plotting table and marked the position that Herdman signalled.

'It's supposed to be here, Bill,' he told Burrows as both men hunched over the chart. He had circled the position allowing for the margin of error. At its nearest, the circle was just thirty miles away, less than three hours' steaming even in this weather. At its furthest, the circle was over 100 miles distant.

'It's a bit close, Badger. And where's it supposed to be going?'

'God knows. They say they'll give us a course in an hour or two. Heading south, according to the signal. Just a guess at the moment, though.'

Until Brocklehurst had a better idea of the course, his current heading would remain sufficient. What surprised him was the closeness of the other ship.

'How's McConnell and his box of tricks?'

'I'll get him on to it.' Burrows left the bridge to find the plump American to run the new radar system, leaving Brocklehurst to puzzle over Herdman's cryptic instruction to be careful: was he ever anything but careful?

Burrows found McConnell in the officers' mess, drinking tea and reading an illustrated American magazine that was unfamiliar to Burrows. McConnell looked up as he walked hastily into the narrow mess.

'Good afternoon, mister Burrows. You look worried. Can I help?' McConnell looked at Burrows over the tops of the big horn-rimmed glasses. The sea seemed to have no effect on the man at all. He looked bright and eager.

'Good afternoon, mister McConnell. Compliments of the captain, sir, and he wonders if it would be possible to try out your new radar machine.'

'But of course, mister Burrows. I would be delighted. When would he like to see it?'

'Now. Right now, that is. If that's all right.'

'Oh. Oh, I see. Right now. Well, if that's what Captain Brocklehurst would like, let's see what we can do, eh, mister Burrows?'

'The captain would be most grateful, mister McConnell.'

McConnell rose from his seat, folded his magazine neatly under his arm and followed Burrows back to the bridge. On *Trent*, the radio room was right behind the main bridge, and it was here that the new radar set had been installed. McConnell, looking important and proud, started up his radar. Like the other systems, it was valve-based and took several minutes to reach normal working temperature. Once the tubes had warmed and a picture started to appear on the screen, McConnell had to adjust the tune and gain controls to get the clearest display. The display itself was the biggest that Brocklehurst and Burrows had seen – a full twelve inches across. The picture flickered as McConnell played with the controls. The motion of the ship was not helping; it shook the valves and caused the picture to fade every time a big sea passed underneath them.

'Mister Burrows, I think we are ready now, if you and the captain would care to come over?'

Burrows and Brocklehurst made their way to the display unit with some difficulty. Just trying to move several yards on the rolling ship involved a steep uphill climb and then, as the sea passed, a sudden change of incline to a steep downhill stagger. McConnell was holding on to the display unit, completely unfazed by the motion. Brocklehurst wedged himself against a bulkhead where he had a view of the glowing tube.

The screen was covered in what looked like green measles; radiating from the centre was a green line that silently swept around the circular tube. The green spots glowed brightly as it passed and then quickly faded.

'It's got spots, mister McConnell,' said Brocklehurst.

'Clutter, Captain. Sea clutter, we call it. The radar is being reflected by the wave tops. Normal, really. And actually, Captain, by now other radars would be useless. Anyway,' McConnell said after a moment's pause, 'we're on four-mile range. It's always worse. Look, I'll switch to twenty-four miles. See what happens.'

McConnell turned a large black knob with a white arrow etched on to its upper surface. It clicked as he turned it. The spots diminished and finally disappeared, apart from one right on the edge of the screen. It was a fuzzy blob, and it seemed to move and fade each time the glowing line swept past it.

'There,' said McConnell proudly. 'All gone. Clear as you like. You're seeing twenty-four miles distant even in this weather. Impressive, I think.'

Brocklehurst ignored the plump American's enthusiasm. 'What's that?' he asked.

McConnell looked where Brocklehurst was pointing. 'That's not clutter, Captain. Definitely not. Not on this set.'

'The captain knows it's not clutter, mister McConnell. So what is it?' asked Burrows.

McConnell looked again at the fuzzy blob. He lowered his glasses so that he could see it more clearly. 'Well, it's an echo of some kind,' he said finally, with a note of surprise in his voice. He spoke as though the blip was spoiling his screen.

'What kind? Size? Range? Bearing?' demanded Brocklehurst.

'Well, goodness me, Captain. Just a moment, just a moment.' McConnell picked up a small ruler and laid it on the screen, scribbled some numbers, looked at the screen again, looked over towards the helmsman where the course was chalked on a board, scribbled numbers once more.

'Range is twenty-three miles or thereabouts. Bearing is twenty-nine degrees from us. Can't give you a course yet.'

'Size?'

'Can't tell, Captain. It's right at the edge of the screen and it's getting distorted. Looks bigger than it probably is.'

'Try.'

'Anything between 500 and 1,000 feet long. Quite high, too, to give that return at that range.'

'Big, then?'

'Oh, yes, Captain. Quite big, in any event.'

'So where's it going? Can you tell?'

McConnell looked at the screen once more. 'Crossing us, right to left, I would say. Maybe angled a bit towards us.'

Brocklehurst looked at Burrows. 'What do you think, Bill?'

Burrows shrugged. 'Could be the bugger, Captain. Looks big enough. Position agrees with London's ideas, or just about. Right on the edge, but then London was never very accurate with these things.'

Brocklehurst had one more question for McConnell. 'Speed?'

McConnell stared at the screen. 'Not fast. Look, it's changing position slowly. Most of that is our speed. Five knots minimum, no more than ten, certainly.'

'Big and slow. Very well, number one,' said Brocklehurst in his formal, businesslike voice that boomed across the bridge, 'set a course to intercept. We'll go and take a look at this chap and see just what

he's up to. Ring action stations,' and he turned to
McConnell with a softer voice as Burrows started
barking out the orders. 'Mister McConnell, you just
keep an eagle eye on that thing and let me know what
it's up to. Can you do that?'

'No problem,' replied McConnell, but Brocklehurst
was amused to see the look of fear that flashed across
the man's round face when '*Action Stations*' was called.

The crew, most of them badly seasick, protested
when the alarms sounded. The chief petty officers
and petty officers were furious that their crews moved
so slowly; they yelled at them, physically hauling some
of them from their bunks. Like a leviathan, *Trent*
slowly started to come alive as reluctant crews
manned unfamiliar gun positions and pulled on
anti-flash gear, though most of them had to be told
where to find it.

'Bloody shambles, Bill,' fumed Brocklehurst, as he
waited for the ready reports to come in. After five
minutes, when by wartime standards the whole ship
should have been ready for battle, not a single gun
position had reported in ready.

'Come on, Badger. You've got a raw crew. Half of
them don't know the sodding ship, and the other half
are seasick,' protested Burrows quietly.

'Damn it, Bill, I don't bloody well care. This could be
real. Get those buggers off their arses and get them
ready.'

'Aye aye, Badger.'

'Do it, Bill. This could be serious,' Brocklehurst insisted.

A pale-looking seaman was hovering near
Brocklehurst with a yellow signal form in his hand.
'Urgent from Sparks, sir. Said you'd want it right now,'
said the young man, looking like death. 'Sparks' was
shipboard slang for the radio officer.

It must be a signal from Herdman. Brocklehurst took the slip of paper and unfolded it.

'Good God,' he said after a moment. He passed the signal to Burrows, who read it with a smile spreading across his face.

'Get Sparks here now,' ordered Brocklehurst to the sailor, who had no idea what the message contained and was wondering what all the excitement was about. He turned to go but Kelly, the radio officer, was already rushing on to the bridge.

'I knew you'd want me. I confirmed it. It's bloody true. Straight from the Admiralty.' Kelly was excited, grinning. The signal he had just picked up – and then, disbelieving the news, requested clarification on – reported the death of Adolf Hitler.

'Well, there's a turn-up for the bloody books,' said Burrows in a loud voice. 'I mean, that's it, isn't it? It's all bloody well over and we've bloody well beaten the bastards. Sir,' he beamed.

'Sparks, any mention of surrender? What's the position exactly?'

'Didn't say, sir,' replied Kelly.

'Get back to them. Ask them if we're still at war or what the hell we're doing. Tell them we've probably found their ship and we're proceeding to investigate. I bloody well want to know if they're likely to shoot at us.'

'Yes, sir, right away,' said Kelly, and he disappeared into the radio room.

'Badger, should I stand the crew down?'

'Not for now, Bill. Let's find out what this means. Besides, it won't hurt them to have the drill. Keep them on watch. But spread the word that old Adolf has gone. We'll find this ship of Herdman's, and then with a bit of luck we're straight off home to Blighty. Let them all know,' finished Brocklehurst.

'Aye aye, sir,' responded Burrows, and went to spread the word around the rest of the ship.

For Burrows, for Brocklehurst, and for the rest of them as they heard the news, it was like suddenly hearing that you'd won a reprieve from a death sentence; that you were supposed to be incurably ill and suddenly you were better; that it was the first warm sunny day of spring after a cold and interminable winter. Every man on board *Trent* thought they had come to terms with war over the past five years; the thought of being killed at any moment, or of finding your family or your friends dead without warning. In truth, no one had come to terms with it at all. It was a constant, grinding fear, a slow trickle of anxiety that ate away at your stomach and your nerves and was never absent, even when you were asleep. And what was worse was that your life was suddenly someone else's to play with. No matter what you had been doing in civvy street before the war, no matter how high or low you had been, suddenly you handed over all responsibility for every decision to the Army, the Air Force or the Navy. You were told when to wake, when to sleep, when to eat, when to shit.

And you were told when to die . . .

Strangely, there were some people who thrived on it. The years between the wars had been hard times for many. If you had spent the last decade without a job, living in cold back-to-back houses in polluted industrial cities, the war suddenly created opportunities along with the risks. Many went on to become institutionalised and would later have major problems taking up the reins of their civilian lives when they came to be demobbed.

But the fear never went. On land, you were scared

you'd be bombed. At sea, you worried about facing action. The worst fear, the deepest dread, was reserved for those ships operating in U-boat-infested waters, which was just about everywhere. You couldn't see them, hear them or even feel the bastards. They were lurking, like great hungry sharks, just beneath your feet. You felt you were always being watched. While you were asleep you could feel them creeping up on you in the dark – all the monsters of your childhood gathered out there in the dark wastes of the ocean.

They had lived on this edge for five years. Many of them had already seen action. Brocklehurst himself had already had one ship shot away from beneath him. And now, suddenly, there it was. Three simple words that changed everything in an instant: *Hitler is dead.* Not many of the men felt the elation of victory. They were just too exhausted. Most merely felt a huge upwelling of relief. *Hitler is dead.* They were alive. The thing was over with. Never again would that worm eat at the guts. Once the disbelief disappeared and the reality came home to them, there was more than one man on *Trent* who disappeared silently into the heads and quietly wept like a child.

Hitler is dead. Over with. Finished. The end. Thank God above.

As Kelly hastily cabled London, the whole ship noticeably relaxed. Even Brocklehurst, waiting on the bridge, looked about five years younger. As if to make the point, the black murk outside the bridge windows was momentarily lit up by a shaft of sunlight breaking through the cloud.

McConnell hardly noticed. He was concentrating on the screen, as ordered. And being an American civilian, the war was something that happened somewhere else, on newsreels. McConnell had not – like the rest of those on board ship – lived with the fear and the terror for five long years.

He watched the blip slowly growing. Brocklehurst had changed course and the radar reflection had now moved to the right-hand side of the top of the screen; *Trent*'s new course put *Hindenburg* on its starboard quarter so that, allowing for the movement of the ships, they would intersect in under an hour. In fact, Brocklehurst had overestimated the other's ship's speed. He had assumed something that big would be moving at least at ten knots, and had adjusted his course to intersect where he thought the German would be. In fact, he was going to sail right past the other vessel's bow.

McConnell recalculated and told Brocklehurst, who ordered a new course. Slowly the other ship's radar image, growing stronger each minute, moved back to slightly off centre. It was now just twelve miles away. In normal weather it would be clearly visible on the horizon; but in this storm, nothing could be seen except the relentless march of the receding waves leaving trails of white foam behind them.

Kelly was having some difficulty in getting through. The radio room at the Admiralty in London was jammed with traffic. Every ship and submarine in the Royal Navy was demanding clarification. 'What the hell is going on?' was being shouted from the top to the bottom of the Navy hierarchy.

'Captain Brocklehurst, sir, I think your ship is now five miles away,' came McConnell's voice from the back of the bridge.

'Bearing?' asked Brocklehurst, lifting his glasses to his eyes.

'Two-eighty', called McConnell after a pause.

Brocklehurst glanced down at the compass and

shifted his glasses to the right, to where the ship should be. The visibility was a little better, but the huge seas hid the horizon. There was only one way to find out what McConnell's box of tricks was picking up. Someone would have to climb to the foretop to get a better view.

'Bill!' called Brocklehurst.

'Sir?' replied Burrows, who had been looking over the charts to see how long it would take them to get home.

'Bill, sorry, but I need someone I can trust up the foretop. I can't see a thing with these bloody seas.'

'Thank you, Badger.' He had served with Brocklehurst for two years and knew exactly what the captain meant. 'Give me the bloody glasses. You'll be buying me gins for the next ten years for this,' said Burrows softly. But he started out for the foretop without a second thought. He pulled on oilskins and a sou'wester and closed the bridge door behind him.

The wind had dropped and the rain blew over in fitful gusts. The motion of the ship was as bad as ever. He had to hold on to every grab rail he could find, and his progress consisted of lurches either uphill or downhill, whichever attitude the ship would take.

He had to work his way towards the squat funnel where the base of the tall mast was bolted into the superstructure. At the base was a narrow steel door, which he pulled open with difficulty. The mast was tubular, and just wide enough to hold a man; inside, welded to the tube, steel rungs disappeared upwards into the darkness. He found the light switch and swung the door closed behind him; there was a sudden silence as the wind and rain were shut outside. He took off the dripping sou'wester and oilskin and dumped them in a pile on the decking. Then he started the long climb to the foretop, forty feet above the bridge. The ship was rocking, but the confined space meant that he was firmly braced against the sides of the mast structure, whichever way the ship moved.

Rung by rung, Burrows made his way up the mast. At the top it opened out into a small viewing station – still sheltered within the mast tube, but with four apertures giving fore-and-aft, and side-to-side, visibility. There was the smell of old urine on the platform, and graffiti – mostly explicit if improbable diagrams of genitalia – was scratched or pencilled on the painted steel inner surface. Officers were not expected to go up here. There were a few ribald comments about Badger. Burrows was oddly pleased to see that he was mentioned too.

He managed to wedge himself into the platform so that both hands were free. He was facing forward. The view from up here, of the ship twisting and cork-screwing in the rolling sea, was not one he had ever seen in weather like this. Now he understood Brocklehurst's reluctance to send anyone else. You would be instantly seasick – the motion of the ship was greatly amplified by the height. And it would take someone of considerable experience to be able to figure out anything in these conditions.

Burrows comforted himself with such thoughts and raised the glasses to his eyes, looking more or less ahead where the ship was meant to be. Almost immediately he saw it. It was low on the horizon, but his view was clear and the shape of the vessel was obvious.

'Jesus,' whispered Burrows to himself. Ship recognition was an area of knowledge where Burrows, like every other officer, had to be more than competent. Too often friendly ships had opened fire on one another, unable to tell if each were friend or foe. Electronic systems had just started to make their appearance, but Burrows was brought up in the old school, which meant that every few months he had to attend yet another course where they looked at silhouettes of ships. Was the mast before or after the funnel? Was there a high foredeck or a low one? How many funnels? Enemy ships had been known to build artificial funnels in an attempt to disguise their identities.

Right now, Burrows knew he was looking at a big battleship. There was no mistaking the long hull, the turrets – although the aft ones appeared to be missing – and the high central superstructure. One funnel: bang in the middle. The problem was that Burrows was familiar, very familiar, with that outline. Too familiar. Three years previously, he had served on *Devonshire*, one of the cruisers that chased and finally sank *Bismarck*. This was the same bloody ship; well, nearly – he couldn't make out the after turrets at all. But in every other respect, it was the same damn ship. Except that Burrows had seen that ship sink; it was lying somewhere on the sea bed, rusting to hell.

Burrows picked up the telephone handset and wound the handle to call the bridge.

'Bridge,' came the tinny reply. It was Brocklehurst, waiting for Burrows's call.

'Badger, you're not going to bloody well believe this.'

'Try me, Bill.'

'Badger, it's big, very big. Battleship, got to be. About three, maybe four miles off. Two forward turrets, none that I can see sternwards. Can't make out any markings. If I didn't know better, I'd tell you which ship it was.'

'Repeat that, Bill. Didn't follow.'

'The bloody ship, Badger. Looks like the fucking

Bismarck. Can't be, of course, but that's what it looks like, I kid you not, Badger.'

'Thanks, Bill. Keep looking,' replied Brocklehurst, and hung up.

Down below on the bridge, Brocklehurst snorted. *Bismarck* indeed! Burrows was mad. But at least he'd spotted the thing.

The next move seemed to Brocklehurst to be obvious. He called Kelly back to the bridge.

'Any luck, Sparks, with the Admiralty?'

'Not yet, sir. I keep re-sending, but nothing comes back.'

'Right-ho. Keep trying. In the meantime, make the following on German frequencies: "HMS *Trent* to German warship" ... quote our position, Sparks. "Am closing from the south. Please identify yourself. We have no hostile intentions. Repeat no hostile intentions. Signed Brocklehurst, Captain." Get that off now and wait for a reply.'

'Yes, sir,' said Kelly and went back to his radio room.

It could do no harm, reasoned Brocklehurst. Whoever they were, they must have heard the news. He wanted to defuse the encounter.

The foretop phone squawked again.

'Badger, that ship – I'll swear it's turning its turrets.'

'To where?'

'Towards us, Badger. I'm really not joking.'

It couldn't be. 'Keep watching, Bill. Tell me if anything happens.'

Suddenly Kelly rushed back on to the bridge, nearly falling over in his haste. 'Captain. Signal from London. Urgent.'

Brocklehurst read the brief signal with a sinking feeling in his stomach.

*

*Herdman to Trent. Urgent. Hitler confirmed dead but
no surrender. All ships should be treated as hostile, and
especially yours. Extreme caution. Take care.*

'Kelly, make to Admiralty. "Personal for Herdman. Treating your ship with utmost caution but looks like a fight.
Ship appears to be *Bismarck* or class. Thoroughly confused. Kindly explain what is going on." Sign it Badger.
Come on man, get on with it!'

'Yes, sir,' coughed Kelly and disappeared from the
bridge to send his signal.

The handset squawked once more.

'Yes,' snapped Brocklehurst.

'Four flashes, Badger. The bastard's opened fire!'

Oh, shit. 'Action stations. Ship under attack!' yelled
Brocklehurst into the crew PA system. But there was
nothing he could do except wait for the shells from
the huge, unknown German battleship to make their
marks.

Brocklehurst and all the rest of them felt the same
cold, gnawing fear that had haunted them for five
years. An ancient monster of the sea seemed to have
come back.

11

Bach had spotted the other ship first. The *Hindenburg* was bigger, the bridge higher in the air, and because Bach still considered himself at war, he had maintained a constant watch in the high mast. *Trent* came into Bach's view a good ten minutes before Burrows spotted Bach's ship. Bach's response was immediate. He ordered his ship to action stations and instructed Kinzel, his artillery officer, to prepare the big guns for action.

Unlike Brocklehurst, Bach had no doubt that this was an enemy ship. He had no idea what or who it really was, but as far as he was concerned any ship was an enemy ship. He was ready to open fire just as Burrows spotted him; once Kinzel advised Bach that the guns were aimed and ready, Bach had no hesitation in giving the order. His intention was simply to frighten the other ship away. It was small, just a light cruiser, less than half the size of his own vessel, and no match at all for his huge guns and massive armour protection. It had probably stumbled on him by chance, reasoned Bach, and it would certainly not expect to be fired upon. In Bach's mind, he had absolute advantage: surprise, overwhelming superiority, impregnable defence.

Kinzel had taken up position in the forward fire control station. The big Leitz rangefinder's arms stretched out thirty feet to each side above him. Heavily armoured, the ends of each arm contained precision optics that gave an exact indication of distance when the images from each end were brought together to overlap on a central mirror. It was the same principle as German rangefinder cameras, such as the Leica, but expanded to a vastly bigger scale; and it was built by the very same people. The range data was fed into the main fire control computer. Situated right behind Kinzel, this machine was fed with range, direction, weather, temperature and wind details, and then calculated through complex differential equations to provide what was known as the 'firing solution' – the precise elevation and direction to set the guns in the turrets so that the shells would hit the target. The first shot was the most difficult. The fire director's main job was to spot the fall of shot and then feed the error back to the machine – so many metres forward or behind, or to port or starboard of the target. This offset quickly improved the accuracy of the computer's instruction. After three salvos, the new data fed back into the machine was usually enough to get the big gun's accuracy to within a ten-metre circle at ten-miles range, enough to destroy most ships with a single salvo.

German guidance technology was easily the most advanced in the world. The Americans had been working on control computers using valves; but the German machines, based on electro-mechanical calculators, were far more robust and could stand up to use at sea and in battle. The American machines, although faster, were delicate and prone to breakdown in poor weather conditions. The Germans could see no future in investing in such fragile technology just for the sake of an extra second or two in getting the firing solution.

Kinzel was cleared by Bach to open fire. His guns were loaded and aimed. He pressed the two big green buttons for turret Anton, warning the gun crews to stand by. Two green lights came on a second later – the signal from the turret crew that all was ready. Kinzel then depressed the two red buttons.

The high-explosive shell sat in the breech of the big gun; behind it were two silk bags, like large hatboxes, containing cordite, a fast-burning explosive. Kinzel's red buttons caused a wire to glow red-hot inside the small detonating cap that, exploding, set off the cordite charges. The shell was hurled along the barrel, accelerating to over 1,000 miles per hour in a few milliseconds as the cordite erupted; the inside of the gun barrel was rifled: thin grooves were cut into the barrel wall, spiralling round from mouth to breech. As the shell was shoved forward, the grooves made the shell spin; as it exited from the barrel it was spinning furiously, helping to keep it on a straight trajectory.

The same sequence of events happened inside turret Bruno. Four big shells were now in the air, climbing fast, reaching the selected height, then tipping over and heading back towards the surface of the sea. Kinzel and his machine had done their jobs well. Even though the howling wind affected the course of the big shells, the correction had been good. The first shell raced down towards *Trent*, fell short by fifty yards and slightly behind the ship. The other shells fell just a few yards away, the computer automatically correcting even for the slight difference in the starting positions of each shell's journey.

In the nose of each shell was a delay fuse which detonated a slow-burning explosive that took several milliseconds before it set off the larger charge. The principle was that with its massive kinetic energy the big shell would be able to pierce the other ship's armour defences and then, once it had penetrated the innards of the ship, would explode, causing the maximum damage.

The effect of the slight delay on the shell's detonation in the water was spectacular. They had time to dig down in the rolling sea, thirty or forty feet deep, before finally exploding. The massive charge created an enormous bubble of hot gas that pushed upwards, erupting into a geyser of water that was flung 100 feet into the air.

From five miles away, Kinzel saw the four spouts leap up into the air. Even the storm couldn't disperse that volume of water quickly, and from a distance the spouts seemed to hang in the air for several moments before collapsing back into the heaving surface of the ocean.

Kinzel quickly estimated the distance of the miss, and called it back to the operator who fed the data into the computer. It took five seconds more to recalculate the equations for the new gun bearings and elevation. The turrets were instructed accordingly as their crew reloaded shells and propellants. Just twenty-five seconds after the first salvo, Kinzel signalled to the bridge that he was ready to fire again.

But Bach hesitated. He too had been watching the salvo. They only just missed; the four waterspouts were near enough to frighten the life out of whoever was on that ship. Let's see what they would do first, thought Bach. If they had any sense, they'd sheer away and try to get out of range. A good captain would not risk his ship in such an unequal fight. Bach certainly wouldn't have done. It wasn't a question of cowardice, just good sense. It would clearly be futile to get into a fight with the battleship.

Once the other vessel turned away, he would let it run a few miles, fire another salvo just to keep it going, and then he would lose himself in the storm. The bad weather was his greatest ally. Bach confidently watched the other ship, waiting for it to commence its turn.

*

Brocklehurst could do nothing except wait for the salvo to fall. There was no point in turning the ship – it wouldn't respond quickly enough, especially in this weather. There was a moment of silence as the entire bridge complement waited; then the four massive explosions, like depth-charges, erupted in quick succession in a neat line off their starboard stern. The fountains of water puffed high into the air, and even the screeching wind couldn't blow them away. They hung for a second of two and then gently collapsed back into the green sea, leaving four white scars on the surface that persisted even in the rolling waves.

'Bastards,' murmured an incredulous Brocklehurst. 'Bastards!' he said again, this time a little louder. He found it difficult to believe what had happened, but now he was angry.

'Burrows, get down here,' he shouted into the telephone. 'Helm, hard to starboard. Call the engine room and tell them I want maximum revolutions. Stand by for action, everyone. The bastard wants a fight, he'll bloody well get one.'

Brocklehurst was not going to do what Bach wanted; he never would have done. It was not that Brocklehurst was any braver than Bach, simply that they came from different traditions. The German Navy since the Twenties was technically superior to almost every other Navy in the world, but control was highly centralised. The battles were not supposed to be fought by the commanders at sea but by the staff back in comfortable offices in Berlin. Donitz, the U-boat supremo, was the greatest exponent of central control: he ran his submarine fleet like chess pieces, the boat commanders little more than drivers following explicit instructions. It worked brilliantly – the highly co-ordinated 'wolf-pack' tactics nearly bringing Britain to its knees. The surface fleet had the same mentality, but ever since the early loss of the new pocket battleship *Graf Spee* in the opening months of the war, Berlin's approach was to protect its assets rather than lose them. Even the mighty *Bismarck* was trying to escape when it was sunk, rather than join a battle. The truth was, the *Kriegsmarine* had few enough capital ships; it couldn't afford to lose any. And so Bach, like the rest of the senior officers, had this mentality drummed into him: avoid a battle at all costs, protect your assets.

The Royal Navy took a very different approach. They all knew they were fighting for their very lives. Losing a few ships didn't matter so long as they won in the end. It wasn't cynical expediency, simply a recognition of the reality of total war. The Admiralty gave its captains much more local control, even though they demanded information and meddled anyway. But commanders were expected to take the fight to the enemy and bring them to battle. That was how Brocklehurst was trained, and that was the way he saw things now. The German ship, bigger and clearly better armed than he was, was offering that battle. It was his job to provide it.

But Brocklehurst was no fool, either. His initial manoeuvre after the first salvo seemed to confirm Bach's view: *Trent* started to sheer away from the enemy ship. Bach watched this approvingly, and so still held his fire. But Brocklehurst was simply bringing his ship round, first to spoil his opponent's aim and second to bring all of his own guns to bear in a broadside.

Trent was turning a full circle. In the heaving seas the scratch crew had to load and aim the guns; they were far from used to it, but the sudden fear and panic transformed them into a highly motivated team that made up in enthusiasm what it lacked in skill. *Trent* corkscrewed wildly as Brocklehurst made his turn. At one point, with sea on its beam, the ship started to heel alarmingly, canting over at twenty and then thirty degrees. Everything loose on the bridge flew to the 'downhill' end; papers, navigation instruments, dirty tin cups, books, binoculars, in a crashing heap. Even Brocklehurst had a moment of worry. But the sea passed and, as the ship continued its turn, it slowly heaved itself back up again.

Burrows made his way through the bridge door as the ship was coming broadside-on to the distant *Hindenburg*. McConnell, the American radar technician, had stayed on the bridge and was calling out the bearings of the battleship. But Brocklehurst could see it for himself now, the tops showing above the waves as *Trent* rode up on a sea.

His gunnery officer, like Bach's, was waiting for the order to fire. Once Brocklehurst was satisfied with his position, he gave the order.

*

Now it was Bach's turn to be astonished. The *Trent*'s main armament was six 8-inch guns, mounted in one forward and one aft turret of three guns apiece. They didn't pack anything like the punch of the big 15-inch guns of the *Hindenburg*, but the *Trent*'s guns could keep up a much greater rate of fire. It was a simple equation between the destructive power of a few big shells and the wrecking ability of more, smaller ones.

The six guns flashed in the gloom. The smaller shells travelled faster; the salvo overshot by several hundred yards and the fall was marked by six white fountains in the water, more widely spread than the *Hindenburg*'s salvo.

'Bloody *useless*,' shouted Brocklehurst encouragingly down the voice-pipe that connected him with the fire control station. 'Next time hit the bastard. I'm going to do a half-turn to upset his aim. I'll bring your other broadside to bear. Make sure you're ready.'

Brocklehurst swung his ship across the waves again. It was a well-timed move and a surprised Bach ordered Kinzel to open fire in response, just as *Trent* started the turn. The computer's aim would have been good had Brocklehurst not ruined it with the sudden change of course. The big guns erupted again, flinging the four massive shells at the *Trent*. They arrived just where the ship should have been, but the British vessel was no longer there. Even so, the shots were close enough, sending cascades of green water over the deck and superstructure of *Trent*.

Now Kinzel's big guns were empty and untrained; it would take him another half-minute to get them ready again. Brocklehurst guessed that with guns of that size they would be slow. 'Two salvos, quick as you can,' he shouted.

The gunnery officer had to wait until the roll of the ship brought his guns to the effective elevation he needed; he did this simply by setting them dead level and letting the ship move to produce the required angle. Just as the roll was getting them there, he fired. Without waiting for the shot to fall, he shouted at his turret crews to reload.

The first salvo was closer but still wide. Fifteen seconds passed. The second salvo was fired. Three shells missed. And then one struck *Hindenburg*'s forward armour belt, just ahead of turret Anton, ricocheted upwards, arched over and then plunged back into the sea, exploding as it hit the water.

But the last two shells struck home. The first of them hit the forward deck. The armour plate held, but the shell splinters from the explosion damaged one of the capstans, suddenly releasing the port anchor. The anchor chain was secured, but the anchor itself was left hanging halfway down the hull, where it started swinging and crashing against the steelwork. The second shell landed further forward, more or less at the very stem of the ship. It did little damage, except to tear away the forward flagstaff and a length of railing.

The explosion had a greater effect below decks. The two bolts on the steel door to Otto Heine's cell were jolted violently by the blast. One came off completely, the other was loosened. And Otto – sick, cold, semi-conscious, his body raging with the pain of holding himself wedged against the motion of the ship – was suddenly shaken back to life.

The shell hits annoyed Bach, but they caused only superficial damage. He was more worried about the anchor swinging free. It weighed several tons and could damage the hull. If his crew couldn't haul it back up, he'd order it cut away. But he simply couldn't understand why this little ship should behave in the way that it was doing. Was it trying to commit suicide? The captain must have been mad. Almost reluctantly, Bach ordered another salvo fired.

Hindenburg's big guns blasted once more. Kinzel had done his best to correct for Brocklehurst's twists and turns, but again he had guessed wrongly. The salvo landed well clear of the port side of *Trent*. Now Bach's annoyance was starting to turn to anger. The master of that ship was a complete idiot. How long did he expect his luck to last? One shell from *Hindenburg*, just one, would send it to the bottom. Why was he persisting? And now look at him, coming round again for another broadside with those puny guns. Bach had had enough. He stormed down to the radio room and pushed open the door.

He was surprised to find Moehle there. In turn, Moehle looked shamefaced and mumbled something about checking the equipment. Bach had no time to ask questions. He ignored him and grabbed the radio-telephone.

In impeccable but accented English, Bach spoke to what he hoped was *Trent*. 'Allied warship, this is your German opponent. Sir, you are endangering your ship and your crew. My ship can totally destroy yours. For the sake of your men, Captain, please depart. We do not even require your surrender.' There was no advantage in sinking the ship and pointlessly killing the men – sailors like Bach, after all. They would report his position, of course, but he would be long gone before anyone else could do anything about it. He would disappear in the endless ocean.

Bach released the transmit switch and listened to the carrier wave hissing from the loudspeaker. There was no reply. Perhaps the ship did not have radio-telephony equipment? Should he send another message in Morse? As he was considering this, he was interrupted by the impact of another three shells, this time from the stern of the ship.

Very well, whoever you are. Your choice, not mine. Bach was not going to allow his ship to be subjected to this. They were like gnat bites – hardly dangerous, but irritating all the same. Furious, he turned to leave the room when the Morse key started chattering. Were they replying? Bach paused to listen, his mind converting the blips and bleeps into letters, then into words. But the message was in German. He stopped now, looking more and more puzzled. Then his eyebrows rose and he looked up at Moehle in sheer disbelief. The Morse key stopped. It was the half-hourly repeat of the message that Berlin had been putting out for some hours now – the message that Moehle had already heard but decided to keep silent about, and that Brocklehurst had already heard, which was why he had – mistakenly – assumed that Bach's ship would not behave as it had just done:

> All ships. Repeat of message. Please relay. The
> German Naval High Command confirms that
> the father of the German people passed away
> at 15.30 Berlin time. Grand Admiral Donitz
> has been named to succeed. Long live the Reich!
> This message will be repeated every half-hour
> on this frequency. Stand by for further orders.

'Did you follow that?' he asked Moehle incredulously.
'No, sir. Too fast,' Moehle lied.
'Good God, man. It was from Berlin. About Hitler. He's dead. Hitler is dead!' Bach stared at Moehle, groping for words. 'Hitler is dead,' he repeated slowly, as though he was examining each of the words for some hidden meaning.

Moehle stood silently, watching the captain. What would he do? Bach was looking directly at Moehle but couldn't see him. There was a look of confusion now in the captain's pale blue eyes. The older man was thinking furiously, trying to fathom out the implications.

Hitler was dead. Donitz had taken over. There was no love lost between Donitz and the surface fleet. There was no mention of surrender. *'Stand by for further orders'* said the signal. Was it a hoax? It was sent in clear, after all.

Bach was not willing to let his world collapse so easily. 'Moehle, you know how to use this thing. Signal Berlin for confirmation. Don't move from here until you get it. If it comes through, get yourself up to the bridge instantly and tell me personally. No one else. Got that?'

'Yes, Captain.'

Bach hurried from the radio room. *'Stand by for further orders'*. What in the name of hell was that supposed to mean? And anyway, did the High Command in Berlin know he was out here? At the original brief-ing, Sluys had made it clear that this was a top-secret mission. Was he just sailing round these seas on his own, on a mission that no one else knew about? And on top of everything else, he had to deal with this little ship that wanted to play heroics.

As he made his way on to the bridge the thought suddenly struck him: did this Allied vessel know about Hitler's death? The message was in clear. Anyone with access to the German Naval frequency would be able to pick it up. Was that why they were being so brave – so downright idiotic?

Well, thought Bach, damn you all! The message might be a hoax anyway. And until he had direct orders to actually stop fighting, he was going to teach this ridiculous ship not to waste his time.

'Kinzel?'

'Yes, Captain?'

'Kindly listen to me. You see that ship? I want it blown out of the water within the next ten minutes. I will manoeuvre my vessel to give you a steady platform. Fire whenever you wish. Helm, come about into the wind. Hold us on that course and keep it steady. Reduce revolutions to steerage way. Warn the crew to expect some impacts. I'm not moving an inch until Kinzel lands a few on that ... fool. Get on with it!'

The great *Hindenburg* slowly began to respond to the helm. The huge steel vessel turned across the wind and the seas until the bow was almost facing the oncoming waves, disappearing into mountains of spray as each wave hurled itself at the ship. On its previous course, beam-on to the big seas, even the *Hindenburg* rolled, making the gun's aim more difficult. Now, head into the waves, the motion steadied, the massive weight and length of the ship responding less violently to the seas. The bow and the stern still seesawed up and down, but with its lower speed – just enough to keep the bow steadily on course – the movement was more acceptable and, the guns being near to the fulcrum of movement, the motion was well within the capacity of Kinzel and his director machinery to correct for.

As Bach well knew, holding this position gave his opponent a perfect target, its biggest profile presented to the other ship – all 800 feet of it. Even a blind man could land a few shells on such a huge target that wasn't even moving. But he didn't care. He knew the *Hindenburg* could cope with whatever this ship could throw at him; their shells were small and his armour was thick. He would hold the position until he had sunk the *Trent*, like slapping a mosquito that dared to bite him.

*

'Now what's he doing?' said Brocklehurst to no one in particular, watching *Hindenburg*'s slow turn through his glasses. The big ship was turning away from him, into the wind.

Bill Burrows had come down from his lookout post on the foremast to join Brocklehurst on the bridge. He too was watching the manoeuvre of the German vessel through his battered binoculars. Both men silently watched the big ship start to take the seas on the bow.

'Turning away, Bill?'

'Maybe, Badger. Maybe he's had enough.'

But then they saw the two big turrets starting to train in their direction.

'Ah. That's it. Spot of trouble coming, Bill, I think.'

'Looks that way,' commented Burrows in the heartiest way he could, trying to conceal the fear in his soul. The German ship had stopped, and was starting to look very serious. He hoped to God Badger would get out of it.

'Time to sod off out of here, Badger?' he asked after a decent pause.

'Well, no, sadly, Bill. No time. If we turn and run, we're just leaving ourselves open. Only one thing for it. Helm, go to port. Centre your wheel when you've got that bastard right in front of you. Bill, tell engines to wind it up. Everything they've got. Keep the forward turret firing just to upset them.'

'Yes, sir,' responded Bill Burrows formally, with his heart sinking. Badger, far from ordering their hasty departure, had instructed his crew not only to head for the German ship but to charge the bloody thing.

*

The door of Otto Heine's cell had been semi-opened by one of *Trent*'s earlier hits. Barely conscious from his ordeal, Heine remained unaware of this until Bach's turn into the wind started the bow rocking up and down, crashing into the oncoming waves. One of the seas caught the bow just as it was starting to descend, and with a violent crash the whole ship shuddered. Heine was thrown into the air; but at the same time the loosened bolts on the door finally gave way and it was flung wide open, clanging against the bulkhead. As the motion changed, the door was flung back again. Backwards and forwards the door swung, with dull clangs each time as it struck first the door frame and then the bulkhead.

Otto's hazy brain started to register the noise. Without really knowing what he was doing, he pulled himself to his feet and stumbled through the door just as it was swinging open. Now he stood in the dimly lit companionway. Aware of the motion of the ship, instinctively he started to head aft, and as he did so the motion gradually lessened.

Being able to move his aching limbs was starting to bring Otto round. As he stumbled down the companionway, holding on to what few grab rails there were, he suddenly realised that he was out of that hell-hole. He walked a few more yards and then paused, trying to gather his thoughts. He had no idea how long he'd been in the cell; he didn't know if it was day or night. His legs, his back, his everything, were all throbbing. Then his head began to swim and, collapsing to his knees, he started retching violently, but there was nothing to come up other than a small mouthful of bile that stung his throat.

He carefully wiped his mouth with the back of his hand and inspected it in the dim light to see if there was blood, but it looked clear. His dizziness passed and the pit in his stomach began to fill itself. He pushed himself to his feet, gripping a stanchion against the movement of the ship which was now less violent.

Then there was a massive crash directly over his head, like a thunderclap. The deck beneath his feet jerked; a fraction of second later, another huge crash, and the deck tried to shake him to his feet. Turret Anton, almost directly above him, had loosed its first determined salvo at the *Trent*.

*

Bach smiled grimly as he watched the other ship turn towards him. Now he knew exactly what its captain was trying to do. He was too close to turn and run, so he was trying to minimise his profile by running headlong at *Hindenburg*, and by closing as fast as he could he hoped to reduce the range to the point where the German ship's big guns could no longer depress sufficiently to get an aim. The secondary armament would probably still function, but Bach assumed that his opposite number imagined that his smaller guns would pose less of a danger, and that his own armament would be more effective close in. It was a tactic that was well known in the theory books, but Bach had never seen it used before. It took a brave man to run headlong at a bigger ship – or else a stupid one. Bach couldn't see much bravery involved. But then, short of surrender, there was no option left for the other captain.

Bach was now determined to resolve the issue and he watched with satisfaction as turret Anton opened up. The great fountains of flame and smoke belched from the barrels. The target was less than five miles off and, he noted, the guns were already within five degrees of their maximum depression. Once the other ship came within three miles, the big guns would be useless. But Bach had no doubt that he would have disposed of the problem before then.

The first salvo fell well behind the *Trent*. But Kinzel was taking his time; it was just a ranging shot.

Bach would have to leave him to it. Now he needed to contact Sluys in Berlin and find out exactly what was meant to be happening to this voyage. If the rest of the officers knew that Hitler was dead, they would certainly want to know why they were continuing the mission. They were not loyal, thought Bach darkly as he made his way down to the radio room. Not loyal, and not determined. And God knows what would happen if the crew ever found out. Moehle knew, but he was a just a youngster and easily overawed. Bach was sure that he could retain his loyalty.

When he pushed open the door to the radio room, Moehle was sitting at the Morse key. He jumped up when Bach came hurriedly in.

'No luck yet, sir. Sorry. I've sent the message three times, asking for confirmation, but there's no reply. They must be busy. Or something.'

'Never mind, Moehle. Listen to me. You must keep this knowledge quiet. For now, that is. It would upset the whole crew. We must obtain more information. I have to get hold of Sluys, in Berlin, urgently. Can you operate this thing to get me through?'

Yes, thought Moehle, I can operate the thing, but it won't do you a blind bit of good because Sluys has long since gone. He's left us both to it, Bach. But Moehle shrugged and sat down at the key. 'I'll try, Captain. I'll try. What's the message?'

'"Urgent for Sluys from Bach." Don't mention the ship. No one's supposed to know. "Request urgent orders in view of developments in Berlin. Am engaged in minor action with small British ship. Advise soonest otherwise will have to consider abandonment." Send that, Moehle. That should wake him up.'

Moehle looked with astonishment at Bach. 'You would abandon this mission, sir?'

'You look surprised, Moehle.'

'No, sir. I mean, yes, sir. You seemed so ... well ... confident just a while ago.'

'Let's see what Sluys says. If surrender is near, I have to consider my position. There's not much point in arriving off Washington if Berlin has given up by then, is there? Not even me, Moehle, if that's what you're thinking. I'll fight to the last, but I won't damn well be doing it on my own.'

As if to confirm Bach's words, turret Bruno erupted in a salvo somewhere ahead of them and the whole ship jerked under the impact.

They let silence return. Bach hoped Kinzel was doing his job well. He was taking his time, he imagined, in order to get his aim right.

'I'll try to get Sluys for you. I'll bring the reply up to the bridge if I receive one.'

Moehle knew that Sluys had probably gone. He hoped Bach would leave him to it so that he could fake a reply ordering Bach to carry on at all costs.

'No problem, Moehle. I'll wait. It's pretty urgent.'

Moehle looked up at Bach, but it was clear that the captain was not going to move. If Bach got no direct orders from Sluys, what was he going to do – give up? And then?

'I'll try,' said Moehle finally. He tapped at the key and then waited. There was a long silence, punctuated by two further salvos from the big guns which made the radio equipment rattle.

'No luck, I'm afraid, Captain.'

'Send it again. He *must* be there.'

Moehle bent over the set once more, but just as he was about to start the key began chattering on its own.

A brief message was arriving and Bach easily deciphered it as it came in:

> To Bach from Naval Command, Berlin. What is your
> ship and position? Sluys has deserted and is to be arrested.
> Report immediately.

Moehle said nothing but watched Bach's face. The captain remained impassive, just silently mouthing the words of the message to himself. He glanced at Moehle and then turned on his heel.

'Captain!' shouted Moehle.

Bach stopped and turned.

'Don't go. There's something you must know.'

Bach looked, his eyes narrowing. 'Moehle? What the hell is going on?'

How on earth do I start? thought Moehle. 'Captain, you had your orders from Sluys. I know that. But I am working for Sluys, too. It is a secret.'

'Damn right it's a secret, Moehle. What do you mean, you're working for Sluys?'

'Before he briefed you – in Berlin, I mean – he had spoken to me. Recruited me, as it were. Into a special plan. Something you weren't meant to know about until we reached our destination; I was only to reveal it then – or if things were going badly. I mean, things are going badly now, so I think I ought to tell you what's really going on.'

'Moehle, for God's sake, what is happening?'

'Sluys has a different mission for this ship. He told you that you were to sail to the Chesapeake Bay and bombard Washington. But he knew it would never happen; the Americans would never let you get that far. Sluys knew that Berlin was about to collapse. He has loaded a substantial amount of gold on to this vessel. You were to be told as we neared the coast so that you could surrender the gold. Sluys by then would have surrendered to the Americans in Germany. The gold was his negotiating weapon, a token of good faith, as it were. To buy his freedom to America. This was the only way he could get that much gold anywhere near them. That's the truth, Captain. Sorry.'

Bach looked at the younger man, his face giving nothing away.

'He didn't want you to know, you see,' carried on Moehle, trying to fill the silence. 'Sluys trusted you to complete the mission, but not if you knew about the gold. He said you would never surrender, not unless the whole thing was finished. He didn't think you would do it if you knew the real reason. He was desperate, you see. Him and the others.'

'The others?'

'Well, Sluys I know about. I know there were at least a dozen others in the conspiracy, but I don't know the names. Once you were well on your way, they would head for the American lines and wait until I had told you. Then all would have become clear.'

'I see. I am just a bloody messenger, then? Driving a load of looted gold to present to the damned Americans?'

'You should not get angry, Captain. He did it with the best intentions.'

'Best intentions, Moehle? Risked my life, your life, even the damned lives of those idiots out there who we're trying to sink? Just to satisfy Sluys's cowardice?'

'I don't think so, Captain. Not cowardice. He wanted to save something of Germany, and this was the only way it could happen. He didn't know we'd get into a fight. He was convinced we would get through unscathed, at least until we neared the American coast, and then we were going to surrender. No one was meant to get hurt. I mean, the whole thing is over, isn't it? Germany, the Navy, everything. Finished. There's nothing left, Captain, nothing. Nothing worth fighting for.'

Bach slumped down on to a chair. Moehle was right, this really was the end. Hitler was dead. Sluys had disappeared. And now he discovered that – far from being the heroic act of defiance he had thought it was – his mission was simply a grubby little theft. There was no duty in this, no honour.

'The gold? Where is the gold?'

'In Anton's magazine. Right at the bottom. Twenty big fifteen-inch shells. And another dozen small ones. Inside them is the gold, not explosive.'

Bach shook his head. 'Well, that's it, Moehle. All is clear. I understand. We stop here, then. A nice quiet surrender, and then back home, eh? It's a funny way for it to end, but there you are. Thanks for telling me, Moehle. I'll go up top and call off Kinzel, if he hasn't sunk those poor bastards already,' and Bach rose slowly to his feet.

'No, no, Captain. You don't understand,' said Moehle anxiously. 'You can't stop now, you can't surrender!'

'Why the hell not? What's the matter with you, man?'

'You must continue. Right to the end. Sluys was always a bit nervous. I mean, in case you found out and wanted to stop. Or if you refused to surrender right at the end, when you were meant to – once you found out what was going on. Sluys has insurance. He's taken it with him. Just to make sure.'

'Insurance, Moehle? What kind of insurance?'

'Forgive me, Captain. Your wife and son. They're with Sluys now. Looking forward to seeing you, in America. When you get there.'

12

Heine needed air. He couldn't catch his breath and the smell of the ship, of raw steel and diesel oil and damp, made his stomach rise. He wasn't sure where he was, but at least he knew which way was forward and which was up, and so he made his way down the length of the long companionway, climbing through the bulkhead doors every forty feet, towards where he assumed the middle of the vessel must be. He had no idea what the huge crashes were overhead. They wrenched the whole ship every thirty seconds; it sounded as if somebody was bombing them.

He reached a set of ladders that disappeared upwards in the gloom. There was a smell coming from above: fresh, salty air mingled with the familiar scent of high explosive, the sort of thing that Heine had experienced many mornings in Hamburg when he awoke in a cellar and emerged into the devastated landscape. Still dizzy after his confinement, Otto grasped a handrail for a few seconds to get his head clear before starting the climb.

Perhaps there should have been revenge burning in his soul. But there was no sense of outrage, no desire to get hold of Schiller, the officer who had imprisoned him. Otto Heine had never wasted time on such feelings. Right now, there were more important things to do. Heine had been torn from his home and bullied on to this ship. He had been abused, sworn at, humiliated. Then he had been thrown into a torture chamber and hurled around like a doll for the best part of a day. And now, by the sound of things, some bastard was trying to bomb them. And all because some bunch of crazy Nazis wanted to play at being heroes when quite clearly all they had managed to do was plunge the country into mayhem.

Quite simply, he had had enough of people trying to kill him and he had no wish to end his days out here. He had plans – to make money, to live a life, to sleep with as many women as he could find, to drink himself stupid every weekend, to watch football, to play cards and win even if it meant a bit of cheating sometimes.

And all that kept happening was that they were trying to blow him to shit in a war in which he had no part and even less interest. Enough was enough. Now he knew he would have to do *something*, before the bastards finally managed to finish him off.

This time he couldn't just shrug his shoulders and wander off, leaving everyone else to their own mess; he would have to take some responsibility. He wasn't scared of the idea; it was just that he knew it would mean other people being involved, and Heine had no great desire to get anyone involved with his plans. They would let him down, screw it up, generally misbehave and very probably fuck up the whole idea; but he had no alternative, no choice. If Otto Heine was not going to end up as a pile of bones on the sea bed, he would have to recruit some help. Once he'd sorted things out, then he could tell them to piss off.

He started the climb up the ladders. There were landings after every short flight and he had to stop to get his breath. He realised he hadn't eaten for over a day, either. And now there was a sharp, stabbing pain across his back every time he took a step upwards. He swore and carried on. The smell of sea air and cordite grew stronger. There was another massive explosion, Heine dropped to his knees on a landing and the steelwork shuddered.

Finally he reached a door, secured by latches operated by a central locking wheel. He paused for breath again and then turned the wheel. The mechanism was stiff, but it yielded with a screech and the two steel pins withdrew from the frame. He pushed again and there was a rush of wind and sea-spray. The door opened outwards and the wind was pushing against it, but the hinges were stiff and rusty and held against the pressure. Heine pushed again and looked at the outside world, even though the wind and the light was making his eyes water. He breathed the air deeply.

He had emerged on to the main deck just aft of the bridge area, close to where the massive uptakes from the engine room ran into the single fat smokestack. The door that he had opened faced directly aft, just hidden from the main guns by a projection in the superstructure. This saved his life. The shock waves from the firing of the main armament were enough to kill a man standing on the open deck anywhere near them, even if the heat from the blast didn't burn him to death. As Heine emerged on to the deck, which was slippery with spray, turret Bruno erupted with another salvo.

Heine couldn't see the turret, but the flash lit up the grey sky with an astonishing brilliance. He felt a sudden searing heat, quickly followed by the blast wave.

Protected in the corner, he fell to the wet deck with the blast echoing from horizon to horizon. Shit, he thought, they're *still* trying to kill me, and this time they're getting serious.

The blast subsided. There was a high-pitched whistling in Heine's ears that wasn't just the howling wind. He pushed himself painfully to his feet. Now he realised where he was, he knew there was a door another fifty yards down the deck that led to the crew's quarters. Could he reach it? The wind was coming from the front of the ship, bringing clouds of spray with it. He sure as hell couldn't stay where he was – unless he went back inside, but that would get him nowhere. What the fuck! He lurched out from behind his protection and staggered down the deck, the wind half pushing him and spray like hot needles peppering the back of his neck.

*

Bach stared out of the bridge window, a dull, defeated look in his eyes. He hadn't spoken a word since arriving back from the radio room. Schiller had been on the bridge while they had positioned themselves to open fire on the approaching British ship. When Bach reappeared, he gave him a hasty report.

'One hit for certain, Captain. Two probables. The rest very close. The trouble is he's still coming and the guns are close to the bottom. We'll have to use secondary armament, but they're all new and never been fired. Kinzel has got some of them manned, but he's worried.'

'Thank you,' was all the reply he got from Bach. Moehle had come up from the radio room, too, and was watching his captain from the back of the bridge. The news that Sluys had his wife and child for insurance had almost floored the man. Moehle could see that Bach had a naïve faith in duty and in his Navy comrades. Now here was not only a betrayal but an act of hostility that was quite outside Bach's experience. 'You must fight on, Captain,' Moehle had urged after Bach had fallen silent. 'Fight on and get us there.'

'Captain?' Schiller had seen the strange look on Bach's face and was worried. What was wrong with the man now? 'Captain?'

Bach slowly turned his eyes towards Schiller. 'Yes?'

'Captain – what are your orders? What shall we do now? We need orders, Captain.'

'Orders?' asked Bach. He looked away from Schiller and out of the bridge windows once more. *God in heaven, I could do with a drink. I could do with a whole bloody bottle.*

The *Trent* was charging directly at them from the port side, about a mile and a half off, visibly rolling in the heavy beam seas, smoke from its straining engines ripped from the funnel and a blacker, thicker smoke billowing from a fire somewhere on the ship where one of *Hindenburg*'s huge shells had caught the cruiser. Every half-minute or so, the forward turret sparkled and smoked. The shots were all over the place: the *Trent*'s rolling didn't give the gunners much of a chance.

Bach gave what sounded like a sigh. Suddenly he seemed to come back to life. 'Schiller, why have we stopped firing?' he demanded.

Schiller looked furious. 'As I said, Captain. The guns are at maximum depression. The ship is too close. Kinzel is waiting for your orders to open fire with the secondary guns.'

'Don't bother. Clear the turrets, quickly. Get the crews inside. Rig the ship for collision. Helm, hard to port, engines full ahead.'

'Captain?'

'Schiller, don't look so worried. If we can't blow him
out of the water we'll run him down. We're five times
his size. We'll sort him out one way or another, eh,
Moehle? We carry on fighting, what do you say?'
There was a strange bitterness in the captain's voice.
Moehle stayed silent at the back of the bridge.

The big ship started to answer the helm, turning
slowly towards the oncoming *Trent*, the engines working up the revolutions. As the *Hindenburg* turned, the
motion began to increase once more.

*

Heine slammed the steel door behind him. The howl
of the wind was suddenly stilled. Now he was on
familiar ground. Just a few days before – it seemed
like weeks now – this was where he had been quart-
ered with the rest of the crew. If any of them were not
on duty, this was where they would be.

He came to the door and pushed it open, but he was
not expecting what he saw. Inside were about thirty of
the kids who had been dragged on to the ship with
him. They had looked brave enough then. But now
they were all sitting on the deck, knees up to their
chins, arms wrapped round their knees, and heads
bent forward. There was a deathly silence in the big
room.

Heine stood for a moment. In a corner he recognised Vogele, the kid who had suggested he lead them
into an uprising to get them off this ship.

'Vogele? You OK?'

The lad looked up at Heine. His eyes were tired and
dull. 'Heine? I heard they locked you up.'

'For a while. Why are you all here?'

'Hiding.'

'From what?'

'Nothing in particular. The guns, I suppose. Or Schnee. Is it true you went for him? His face is a mess.'

Heine ignored the question. He was surprised that Schnee was on his feet after what he'd done to him. He would have to be careful; the chief petty officer would be wanting his revenge. 'What's been happening?'

'Some sort of battle. A British warship turned up and we started firing. The big guns. We were told to get under cover and stay off the deck. The other ship's coming in close, Otto. I suppose we're going to get sunk or blown up or something.' Vogele spoke with a resigned fear. The lad was clearly convinced that he was going to his grave.

'Like fuck we are,' replied Heine. 'I've had enough, Vogele. I am not going to stand here and get shot to hell. Neither are you.' He raised his voice so that the rest of them could hear. 'Listen, all of you. I'm going to sort out this mess. We need weapons. You remember where the armoury is? I need two or three of you to come with me. We'll get the keys off one of the bastard officers and then we meet back there. Give us half an hour. Then we'll figure out what to do.'

Vogele remained sitting. 'Otto, don't be stupid. There's no way.'

'You want to sit there and get killed? Do the rest of you? Listen, I've broken into more places than the rest of you have had hot dinners. Don't worry, I know exactly what I'm doing. It's so easy you wouldn't believe it. We go up to one of the officers. He's distracted by the battle up there. We make things easy for him. A little force, a little determination. I've done it hundreds of times. People always give you what you want if you threaten them. They're scared to hell. Believe me.' Otto Heine had broken into many places, though he had never once done what he was suggesting now. But he sounded totally confident.

Vogele looked up at Heine. 'You're serious, aren't you?'

'Of course I'm serious. I don't plan on having my funeral right now. It's that simple. You in or out, Vogele? The rest of you?'

They stayed silent, sitting on the deck, looking up at Heine. Nobody moved.

'For Christ's sake! Listen, you get one chance and one only. You know what's going to happen? They're already attacking us. Do you really think that we'll get any further? Bach is mad. He's convinced he'll get through, and he'll kill us all before he gives up. You want to sit here? Go ahead. They'll shell you. High explosive. You'll get arms blown off, you'll get legs blown off. You'll get your eyeballs burned. You'll get your fucking balls blown off. You'll die nice and slow. Then when you're screaming because bits of you are hanging off, you'll get thrown into the water or become trapped inside the ship as it goes down. You'll hear the water outside and you'll know you're going down, and you'll live for another few hours as the water comes up or the air runs out – and you'll know you can't get out. *Ever*. Shit, what do I care? I'm not going down with you people. I'm going to get out. Now.'

Heine stormed out of the room and slammed the steel door behind him. Then he stopped and waited.

Ten seconds. Twenty. One minute. Nearly two minutes. The door behind him opened slowly. It was Vogele.

'I thought you might be waiting here,' said Vogele quietly, with a slight smile.

'I thought you might think that,' replied Heine, but with a wide grin.

There were four others behind Vogele, looking expectantly at Heine. He knew how much courage they would have had to screw up to make the move.

'Listen. Just keep quiet and follow me. Don't worry about a thing. I know exactly what I'm doing. Ready?'

They nodded nervously.

Heine led them quietly down the companionway to the door that opened to the main deck. The big guns had not fired for some time, and the motion of the ship had changed from the crashing of a headlong course into the wind to the deeper side-to-side roll of a beam sea. The *Trent's* fitful and optimistic shots came nowhere near the ship, falling in silent white blooms hundreds of yards away. When Heine opened the door and looked out, the screaming wind was completely gone; this was the door on the lee side of the ship and the superstructure sheltered them. Nobody was outside. He led his party carefully forward, keeping tight in to the rusting steelwork that formed the central section of the ship. Some of the portholes had never been finished, and the ship had left Hamburg with wooden planking poorly nailed over the frames. The weather had loosened the wood and in some places the portholes were completely open to the elements. In others, sheets of canvas had served the same job, and now most of them were flapping in the loose gusts that now and then crept round from the weather side of the vessel.

Still the main deck remained deserted. Everyone seemed to have moved inside. Heine moved along to the wider section of the superstructure at the forward end, where sets of ladders led to the bridge several decks up. He needed to find an officer – any of them would do – with his keys for the armoury. They were most likely to be around this part of the ship.

'Wait here,' ordered Heine. He left Vogele and the others and climbed the first set of ladders. His aching legs and back seemed less troublesome now. When he reached the top of the first flight, there was an exposed landing and then another set of ladders. He stopped on the landing and looked out ahead. For the first time he saw in the distance the *Trent* steaming towards them. But he took little notice of the cruiser. Heine had other things on his mind. Where were the officers? They must be here somewhere.

His question was answered. An officer suddenly came clattering down the ladder and stopped immediately he saw Heine.

'What are you doing? All hands have been ordered inside.' It was Jensch, the communications officer.

'Sorry, sir. Bit of a problem back there. I was sent to find an officer. Urgent, sir.'

'What sort of problem? Who sent you?' asked Jensch. Heine looked a mess – unshaved, stained, with staring hollow eyes.

'Schnee, sir. Said it was very urgent and an officer was to come straight away. Dangerous situation.'

'Very well. Take me there. Look sharp, lad!'

'Yes, sir. Right away, sir,' replied Heine. 'This way, please.'

Heine led Jensch back down the ladder, where Vogele and his companions were standing at the bottom. Jensch followed Heine; he didn't take any notice of Vogele, and just passed through the middle of the group as though they did not exist.

Suddenly Heine stopped and turned to face Jensch.

'Come on, come on,' Jensch urged.

'Take it easy, take it easy. I need something. Now, you want to do this the easy way or the hard way? What's your name?'

Jensch suddenly looked confused. This wiry, scruffy seaman was talking to him as though he was an underling. Jensch was not a stiff military man by background. He had been a scientist before the war, specialising in electrical systems, and he was – for a Navy officer – unusually mild-mannered. But he still knew his place in the careful hierarchy of position, and Heine talking to him like this – and being so confident and self-assured into the process – upset his world. That was Jensch's undoing. Any normal officer would have reacted violently and would almost certainly have scared off Vogele and his uncertain band. But instead, Jensch looked and sounded nervous himself.

'What do you mean? You mustn't talk to me like that.'

Heine reached out casually, gripped Jensch's tunic lapel and pulled the man towards him. 'I said, what's your fucking name?'

'*Oberleutnant sur See* Jensch . . .'

'Well now, Jensch, I need your help. You've got keys?'

'Of course, but . . .'

'Good. Come with us. But quick. Or else I'll push your fucking eyes out, got that?'

Jensch was now starting to look worried. Heine seemed so self-confident and the others around him were beginning to look menacing, too. The threats of violence were made with a cold, hard edge to them, which sounded to Jensch quite convincing.

Heine didn't wait for the reply. He knew he had to keep his man on the move. Never let them stop and think. Threaten hard and push hard. People usually did what he wanted without recourse to violence, and Heine saw instantly that underneath the uniform Jensch was just a frightened little man, like the rest of them. He grabbed the officer by one arm and pulled him along, away from the ladder leading to the bridge. The others gathered round in a tight group. They made their way quickly towards the after end of the ship, keeping close in to the upperworks.

The armoury was located in the petty officers' quarters in the middle of the ship. The heavily armoured room could only be reached through the petty officers' mess.

Heine pulled his captive through a door that opened on to a long companionway, and stopped him suddenly outside the mess. He hoped to God that no one was inside. He opened the door. Empty. He pushed Jensch through and hustled the rest of them inside, closing the door after them and pushing down the locking latches.

'Keep going, keep going,' shouted Heine.

But Jensch had stopped and was looking stubborn. 'Listen, you can't do this. I'm an officer. You really can't treat me like this.'

Heine only had one option and he regretted having to do it. He quite liked this mousy officer. What was he doing on a ship like this? But Heine had to assert his authority, not just to make Jensch behave but also to reinforce his position with Vogele and the rest of them. And it must look convincing.

Heine walked up to the officer, stood very close, and looked at him in the face.

'Jensch, you're a nice fellow but you're behaving like an idiot. You know what I'm going to do?'

Before Jensch had a chance to reply, Heine brought his knee up into Jensch's groin with a sudden sharp and violent blow. There was no anger on Heine's face, just a look of deep regret.

The officer's eyes widened and his mouth fell open, but not a sound came from the man as he wobbled for a second and then collapsed to his knees where he remained for a moment, silent but goggle-eyed, before he rolled over on to the deck. As if in slow motion his hands moved towards his groin, but they hovered, not daring to touch. He started to make a gurgling sound.

'Vogele, help the officer up,' commanded Heine.

With some distaste he watched as Vogele and the others, fascinated and frightened by Heine's ability to inflict such violence without seeming even to think about it, instantly obeyed his orders.

Jensch was helped to a kneeling position where he gasped for breath. His face had gone pale with shock and pain.

'Now, Jensch, you listen to me. You do exactly as I say. Not one word from you. Understand?'

Jensch didn't look up at Heine but nodded, slowly. Heine waited until he got to his feet and then silently led his group to the back of the mess where another door led into a large room. At the rear was the entrance to the armoury, with two locks, one at the top of the door and the other at the bottom.

'Open it,' ordered Heine.

The officer had to obey and pulled a small bunch of keys from his tunic breast pocket, held on a chain. He fumbled with the keys on the ring, but selected the right one and opened the top lock. Then he leaned down and selected another key to open the lower lock. The locks gave a curious springing sound when they were released. Heine grasped the latching lever and pushed it upwards, then pulled on the door, which swung easily open. There was a light switch inside, and he snapped it down.

The armoury was small. The bulkheads were lined with racks. On one side, long rifles of gleaming steel and polished wooden stocks were lined up in a precise pattern; on the other, stubby sub-machine guns with metal frames and perforated barrels.

'Ammunition?' asked Heine.

Jensch nodded and bent down to pull open the drawers along the bottom of the racks. Grey steel boxes inside the drawers held the magazines for both weapons.

'Vogele, run and get the others. Quick! The rest of you, start getting these things loaded.'

Vogele disappeared at a run but the others stayed motionless.

Heine grinned. 'Fucking sailors, eh? Come on, Jensch. Show these brave seamen how to load these things.'

Jensch was quick to comply. He remembered his training from the officers' academy. He loaded one of the sub-machine guns with its long magazine, pulled back the bolt to cock it, keeping the safety-catch on. Then he did the same with a rifle. His class watched carefully and, to Heine's silent amusement, they all did as they were shown, with Jensch now peering fussily over their work and correcting them when they went wrong.

By the time Vogele returned, they had twenty sub-machine guns and a dozen rifles loaded. Heine had found himself a small automatic pistol, which he stuffed into the loose waistband of his trousers. Vogele's crew stood nervously in the mess as the weapons were handed out. Most of them had never touched a gun in their lives, and Heine made sure that Jensch gave them enough instruction to enable them to look reasonably convincing. Heine was sure they'd never have to fire the things; God knows what sort of mess they would make if they did. But they needed to look as though they might be prepared to use them. That was all that he wanted.

Eventually satisfied, Heine ordered Jensch into the armoury.

'Listen, Jensch,' he said softly so that no one else could hear. 'You'll have to stay here. I've got to take over this ship before your fucking captain kills us all. As soon as we've sorted that out, I'll come back and get you. Just stay quiet and everything's fine. Got that?'

Jensch nodded miserably. Heine shut the door and locked it with Jensch's keys, then joined his crew in the mess. He looked at them. Not one of them was over the age of twenty; most of them looked younger. They all looked worried and uncertain, even if the guns in their hands had started to give them bravado. What the hell, thought Heine. It's the best I'm going to get. Better get on with it now.

'Pay attention, all of you. Now, you saw how easily the first part happened?'

They all smiled and nodded. Just as Otto Heine had said. No problem. This was getting *good*.

'Right, the next part is even easier. You're all armed. You look fucking scary. Believe me, you won't have to use those guns, not unless I tell you to. Got that? Just do as I say and everything will be fine. In a few minutes we'll have charge of this thing and then everyone can go home. You want that?'

One or two brave souls shouted that yes, that was what they wanted.

'You all want that? Going home, safe?' shouted Heine, trying to get something going inside their souls.

Now a rustle of enthusiasm passed through the group like a current; it fired more of them up. Voices were raised, and joined by others. Rifles were brandished. Suddenly the party came alive and started to move like a single organism. The crowd had taken over.

Heine pushed his way through them and marched out to the companionway and on to the main deck. He didn't turn; he could feel them behind him, their eyes gleaming. For the first time in his life, Otto Heine found himself leading a group of people for a common purpose. The worst thing, he reflected to himself, was not that he enjoyed it but how curiously easy it was, and how well he fitted the role.

He hadn't really formulated a plan at all. But as he walked confidently at the head of his small army, he quickly worked out what he should do. They made their way forward, up the deck of the rolling ship until they reached the ladder that had brought Jensch down to them.

Heine now split his army – one section staying with him on the port side, the other to work its way around the front of the superstructure to assemble at the ladder on the starboard side. He had to trust Vogele to do the job; the youngster seemed proud to be given the responsibility.

He gave Vogele a few minutes to get round. This would mean that both outside escapes from the bridge area were covered. The only other way out was through the enclosed upper decks, and access was limited. Heine could station just a handful of his men at the four exits, and then the whole bridge area would be sealed. He assumed Bach and the rest would be there.

There was still nobody on the deck. As Heine waited for Vogele to get into position, one of the youngsters pointed out the approaching British cruiser and Heine looked out over the bow. The ship was much closer now, heading directly for them. He shrugged. He didn't know what Bach or this other ship were up to, and he didn't care. He just wanted to get on to the bridge now before anything else happened.

*

'Two miles, Badger.'

Brocklehurst was fixed to his glasses, watching the approaching monster. The other ship was huge. He had ordered his single forward turret to cease firing – the fall of shot wasn't even getting close to the German because his own ship rolled so much, and he was in no mood to waste any more shells. The closer he got, the more damage he would be able to inflict. But what surprised him – and continued to do – was that the German vessel was also holding its fire. He could see that the big guns were useless; but they had other, smaller guns. Why didn't they fire? And why had the other ship suddenly turned towards him? It was becoming a test of whose nerve would give way first, and Brocklehurst was damned certain it wouldn't be his. One way or another he would stop this German. Five years of war at sea, and five years of returning home on shore leave to find streets wrecked and schools full of children bombed, had given him a powerful sense of revenge. Now he had one of the bastards in his sights, he was not going to let him go.

'Close enough, do you think, Bill?' he asked quietly.

'Any closer and we can throw the sodding shells at him by hand, Badger,' replied Burrows.

Brocklehurst considered for a moment. 'Right-ho, Bill. Everything you've got.'

Relieved, Burrows seized the handset and cranked it furiously. 'Guns? All fire and maintain fire, please. Soon as you can.'

There was a short silence. The ship continued its steady rolling to starboard, lifting itself almost upright before rolling back to starboard again, pausing as the green sea slopped over the gunwales and then pulling itself gently back once more.

As *Trent* came back to the upright position, the forward turret fired its guns. Smaller than the 15-inch monsters on *Hindenburg*, the firing was less spectacular; instead of huge explosions there were just two sharp cracks as the guns, aiming more or less directly at the approaching battleship, let loose.

Brocklehurst knew that even his best armour-piercing rounds would do little damage to the German. Instead, he ordered shrapnel rounds – normally used to bring down aircraft – and ordered his men to aim for the bridge. Quite simply, he was trying to maim and kill as many of the men on the ship as he could in an attempt to stop it.

The two shells, soon to be followed by more rounds, whined as they sliced through the wet air separating the two ships.

*

Heine's plan was for his party and Vogele's to head up the ladders, leaving half their group behind at the bottom to catch any stragglers from the bridge and to prevent anyone else from coming up. Once he reckoned that Vogele had got into position, he ordered up his own party. Heine took the lead and six others followed him, feeling both nervous and excited. He personally made sure the safety catches on their weapons were turned on. The last thing he wanted was one of them accidentally shooting the rest of the crew, which he felt was probably the greatest risk of the whole enterprise.

Heine climbed the ladder until he reached the first landing. There, it turned back on itself, and the next flight upwards was concealed behind the super-structure. Heine was leading his crew up when there was a whistling sound, suddenly growing louder. He was just turning when there was a loud explosion from below, and he and his crew ducked down. A blast of hot air like an oven door opening washed over them, then the air was filled with whining sounds, and then with the howl of ricochets. Silence fell.

'What the fuck was that?' asked Heine of nobody in particular.

'Sir, look, behind us,' called one of his crew. They had already taken to calling him 'sir'. There was a quaver in the youngster's voice.

Heine pushed past the others and looked down from the landing.

'Oh, shit,' he murmured. He had left six youngsters down below. None of them were still standing. He could see only four of them. One was just a torso, his bloody head rolling gently from side to side as the ship rolled with the waves, leaving a bright red arc across the deck. Another was sprawled against a bulkhead, but the lower parts of both arms were missing, and bright red blood was flowing from the shredded sleeves, creating a slowly growing delta across the deck. The other two remaining were hunched together, their faces hidden, but from them came a choking, sobbing cry. There was a sharp smell in the air. Heine heard another whining sound; then there was a series of four sharp explosions, but this time further back on the ship, somewhere near the after deck.

'Get back up,' he ordered, looking directly at the youngster who had called him. The lad stayed stock-still.

'NOW!' he shouted. 'There's nothing you can do. Hurry up before another one lands. Come on, fuck it,

come ON!' he urged. Now he had just one desperate
need: to reach the bridge and get some solid steel
around him before anything else happened. The others
needed little urging as Heine headed up the next set of
ladders, taking them two at a time. There was another
landing, then a short walkway. Finally he reached the
bridge door, closed against the elements.

Heine turned to the others and signalled them to
keep quiet. He edged along the outside until he reached
the window in the door, and carefully peered inside.
He could see Bach, right at the front of the bridge.
There was Schiller, too. He could see Moehle and the
others, but wasn't sure of their names. The only officer missing was Jensch, and Heine already him under
lock and key.

There was another shrill whine, close this time. One
of *Trent*'s small shells smashed into the smokestack
behind them with an echoing crash. He could see the
bridge crew duck.

There was no time to think. He pulled on the handle,
slid the mahogany door towards him and walked inside, pulling the automatic pistol from his waistband
as he did so.

Bach didn't look at him, neither did Schiller at first.
Their attention was fixed firmly on the oncoming ship,
now just over a mile way, its guns silently sparkling as
it fired another salvo. Heine was just another crewman coming on to the bridge.

For a moment Heine wasn't quite sure what to say.
They all seemed engrossed in the action. Bach was
ordering the helmsman to hold his course, but there
was something odd in the way he spoke.

Heine hefted the gun. Still nobody took any notice
of him.

'Bach! Schiller!' he shouted suddenly. Then he pointed

the gun at the nearest window and fired a shot. The window burst in a shower of glass and the sound of the shot rang around the room. The bridge crew all ducked; their nerves were shredded.

There was a second or two of astonished silence, then Bach and Schiller slowly straightened up, looking with disbelief at Heine. Bach remained where he was, but after a moment, Schiller started towards Heine.

'Schiller, don't,' warned Heine. 'Nothing would give me greater pleasure.' He pointed the gun at Schiller's face and the officer, now recognising Heine, stopped, unsure what to do.

'Heine, what in the name of hell do you think you are doing?' he asked.

'What does it fucking look like, Schiller? Use your eyes. Now, listen to me very carefully. I've got thirty armed sailors around this place and you're trapped. They're all loyal to me. We're taking over this ship right now. All of you, move to the back. You at the wheel, turn this thing around now before we all get fucking killed.'

The helmsman looked uncertainly at Bach, but got no response.

'If this is a mutiny, Heine, you've got to be joking,' growled Schiller.

'Does it look as if I'm joking? Take a look outside. Both sides,' invited Heine. Schiller looked. Behind Heine he could see one team; now peering through the other bridge window he could see a worried-looking Vogele and his party. All were armed, just as Heine had said.

'Now, do as I say. Move back and turn this fucking thing round,' repeated Heine. His first concern was to get as far away from the rapidly approaching cruiser as he could.

'Heine, can you see that ship out there? If we turn

now we get blown to shit. We'll all get killed,' Schiller shouted.

'Bullshit! We're going to get killed anyway. Turn the ship round. Now. And then I'll give you your new orders.'

Schiller glanced at Heine, then at the helmsman. Then he turned to Bach with a questioning look. Bach looked at Heine. Slowly a smile spread over Bach's face. To the astonishment of both Schiller and Heine, the captain started quietly laughing.

13

Schnee was making his way with some difficulty along the swaying deck. The right side of his face was hidden with grubby cloth that served as a bandage, and his left eye was a livid red slit through which he could see little.

Schiller had ordered him to stay in the sickbay; but when the ship changed direction and the first of *Trent*'s shells struck, the sickbay was the last place Schnee wanted to be. If there was going to be a battle, he didn't intend to sit and wait to be blown to hell. The sickbay was located aft where the armour was at its thinnest; it never occurred to him that its position was deliberate.

He had pulled himself from the iron bedstead and made his way up a short companionway to the outside. Now he emerged on the windward side and the spray lashed at his swollen face. Schnee didn't care; he wanted to get forward where the rest of the crew would be. He could hear the whining of the shells as they dropped into the sea around the vessel, and the explosions as some hit the ship. Most of them seemed to fall forward of where he was, so he felt in little danger.

Who was firing them? Why were their own big guns

silent? Why had the ship speeded up? They had given him a shot of morphine to quieten the pain from Heine's assault on him, and it slowed his dull brain down to a near-bovine level. He wasn't even sure where he was going, other than getting away from somewhere he knew would be dangerous.

Schnee struggled along the deck, slipping once on the wet planking and mumbling a few swear words. He pulled himself up again and continued his slow progress. Another shell landed on the ship, although he wasn't sure where, and a few shards of shrapnel rang on the steelwork above his head in a brief gust of metallic hail. He stopped to see if anything else happened, but other than the steady roll of the ship all was still and silent. Once more he resumed his confused progress until he finally reached the starboard ladder that led up to the bridge and the upperworks.

He paused to get his breath. The effort of getting this far on the rolling vessel had exhausted him and he leaned against the flimsy steel guard rail. He looked upwards; it seemed a good place to go. He gripped the guard rail and started up the ladder.

*

Heine was confused. So was Schiller. Bach must have gone mad. Only Moehle, still standing quietly at the back of the bridge, knew why Captain Erich Bach had started laughing out loud.

'What's so funny?' demanded Heine.

Bach just shook his head, still laughing. It was an eerie sound; there was no humour in it.

'Order the ship around,' ordered Heine, trying to take control again. He lifted his gun in a way he hoped was menacing. He couldn't afford to let this madman divert him.

'Fine, fine. Have it your own way. Helm, hard to port and come about. Hang on, everyone.' Bach was still smiling as he gave the order.

The helmsman looked uncertain but did as he was told. As he wound the wheel round, the polished brass rudder indicator on the dial before him slowly moved to the left. The ship started to plough once more into the oncoming seas, and began to shudder as the angle of the waves became more and more head-on. Clouds of spray started flying up in the air, obscuring the oncoming ship.

'Heine, don't be stupid. Look at that ship. We're leaving ourselves wide open,' pleaded Schiller.

'Schiller, don't interfere. Just get us away,' shouted Heine.

'He won't let you, Heine. Look at him. He's coming straight in!'

The turn had slowed the *Hindenburg*. Even Heine could now see the *Trent* coming in at them, less than half a mile off. The forward guns were still sparkling as Brocklehurst kept up his fire.

'Damn it, what's he supposed to be doing?' asked Bruller, the navigation officer, who alone of the bridge crew had kept a careful watch on the other ship as it came in.

'Wants to ram us by the look of things, young Heine. What shall we do now? Any ideas?' smiled Bach, giving every appearance of enjoying the situation.

'Heine, for God's sake ...' Schiller started.

But Heine refused to panic. He didn't know if they were telling him the truth or not, but he wasn't going to be diverted from his mission. He was determined to escape.

'Keep turning. Fire on the ship. Use the guns.'

'Can't. Too damn close,' smiled Bach.

'Fine, you're the fucking genius, Bach. Suggest something and I'll see if I like it.'

'Turn back and ram him instead. It's the only way. If he catches us on the beam or stern he could turn us over in a sea like this. We've just got time to turn back and slice right through him.'

'You'll sink it.'

'That's the general idea. Unless you want him to sink us?'

Heine had no choice. Bach seemed to know what he was talking about. And the other ship was charging directly at them and gave no sign of wanting to turn away. 'Fuck it, Bach. Order the turn, then. And you'd better be right.'

'Helm, hard to starboard. Brace for impact.' Bach issued the order instantly. Heine watched, gun in hand, as the helmsman wound the wheel back again and the spray started to lighten. Heine didn't want to sink the other ship. This was not out of sympathy, but simply because he just wanted to get away. And now here he was, trying to organise a simple mutiny, trapped into carrying on a fight that other people had started.

The view through the windows cleared as the spray subsided. The bow of the *Trent* was now aimed directly at them, a crisp bow wave curling away from the forefoot as the British ship headed for them at speed.

With an agonising slowness the giant battleship's own bow came round. The *Trent* was closing fast, just a few hundred yards now between the ships. Vogele and his party started to crouch, waiting for the impact.

Bach's bow was still swinging into the other ship's line. The angle was narrowing, but not fast enough.

'It won't make it,' hissed Heine.

'Don't worry,' said Bach, still smiling. 'Just watch.'

A hundred yards; seventy-five; fifty. The vessels

were so close now that Heine could see figures on the bridge of the other ship peering out of their windows. Did they feel the same certainty as Bach? Who was right?

The bow of the *Hindenburg* was still not square on to the *Trent* when the ships struck. The rise and fall of the sea made the bows of each ship move violently against each other. The British cruiser's bow rose and moved to starboard as that of the German ship fell and yawed to port. As the *Trent* rose high into the air, it pushed its way into the side of the *Hindenburg*'s bow.

There was no feeling of impact. No slowing, no crash, no sudden jarring when the vessels smashed together, not even any sound that Heine could hear. But as the ships connected, he could see sheets of steel being peeled away and stanchions and guard-rails silently folded up. The rising bow of the *Trent* peeled the steel upwards and then started to fall, dragging the debris down with it so that it disappeared.

There was a growing gash in the *Hindenburg*'s forward starboard side as the *Trent* silently pushed inwards. But then the overwhelming inertia of the *Hindenburg* started to tell. The bow was still turning, even under the impact of the cruiser. While the German ship remained upright, the much lighter British ship, now with its bows caught, was being pushed steadily to one side as the *Hindenburg* continued the turn. Unable to break free, the *Trent* began to lean to starboard, the list developing quickly. Bach saw what was happening.

'Helm, keep the wheel over.'

Now the *Hindenburg* was starting to wrestle the other ship down. The stern of the *Trent*, free to move in the waves, was coming round to port quickly while the bow remained held firmly in place. The whole

British ship was not only being pushed over, but was now slewing round broadside on to the German. Still the huge battleship continued to press down on its flinching prey.

Now the *Trent* was coming round almost beam-on. Suddenly the huge stress forced its bow out of the gash; sheets of steel flew silently into the air and cables from one or other of the ships' bowels snaked up and around, flailing violently. The freed bow swung round even more under the onslaught of the battleship. Now it was the *Trent*'s turn to be pierced.

The sharp bow of the *Hindenburg*, damaged only on one side, was taller than the British ship and it drove cleanly into the exposed side of the *Trent*, just aft of the crumpled bow section, carving through the metal like a sharp knife.

The *Trent* heeled even more. The German ship began to rise, partly in response to the waves, partly in response the leaning mass of the *Trent*. It was like an icebreaker heaving itself over an ice floe.

Trent was stricken. Unable to rise, the point of equilibrium was reached and now it began to topple over of its own accord. The German ship continued to cut into the fresh steel which the capsizing cruiser presented to the blade of the bow. Now the whole bow section of the *Trent* was almost severed. Finally, with the British ship now on its side, the *Hindenburg* cut through the remaining plating. The bow fell away, and the sea began to pour into the mutilated corpse.

Hindenburg continued as though it had passed over a raft of seaweed.

Heine and the others watched from the port windows as the *Trent* continued its death roll. With a stately slowness, the ship gently rolled over, showing the red anti-fouling on its bottom, newly applied and bright as blood in the grey and green; the twin screws at the after end of the ship were still turning, throwing off spray. Then a slow roll back in the other direction started, but the ship was now completely capsized and would never rise.

'Helm, hold your turn and come around. Now, young Heine, what would you like to do? See, you've sunk your first ship. A great victory for the German Navy. You'll get a medal.' Bach was still smiling.

'Bach, you're mad. Stop this thing and pick up the survivors.'

'Forget it, Heine. There won't be any. Watch.'

The *Trent* was already sinking. The stern, upside down, was now twenty feet into the air and coming up rapidly. Filling with water from the severed bow, the ship was going down fast; it had capsized so quickly that none of the crew could possibly have escaped.

Within a minute, as Heine and the others watched, the stern of the British cruiser rose into the air, streaming water, where it paused for a moment, almost vertical, and then started to slip downwards, slowly at first and then with gathering speed. As it vanished finally beneath the heaving sea, a puff of spray rose high into the air, which soon blew away in the wind, and then there was nothing to mark the place where the *Trent* had been other than a scattering of debris that bobbed on the surface. Bach was right; there was no sign of survivors. Heine was suddenly keener than ever to get out of this place. It was like watching his own death.

Those on the bridge had watched in silence as the ship sank. Now, suddenly, Heine pulled himself back into action.

'It's all over. You officers, move to the back of the bridge and stay together. Vogele, search them.'

Bach, Schiller and the others shuffled back to join Moehle. Vogele nervously moved forward and checked each of the officers for guns, but found nothing.

'Now, listen. Here's what we're doing,' started Heine. 'First, you have a simple choice. You either follow my orders without hesitation or you get locked away for the voyage. Schiller here has introduced me to a nice little place, haven't you, Schiller? Everyone understand?'

Bach spoke immediately. 'It rather depends on what your orders are,' he said.

'That's the easy bit, Bach. I want you to turn this ship round and take us back to Germany. Fast as you can. Once we're near the coast, we take a small boat and we get off. You can sail this thing back in and we'll leave you alone. That way we all survive. Me. These kids here. You as well. That's all we want. We sure as hell aren't going any further.'

Schiller, Bruller and the rest of them looked at Heine with something of a sense of relief. They weren't going to say anything, not in front of Bach, but it was exactly what they themselves wanted to do. And now with Heine holding a gun at the captain's head, the old man surely had no choice.

They waited silently, wanting to see what Bach would do now. But his obstinate sense of duty, which had brought them this far, was now replaced by a bitter sense of betrayal. Sluys had not only sent him on a false mission, but had lied to him. And on top of that, he had taken his family as hostage.

The bottles in Bach's cabin were empty now. There were just a few mouthfuls left in the flask, hidden away down below. God in heaven, he said to himself, I could do with a drink right now. His nerves were ragged enough without all this happening. Bach's emotions now seesawed violently between bitterness, anger and determination.

That was why Heine's mutiny struck him as so funny. Once he had learned about the real nature of his voyage, he would have abandoned it, just as Heine wanted him to do. And now he had to continue, whatever he felt. The voyage had to be completed. The gold must be delivered. It was as simple as that. Much as Bach now agreed with what Heine wanted to achieve, there was no possibility of giving in to him. Had he struck just a day before, he would probably have shaken Heine by the hand. This would at least have saved him from the shame of turning round on his own orders. Heine was too late.

And now Bach would have to lie in order to gain some time. He had seen men close to mutiny before. They were hot-headed; tempers flared. Once they had time to cool down, they would start to feel foolish and want to get back to normal. In the meantime, Bach needed to keep his ship headed towards its destination.

'Heine, it's not that simple,' said Bach eventually. 'You clearly do not understand these things. Let me explain. First, Hitler is dead. I see you didn't know this? We had news of it just now. Donitz has taken over. This means that Berlin is about to fall. If we sail back, the only port we can enter is Hamburg, which is certainly in the hands of the Russians. We'll all get caught, Heine. You might escape, but we won't. We're all German officers and they will probably murder us on sight. There is nothing you can do to us that the Russians won't. Frankly, I'd rather be shot by you, out here, than get tortured by those barbarians.'

'So? We don't go to Hamburg, then. Somewhere in France would be fine. The Allies won't be so bad.'

'Come on, Heine. The French don't like us much. What chance would we stand there? And come to think of it, how far do you think you would get, speaking German? Sorry, Heine, that won't work either.'

'Well, maybe I'll just fucking shoot you here and now and get on with it myself.' Heine was getting angry with Bach's explanation, the more so because he saw that the captain was telling the truth. This would not be as easy as he imagined.

'Heine, you *can't* get back to Europe anyway,' interjected Moehle, with an exasperated note in his voice. 'There isn't the fuel. This was a one-way trip, remember?'

It was the final straw. Unarguable. And no less infuriating for being true. 'Fuck you. So where's the nearest land? You, Bruller, you're supposed to be the fucking navigator. Get a chart and show me where we are.'

Bruller shrugged and went to the navigation table for the big chart.

The position of the ship was marked with a pencil circle. 'That's us, here. Nearest I can get it.' The chart showed the northern half of the Atlantic Ocean, Newfoundland at the bottom left-hand corner and the British Isles at the bottom right. A pencil line, in short sections drawn at different times, traced the progress of the ship over the tip of Scotland, north to the ice cap, then west, suddenly heading due south until it terminated in Bruller's circle.

Heine was no navigator but he could read a map. From Bruller's position to the coast of America – or, more correctly, the eastern tip of Newfoundland – was about 900 miles off: just under three days' steaming for the *Hindenburg*. It was another day's steaming, or more, to reach America proper.

'Heine, we *have* to go on,' said Bach. 'We cannot turn. There is no nearer land than America. We can make our way to the coast; there we can surrender. I promise you, no fighting. We will give up the ship to the authorities and we can all live. There. You have my word.'

Heine was not the only one to look surprised at Bach's sudden change of heart. Schiller and the others seemed equally astonished.

But there had to be a catch. Heine was too cynical to believe that someone like Bach would give up so suddenly. What was his plan? Why would he want to go to America? What would be the effect of this huge battleship turning up on the doorstep of people who had been bombing shit out of his homeland for the last few years? How would they treat Heine and his mutineers? It didn't make any sense to him. They would arrest everyone. Frankly, he knew that while the officers might get away with it, he would not. He didn't trust Bach. He didn't trust the Americans; he had not gone through all this just to end up in some American prison for the next ten years. He had seen the films. American prisons were not nice places; American prisoners were not nice people.

But where else? If he had fuel for only three or four days' steaming, it must be somewhere about the same distance away. He looked at the chart. Nothing to the south. Iceland was just within reach, but it was full of Americans and British. Canada had the same problem, and as far as Heine was concerned it was just another part of America anyway.

There was only one other land mass within reach. Greenland, and the ice.

It was remote, deserted. Nobody could trace them there. Heine had never been to Greenland, but he knew enough to be aware that of all the places on earth, it was just about the only one where he would be able to conceal a ship of *Hindenburg*'s size for months, even years, maybe for ever. If he could get the ship there and dump it, then make good his escape, the rest of the world would assume that the battleship had gone to a watery grave. Which meant that nobody would be looking for Heine. Quite how he would make his way home was another question. But then, why home?

If it was true that Hamburg was now full of Russians, he had no real desire to return. On the other hand, if he could make his way secretly to somewhere like America, given a chance to make a new identity for himself, he would be home and free. He couldn't do it by turning up on this ship; but he could manage it if he sneaked in unnoticed. It was the kind of thing that Otto Heine knew he could do easily. He had got away with far worse in the docks of Hamburg. America would be easy. Of course, he didn't know a word of English; he would simply have to learn. How difficult could it be? He would have to take the chance.

'How far to *here*?' he asked Bruller, jabbing his finger at Greenland.

Bruller measured off the distance with a pair of brass dividers. '860 miles,' he replied.

'That's where we're going. Head for it.'

'Greenland?'

'That's the place.'

Captain Erich Bach could see that this was not going to be easy.

*

Schnee had watched the sinking of the *Trent* with huge satisfaction. He had secured himself on the first landing of the bridge ladder by wedging himself against the guard rails in order to better follow the action. His fuddled mind was slowly clearing. As the ship upended itself and disappeared beneath the waves, Schnee pulled himself to his feet and cheered loudly, only to discover that his face felt as though it was covered in dry concrete and if he moved too quickly stabbing lances of pain shot through his head. He stopped cheering.

There was still nobody about. The deck was strangely quiet. Schnee decided to carry on up to the bridge to see what was happening. Those lazy bastard officers were staying out of the wind and the rain, keeping themselves warm and comfortable as usual. He still found walking difficult, and now the morphine was wearing off the pain grew, and his head jarred with each step. But Schnee wanted to find out what was happening.

He pulled himself to the top step. Now he was higher up, on the same level as the bridge. He moved down towards the bridge door. He was intending to walk straight in, but some sense of caution made him stop and look inside.

*

The officers looked at Heine with some surprise. Not all of them thought Greenland such a bad idea. Schiller could certainly see the benefits; so could Bruller. Neither of them wanted to take the ship to America. Like Heine, they foresaw nothing but imprisonment; if Hitler was dead, there was no real chance that the original rescue by submarine would take place. And they knew that the fuel would not allow them to get back to Europe. Heine's idea was not such a bad one. They had small boats, they had supplies, they even had winter clothing in the storerooms. They could survive a week or two in the northern latitudes, more than enough to return to civilisation. And Schiller spoke good English, too. He would make his way to Canada.

But Bach could have none of it. Heine must be stopped.

'Bruller, how do we get to Greenland?' asked Heine.

Bruller was standing behind Bach. The navigation officer waited a second and then turned to the chart table at the back of the bridge, getting ready to work out a new course for Heine.

'Do no such thing, Bruller,' ordered Bach. The smile had gone now. Bruller stopped and watched.

'Bruller, get on with it,' said Heine, calmly and softly. At least Bach was behaving now as he had imagined he would.

'Captain?' asked Bruller uncertainly, still unable to shake off the ties of authority.

'Bruller, you are still under my orders. This ship is not going to Greenland, mutiny or not. Not while I'm the captain. You'll have to kill me first, Heine.' Bach knew the sailor's mind, he told himself. Always complaining. Always upset. Always mumbling about not putting up with this or that. It was natural. The order of things. But deep down, they respected … no, they *craved* authority and leadership. Every now and then a Heine would appear, but firmness was all that was needed. Once people like Heine realised that you would not be pushed around, they would give way. Now was the time for Bach to reassert his authority. And now he had every reason to do it too. Heine would back down, he was sure of it.

Heine looked at Bach. The man was confident, with an air of assured authority that came from years of command. He was the sort of man whom Heine had had trouble with ever since his days at school, when he was confronted by an overbearing master and had decided not to submit. In truth, Heine was equally confident, perhaps more so. And he found it impossible to accept authority, especially from men like Bach, even if the captain did seem more likeable than he should have been. And there was no way that Heine was going to America, not after all this.

Heine and Bach stood facing each other. In the background, in the shadows of the bridge, the other officers watched silently. The tall, aristocratic Bach, uniformed and severe; wiry, scruffy Heine, with his torn clothes, unshaven chin and a good six inches shorter than the captain. Who was going to win?

'Well, Captain Bach. I'm certainly not going to kill you,' said Heine finally. 'Schiller, come over here.'

Schiller slowly walked to where Heine and Bach were standing.

'Schiller, take my gun.' Heine held out the automatic, butt first. Schiller, mystified, took it. Heine turned round and took a sub-machine gun from one of the youngsters. He pulled the bolt back and flipped off the safety-catch.

'Now, Schiller, there's Captain Bach who wants to take us all to our deaths. I want you to point your gun at his feet. When I give the order, shoot one foot and then the other. I'll count to three. If you haven't opened fire by then, I'll shoot your friends at the back of the bridge. Then I'll shoot you. I won't kill any of you. I'll just shoot your legs. None of you will walk again. And if you don't believe me . . .' and still looking at Schiller he suddenly pressed the trigger of the gun. With an ear-splitting crackle the gun fired off six or seven rounds in a brief burst. The bullets smashed into the wooden deck of the bridge. Dust, splinters and smoke from the gun flew into the confined space.

'Jesus,' breathed Schiller. 'For God's sake . . .'

'Shut up, Schiller. You locked me in the fucking cell.

I would just love to blow your face away. Give me a chance, *please.*' Heine's face was impassive but there was a dangerous, cold look in his eyes.

Hesitantly, Schiller lifted the gun.

'Come on, come on,' shouted Heine, and he re-cocked the machine gun and brought it to aim at the legs of the officers. Speed was everything. They must have no time to think, no time to react. No time for heroics. Heine had done this sort of thing before. Keep the pressure up, look serious. They always broke in the end.

'So, Schiller, you have exactly three seconds. Bach? You understand? In three seconds' time you'll be responsible for all your officers being mutilated.'

Bach looked impassively at Heine.

'One ...' and Heine loosed another burst of gunfire into the floor that made everyone, even Bach, jump visibly. He pulled back the cocking mechanism.

'Two ...' and he let rip with another burst, this time into the back of the bridge where books and manuals were kept on shelves; the paper was shredded and flew into the air like confetti. Bruller and Moehle were now cowering, half-kneeling. Schiller had gone pale and his eyes were wide.

Heine pulled out the magazine of the sub-machine gun, almost spent. He dropped it on the floor and held out his hand without taking his eyes off Schiller. One of the sailors, fascinated, immediately passed a new magazine to Heine, who slowly and carefully loaded it. He drove it home with a metallic crack, then started to pull back the cocking lever.

'For God's sake ...' shouted Bruller. Heine raised his eyebrows and brought the gun up.

A million thoughts flashed through Bach's mind. He could not let this young fool divert them. Sluys's blackmail had ensured that, whatever his feelings, he had to see the voyage through. He had thought that he could cow the youngster; but he could see now that Heine was made of something that he had not expected. He was as stubborn and determined as Bach himself. Even if the lad was just doing this for show, it was bloody well working – even Bach had to admit that. The kid really seemed serious. Bach had to buy some time, make a bit of space. Maybe the boy could be reasoned with … not now, but later. Let him calm down. Appear to give him his head. Then? He would simply have to be let into the secret, the gold and all. Maybe he could be bought off?

'Heine, very well, very well,' said Bach softly, with a note of resignation in his voice. As if in some kind of ritual of surrender, the captain slowly took off his cap and held it under his arm.

Heine breathed again, but hoped nobody noticed as he tried to calm his thumping heart. 'See. Not difficult, is it? Now, Captain, if you would care …'

Suddenly the bridge door was flung open. Schnee launched himself through it, rage on his battered face. He grabbed one of the young sailors and pulled the rifle from his hands.

'Heine, you fucking little shit, I'll fucking cripple you …' and he pushed the other surprised sailors out of his way. He was heading for Heine and starting to level the rifle. Heine's crew began to melt away in the face of this screaming, bandaged monster.

For all his bravado, Otto Heine had never shot a man. His combination of charm and aggression had never made it necessary. He'd hit a few – some, like Schnee, with as much force as he could muster. And he'd held many guns. But now he had half a second to open fire before Schnee could get as many bullets into him as he could manage.

Heine's world slowed down. There was only one person in it, and that was the gibbering, red-faced, shaking figure of Schnee, fumbling with the safety-catch on the rifle. The man's actions seemed ponderous and heavy. Heine knew what he had to do. The magazine on his sub-machine gun was full and the cocking lever already pulled back. Heine brought the stubby gun up to his chest and pointed it at Schnee as he closed his finger around the trigger.

Schnee, still in slow motion, was bringing the rifle up to his shoulder. His damaged face made it difficult to aim, but his rage was so strong that he was past caring.

Then Heine pulled the trigger and kept it held back. The spring, tensioned by the cocking lever, drove the mechanism that pulled the cartridge into the breech, fired it, pushed out the spent case and pulled in the next one, repeating the action four times each second. The magazine held twenty-four rounds and, to Heine, the gun fired each round so slowly that he had the time to move the gun up and down, and from side to side, describing a small circle covering the man's chest.

The bullets punched into Schnee, each one splashing a small red puff as it struck home.

Schnee was pushed back each time a bullet struck, but he either didn't feel it or didn't care. He stayed upright, trying to aim the rifle, but the bullets kept knocking him back. After the sixth bullet, he began to lose control of his legs and started slowly to kneel. But he still kept trying to aim the rifle.

Heine kept his finger firmly on the trigger, and the gun kept spitting at Schnee.

Schnee was now looking confused. His legs then gave way completely and he slumped on to the floor like a schoolchild, staring stupidly up at Heine with a puzzled expression. Now he let the rifle drop and decided he needed an arm to hold himself upright. But that arm wouldn't move and he slid sideways to the floor.

Heine kept the trigger pulled, but the gun stopped. The magazine was empty. The bridge was misty with the smoke. Schnee rolled over on to his stomach. He made no sound. One arm reached out for something, but stopped; his plump body then gave a short shiver. There was a sudden foul smell in the air; Schnee's bowels had emptied themselves. A dozen small rivers of dark red blood began to crawl from beneath the still figure, creeping steadily across the chipped wooden decking.

Heine was now aware of the others on the bridge. They were all looking at him with a mixture of fear and horror.

He felt a sudden coldness sweep over him and a damp flush of perspiration prickled his back and face. The gun felt heavy.

'You – Bruller – check him.'

Bruller hesitantly moved over to the body and knelt beside it, carefully avoiding the blood on the deck. He put out a hand and touched Schnee's back to see if there was any sign of the man breathing. Having left it for a few seconds, he then moved his hand up to Schnee's fat neck. He touched the side of the neck, then pressed hard through the folded flesh to feel for a pulse. There was nothing. He didn't want to touch him any more and stood up, saying nothing, and walked back to the captain.

'Vogele, get a party together. Shift the body off the bridge. Clean this up,' ordered Heine in the awkward silence. The youngster, who had been pushed aside as Schnee burst in on the bridge, nervously turned round to find some others to delegate the task to. He picked six of his party and they shuffled forward.

Heine watched them for a few moments; then he suddenly propped the gun against a bulkhead and turned quickly. Without a word he walked from the bridge door on to the wing, looking out across the open bow of the ship. He felt faint. Seeing the rolling sea, he felt worse. But the wind was still blowing and the cold air suddenly brought him round again. He gripped the handrail and looked out, and took several deep breaths. He hoped nobody could see him.

Shit, he thought. It wasn't killing Schnee that worried him. It was killing anybody at all.

Then his fingers, then his arms, and then the whole of his body started to shiver. It was completely uncontrollable, as though he was being given an electric shock. He gripped the handrail even more tightly, but the shaking continued. Then the light-headed feeling started to come back. His head began to swim. Oh God, let me die quickly.

With no warning, his stomach suddenly contracted and he threw up violently.

He had not eaten since before his enforced stay in the cell at the bow of the ship, and there was nothing to come up except for a thick green bile that burned the back of his throat. He retched again, doubling over and gasping for air between the spasms that gripped him. And then again. Finally his stomach seemed to relax and he paused for air, wiping away snot and tears and dribble from his face on the back of his filthy sleeve.

When he looked out across the bow once more, the ship had stopped in the water and the green waves were now coming on them from the stern. All Heine could see was the backs of the seas as they marched steadily past them and onwards towards the horizon. It felt as if the ship was moving backwards.

He shook his head, as much to clear it as to express his disgust at the situation he found himself in. Straightening up, he wiped his mouth once more, and then marched back on to the bridge where a sudden silence greeted him.

Bach looked at him. 'Feeling better, I trust?'

Heine scowled at the captain. Bach managed to maintain an effortless air of superiority that irritated him. In spite of himself, Heine started to feel small and foolish, like a schoolboy. He fought back the feeling.

'Much, thank you. The show's over. Now, set a course for Greenland and get this ship under way. All officers get below. Vogele, see them down and lock them up. Get on with it.'

The men on the bridge paused, then started to move, obeying the orders. Bach was the last to leave and turned to look at Heine as he was hustled out of the bridge by Vogele. Heine didn't see him. He was standing at the front of the bridge, looking out across the empty sea.

Captain Otto Heine now had command of his first ship.

14

The wind had dropped to a fitful northerly breeze, but the skies remained grey and low and the big seas still rolled steadily onwards, now smoothed to glassy undulations on the ocean, uncoloured by foam and spray. The *Hindenburg* had settled to a course a little west of north, and the westerly set of the seas rocked the huge ship gently from side to side in a regular movement like a pendulum.

For an hour, perhaps longer, complete silence reigned on the bridge after Schnee's body had been removed and one of the sailors had mopped up the blood with several buckets of water that turned bright red. The damp stain on the wooden planking marked the spot like a gravestone. Everyone tried to ignore it, and nobody would tread on it. They stepped over it, or round it, but never on it. Not even Heine. Now there was just Heine on the bridge, together with the helmsman, and Vogele standing quietly at the back.

Vogele had returned from escorting the officers to their prison down on the main deck. Bach had followed meekly enough, but his mind was seething as Vogele closed the steel door behind him and his men. He knew he had to do something quickly, before the ship got too far and used so much fuel that it would be impossible to make landfall in America. Every hour took them further and further away.

Force was no longer a possibility. Bach and the ship were now entirely in Heine's hands. But Bach had watched Heine in action. He was a strange character. The boy had guts, that was for sure; he was bright, too. If he had been born of a better family and gone to a better school, he would have been excellent officer material – the sort of man the Navy needed. I could have made something of him, thought Bach.

Schiller and the others remained quiet. As far as most of them were concerned, this was not such a bad deal. They would rather not be locked up, but at least it meant that Bach's demented, inflexible determination to reach America was finally overcome. They had a chance of escaping alive.

But Moehle quietly sidled up to Bach.

'You have to do something, Captain,' whispered the younger man.

Bach felt like shouting at him, but he kept his voice down. 'Thank you, Moehle. You have any suggestions?'

'The gold. Tell him about the gold. Tell him he can have some of it. He's just a petty crook; he won't be able to resist it,' Moehle murmured close to the captain's ear.

Bach knew he was right, that it was the only chance they had. He had to speak to Heine, make him see sense, before it was too late. Now the other officers were out of the way, he could have a proper talk with the lad away from the accusing stares of Schiller and the others. All he needed to do was to get out of this place.

They were locked in a small compartment at the front of the ship, on the main deck. It was designed as a storeroom and had no windows, just a steel door latched from the outside.

Surely they must have posted a guard, thought Bach. One of the sailors, one of the younger ones, would be given the duty.

Bach looked around. There was a galvanised steel bucket in a corner, strongly made to *Kriegsmarine* specifications. He picked it up without warning and swung it violently against the inside of the door. Schiller and the others stood back in alarm. What in the name of God was this madman up to now?

Bach swung the bucket again and again, keeping up a beating on the door that was deafening to everyone inside. Schiller was moving forward, getting ready to restrain the captain, when Bach's efforts were rewarded. With a squeal the latches were lifted and the door was opened, just six inches. The barrel of a rifle was poked through.

'What's going on in there?' asked a nervous young voice.

'What's your name?' demanded Bach, shouting through the narrow gap, his voice ringing with years of authority.

'Lempe. Now what's going on? What's the noise all about?'

'Lempe, you address me as "sir". I am the captain of this ship and don't you dare forget it.'

'Yes, sir. But you are making a noise.'

'Of course I'm making a noise, Lempe. We've been in here for two hours, and we have not had a bite to eat or anything to drink. Listen to me, Lempe. You get Vogele or Heine and tell them from me that we want food and drink and quickly. Got that? At the double, lad, at the double.'

'Yes, sir. But I'm supposed to stay here. I'm not allowed to move.'

'Lempe, I gave you an order. Are you disobeying my order?'

'Well, not really, but Heine is supposed to be in charge now. I mean, I was told to stay ...' His voice tailed off, not knowing quite what to do.

Bach grabbed the edge of the door and pulled it hard. Lempe held on, but the gap widened until the captain and the young rating were looking at each other.

'Lempe, listen to me. I am Captain Erich Bach and I am giving you a direct order. Get someone here within the next thirty seconds, or by God you'll wish you'd never been born. I won't give you another chance, lad.'

Lempe backed away as Bach hissed his threat through the gap. He pulled the door closed, latched it, put down his rifle and ran.

Breathlessly he burst on to the silent bridge. 'Sir, it's the captain. He's sent me.'

Heine turned, even though Lempe was talking to Vogele. 'What's the problem? You're supposed to be guarding them.'

'I know, but he insisted. Wanted to see someone.'

'Tell him to shut up. I'm in charge of this ship.'

'I know, but can you tell him?' pleaded the lad, terrified of having to face the wrath of the captain alone, even if he was locked up.

Heine swore and followed Lempe off the bridge, down the several flights of ladders and back a short way along the main deck to the doorway. He banged on the door with his fist. 'Bach?'

Silence.

'Bach? *Bach*?' he shouted again. There was no reply.

'Lempe, give me that gun. Go off and fetch some of the lads, make sure they're armed and get them back here at the double.'

Lempe handed over the gun and raced off, delighted to be out of the way. Heine shoved up the top and then the bottom latch, and hauled open the rusting door, keeping the rifle at his hip and his finger on the trigger.

It was pitch black inside. They had turned out the lights.

'Bach, this is a pretty obvious trick. You don't really expect me to fall for it, do you?'

Suddenly Bach appeared in the gloom. 'No, Heine. It's not a trick. I need to see you.'

'You can see me. Here I am.'

'I need to see you and talk to you. There are things you should know,' and Bach was dropping his voice as he came closer.

Heine pointed the gun directly at him. 'Tell me.'

'Not here. In private.'

'Fuck off, Bach.'

'On my own. I'm not armed. I'll come out.'

Heine looked at the captain. He sounded serious. Lempe and his boys would arrive soon enough, and Bach wasn't armed; he could do no harm. 'OK. Hands on your head. Come out slowly.'

Bach carefully placed his hands on his head and walked forward, out over the sill of the hatchway and into the grey Atlantic daylight.

Heine quickly closed the door behind him, keeping the rifle trained. 'Well?' he asked, as he pushed the bottom latch into place.

'At least do me the courtesy of taking me somewhere private, Heine.'

Heine shrugged. 'Come on, then. Your cabin. Your *old* cabin, that is. Lead the way.'

Bach marched stiffly along the deck, followed by Heine, turning into the centre of the ship and down companionways and ladders until they reached Bach's cabin. They went inside and Heine shut the door. He leaned himself against it, the rifle still in his hands.

'May I sit?' asked Bach.

'Do what the hell you want, Bach. What's this all about?'

'Very well,' said Bach, sitting anyway. 'Before you set off for Greenland, I thought you should at least know the real purpose of this voyage.'

'I know the real purpose of this voyage.'

'You think you do, but you don't. You don't know, for example, about what's stored in the forward magazine, I take it?'

Heine didn't. He looked at Bach. 'What are you talking about?'

'And you don't know what is going to happen when we get to America. Or should I now say, *if* we get to America. And we're certainly not talking about shelling Washington, Heine.'

'Bach, what the fuck are you talking about?'

'Heine, this ship has a special mission. Loaded in dummy shells in the forward magazine is over ten million dollars' worth of gold, fresh from the Reichsbank – or what is now left of it. There's enough gold on this ship, Heine, to make millionaires of everyone on board.'

'Bullshit.'

'Suit yourself, Heine. You want to see it?'

'Why on earth would we be carrying this gold, Bach?'

'Because I was taken for an idiot, Heine, that's why. I was asked to command this ship on its last voyage to shell Washington. Something that was for the good of the Fatherland, something that was honourable even if it was bloody suicide. Then I found out a day ago what the real job was.'

'And?'

'Admiral Sluys and a bunch of his friends have already fled Berlin. You don't know Sluys? My boss, Heine, or one of them. Spent the war sitting in Berlin telling people like me what to do. They had the gold loaded on this ship, without my knowledge. The plan was for me to arrive off the coast of America, where I was supposed to surrender to the authorities and tell them about the gold. Sluys by this time is in the hands of the Allies; he does a deal with them to save his skin.'

'And why on earth didn't he tell you?'

'Don't be stupid, Heine. Do I look as though I would sail across the ocean with a load of gold to surrender to the Americans? They had to keep me in the dark until it was too late. They sent Moehle along.'

'Moehle?'

'He's one of them, Heine; he knows all about it. He was sent to keep an eye on me, just in case I decided it was a bad idea.'

'I can see their point, Bach.'

'I shall take that as a compliment.'

'Why choose to move it by sea? Why didn't Sluys just plan to hand it over when the Americans turn up?'

'Too much of it, Heine. We're talking about eight and three-quarter tons of the stuff, not a few boxes. Too risky. There's a war on, in case you hadn't noticed.'

'And this gold is still here?'

'Down in the magazine, right now. There are twenty big shells on the bottom racks in Anton's magazine, and another dozen smaller ones, easier to carry in case something goes wrong. You can tell them because the cases are unmarked. The real shells all have part numbers stamped on them, near the nose. The gold was melted into the steel cases.'

'So? Sounds to me as if I've saved the lot of you.

Instead of handing it over to Sluys, we get to keep the stuff . . . if you're telling me the truth.'

'It's not that easy, Heine. For one thing, how the hell are you going to move that gold from bloody Greenland? You'll never shift it.'

'Just a bit of it would do me. I'll take the smaller ones.'

'And leave the rest of it here? It's worth a fortune, man. More money than you'll ever see in your life. You really want to go off with a tiny bit of what you could have? Think of what you've been through. It's your chance, Heine, and your only one. Sorry, but the only way you'll get to see *real* money is if you go through with the original plan. Sail to America and surrender.'

'No problem. We hand ourselves over to the Yankees and you're a fucking hero, and what about me? Don't be ridiculous.'

'For God's sake, Heine. I'll look after you. Work with me on this and I'll make sure you're protected. I'll make sure you get a good share of the gold and you can disappear quietly, start a new life. You won't get a better opportunity, you know that.'

Heine paused for a moment, perhaps thinking over Bach's offer. 'You really believe it's that simple?'

'Of course. The whole thing is arranged.'

'Listen, Bach, let me tell you something. You and I, we come from different planets. Where you live, good things happen. People have happy lives. They get on with their parents; they go to good jobs, earn money, settle down, have nice kids. Money is always available. I mean, even if you haven't got any yourself, you can borrow from your parents or from your aunt or uncle; and if you go along to a bank – they look at you, nice accent, nice clothes, good background. Take the cash, pay me back sometime. Even the fucking sun shines when you go on holiday. Now let me tell you about my world, Bach. You live in a house that's so cold in the winter that it freezes up indoors. Your folks are always shouting at each other. If your dad's got a day's work at the docks for a few marks he goes out drinking, comes home late and beats up your ma. You don't eat every day, Bach. You go to school, where they beat shit out of you and you can't wait to quit. Money is something you steal. You never get it otherwise, because there are no jobs for kids like you. If you don't want to starve, you steal. So then everyone chases you. You get arrested, you get jailed a few times, you get out. The fucking Navy is always trying to haul you in. Then the fucking war starts. You people are out there having a good time. I'm left in the rubble trying to make a living. Different worlds, you see that? Sorry, Bach. The moment I set foot in America I'm the sort of the person that they'll arrest and throw into Alcatraz for the next hundred years. That's what happens to people like me. People like you, Bach, probably get a fucking medal.'

It was Bach's turn to be silent. Other than giving them orders, he had no idea how the likes of Heine lived and died. He looked at the younger man. He was short, skinny, his clothes were torn and he was dirty. His accent, even his actions, the ways he moved his head and his hands, were rough and suspicious. Yes, Bach could see, Heine was perfectly right. The moment he set foot on the shores of America he would be a problem.

'Very well, Heine. I understand what you say. But listen to me. They have my wife and my child, Sluys and his people. As hostages. To make sure I arrive.'

'Jesus, Bach. You expect that to work on *me*, after everything you've done?'

'Perhaps. You are an intelligent man, Heine. You must have feelings.'

'Feelings? Oh no, Captain Bach. We have no feelings. That's why it's fine to starve us, to shoot us, to kidnap us off the streets and send us to a war that we had no part in starting and will have even less part in who-ever wins or loses. We're always the losers, Bach. We don't feel a damn thing.'

'I'm sorry. It was the wrong thing to say.'

Heine just shook his head.

'Well?' asked Bach, after a pause.

Heine thought for a moment. 'So, Captain Bach. Here's what I will do. The ship and the crew go to Greenland – with the gold. Look on it as compen-sation. You, Bach, if you don't want to come and take your chances with the rest of us, I'll give you a boat and you can make your own way. Take Moehle with you. I don't trust him, not now.'

'I cannot leave my ship.'

'Not *your* ship, Bach. Not now.'

'It's surrender.'

'It's your only fucking chance, Bach, is what it is. I'll give you a good boat, plenty of supplies. I'll even send out a distress message for you so you'll get picked up.'

'And when I get picked up? What happens if I tell them? About you and the gold?'

'Of course you will. But you won't know where I've gone, will you? Greenland is a big place. By the time they catch up, I'll have disappeared. Don't you worry about me, Bach. I'll be fine. I always am.'

'You can't do this, Heine.'

'I can and I will. You make your own way, Bach, same as I've had to do.'

Bach suddenly straightened up. 'Very well. If that's what you wish. I presume I may invite my other officers?'

'Take who you like. Get rid of the lot of them –
especially Schiller.'

'Thank you. May I go?'

'You may. I'll get things ready.'

Bach stood up, to attention. Heine opened the door
and let him march stiffly past, out into the companionway and up the ladders until they returned to the
main deck where the officers were being held. Bach
didn't once falter in his step, and didn't turn. He had
made up his mind. So had Heine.

*

Nearly a day had passed before they were ready. The
ship continued its steady northern progress and the
air had grown noticeably colder. Icebergs were coming into view. These were not floating cathedrals of
gleaming ice but low, slushy, grey monsters that rolled
around in the sea, barely showing themselves above
the swell until every now and then one turned over
like a lazy whale, showing its sea-eaten belly before
slumping back down into the water.

Under Heine's orders, they had started to get one of
the boats ready. It was a naval tender, a steel craft about
ten metres long with a large open deck behind high
gunwales and a small cabin at the stern. Powered by a
big diesel, it was designed to ferry men and equipment
to and from the dockside when the big ship was on
a swinging mooring. It was big enough to hold Bach's
officers and plenty of spare fuel. Vogele had already
begun the slow process of siphoning off jerrycans of
diesel oil from the large tanks at the bottom of the ship.
Several hundred litres of fuel would make little
difference to the tonnage carried on the *Hindenburg*.

The tender had a powerful engine but limited tank-
age, so Vogele was having to store the cans on the open

deck. Heine had no idea how much to give them; he simply ordered Vogele to stow as much as they had cans to hold. For some reason there seemed an endless supply of brand-new cans down in one of the store-rooms, and Vogele already had filled and stowed twenty of them.

They had found clothing, too. If they were going to stand any chance of surviving at all, they would need to keep warm. As for shelter, at a push all the officers could squeeze into the small cabin. What the hell, thought Heine: they didn't worry about putting me in that fucking cell a few days ago. It will do them no harm.

The clothing was standard-issue oilskins and wool-lens. Like the oil cans, there seemed to be an endless supply; they were loaded into the small cabin like bedding. Then came the food. There was nothing fresh, and hadn't been since they left Hamburg. It was all in tins, large ones, and was mostly fish stew. Nobody liked eating it but they had no choice, and as many as could be lashed on to the open deck were secured in place. And then another dozen jerrycans of water were wedged underneath part of the gunwales.

Once Vogele had finished, Heine went to inspect. The day was dying and it was starting to grow dark.

He arrived at the tender, slung high on the super-structure and movable only with the big crane that was nestled above it. He climbed the ladders and got on board the small boat. It looked comfortable enough to him. It was strongly built of good plating and the main deck, although wooden, was as thick as railway sleepers. It was built to take hard work and ought to stand up to a few days on the open sea.

He went inside the cabin. It consisted of a wheel-house and a small area below, equipped with some hard wooden benches covered with oilskins – slashes of bright yellow in the gloom. Underneath the cabin area was the single engine.

'Have you tried it?' asked Heine.

'Yes. It works OK. Bit smoky, but I got one of the engine-room lot up to take a look. He says it's fine. Nothing to worry about.'

'I wasn't worrying,' laughed Heine, but it wasn't true. He couldn't help himself. Much as he felt a deep anger about Bach's patronising offer, and much as he would like to pay Schiller back, Otto Heine was not really the sort of person to send Bach and his men to their deaths. He wanted to make sure they stood a good chance . . . but not too good.

'Is there a radio?'

Vogele showed him the VHF radio set, used for short-range communication between the tender and the ship. It was a large grey cabinet, mounted on big bolts to the side of the wheelhouse. Heine knew nothing about radios, including the fact that this set had an effective range of no more than a dozen miles and it would be useless for broadcasting a rescue message.

'Get it out of here. Sling it overboard.'

He left Vogele to remove the set and made his way back to where the officers were being held. He ordered the sentry, Lempe, to open the door.

'Bach?'

'Yes.'

'Very well. We are ready for you. Follow me.'

Bach started forward, but nobody else moved. The officers shuffled. Then came a voice from the back. 'Hold on, Heine, hold on. We don't all want to go.' It was Schiller.

Bach looked at Schiller with surprise for a second, and then with outright contempt. This was the first time that Schiller had said a word to him.

'What do you mean?' asked Heine.

'What I mean is that we don't all want to go with Bach. I'm on your side, Heine. I'll help you get to Greenland. I've had enough of this madman and I'm certainly not going to America.'

'Schiller, you are a fool and a traitor. Heine, he speaks just for himself,' spat Bach.

'Well?' asked Heine of the others. 'Bruller?'

Bruller, the navigation officer, looked sheepish. 'I don't want to go with Bach, Heine,' he replied quietly.

'And the rest of you?'

Ecke, the engineering officer, still in overalls, was next. 'I will stay with the ship. I will not go with Bach.'

'Nor will I,' said Jensch, the communications officer.

'And neither will I,' added Kinzel, who had been in charge of the artillery.

Moehle, the youngest of the officers, walked over to stand next to Bach and then turned to face the others. 'Fools, all of you! You will die on the ice. You cannot desert the ship.' He was desperate now; it was his last chance to salvage the voyage and perhaps his own life. He turned to Heine. 'Listen, Heine, you'll kill everyone. You cannot survive. Let's sort this out. You have a good point. We'll help you sail this thing to America and then we'll make sure you go free. I guarantee it.'

'That's good of you, Moehle,' replied Heine.

'You'll stop all this nonsense?'

'Moehle, do I look like an idiot? I know what this ship is meant to do. Bach's told me everything. Now, Moehle, you don't get the choice. You go with Bach.'

Moehle came closer to Heine and he dropped his voice so that the others couldn't hear him. 'Listen, Heine, I'll do a deal. If you know what's really on this ship, you get a share. A big one. I'll see to it.'

'Moehle, you'll see to nothing. We'll never get there. You're out of your mind.'

Moehle looked at Heine, whose face was calm and impassive.

'Fuck you, Heine. Rot in hell!'

'You'll be there before me, Moehle. Now get in that fucking boat.'

Moehle turned away.

'Looks as if you and Moehle are on your own,' said Heine to Bach, but he found himself slightly disgusted with the officers and certainly didn't trust them. 'All of you, out. Lempe will lead the way.'

With a nervous-looking Lempe in front, the party filed out with Heine covering them from the rear, and they all walked steadily down the deck to where the tender was slung out above them.

'Well, Schiller, we've got to launch this thing. You can sort it,' ordered Heine.

Happy to serve his new master, Schiller clambered up to the crane. There was an intercom handset, and he called the bridge to order the ship to stop engines and come around, so that the bulk of the *Hindenburg* created a lee, a pool of calm water into which the tender could be launched. With the help of Ecke they started the crane and positioned the hook above the wooden cradle that held the tender in place.

Bach stood on the main deck watching the actions of his traitorous officers. His hands were clasped behind his back. Only Moehle stood with him, a sour look on his face.

There was a huge groan and the tender was lifted clear of its seating, still in its wooden cradle. The boat quivered now it was free of the restraints. The crane jib started to lift and the tender moved slowly upwards.

Once clear of obstructions, the jib slowly began to

swing outwards, carrying the tender over the main deck and then out over the gunwales. There it stopped, hanging out over the sea. It gave a shake and then started a slow progress downwards. Two groups of sailors had caught hold of restraining lines, one attached to the bow and the other to the stern, to stop the boat swinging around. Steadily the tender dropped down until it was level with the main deck, still hanging out over the water.

The darkness was deepening quickly now. One of the crew switched on the deck lights, and someone up on the superstructure turned on a small searchlight. A brilliant pool of yellow light suddenly illuminated the tender, swinging slowly over the dark ocean.

Another party of crewmen was busy getting scrambling nets into place – heavy rolls of rope netting manageable only by five or six men, which had to be secured to cleats on the deck and then heaved over the side where they lazily unrolled down to the sea, hitting the water with a damp splash. They were meant as a rescue device, to help survivors in the water climb up the sheer sides of the big ship. But Heine had decided that Bach should use the nets. It would take too long to get the gangway rigged.

Once the nets were in place, Schiller slowly let the tender down to the water.

More crewmen made their way carefully down the nets. Once the tender's cradle touched the sea, the job was to float the tender off and then haul the cradle back up to the deck. The operation was slow. None of them had done it before and it took fifteen minutes before the tender was finally moored alongside, rising and falling in the gentle sheltered swell, and the cradle was disappearing upwards. Finally, as the sky was all but black, the tender was ready.

All the while Bach remained standing stiffly by the guard rail. His presence had disconcerted everybody. He simply stood and glared. Schiller had come down from his crane to watch the departure.

There was a tense, sullen atmosphere.

Heine walked up to the captain. 'Very well, Bach. On your way. And you, Moehle.'

'Heine, let me get something from my cabin. It's personal,' requested Bach.

'I'll get it for you,' replied Heine.

'No. I will get it. Do this for me as a last favour. You have condemned me, after all.'

'Very well. I'll come with you.'

Heine and Bach walked off into the gloom. In silence they made their way along the deck, through the doors, down the long companionway until they arrived at Bach's cabin. Heine followed as Bach opened the door.

'You are going to watch me, Heine?'

'I don't trust you. Sorry.'

'Suit yourself,' shrugged Bach. He had no shame, no pride any more. He went to his bunk and pulled out a leather case from underneath it. Then he produced a key from his pocket and opened the case. He fished out a silver flask, opened the cap and drank the contents. When he had finished, he threw the empty flask on to the bunk.

'Now you know. We all have weaknesses, Heine. My life is not quite so wonderful as you think it is, perhaps.'

'I had no idea.'

'I hoped not.' Bach's large ears had gone pink. He looked less strained now. 'I'm ready now, Heine. And thank you, at least, for that.'

In silence Bach led the way back, up on to the deck where everyone was waiting.

He didn't say another word but turned round to make his way down the net, followed by an equally silent Moehle. Bach's crew-cut head disappeared over the side of the ship.

'Schiller?' asked Heine, quietly.

'Yes?' replied the officer, eager to undertake whatever new task he was given.

'You too, Schiller.'

'Sorry?'

'You. On the boat. I don't want you on my ship.'

'Me? But I'm with you, Heine,' he said. There was a sudden note of pleading in his voice.

'Oh no, Schiller. You're not with me. Go and look after your captain. Do your fucking duty. Isn't that what you Navy people are always on about?'

Schiller made a sudden grab for Heine's rifle, held slackly. He seized the barrel and wrenched it away, spun it round and was pointing it at Otto Heine's head before he could do a thing about it. But almost as quickly, four of the sailors who had been watching levelled their guns at the back of Schiller's head.

'Look behind you, Schiller,' said Heine, in what he hoped was a relaxed voice.

But Schiller didn't need to look, he could feel the guns aimed at him. He lowered the rifle and laid it on the floor at Heine's feet. 'Fuck you, Heine,' he spat and then turned to make his way down the net.

'And fuck you too, Schiller,' called Heine after him.

The searchlight couldn't illuminate the boat, so close in under the sheer steel cliff of the ship. There was just enough light in the sky to see the shadowy figures make the jump from the net across the narrow finger of sea on to the wide deck of the smaller vessel.

Bach, Moehle and Schiller were finally off the *Hindenburg*.

'Let go the lines,' ordered Heine.

The two crewmen who had gone down the netting to secure the tender slipped the knots. In the gentle swell the tender stayed firmly alongside the mother ship, until there was the sound of the engine turning over and then firing up. The rattle of the small diesel floated up to the main deck. The engine was engaged and slowly the tender pulled away, stern first, until the bow was clear. The engine note changed again as 'Ahead' was selected, and the nose of the boat turned out and away into the darkness. Now the searchlight could pick them up, and the yellow glare surrounded Bach's new command.

*

It was Moehle who got into the cabin and started the engines and who finally pulled the craft away. Bach simply stood in the middle of the open deck, silent, with a strange look in his eyes.

It had finally come to this. He had joined the Navy when Germany was a great power, with a fleet to take on the world – the dream that had died at Scapa Flow with that unforgettable surrender. And then Adolf Hitler had arrived, hated by the armed forces and most of all by the Navy, a man they looked down on and whom they assumed they could easily control. It was in 1938 when Bach saw the strange little man in his raincoat and his hat alongside the venerable but hopelessly aged Hindenburg, namesake of the great ship. Then he realised where the real power lay. Like all his class and generation, he had assumed they would not go to war, least of all against England. But when war came it was duty that drove him. Not to Hitler, but to the traditions of the Navy. Now he had to fight, he would do so until he won. No more surrender – that was the key. Not after Scapa. Never, never again.

But even before his last orders were given to him in the bunker in Berlin, Bach's sense of duty was being strained, though he himself would not admit it. The war was clearly lost, his country was being turned into a ruin. Where was the duty in this? But he told himself he had to keep going. No surrender. Never again. He took on this last voyage because (he told himself) it might be hopeless but it was a sign that surrender could never be considered. Perhaps he even felt that there was something hopelessly noble about this final act. There was the sense of the Wagnerian twilight, a *Götterdämmerung*, that was a powerful part of Bach's background. If it was going to end, then it should end like this, with honour, with duty being done, even if it meant certain death. Not for Hitler; he was nothing to do with it. But for Germany.

He had forced the ship onwards, even when it was clear that the others didn't want to go – even when it was clear that the mission was insane. But Bach could not give up.

Even the news of Hitler's death didn't change his mind. That fool had broken Germany, and now it was left to the likes of Bach to rescue something from the wreckage.

Then Moehle had told him what the real voyage was. In those few simple words, Bach's whole complicated systems of values, of loyalty to the Navy and to the Fatherland – deeply held, not mere slogans – evaporated like smoke from a gun. Then his wife and his child, held as hostages by the man he had trusted. Was he the last man with any honour left?

He had tried to convince Heine to continue, but deep within himself Bach had realised that he didn't want to, not now that he knew he was nothing but a driver hired to deliver looted gold to the enemy.

He had no future, no wife, no country, no Navy. And, towering above him but receding slowly as the diesel rattled beneath his feet, was his last command, destined for God-knows-what final fate in the hands of a grubby street urchin from the docks of Hamburg in front of whom he had just been forced to reveal his last, deepest secret.

'Captain?' It was Schiller, calling to him from the wheelhouse. 'Captain?' called the voice again.

Bach had no interest in hearing the urgent voice. He stood in the middle of the deck. He had reached his decision. Slowly he unbuttoned his tunic, his long fingers unhooking the silver buttons one by one. He lifted one leg and tugged off one leather boot, then the other, and stood them neatly side by side. He shrugged off the tunic folded it neatly and laid it at his feet. Then he unbuttoned the trousers, removed the leather belt and stepped from them; they too were neatly folded and added to the pile. He was wearing grey woollen underclothes. He removed these, first the long-sleeved vest, then the long pants, and placed them carefully before him. Last of all were the thick black socks.

Erich Bach stood there, white and naked.

'Captain, what on earth are you doing?' It was Schiller again, shouting through the door of the wheelhouse.

But Bach showed no sign of hearing. Calmly he walked to the side of the boat furthest from the *Hindenburg* and then climbed up a short ladder. He stood for a second on top of the gunwale and then, making no sound that anyone could hear, he eased himself down into the dark water of the Atlantic Ocean, disappearing in moments in the darkness.

*

Otto Heine had turned away from watching the small craft when something inside him made him turn back again. The searchlight was just strong enough to illuminate the vessel with a weak yellow cast. As he turned, he saw Bach complete his undressing and climb to the gunwale. Heine knew what he was going to do. In a split second, Otto Heine finally understood Erich Bach. He watched the naked captain quietly slip over the side in his final moment of duty and honour.

'Fuck you, Bach,' murmured Heine as he turned away. The wind had gusted into his eyes and made them moist.

15

Greenland is not one but several large, rocky islands: the permanent cover of ice, in places over 1,000 feet thick, turns it into a single continent-sized slab with its southern tip just grazing the last dying eddies of the North Atlantic Drift and the northern coast buried deep beneath the polar ice-cap.

In the long winter, the ice covers not only all the land but much of the northern part of the surrounding sea as well. Even during the height of summer merely a narrow coastal strip thaws, and that only in the south.

The Vikings first made settlements on that coast, surviving the harsh winters through sealing and whaling. To this day, Greenland remains a dominion of its Scandinavian past, administered by Denmark. The population of Greenland – never more than a handful, either of Europeans or of Inuit on the western side nearest Canada – fluctuates with the weather. Around AD1000, when there was a brief warm spell, the Vikings arrived and stayed. By the 1500s, as a mini ice age meant that even the southern coastal strip remained barely above freezing by July, the population had dwindled to less than a couple of hundred brave souls. As the twentieth century approached, the population rose again. Settlers from Iceland and from Canada, reinforced by weather outposts, meant that by 1945 a few small settlements once more existed on the southern coasts, even during the winter. But in the far north, where the pack ice stayed all year round, the coasts were empty.

It was Bruller, the navigation officer, who explained to Otto Heine the possibilities offered by the Greenland coast for hiding away his huge ship.

The southern coast was rejected. It was too close to sea-going traffic, too near weather stations that belonged to the Allies, and not as ice-bound as Heine needed to conceal the ship. The eastern coast, stretching northwards, had plenty of hiding places, but then they would have a long and dangerous journey across the ice cap, or an even longer journey by sea, to get to the islands north of Canada which would eventually take them to safety.

But the western coast, facing the northern outposts of the American continent, offered Heine and his men the perfect place, or places. For mile after mile, the near-deserted coastline weaved in and out in an almost endless series of rocky bays, inlets and fjords. The geography was what had attracted the Vikings in the first place.

The sheer scale of this coastline was awesome. From the southern tip to only halfway up the western coast was a greater distance than the entire western seaboard of France, from Biarritz to Brest. And in all of that distance there were no more than a dozen small settlements, and most of those were concentrated in the relatively warmer southern latitudes.

It was late April, and the pack ice was still clinging to much of the northern part of the coastline, but it was already thinning and starting to break up. Only those parts closest in to the land were still solid; even a few hundreds yards offshore the glistening white sheet was already slushy and cracked, and the gentle ocean swells made it undulate like a slowly breathing giant sea creature.

On the chart they were using, the firm black line that denoted the coast ran out after a few hundred miles and turned into a pecked line.

'Unsurveyed,' replied Bruller to Heine's question. 'It was either hidden under pack ice when the surveyors arrived, or they never even got there. Same with the soundings, look.'

Most of the areas of sea were covered in tiny numerals, showing the depths of the water in various places. Even the deepest water was sounded. But where the pecked lines took the place of the coastline, the soundings were also missing, leaving the upper half of the chart virtually a blank.

But Bruller was enthusiastic. He had been in the Arctic before.

'My bet is that we can get quite a way up, Heine. This ship is made of solid armour plate. It's like an icebreaker. We just keep ploughing through, as far north as we like. The ice is melting and we should be able to go a long way.'

'How do we get rid of this thing?' asked Heine.

'Just scuttle the ship. Dump it. Look at all the inlets. Sure to be the same sort of coast further up. We run the ship into one of the inlets, open the seacocks and let it settle. Then we just walk off the thing and get away. Ship's left on the beach. The ice will cover it up in no time. Nobody will ever find it.'

'And how do we escape?'

'By boat. We'll have left an open channel behind us.

It won't freeze up, not at this time of year. We have enough boats to get away. We go south and make our way to the Canadian islands. Anywhere you like.'

Heine nodded silently. Yes, he thought, the plan would work. Except for the gold. How the hell was he going to transfer several tons of gold to some small boats and get it to civilisation? Without anyone else knowing?

*

Earlier, Heine had been down to the magazine under the forward turret. It was a circular room, almost the same size as the turret above, deep in the middle of the ship and surrounded by thick armour plate. The big shells rested in racks lining the sides of the room, as well as in the middle. They were stored upright like grey steel bottles, two deep, with steel straps holding them in place. In the nose of each shell was a lifting hook, screwed into the recess that would take the fuse when it was made ready for firing. A circular girder, bolted to the deckhead, created a track for an electric winch that would haul each shell out by the nose and deposit it on a set of rollers, still upright. The crew would slide the shell along the rollers on to a hydraulic lift and then close the armoured door, which acted as protection against the flash of the big guns. The shell would travel aloft to a shell-handling room, immediately below the turret, where the nose fitting would be replaced with the required type of fuse and then armed; next the shell would pass up into the turret itself, where the crew would load it.

There were three types of shell on board the ship. Each was clearly marked with part numbers and brief descriptions incised as small letters around the nose of the shell. The ordinary high-explosive type was designed to detonate on contact, like a bomb. Then there was an armour-piercing variety, with a reinforced case, and normally fitted with a delayed-action fuse that would detonate the shell a split-second after it penetrated the other ship's armour, exploding inside the vessel where it would do the most damage. Lastly there were a few shrapnel shells, designed to explode into thousands of small, sharp, deadly fragments. These would bring down distant aircraft or would decimate the crews of another vessel.

In addition to the big shells, the magazine also held ammunition for the other armaments. Steel boxes contained belts of machine-gun ammunition and wooden boxes held shells of other calibres, stacked away in neat piles and clearly marked.

On the bottom level of the main racking sat twenty ordinary-looking shells, but with no marking on them at all. Heine had touched the dull surface of one of them, wiping his finger through the thin film of oil that kept the steel from rusting. Was Bach kidding him about the gold? They looked perfectly normal to Heine.

He looked around for some means of getting inside the casing. There was a small workshop outside the magazine, designed for maintenance crews to work on the hoists and cranes in battle, to keep the ship firing. He found a hand drill and some bits, and returned to the magazine. He hoped to God these were the right shells. If he drilled into a shell packed with high explosive, the whole ship would go up. But Bach had been specific. Unmarked, he had said. These were the only ones.

He held the drill to a shell and gently started turning the wheel. The steel was oily and it took increasing pressure, with Heine leaning against the drill, to finally get it to bite. Small shavings of steel curled away from the bit as it began to cut into the metal. He paused every few seconds to make sure the bit didn't get hot, and spat on the growing hole to help cool it. If it was the wrong shell, he didn't want a red-hot drill suddenly hitting something explosive.

How thick was a shell case? Thick or thin? Heine had no idea. But he had to satisfy himself about the gold. He kept turning, stopping, spitting, turning some more. The curls of steel were like shiny pubic hairs gathering in a small bush beneath the hole. Suddenly the consistency changed. Instead of hard steel it felt like ... butter? The drill started to cut through much faster. Before Heine could stop, thinking he must be cutting into explosive, the curls of metal changed. Now they were a deep yellow, shiny. And instead of clinging to the shell casing and the drill bit, they fell to the deck.

Heine picked up one of the curls. It was soft, like something organic, but it was heavy. The yellow metal gleamed. He had seen gold before, although not much. If this wasn't gold, then Otto Heine wasn't German.

He unfastened the steel strap that held the shell in place, then grasped the hook screwed into the nose and attempted to move the shell, but however hard he tried it remained firmly in place. He couldn't even rock it. Bach was right again. They were going to be difficult to move. Downright bloody impossible unless he had help.

He looked around at the boxes holding the other ammunition. There were supposed to be another dozen shells, 6-inch calibre, easy to move by hand: realising how unwieldy the big shells would be if they had to be moved in a hurry, the plotters had thoughtfully produced the smaller shells in case something went wrong.

These were easy enough to find. There was a stack of boxes holding the six-inch ammunition, and the first six boxes on the pile contained unmarked shells like the other false ones. Heine lifted out one of the small shells and subjected it to the same investigation. Just like its big brother, a small curl of buttery yellow metal oozed out as he drilled it.

Heine carefully replaced the shell and the lid, and then swept the shavings behind the racking, pocketing the small curls of gold, and filled the drill hole in the big shell with a small plug of oily rag he found on the deck. Nothing showed unless you looked closely. He retreated up to the bridge, thinking all the while about how he would get twenty solid gold shells off the ship and take them somewhere where he could turn them into hard cash.

He was rich now. Extraordinarily rich. Judging by what he had just seen, a significant slice of Germany's gold reserve was sitting quietly in the magazine deep below him. He was not just a millionaire, he was a *multi*-millionaire. He had dreamed of being rich since he was a small boy, and had never really come anywhere near achieving even modest wealth. Until now. Suddenly, he was richer than he had ever thought he could be.

And here, for one of the few times in Otto Heine's life, his natural judgement deserted him. Perhaps the success of his mutiny and the scale of the wealth beneath his feet affected him. He was normally too cynical, too worldly-wise, to fall into such traps. But, for whatever reason, fall he did.

It was his gold, he told himself. No one else's. He was damn well not going to share this, not after all he had been through. It was a just reward for the dangers he had endured. He *deserved* it.

Nobody else knew about the gold apart from Bach, and he was dead now, his body drifting out there in the cold Atlantic wastes. Heine would keep it to himself. He would just have to move the gold without help, without letting anyone in on the deal.

He just hadn't quite worked out how.

The ship made its way steadily northwards. The ice floes had turned to bergs proper, and they now populated the sea. Every two or three miles a white island drifted in the long swell. The weather was quieter. They had moved beyond the track of the normal Atlantic depressions and were in that corridor where the sea was usually calm and sudden banks of fog could wrap them in a cold and clammy silence.

'Heine?' called Bruller softly later that afternoon.

Otto Heine was sitting at the back of the bridge, peering at a large-scale chart of the North Atlantic. He looked up.

'Come and see,' said Bruller.

Heine got up and went to the front of the bridge. He took the binoculars that Bruller handed him and scanned across the horizon, littered with bergs. Then he saw it: in the far distance, floating disembodied above the horizon, a black smear, with ridges. Land. Greenland.

'It's the southern tip. There must be fog hanging around the coast. You can see the high stuff.'

'How far?'

'Twenty, thirty miles maybe. A couple of hours away, at any rate.'

'Will we be seen?'

'Not with that fog. But we should alter course now to stay this far off the coast. If we keep it in sight it will make navigation easier.' The *Hindenburg*, hastily bolted together for a one-way trip, was equipped with one of the rare radar sets available, but Moehle was the only one of them who could ever get it to work, and he had gone with Bach. Bruller was left to navigate with much the same equipment as the Vikings – compass and dead reckoning – and in these northerly latitudes the compass became increasingly difficult to use. In theory the needle pointed to the north, and in most waters that was essentially true. But in reality it didn't point to 'true' north – the north pole – but instead to the magnetic north pole, and that could be as much as five or six degrees away from the real north pole.

Corrections were published on charts, showing navigators the difference between 'true' north and 'magnetic' north, so that they could compensate accordingly. The trouble was, the nearer you got, the more the difference mattered. At the equator you would only need to add a few degrees, more or less, to your heading, for reasonable accuracy. But up in the far north, where the difference between the magnetic and true north poles was more significant, you needed to correct not only for degrees but for minutes as well. On top of that, Bruller's charts were based on old surveys. Things were not always where they were meant to be.

He had his sextant of course, an instrument that would determine his position from the angle of the sun on the horizon. But you needed to see the sun, or some stars, and the solid grey overcast made that impossible. Bruller would do what the Vikings did – navigate by touch and by guesswork.

They would go as far north as the massive steel ship could clear a path through the melting ice, and then take it into the nearest convenient inlet.

*

Heine paid another unseen visit to the magazine deep below the forward turret. He had worked out a plan for getting one or two of the big shells off the ship. The small shells were easier to move, but Bach was right: why risk all this for a handful of the stuff when there was a much bigger fortune to be had?

He spent two hours in the gloomy dungeon trying out the electric hoist. He quickly worked out how to get the hook on to the nose and operate the button that moved the hoist up and down, and along the railing. On his own, he had already moved one of the shells to the hatch where the lift would take it up to the turret. Now he was trying to figure out the lift. There was a mass of buttons and switches, but none of them made anything happen. He stood there, trying to think it out; and then it occurred to him. The lift wasn't operated from down here at all. It must be operated from above: the turret crew would want to control it. So the switches and buttons down here must be signals only.

Shit, thought Heine. He made his way from the magazine up through several decks, climbing steep sets of ladders. Although the lift ran directly up into the turret, there was no access for crew other than through the armoured hatch at the rear. He emerged on to the main deck into the chill air and made his way inside the turret. Here the mass of stainless steel pipework, bronze fittings and tangled loops of cabling made his heart sink. He finally found the cradle that brought shells up to the breech. But while the shell he had left below was upright – and the lift was designed to carry it in such a position – the cradle here could only carry a shell on its side, ready for loading. Heine swore again. Some intermediate stage was missing, and he didn't know what.

There was a hatch going below, so he unlatched it and went down. Directly below the turret lay the shell-handling room. In fact, the shells from the magazines came here first; they were pulled off the lift, and the hooks in their noses were unscrewed and the required fuse fitted in its place. Then they were moved to another cradle, a horizontal one, where they were sent up to the turret for loading. At last Heine understood the process. But it didn't make his task any easier.

An experienced crew could easily get shells up fast enough to match the rate of fire of the big guns. But for Heine, on his own? The thought of involving other people still did not cross his mind. This treasure was his, and his alone. Whatever it took, he would do it.

He had already decided that just a couple of the big shells would be enough. If he could load those on to a boat, and get them back to civilisation, he would have more than enough money to enable him to come back later, when the war was over, to collect the rest.

It would take him around an hour, say two, to get the shells up to the turret. He'd already discovered some shell-handling trolleys down in the magazine; he would bring those up. If he could lever and roll the shells on to the trolley ... however he did it, he'd need more or less a whole day to get the two shells out, and then he'd still have to get a crane to drop them down on to a boat.

What the hell! He'd come this far, and he was pretty sure he'd be able to figure something out nearer the time. But now he had discovered how to lift the shells,

Heine set to work to bring his two trophies up from the magazine and into the turret.

*

Bruller was on the bridge, waiting. He had asked Ecke, the engineering officer, to come up while Heine was elsewhere. Bruller was worried, but he didn't want to admit it in front of Heine. His pride would not allow him to show weakness in front of a mere seaman, even if by a quirk of fate he was now in charge of the ship.

What Bruller was very worried about was the fuel situation. His plan for going north through the ice was fine in theory, but he knew they were limited on fuel. Oil was scarce in Germany when they left, and they had only been allowed enough to make the one-way trip. He hadn't been told how much they had taken on in Hamburg. Bach would have had the fuel manifest, but for some reason Heine had insisted on locking the captain's door; he wanted nothing disturbed.

Bruller would simply have to dip the tanks. There were no fuel gauges on the ship, no means of finding out how much fuel was on board other than physically pushing a dipstick into the tanks and reading off the levels. It was a simple enough process but, with the crew they now had, Bruller doubted that anyone on the ship knew how to do it accurately other than Ecke. And right now, accuracy was important.

When Ecke walked through the bridge door, Bruller took him to one side and explained his problem. Ecke nodded. Bach had not told him at the outset what the fuel load was, presumably because he was trying to keep it secret: it would have been obvious to Ecke, as engineering officer, that the ship was only going one way, and Bach had wanted to keep that quiet at the

beginning. And in the intervening period, Ecke had
simply never asked Bach. It never occurred to him to
do so.

Ecke immediately set off down through the decks.
The bunker tanks were at the very lowest level, just
above the inner layer of the triple bottom. The tanks
were divided up into compartments, and the compartments were pumped into a day tank which fed
the diesels directly.

Hindenburg had set off with only four of the
bunker tanks filled. Ecke finally reached the fuel tank
level and set about dipping them. He knew tanks one
and two were empty, because he'd ordered the day
tank switched once those were dry. He was now running on tank three.

The long wooden rods, weighted with lead at the
end, were clipped to the tanks, the dimensions and
therefore the rod for each tank being different. Ecke
had to assault the screw cover of the first tank with a
wrench to get it to shift. The tanks had never been
dipped.

Ecke dropped the long rod down and it gave a dull
clang as it hit the bottom. He carefully lifted it up,
hand over hand. Almost empty; not enough to fill the
day tank next morning.

He screwed the cap back and re-clipped the long
rod, he found the fourth tank. Once again he had to
wrench the cap off, and once more dipped the tank.
This one should be full, but he could tell from the
sound the rod made that it wasn't. When he pulled the
rod back up, it registered less than one quarter full.
Ecke's brow furrowed. There was damn-all fuel on
this ship.

He looked at the capacity plate on the top of the
tank: 8.2 tonnes when full. It took Ecke all of a second

to work out how far they would get. He hurried back up the ladders to find Bruller and give him the news.

*

Heine had just managed to get the first shell up to the handling room, sweating and swearing, when the public address speakers all over the ship started squawking. The voice that came from them was artificially high-pitched; somebody had decided that a shrill voice carried better in the din of battle.

'Heine, bridge here. You're needed urgently, Heine.'

Heine looked around. There was a handset, but he had no idea how to use it. He had no option but to drop everything and make his way to the bridge.

*

The *Hindenburg* had already started to plunge through the ice; it was breaking up into enormous plates, but each plate was three feet thick and although the weight of the ship and the massive armour plating were easily enough to push through it, the big diesel engine found the propeller harder and harder to turn against the heavy pressure of ice.

The young crewman in the engine room noticed the gradual drop in revolutions, and saw that the exhaust gas temperature was steadily climbing. Ecke was gone. He used his initiative and opened a valve to increase the fuel flow. Slowly the speed built up once again.

*

'Eighteen hours? What does that mean, for Christ's sake?' demanded Heine, looking confused.

'It means that in eighteen hours we're out of fuel. We're running at twelve knots. We can go another two hundred nautical miles before we're finished.'

Heine paused, thinking. He'd just about moved one shell. 'Are you sure?' he asked.

'Ecke here has dipped the tanks. That's all the fuel we're carrying. And you'll need some for the boats.'

'How far does that take us, Bruller? Two hundred miles?'

'Here, somewhere,' replied Bruller, handing over a chart with a circle pencilled on the coast. But it was just beyond the place where the chart surveyor's knowledge ran out.

'You're sure? Is it any good?'

'Good as anywhere, Heine. But we need to start getting ready now.'

Heine left the bridge. It was beginning to get dark. Eighteen fucking hours? How the hell was he going to move those shells?

*

Heine had slept and was up the next morning as early as he could manage. Ten hours of the eighteen had passed. But now, at least, he had his solution. It was all he could do – but it should just work. He would box the two shells in wooden cases, which he could just about manage to do on his own. Then he would need help. His plan was to use the remaining four boats to get the crew and officers away. Three were big boats; the fourth was small and would take the two heavy boxes and Heine, with perhaps three or four other people. He would get the three big ones away first, then with Vogele and some crew would get the boxes loaded. What was in them? Weapons and ammunition for all of them – that would account for the size and the weight, or some of it anyway. Vogele was a trusting soul and wouldn't ask too many questions.

The fourth boat would be last away. Heine had

decided that he would make his own way from there. He would catch up with the others, order Vogele and the rest of them on to another boat. Then he'd leave them all to it. He'd done his bit for them. He'd got rid of Bach, taken over the ship, saved their fucking lives. He'd done enough for them. They wouldn't blame him.

He made his way up to the bridge where he gathered Vogele, Bruller and the other officers and explained about the boats. They all listened carefully and nodded in silent agreement, then checked back the times. They would launch the boats as late as possible so as to get as far north as they could. There being now seven hours of steaming time left, they would plan to launch in around six hours' time. They departed from the bridge to get the rest of the crew ready.

*

The ice was slowly growing thicker. Now the big ship was having to carve through solid sheets, the damaged bow cutting through the white crust like a can-opener – leaving behind it a jagged, clear track that wouldn't re-freeze in the warming water. Down in the engine room, the same young engineer was back on duty and noticed that the revolutions had dropped once again.

He opened the fuel flow valve a little more, and the huge diesel engine picked up speed to maintain a steady twelve knots, as he had been so clearly instructed to do.

*

The *Hindenburg* was now buzzing with activity as everyone plunged into the process of leaving the ship. The boats had to be fuelled and the engines checked; food and water had to be brought up from the stores and stowed; most importantly of all, the warm clothing had to be sorted out and everyone issued with what would be necessary for the last stage of their journey.

Bruller had drawn up instructions for the leader of each boat and was taking them through the plan. Once clear of the ice pack, which he reckoned would take about two days, they would make their way west and south to the nearest settlements. Each boat was given a course for a different place in the Canadian north. There they would tell the locals that they were survivors of various German ships sunk or abandoned in the last days of the war – a weather ship, a submarine, a freighter. All signs of the *Hindenburg* were wiped out – names, serial numbers, anything that would identify them. Survivors arriving in far-flung coastal villages were not unusual at that time and were treated well enough. The Germans were normally detained in local prisons, if there were any, before eventually being taken to camps. It was assumed that they would be repatriated without great fuss when the war was over.

Almost every man on the *Hindenburg* simply wanted to go home to Germany, no matter what state Germany might be in. They would put up with anything to get back. Internment, after what they had been through, was a comfortable option. Even if Germany was reduced to rubble and occupied by Russians or Americans, it was still home where they had families, lives, memories and identity. The dream of returning gave every man on board a powerful motivation to make the operation go smoothly.

Only Heine was not going home. Perhaps he would have liked to, in a way. He would return a wealthy man, show all those people who had pushed him around just how successful he had become. But he knew it was impossible. Now he was a murderer and a mutineer, even if he had good reason to be so. Defeated or not, the German naval establishment would never let him get away with it.

So he would be rich in America, where he could easily get an expedition together to come back to the ship and bring home the rest of the gold.

With just a few hours left to him, Heine was busy building the crude wooden boxes around the shells. Carpentry was a strange skill for him to possess, but a two-month spell in a youth camp – courtesy of the Hamburg police – had forcibly taught him the rudiments of the craft. He found himself curiously proud of his work.

He had completed one, and was struggling to roll the last shell on to the wooden base of the second box, when he suddenly stopped and listened.

Something had changed. Something was different. What?

He looked around. Everything appeared normal. No one had come in. Shit, Otto, you're imagining things. He carried on with his carpentry.

A minute later he suddenly realised what it was. The ship had slowed down. The vibrations of the engine had become part of the background, unchanging for hour after hour. But now the soundless vibration, felt and not heard, had changed. What was going on?

Heine made his way up the ladders from the magazine, and emerged on to the main deck. The normally quiet decks were filled with crew who were running backwards and forwards. Everyone was looking scared.

Heine caught one of the crewmen. 'What the hell is happening?'

The boy, no more than eighteen, pulled away from Heine's grasp. 'Get to the boats – orders!' he shouted, and ran off.

Heine looked at his watch. There were still five hours to go – what the hell was all the panic about? Now he started running forward, reached the ladders leading to the bridge and hauled himself up them two steps at a time, bursting through the bridge door where Bruller and Ecke, looking worried, were talking.

'What the fuck is happening?' demanded Heine.

'We were looking for you,' Bruller replied.

'I was busy. What's going on?' he repeated.

'Ecke, you tell him.'

'It's the fuel situation. We are very low. The ice slowed us down, so one of the crew opened the throttle to maintain speed. It used more fuel than I had calculated.'

'How much fuel have we got left?' Heine was wondering how long he had to complete his task. He needed another hour, maybe half an hour if pushed.

'Very little. We're very low. I mean, I think the tanks are probably nearly empty.'

'You think?'

'Empty. The tanks are just about dry.'

'You're joking.'

'He's not,' replied Bruller. 'We have just a few minutes of power left, if we're lucky. I've ordered the boats made ready to launch now. That's it, Heine. We have to go.'

Heine stared at the officer, but Bruller just looked sad.

'What about beaching the ship?' Heine asked.

'We don't need to. Just get the boats off and let it drift.'

'We beach the ship, Bruller. We have to fucking well beach it.' The last thing that Heine wanted was his precious cargo drifting around the high seas. The ship *had* to be beached, so that he could come back and find it.

'Why, for God's sake? We don't have the time, man.'

'Beach it. Don't argue,' shouted Heine, angry and worried all at once.

'Then we have to do it now. But I don't understand why you want to beach it.'

'To keep it out of the way. Just do it, Bruller, for fuck's sake.'

'It'll float off. The tide's low. If you want it done, we have to open the seacocks right now. We're half a mile off the coast. We can just get it done – but for God's sake, Heine, the crew is panicking to get off.'

'I don't give a damn. I'll do it but I'll get some help. You just get us there.'

'What about the boats?'

'Launch them when you like. Leave the last one until I'm back. Do what you like, Bruller, but beach this pile of shit now.'

'We have to go slowly, to get the boats off. We have to stop at some point.'

'Do what you need to. I'm going.'

'Heine?'

Otto paused at the bridge door and looked back at Bruller.

'Good luck, Heine. I think you're crazy. But good luck anyway.'

'Thanks, Bruller. And to you. And give my love to Hamburg.'

*

The following ten minutes passed as a blur. Heine raced back down the deck as the big ship started a slow turn towards the nearby coast. He found Vogele and another two lads. Ecke had told him where the main seacocks were and what he had to do, but finding them on the huge ship was not easy.

There were four, but they were arranged in separated pairs, one pair amidships and another towards the stern. He went for the amidships ones first. Heine and his party had to descend through all the decks, down ladders and deserted companionways that had never been finished or even cabled for light. They'd brought a couple of flashlights with them.

It took them five minutes to find the first pair. The valves were controlled by hand-wheels, and they hadn't been touched since the ship was built. The damp air in the bowels of the ship had rusted them to a stiffness that human muscle alone was never going to budge. Ecke had warned him about this, and Heine had found some steel bars. Now he inserted one between the spokes of the hand-wheel and all four of them leaned on it. The rusty steel groaned and then shrieked, but finally the hand-wheel started to shift. Once freed, they could move it by hand. A thin stream of water dribbled from the six-inch-wide pipe, and then gathered force. The wheel spun easily now, and the water started to gush, cold and clear, as the icy sea outside the hull began to push through. They moved to the next valve, a few yards away on the other side, and repeated the process. Within minutes the freezing water sloshing around the bilges was a foot deep and Heine and his men were wading through it, their feet and legs quickly numbed by the sudden cold. Satisfied with the first part of the operation, Heine now led them on a race down the ship towards the after sections, where the second pair of seacocks was located.

Halfway along the gloomy companionway, Vogele suddenly called to Heine.

'Heine, please stop for a minute.'

'Come on, we have to hurry.'

'Heine, no. I'm not going any further.'

Heine stopped. 'It's not far. Come on, Vogele.'

'You don't understand. I want to get off the ship; I don't want to stay here. It's time to go. If we don't go now, we'll be stuck.'

'Don't worry, Vogele. I'll make sure we get off. I need your help.'

'No, Heine. Sorry. I've had enough.' And Vogele turned and started walking quickly away. They had just passed a set of ladders leading up to the fresh air, and Vogele now began climbing them. The other two were following him.

'Come back!' shouted Heine. 'Damn it, Vogele, it was you who suggested I take over the bloody ship in the first place. You can't dump me in it now,' he called, but Vogele was not stopping to listen.

'Sorry, Heine,' came Vogele's voice, echoing down the long companionway as he and his men disappeared upwards.

'Bastards,' muttered Heine to himself. There was no chance of getting them back.

Now, he finally realised with certainty that he had lost it. The two gold-filled shells, sitting in the shell-handling room, were going to stay there. He couldn't get them out on his own; it was impossible. He smashed his fist against a steel bulkhead in frustration and swore several times.

So, what now? he asked himself. There was only one thing he could do: make sure the ship was safely beached, and then one way or another he would come back and rescue the gold, make his fortune. He would be able to take the smaller shells. They were full of gold, for heaven's sake, enough to give him the cash to enable him to return at his leisure. He could manage one or two of them, no trouble.

But he knew that he had to open the other seacocks

to make sure that the ship was finally beached, keeping his gold safe on a deserted Greenland shore until he could return.

Now, in the dark, Heine worked his way aft until he reached the compartment below the main engine room. He could hear the big diesel slowly thumping above him, drinking the last drops of fuel oil and pushing them the last few hundred yards to safety. Keep going, keep going, he prayed. Give me just a few minutes more to get my damned gold. Once more Heine forced the hand-wheels open and the cold Arctic sea started to flood into the deep, oily bilges of the ship.

As he had just opened the last valve, and the sea gushed in, the steady 'thump-thump-thump' of the engine slowed dramatically. It could mean only one thing; they were slowing the ship down to disembark the crew on the boats. But his task was finished. The sea was flowing steadily into the bowels of the great vessel.

Heine – exhausted, sweating, nervous and frustrated – hauled himself up seven decks until he finally emerged into daylight. The main deck was quiet. He had to make his way forward as quickly as he could and get down the magazine below Anton. His head was splitting.

He started running down the deck.

'Heine!' came a distant voice. It was Bruller, running down the deck from the opposite direction, coming straight towards him.

'Heine, I was looking for you. Get on the boat. I've lashed the wheel and Ecke has set the engine to full speed. We'll beach in a few minutes.' He didn't wait for a reply and started climbing over the rail, where scramble netting led down to a waiting boat. Turning to look at Heine, he stopped when he realised that the other man was not following.

Heine looked forward, out across the bow. The huge ship was gathering speed, aimed at a small inlet on the coast. The last of the boats below was running its engine to keep pace with the ship.

'Come on, for God's sake!' called Bruller.

All that gold, just sitting there ... Otto Heine was fabulously rich. It was all his. Everything he had ever dreamed off, just waiting for him. He needed only two – maybe even only one – of those small shells, just to keep him going.

'Give me five minutes,' he shouted to Bruller, and started running forward towards the turrets and the access hatch to the magazines. Before he had moved more than a few paces, he was suddenly gripped from behind. It was Bruller.

'Heine, come now, for God's sake. It's the last boat and they're going to leave. They won't wait. If you miss that, you've had it.'

'Leave me alone. There's something I have to get. Tell them to hold on,' shouted Heine, struggling to free himself.

But Bruller held on, and tightened his grip. He was a big man. 'Heine, *now*!' he shouted. 'They won't bloody wait. They're scared to death they'll be trapped. Come on, man, for God's sake,' he pleaded.

It was all going terribly wrong. His plan had been so carefully worked out but now it was collapsing. 'Bruller, I have to get something. It's vital.' Heine was almost begging now.

Bruller looked at Heine. 'Sorry,' he said, and then swung his fist into Heine's face. Heine tottered and sank to his knees with blood welling from his nose. Bruller grabbed his arm and shuffled him back along the deck, unresisting, to the railings where he shouted for help. One of the crewmen scrambled up the ladder, gripped Heine's other arm, and between them they manhandled the groggy man down into the boat.

'Go!' shouted Bruller, and the sailor opened the throttle which took them quickly away from the ship. Heine, still too shocked to resist, mutely watched the massive bulk of the *Hindenburg* head for the inlet, gathering speed all the time. Already the ship was visibly lower in the water as the inrush of ocean from the opened seacocks gradually filled its dark interior.

It took five minutes for the ship to finally die. The lifeboat was nearly a mile off when the *Hindenburg* mounted the beach at full speed. Heine could see the smashed prow suddenly heave into the air as it ploughed into the shingle, and the whole vessel shuddered as it came to a halt. The stern was low. Over the next few hours, as the water filled the ship, it would sink even lower.

The last voyage of the *Hindenburg* was finally over. As Heine's small boat motored gently away, as if in some operatic finale the clouds closed in over the distant ship and a sudden snow shower descended like a fog. Sweeping across the smashed ice, the snow obscured Heine's final view of the ship. Then he doubled up in the bottom of the boat and passed out.

The *Hindenburg* disappeared in a white, whirling haze; and for fifty-five years that was to be the last glimpse that Otto Heine would ever see of the ship that nearly killed him and would one day, he hoped to God, make his fortune.

16

OFF THE GREENLAND COAST
9 AUGUST 2000

Billy Tan had spent three weeks waiting. His repair crews had closed the rusted seacocks and pumped millions of gallons of cold, oily water from inside the ship. The smashed bow had been patched up and made watertight. Now the *Hindenburg* was as ready to start on the last stage of its journey as it would ever be. He was only waiting for two things to happen – one certain, the other less so.

The certain event was the next day's tide. It would be a spring tide, the highest of the month, when the extra few centimetres of water would make the task of pulling the dead weight of the huge ship off the clinging shingle an easier job. Pumped out, the old hulk of the *Hindenburg* was already floating in the water. Only the bulge beneath the damaged bow was still anchored deep in the soft Greenland gravel, and the massive power of the *Zuider* – the Dutch salvage tug that had been Tan's base for the last three weeks – was meant to be enough to pull the ship off the beach.

The less certain event was the arrival of the Russian nuclear icebreaker *Lev Semoyovitch*, chartered at no little cost from a Moscow shipbroker whom Tan didn't trust one inch. It was supposed to have arrived last night, to break open an escape route for the ship through an ice cap that was already melting in the brief Arctic summer. The *Hindenburg* alone could have smashed through it, but for all its power, the huge salvage tug *Zuider* simply lacked the sheer brute weight to take them both through.

Tan was already on the satellite phone to Moscow.

'Yuri, you're giving me shit. I paid you good dollars for that fucking ship: if it's not here in one hour, I will take a helicopter and I will fly to Moscow and tear your fucking balls off.'

'Billy, just relax, will you? You'll get ulcers. I spoke to the captain only a few moments ago. He will be with you by tonight.'

'The captain is a drunken fool that I wouldn't trust with a fucking rubber duck in my fucking bath, Yuri.'

'That's harsh, Billy, very harsh. You know that Captain Igor is a good man. Perhaps he drinks a bit. For God's sake, Billy, he's a Russian. He has every reason to like a drink now and then.'

'Is he smashed, Yuri?'

'He's on his way, Billy. Don't worry.'

'Is he smashed?'

'He's verging on the unconscious as we speak, Billy, if you want the truth. But Igor drives that thing much better when he's drunk than when he's sober. He'll be there. Promise.'

'I want my money back.'

'Bit of a problem with that one, Billy.'

'Fuck you, Yuri.'

'Thank you, Billy. Igor will be there. Calm down.'

With that less than helpful advice, Billy Tan slammed the satellite phone down. Now all he could do was wait.

The high tide was predicted for one minute past twelve midday tomorrow. If the Russian ship was not with them by then, they'd have to wait another two weeks for a tide that even then wouldn't be as high as they really wanted. And Billy Tan was in no mood to pay De Wit and his dour Dutchmen another two weeks' charter money.

He was fuming when he ran into Louise DeAngelis on the way down to his cabin.

'Billy, you look pissed off,' said the blonde.

'Don't talk to me about it.'

'Buy me a drink and reveal all?' Was there an interesting angle in all this?

'In my cabin?'

Louise DeAngelis was torn between her professional need to get a good story and a deep reluctance to get involved with Billy Tan. She didn't simply not fancy him, she actually found him repulsive. But as always with Louise DeAngelis, the story won.

'Sure. Why not?' With a sinking heart she followed him to his cabin.

She watched as he closed the door behind him. He actually had a smirk on his face. He poured two large Bourbons and ice, and sat down to her very, very close.

'So, what's the story, Billy?' she asked nervously, moving slightly further away.

'The story, Miss DeAngelis, is that you're a beautiful woman. I think I'm in love with you. Here we are alone on this ship. I feel romance is in the air. What do you say?'

Louise DeAngelis breathed hard. She wasn't sure if he was joking or serious. 'Listen, Billy . . .'

'Just you, me, and more ice than you could dream of. Come on, Louise, drop the hard-bitten TV reporter act for five minutes and relax.' He moved closer and put his hand, firmly, on her knee.

She edged away, unable to help herself.

'Don't want to play?' asked Billy, moving along the sofa after her.

'A bit sudden, Billy, that's all.'

'Come here, then.'

'Billy, I don't think the time is right ...' And then the phone buzzed insistently. Billy Tan tried to ignore it, but it wouldn't stop.

'Fuck it,' he muttered, and wrenched the phone out of the cradle. 'Yeah?' he growled.

The Russian icebreaker's captain's sense of timing was perfect. 'Mr Tan, De Wit here. You wished to know if the Russian ship was arriving?'

He would kill the famous Captain Igor. 'So?'

'The ship is here, Mr Tan. I have instructed them to drop anchor nearby. The captain seems strange. Perhaps it is the language?'

Language? It was the fucking vodka, not the language. 'Thanks,' and he put the phone down, turning his attentions back to the delectable Miss DeAngelis who for some reason was now standing and walking towards the door.

'What's up, baby?'

'Er, nothing. Just the time of month, you see.'

'Oh,' said Billy Tan, disappointed. 'Well, maybe next time then.'

'Maybe,' replied Louise DeAngelis, and vanished out of the door.

'Bitch,' he muttered to himself. Louise fucking DeAngelis? What sort of name was that anyway? Just a stage name. In that assumption, at least, Billy Tan was correct.

*

While Billy Tan was waiting, it had taken Otto Heine the same three weeks to track down Tan's firm of lawyers. Heine had assumed it would be easy. Lawyers lived on Wall Street, as everyone knew. All he had to do was call each one in turn, asking them if they worked for Billy Tan, until he came across the right one. Then he would put his proposition. Then, doubtless he would be whisked off to the ship to speak to Mister Billy Tan in person.

It didn't take Heine long to realise that finding Billy Tan's lawyers was going to be a difficult proposition. First, the listings in the phone book ran to page after page and he had no idea where to start. And not all of them, by any means, were on Wall Street. So he picked one with the most impressive name he could find and called them.

'Hermannbaileycohenlawrencesimpsongottesmanpeakeandcompany, how can I help you?' came the bored voice.

'I'm looking for Billy Tan.'

There was a brief pause. 'I'm sorry, we have no Billy Tan, we have Amanda Tan, shall I connect you?'

'No, you don't understand. I'm trying to find out if Billy Tan is a client of yours?'

'Sorry, we cannot divulge that information, thank you for calling, have a nice day,' and the phone went dead.

He made a few more calls, with exactly the same result. Heine had little experience of lawyers, but it was clear that he was going to get nowhere. The thought of calling the TV station to get hold of Tan horrified him; they would ask him what it was all about – the last thing he wanted was his story broadcast over the airwaves for every crook in the country to latch on to.

Having spent the afternoon at the bar, he was just going home when he saw Hans, who owned the place.

Hans was a man of business; he would know about lawyers.

'Hans, how would I go about finding someone's lawyers? You understand that sort of thing.'

'Lawyers, Otto? What you want lawyers for? Someone owe you money?' and he dissolved into laughter.

'Something like that. I'm serious, Hans.'

'Ho, serious, is it? Simple. Go to a law centre. There's one down the street; you know the place. Tell them you want to sue whoever-it-is. They draw up a writ, serve it, and if whoever-it-is has lawyers they'll respond within the day. Mine do, anyway.'

'What if I don't know where this character lives?'

'Don't you worry, Otto. Lawyers have ways of finding out these things.'

Otto Heine finished his beer. He went home, slept on it, and next morning took $1,000 in $100 bills from the steel box hidden behind the big fridge in his kitchen, and by nine was sitting in front of a keen young female lawyer, fresh out of law school, eager to fight the battle for the poor and dispossessed of New York city.

Otto instantly identified the type, and proceeded to tell her the harrowing tale of Billy Tan – the famous one, she must know him – whom he had trusted with his life savings and who had vanished – and how could he get his money back?

She looked duly concerned, nodding sympathetically at this old man, a poor migrant, being taken for a ride by no less a person than Billy Tan. If this didn't make her reputation, nothing would.

After Otto Heine finished his story the girl looked angry and delighted at the same time.

'Disgraceful, Mr Heine, absolutely disgraceful! I'm sure we can help. What we need to do is serve a writ on this Tan fellow straight away. Do you know where he lives?'

'No, I'm afraid not.'

'Never mind. We'll find him. Don't you worry now, Mr Heine. Leave it with me. Go home and try not to think about it. I'll let you know the moment I hear something. This Mr Tan needs teaching a lesson.'

'Thank you so much. Look, I have brought some money ...' mumbled Heine piteously, fumbling inside his jacket.

'Gracious no, Mr Heine. Don't think about it. We'll get Mr Tan to pay every penny.'

Heine mumbled something again, left the office and went back to his apartment, where he put the wad of $100 bills back in the box and pushed the refrigerator into its normal position. He smiled to himself. He would never understand the extraordinary simplicity of these Americans.

It took her twelve days exactly. Then she called him and told him to come into her office. He did as was instructed.

She looked less enthusiastic than she had before.

'Well, I've had a reply. From Mr Tan's lawyers. Here, have a look.'

The letter expressed astonishment that she would try to strong-arm their client into paying money to someone that he had never heard of, and stated that her writ would be contested most vigorously. Heine scanned the text briefly – but read the letterhead carefully, and especially the telephone number, memorised it, and handed it back.

'Sounds very strong, Mr Heine. Are you sure you've got the right man?'

Heine looked as sad as he could manage. 'It's a common name, Miss. For Orientals, I mean. Perhaps it's the wrong one, after all.'

'You did say the famous one? The financier?'

'Oh no, Miss. Not a financier. Not my Mr Tan. No, he was a famous ... painter.'

'I see. I think this is probably the wrong one. Can you remember more about your Mr Tan?'

'I'm afraid not. It was many years ago now.'

'Well, Mr Heine ...'

'Yes, I'm sorry to have wasted your time.'

'No trouble. About the fee?'

'Ah. Yes. I have ten dollars. Will that be enough?'

'Never mind, Mr Heine. Don't worry. Come back if you remember anything, all right?'

'Thank you, Miss,' and a sad-faced Otto Heine shuffled out of the office and went straight to a phone booth.

'Hoggins Banks O'Shea,' came another receptionist's cold tones.

'Mr Banks, please. It's about Billy Tan,' said Heine. Banks had signed the letter. A senior partner, no less.

A moment later the phone was picked up. It was a precise Massachusetts drawl.

'Banks here.'

'Mr Banks, my name is Otto Heine. I understand you represent Mr Billy Tan?'

'That is correct. How can I help you?'

'Right now Tan is sitting off the Greenland coast. I saw him on the television. He's trying to salvage an old German ship. He might be interested to hear from me. I was on that ship. In fact, I was the one who left it there.'

There was a long silence. 'You left it there, Mr Heine? Could you tell me in what way you left it there, exactly?'

It was a question that Heine had been expecting. The ratings on Louise DeAngelis's live broadcast had dropped and, in order to spark up some interest, she had deliberately started to play on the legal issue that faced Tan: if the ship was wrecked, it was fair salvage, but if it had been scuttled it was still German government property. She had managed to make quite a controversy out of it, even getting some inches in the better-quality press, which helped the show's figures to recover. Irritated as Billy Tan was by it all, he needed the publicity so he went along with it. Besides, nobody could prove it one way or another. And as he had already covered up the evidence of the opened seacocks, he was on safe ground. Or so he thought.

'No, I couldn't tell you in what way I left it there,' replied Heine.

'Beg pardon?'

'No. Not to you. To Tan. In person. I want you to fly me out there.'

'Sorry, Mr Heine. You could be anybody. How do I know you're telling the truth?'

Heine had thought about this too. It was just about the only thing he could remember from fifty-five years ago, and it was burned into his memory.

'Tell him to look in the first gun turret on the ship. Just below, in the place where they got the shells ready. He'll find one wooden box with a shell inside, and another sitting on a wooden base. Tell him not to touch the shells, they might go off. If I'm right, call me on this number ...' and he gave his home number '... this time tomorrow. Understand?'

'I'll pass the message on.'

'Do that,' replied Heine and put the phone down.

*

That was not the only call about Billy Tan that Erasmus Banks, senior partner of Hoggins Banks O'Shea, had fielded within the past few days. One day earlier, his secretary had put through an urgent call from Bonn, Germany. It was Bethe Fischer.

Bethe had escaped from Lil Beasley and her evil dog and her even worse cottage, minus the manuscript, and returned to Germany. The story she had read, according to Lil's researches after the war, was almost the whole tale of the *Hindenburg*: the voyage, the mutiny, and ending with the suicide of Bach. Nothing was said about the gold. Nothing was said about the final days of the ship, which was what Bethe was really interested in. Lil had pieced everything but that together, mainly from Schiller's report: he was the only one to survive and he managed to tell most of the story before he too died.

If Bethe wanted to stop Billy Tan dragging the old wreck out of the ice – and that was exactly what her masters required, given the approaching election and their natural reluctance to let the past haunt the present – then she needed to able to prove that the ship had been deliberately abandoned, in which case it remained the property of the German government and could not be touched. On the other hand, if it had been wrecked, then Tan could safely salvage the hulk. Lil Beasley's fascinating tale shed no light on the final fate of the ship; but when German intelligence reported that the *Lev Semoyovitch* was nearing the site, Bethe Fischer was told in no uncertain terms to do something. Anything. Just stop him.

Like all good lawyers faced with a hopeless case and a client screaming for a result, she had to fall back on bluff. She decided to call Billy Tan's lawyer in America and see what she could conjure up out of thin air.

'Mr Banks, your client is about to get himself in very big trouble. I hope you appreciate this fact,' she started almost straight away.

Banks was used to threats, especially where Billy Tan was concerned. 'Oh, Miss Fischer, thank you for your concern. Of course, you cannot be expected to be familiar with US law – being a German, I mean. But here, Miss Fischer, we have something called due process. Our courts take it quite seriously.'

'Mr Banks, you clearly do not know that I took my original law degree at Harvard. American law is something I am extremely familiar with.' It was a downright lie.

Banks was silent for a moment. Did this woman have something on Billy after all?

'I see. So how can I help you?'

'It's how *I* can help *you* and your client, Mr Banks. That is, if he wants to avoid a several-hundred-million-dollar lawsuit from the German government for stealing our property, and also charges of criminal damage to an historic monument.'

Banks gave a patronising sigh. 'Miss Fischer, the fact is that my client and I have investigated the whole matter. My client has been at that ship for three weeks. The vessel was clearly wrecked, there can be no doubt about it. As such it is nobody's property. My client is fully within ...'

'Mr Banks, there is *every* doubt about it. You do not perhaps know that I have visited a retired member of British Intelligence who has a complete history of the ship and its last voyage? She has records of interviews with one of the officers who was on that voyage, an officer named Schiller. He survived, do you know that?'

Banks remained silent. Good God! No, he fucking well did not know that. Neither did Billy Tan. Or if he did, he hadn't told him.

'She managed to reconstruct the whole story, Mr Banks. I think an American court would find her evidence very interesting.'

Bethe Fischer chose her words carefully. She had

lied once; but now she told the truth – if Banks wanted to read between the lines, that was up to him.

'Well, Miss Fischer, thank you for bringing this to our attention. Obviously, if you have proof that the ship was *not* wrecked after all then I am sure my client would find the information most useful. My client wishes only to act within the law, you understand.'

'Tell your client, Mr Banks, to leave our ship alone. If he does not, I will be instructing our people in New York to file immediately.'

'Perhaps I can discuss this with my client, Miss Fischer.'

'I think that would be a very good idea. You have, I think, perhaps forty-eight hours. Otherwise I shall instruct.'

'Goodbye, Miss Fischer.'

'Goodbye, Mr Banks.'

Erasmus Banks felt like slamming the phone down, but did not. He disconnected the call, then waited for his secretary to come on the line. He was talking to Billy Tan within five minutes.

*

Following Heine's call, the traffic via the satellite dome on top of the *Zuider* was intense. First Fischer's threat. Then the old man with the German accent. Tan had himself taken to the hulk on an inflatable and made his way to the forward turret, alone. He found the shell-handling room where, with a sense of astonishment, he saw there was one wooden box, sealed, and a dull grey shell sitting on some planks. He levered off the top of the completed box. Just as Heine had promised, there was the shell. It was a voice from the past. Suddenly the rusting wreck was coming to life.

Banks told him that the old man said he knew how

the ship came to be there. That would help his legal case. But in Billy Tan's mind he could see endless other possibilities – he would get that bitch to interview the old man on the ship, tomorrow, and the ratings would go through the roof. It was like striking gold, he thought, as he covered the shell carefully, went back to the main deck and climbed down the ladder to the inflatable.

By eight that evening, as instructed, Heine had reported to a small private airfield in New Jersey where a twin-engine turboprop was waiting for him. He was the only passenger. With a mounting sense of excitement, he sat back in the luxurious seat and the small aircraft took him north where, early in the morning, it touched down at the small settlement of Clyde, on Baffin Island; there a chartered Russian long-range helicopter was waiting to fly him 400 miles across the breaking pack ice of Baffin Bay to where the *Zuider* was waiting.

It was eight the following morning when Heine, exhausted but elated, finally stepped from the door of the helicopter on to the deck of the *Zuider*. In the near distance the looming grey bulk of the *Hindenburg*, tow-lines hanging from the stern, was sitting in the inlet, just as Heine had finally left it all those years ago. His dream was coming true.

'Otto Heine? Pleased to meet you. Delighted, in fact.' It was Billy Tan. He was much shorter than Heine had expected, but the thick, shiny black hair and the round face were familiar. Heine instantly distrusted the man. When he was younger he would have taken pains to avoid showing it, but now he couldn't be bothered with such pleasantries. He wanted his gold and he didn't have much time.

'You're Billy Tan. I have some interesting things to

tell you.'

'Good, good. Come below, have something to eat.'

Heine followed Tan down from the helicopter pad to the interior of the ship. He had only been on one ship before – the *Hindenburg*. This vessel was completely different. It was like a luxury hotel. Thick carpets, curtains, heating ... it wasn't like a ship at all. They arrived at the mess where Tan settled Heine into a chair and coffee was brought. Heine was hungry and kept quiet until he had some food inside him – Danish pastries and some cheese.

Tan waited patiently until his man was ready. Finally Heine started to speak.

'I know how that ship came to be there. I was on it, you see.'

'So I understand.'

'You know also that you have a problem, Tan. I know the ship wasn't wrecked.'

'Indeed? And how is it you know that?'

'For the simple reason that I was the last person on the *Hindenburg*. I drove it to this inlet and let the crew off, and then I went below and opened the seacocks. The ship was scuttled, that's what they call it, Tan. Not wrecked. Not salvage, you see.'

Tan nodded and stayed silent. What did the old man want? He wouldn't have come all this way just to tell him that.

'So. Now you know this, you must not move the ship. It's not yours to move.'

Tan remained silent.

'But perhaps I can help you,' Heine continued.

'In what way?' asked Billy, in what he was trying hard to make a friendly voice.

'I can keep the truth to myself. I am the only person who knows what really happened. I can say the ship was wrecked; this makes it completely legal. But for this I want something in return, Tan.'

'Which is?' This was the sort of thing that Tan understood. He just hoped the man's demands were not going to be crazy.

On the flight over, Heine had been giving some careful thought to exactly what he wanted. He knew how difficult the gold was to move. He had no illusions about the problems of shipping it off the old boat and then trying to cash it in. That was the mistake he had made fifty-five years ago, and it had cost him his fortune. Now he had only a few years left to enjoy it and he didn't want to waste time. Now, he would have to share the gold. Almost . . .

'On the old ship, Tan, there is something very valuable. Worth millions of dollars. Maybe hundreds of millions of dollars. I know where it is.'

Oh God, thought Tan; the man really was crazy.

Heine must have seen his expression. 'Let me show you. I need to get to the ship.'

'Listen, Herr Heine. Thank you for telling me about this. But I've been over the ship several times and I can assure you that . . .'

'Tan, don't fuck me about. I don't have the time. I left a written account of the whole voyage with my lawyers in New York, scaled. If they don't hear from me in twenty-four hours they will release it to the German and US governments. The whole fucking story, Tan, especially how the ship was deliberately scuttled.'

'Why should they believe you?'

'For the same reason that you had a private plane fly me up here. I can *prove* it, Tan. I know all the details, you see – things that only someone who was actually on the ship *could* know. Serial numbers; where certain things are; that sort of thing. Don't worry, Tan. They'll believe me just as fast as you did. Now get me to that fucking ship.'

Half an hour later, Tan was following Heine down to the shell-handling room.

Heine remembered every detail vividly, except that the whole room seemed to be only half the size it had appeared when he left it. There was the unfinished box, and there was the finished one, the lid still sitting askew where Tan had replaced it without nailing it down.

'Take the lid off, Tan.'

'I've seen inside, Heine. You were right.'

'Take the lid off, for Christ's sake.'

Tan shrugged and did what he was told. In spite of himself, he was fascinated by what this strange old man was telling him.

'Take a look.'

'It's a shell. I told you, I've seen it.'

'Take a look on the side. Near the top.'

Tan peered at the nose of the shell in the yellow beam of the flashlight.

'There's nothing. Just a small hole.'

'Get a drill. You'll find one below, several decks down, inside the magazine. I left it there.'

'I'm not going to drill that fucking thing, Heine. It'll go off.'

'Just get the drill. I made the hole. Don't worry.'

Tan disappeared down the ladders; he re-emerged fifteen minutes later, panting and sweating. 'Jesus, Heine. It's a long fucking way down there.' But he had the drill.

'Now, drill into the hole. It's quite safe.'

'You drill. I'm not doing it.'

Heine grabbed the drill from Tan, plunged it into the hole, and vigorously started turning the handle.

Soon the turning drill began to extrude a soft, dull yellow metal. Heine kept twisting the handle until he had a handful of the swarf, which he handed over to Tan.

'There. Take a look.'

Tan took it in his hand, looking doubtfully at it. It felt curiously heavy. He peered at it more closely, then he took a shaving and bent it. Instead of breaking, it gave, like soft putty. The metal had a yellow gleam to it.

'What is it, Heine?'

'What the hell does it look like?'

'I dunno. You tell me. It's not what I think it is – is it?'

'That's exactly what it is, Tan. Gold. That shell is solid gold. So is the other one. And down below there are another eighteen like those. All filled with solid gold, Tan.'

Tan just stared at Heine, unable to comprehend.

'That's what the voyage was all about, Tan. It was the end of the war, you see. The rats were leaving the ship. Some high-ups in Berlin got hold of this lot, melted it down, hid it on the ship and found this man Bach. He was a strange man. Sense of duty, all that crap. Knew nothing about the gold, thought it was a chance to do something for the Fatherland. Halfway across things began to get bad. He was going to shell fucking Washington and he would have killed us all. I had to do something, so the crew chucked him off. Then we dumped this thing up here. I tried to get the gold off then, but it was too late. I've been sitting in New York for fifty-five years, Tan, dreaming of this stuff. And now here I am again.'

'Jesus. You're not joking, are you? How much is here?'

'Twenty shells all told. Eight and three-quarter tons in total. But you can't move them, not by hand. Too fucking big and heavy.' For some reason, Heine thought it better not to mention the existence of the twelve smaller shells, which were still sitting in the magazine in their wooden boxes.

'So, what's the deal, Heine?'

'It's this. I'll play ball, keep silent about what happened. I'll say it was wrecked. All you've got to do is buy the gold from me.'

'How much?'

'Twenty million dollars. Into a Cayman Islands account. I presume you've got an account like that as well. Just transfer the money, and nobody finds out a thing. You get the ship, you get the gold, and you get Otto Heine saying good things about you.'

Tan ran the numbers through his head. The gold had to be worth far more than twenty million, but converting it into cash was another question. Still, the discount that Heine was offering should take care of any problems. And he still had the ship – and the man who was last to command it. Louse DeAngelis would lap it up.

'Herr Heine, you got yourself a deal. Just one condition.'

'Which is?'

'You stay on the ship until we get back. The moment we're safely tied up, you get your cash.'

Heine looked at Tan; he nearly smiled. He'd organised a mutiny and nearly got himself killed to stop the ship getting to America. Now he would be on board as it completed the final journey. Somehow, he didn't mind.

'Tan, I accept.'

'Great. First, I want you to get back to the salvage ship and do a TV interview to call the dogs off. The Germans are threatening to take me to court.'

'Fine by me. Just remember, you fuck me about and

the whole story gets released. Even the gold, Tan. I'm
nearly too old to care.'

'No problem, Otto.'

*

Christian Bach, like Otto Heine, had also been watching the progress of Billy Tan. He scowled every time
the Oriental came on the screen with the latest news
from the *Hindenburg*. He had watched the unfolding
story for two weeks; there was no point in making his
move just yet, Bach reasoned – wait and see if he was
going to be successful – and besides they were too
damned far away. It became clear that Tan was not
being put off, even by the reported activities of the
lawyers, and he would very probably succeed. Bach
decided it was time to make his move. He locked up
the shop and took a plane to New York, where he
made his way to the cable station that was broadcasting the story.

His first attempt to get through was rebuffed.
When he had walked into the reception area, the girl
at the desk had virtually threatened to call the police
even before he got his story out. Christian Bach was a
big man, bigger than his father, bigger than his
grandfather – although he inherited the same protruding ears – and, dressed in dirty jeans, boots, a
worn combat jacket and a baseball cap with a hand-
gun printed on the front, he was a far-from-friendly-
looking character.

The last thing he wanted was trouble from the
police, so he backed off and returned to the grubby
hotel near Times Square where he was staying. This
was not going to be as simple as it seemed.

It was time to try another approach. He had
brought with him the picture that hung in the shop –

the old photograph of the *Hindenburg* – and an old notebook in which his father had jotted down some of the story of the last voyage. He slipped them into a brown envelope, and slowly wrote a letter on a sheet of cheap hotel letterhead. It was in capitals because Christian Bach was never very comfortable about writing.

> *HERE ARE SOME ITEMS ABOUT THAT SHIP ON YOUR PROGRAMME. THE OLD GERMAN SHIP. MY GRANDFATHER WAS ERICH BACH WHO WAS THE CAPTAIN OF THAT SHIP IN THE WAR. I AM STAYING AT THE ABOVE PLACE. I KNOW SOME GOOD THINGS ABOUT THE SHIP. I AWAIT YOUR CONTACT.*

Bach signed it carefully, slipped the letter inside the envelope and sealed it. Then he walked out of the hotel, down six blocks, and posted it in the mailbox of the cable station. He returned to his hotel to await the call.

*

The FBI noted Bach's departure from his home airport to New York. They routinely had people at the airports, and a wide-awake young trainee spotted his name on the list.

The information was relayed to the New York office, where the local people watched him off the plane and followed him to the hotel. They didn't bother watching his visit to the TV station and then, later, his journey with the envelope. Although Bach was considered a risk, he was not a high one. There was no damage he could do in New York; there were no politicians or other possible targets in town. Washington would have been a different story. The President was at the White

House, and Bach's presence there would have got the temperature rising. But right now, even though they kept an eye on him, Christian Bach was considered harmless enough.

17

They had made Otto Heine stand on the foredeck of the battleship and were trying to get some make-up on him. All he did was swear sullenly at them in German and they gave up. Louise DeAngelis fussed around with the camera crew as they tried to improve their angles. Otto stood patiently beneath the drooped guns of turret Anton and waited for them to finish whatever it was they were meant to be doing. They were, he thought, very strange people.

The bustling stopped, a light came on, and Louise DeAngelis's face changed in a second from tight-lipped to wide smile. They were on the air.

'I'm here with Otto Heine, probably the last man to see the mighty *Hindenburg* before it was lost to the world. Mr Heine, you were actually on this ship's last voyage, is that right?'

'That is correct. I was with the ship when it sailed from Hamburg in 1945 just as the war was ending.' Heine spoke with a slight German accent that delighted DeAngelis. He sounded perfect.

'So you were in the German Navy?'

'Not really. I think the term is press-ganged. I was forced on to the ship at gunpoint. Things were very different in those days; they needed some crew, and I happened to be in Hamburg at the wrong time.'

'So, can you tell us exactly what happened to the ship?'

'Oh, yes. There was some problem with the engines; I don't know what. They stopped and we had no power. We started to drift. Then the captain – Bach, I think his name was – ordered us to abandon ship. I was one of the last off, just as the ship was getting near to the ice.'

'So it was definitely wrecked? Not scuttled? Not deliberately beached?'

'Absolutely not. We had to get off and leave the ship to its fate. We were adrift, you see.'

And that was exactly what Tan wanted to hear. Heine had kept his side of the bargain. DeAngelis carried on with Heine, getting the rest of his story – how he had arrived in America – but Tan had lost interest. Now he could get to work without fear of interference.

*

There were four steel cables, each one a foot in diameter, running from capstans on the aft deck of the *Zuider* up over the stern of the *Hindenburg* to where De Wit's crew had secured two of them to massive bollards newly welded to the deck. The deck was so rusty that they had to cut through to the underlying steel beams to get a secure fix. The other two cables had been secured to the two stern anchor capstans; the stern rails had been cut away to allow the massive cables plenty of room to swing and roll.

De Wit had positioned his own ship 500 yards off the stern of the wreck. His ship's computers, taking constant satellite fixes, had juggled the four main screws and the bow thrusters to maintain an almost unvarying position for the six hours it had taken to finally secure the cables. Now De Wit, given the final go-ahead by Tan, ordered dead slow ahead power; the four cables slowly rose dripping out of the cold sea, and began to take the strain as the *Zuider* gently pulled on the captive ship. De Wit's engines were two 24,000-horsepower MAN diesels – the 'fathers' – running the two inboard screws, and two 5,000-horsepower 'sons' running the outboard screws. Under full power, the *Zuider* had enough static pull to rip a concrete quay out of its foundations. It was the most powerful salvage ship in the world, and Tan was paying dearly for using it.

The tide was now right at the top. It had reached that gentle pause, no longer than ten minutes, when the flood ceased, turned, and started to ebb. The hull of the *Hindenburg*, now pumped clear of water, floated freely along all its length apart from the forward 110 feet. The ship was designed in such a way that the bow was the deepest part of the hull, with a bulging forefoot. While the top sections had been ripped open by the collision with the *Trent*, the lower sections were intact. And this was the part that was still deeply embedded in the clinging gravel of the inlet, rammed tightly in fifty-five years ago.

De Wit's plan was simple. Rather than the massive strain of trying to haul the ship straight out, he would pull it from side to side a few times. The movement of the huge hull and its sheer inertia would then tug the bow free. This would impose less strain on the cables and on the ship.

De Wit knew what he was doing. He and his brothers – and his father, and even his grandfather – had all been involved in the salvage business. The risks were huge. 'No cure, no pay' contracts were still common, and he had to be prepared to sail to maritime disaster scenes – without being asked – in the hope of getting a contract that might earn him a fortune or else could prove a total waste of time and fuel. But for every half-dozen failures, he would have a success big enough to pay for a whole year of running the ship and the crew. If he could rescue a drifting supertanker with its cargo intact, the insurers would be obliged to reward him with a massive salvage fee. He had bought the *Zuider* four years ago from the proceeds of a single salvage in the Indian Ocean.

De Wit looked out from the bridge over the stern. The cables drooped across the calm sea, as taut as they would get.

'Full ahead fathers. Bow full starboard.'

The giant diesels responded quickly, picking up revolutions, and the two screws bit powerfully into the water. At the same time, the bow-thrusters pushed the prow of the ship out to starboard. De Wit watched the stern of the wreck slide easily round under the pull.

'Bow full port,' he ordered.

Now the *Zuider* moved across the stern of the *Hindenburg* and started pulling from the other direction. The German ship's stern obediently followed.

De Wit repeated this manoeuvre seven times. Each time the stern of the *Hindenburg*, floating easily in the water, swung smoothly around. At the other end of the ship, the bow was being worked out of the deep gravel, forcing the bow first to one side and then to the other.

'Bows stop. Sons to full, fathers to full. Tell the fucking Russian to watch out. We're coming.'

Now all of the *Zuider*'s four screws were brought

into play for what De Wit hoped would be the final pull. Billy Tan, Otto Heine and Louise DeAngelis watched from a deck below the bridge, with the camera crew trying to get close-ups through a shaky telephoto lens. Captain Igor Davidovitch, nursing a bad headache, was watching over the stern rails of the icebreaker *Lev Semoyovitch*, and just grunted when a crew member told him of the warning to stay clear. He was fine. No problem. Don't bloody fuss. They were over a mile away, having cleared the start of a channel, just as instructed.

The *Zuider* took the strain. Nothing could be heard above the whine of the huge engines, now running at full power. The stern was a mass of churning white water, boiling up in huge domes as the screws beat the sea into a foam. The mighty battleship was still reluctant to give up its berth. The *Zuider* was not moving; the bow was starting to push itself up into the air under the strain. De Wit watched his cable carefully. The catenery – the bow of the cable under its own weight – should be enough to absorb a lot of the strain. But De Wit had seen cable this thick part like string before now. He would let the engines run another twenty seconds and then he would have to stand down to check the cable anchor points.

Suddenly, the distant stern of the *Hindenburg* dipped down into the water, and then a clean bow-wave started to curl away from the round hull. The huge ship was finally moving. The whine of the engines on the *Zuider* dropped as De Wit instantly ordered three-quarters power; but the old ship, now freed of the cling of the inlet, started moving fast, and the *Zuider* in turn began to accelerate into the water.

Tan was cheering loudly. DeAngelis and the crew, beaming the story live to New York, were getting

equally worked up. Only Otto Heine stood there
silently, watching the grey hulk slide down off the
beach and settle itself smoothly in the water. If it had
happened twenty years ago he might have been cheering with the others. But now it was just something that
he had to get over with, as quickly as possible.

The *Zuider* gathered speed. De Wit was watching
the cables when one of his crew turned to him.

'Sir, the Russian!'

De Wit spun round. Out of the forward bridge
windows the Russian icebreaker was sitting dead ahead.
The *Zuider*, with its massive engines, was moving
down the channel a great deal faster than Captain Igor
Davidovitch had expected, and even now he was
screaming at his crew on his bridge, breathless from
running up the ladders, to get the ship moving.

De Wit was horrified. He could not stop the *Zuider*,
even if he wanted to. The *Hindenburg* was running
loose behind him, and there was no way he could
prevent the German ship from smashing into his
stern if he tried to stop.

He picked up the VHF handset and started yelling at
the Russian ship. This created even more panic on
Davidovitch's deck. The *Zuider* was now less than half
a mile from the Russian. De Wit leaned on the ship's
horn and the mournful blast echoed across the icy
wastes in the still air.

Billy Tan leaned over the railings to see what was
going on.

'Fuck,' he muttered. The Russian ship was sitting
dead ahead of them.

But Igor Davidovitch always cut things fine. Maybe
now and then, he had to admit, a little too fine. Like
that unfortunate incident with the ferryboat near
Murmansk – but that was not altogether his fault,

damn it. But he usually got away with it. OK, he was screaming at his crew right now and giving every impression of panicking, but it was just his way. He liked to wind them all up a bit. And maybe that idiot Dutchman was racing down on him too fast. He should fucking slow down, he shouted back down the VHF.

Igor Davidovitch crossed himself and started muttering a prayer when the deck-plating began to vibrate violently. They had got to the engines and now they were running, faster and faster. He crossed himself again. He could feel his ship start moving. One more prayer, just to be on the safe side. The *Lev Semoyovitch* gathered speed and started crushing its way through the ice.

Igor paused, and looked back. The *Zuider* and its tow, although close, were not getting any nearer. He watched for several minutes to make sure, then breathed again, ordered the mate to maintain speed and went below. He badly needed a drink.

*

The call had come for Christian Bach, but it was not quite what he had expected. What he had imagined was a stretch limo and instant stardom as a celebrity on the cable station that was broadcasting Tan's efforts. What he got was a telephone call the next morning from the one-eyed Hispanic in the hotel's reception, telling him someone wanted to see him right away.

Bach ambled down the shabby staircase and found a young man, neatly dressed in a Ralph Lauren blazer, designer glasses and slicked-back hair.

'Mr Bach?' asked the young man eagerly, holding out a hand.

'That's me,' replied Bach unenthusiastically. He ignored the hand.

'From Newsworld. Sam Lauder. It's about your note. And your picture. Can we sit down?'

'Sure,' replied Bach, sounding disappointed. He led the keen young man to two grubby brown plastic armchairs.

'We got your package,' started Sam Lauder. 'Very interesting. Can you tell me more about it? The story, I mean?'

No limos. No stardom.

'And who exactly are you?'

'A researcher. Amongst other things. I work on the *Hindenburg* programme. Your stuff was very interesting. I'd like to know more about it.'

Bach was now feeling pissed off. They were not taking his story seriously; they had sent this young kid to see if he was talking horseshit. The thought crossed his mind that he should just get up and go back home, but then the whole journey would have been a complete waste of time. And then he thought about the money that his story was worth. He calmed himself down and tried to be nice to Sam fucking Lauder, smart little Ivy League shit.

So Bach told him the full story of his father and his grandfather, and about the tales he had been told of how Captain Erich Bach had been sent to his death, and how his son (Christian's father) and the captain's wife (Christian's grandmother) arrived penniless in an unforgiving America. Christian Bach knew how to sell; he had stood in his gunshop and watched customers who had walked in with no real intention of buying walk out half an hour later having spent $1,000. Now he sold his story to Sam, amplifying the characters – how hard life had been, how that ship had haunted their family, and now here it was coming to life again.

He had the perfect audience in Sam, who not only looked fresh out of college but really was. This was his first job. He had started just two months ago and he was keen to impress. And Christian Bach's story sounded to him like absolute dynamite, the way Bach told it.

An hour later, Sam had returned hotfoot to the editor's office and was re-telling the tale. He was bubbling over with enthusiasm.

Zee Prebble, the fiftysomething news editor on the station, was less enthusiastic and a great deal more cynical. But she listened carefully to the story and started to catch a taste of something more interesting, a human angle to run alongside DeAngelis's little old German guy. She was a great deal less interested in the story itself than in the pure TV possibilities that were right now flashing in front of her as Sam Lauder wittered on.

So, DeAngelis already had Otto Heine, the man who had led the mutiny and lost the ship whose rescue they had been covering. And now here was the grandson of the man whom Heine had sent to his doom, the original captain of the *Hindenburg*. She could visualise the old hulk anchored somewhere in Chesapeake Bay, with Washington in the distance. On the deck, beneath the towering guns, an emotional reunion: the man who stole the ship meeting the last of the Bach line. Old meets new. Generation meets generation. Nazi meets American hero. The possibilities were endless. It was a story that had, as they said in the trade, 'legs'.

Sam was still burbling about the injustices America had done to the Bach family.

'Sam?' said Zee, with a patient smile.

'Yes?'

'Shut the fuck up and get your man Bach here now. In person. Now disappear,' she added, turning to the phone. She hoped that spoilt bitch Louise DeAngelis was out of bed. The image of the handshake in the shadow of the guns was haunting her mind. She could run trailers for the rest of the week. The press would eat it. Zee Prebble, who had been fired from the staff of a tabloid paper for being too old, could barely restrain herself.

*

The *Lev Semoyovitch* led the way. The Russian ice-breaker drove itself over the top of the ice and its sheer weight crushed a passage through it. It was not too difficult a task; the ice was thin and breaking up anyway, other than in a few patches where it had remained stubbornly thick. The channel it left was littered with smashed ice that turned a dirty, slushy grey in the green sea.

De Wit's *Zuider* followed, keeping more than the normal distance aft of the Russian. No one trusted them. Now he had turned off his small 'sons', keeping the two big 'fathers' running to provide enough power to drag the hulk behind them at less than five knots. His four tow cables hung down, just touching the smooth water, while the massive grey bulk of the *Hindenburg* followed steadily behind, travelling stern first, its rudder having been cut loose and dumped by Tan's divers to make it more steerable. There was no point in trying to turn the ship; besides, with the damaged bow, the passage of time could have weakened it to the point where it might spring open and let in the sea if it was travelling bow-first. To Otto

Heine, watching from the deck of the *Zuider*, the old ship looked reluctant, as though it was being forced away from its berth against its will.

'All OK?' asked Billy Tan.

'Fine, Mr Tan. No problem,' confirmed De Wit with his usual Dutch lack of enthusiasm for anything.

'All on time?' asked Tan anxiously.

'All on time. Nothing to worry about.'

'I'll leave you to it then.'

'Yes, that's fine. Thank you,' said De Wit politely, hoping the American would get off his bridge and leave him alone. He was paying good money – a fee, too, not the usual 'no cure' stuff. Customers like Billy Tan didn't turn up every day and, irritating as he was, if he wanted to dance a hornpipe on his bridge then De Wit was not going to argue with him.

To the Dutchman's relief, Tan turned away and left the bridge. There was an almost audible sigh of relief from the bridge crew.

Now they could talk in Dutch. Bakker, De Wit's second-in-command, came along with a mug of coffee and seated himself in the comfortable swivel arm-chair next to De Wit's, looking out over the instrument console and the bridge windows.

The *Zuider* was state-of-the-art. Every known electronic aid was built into the gleaming steel console, and it looked more like a TV studio control room than the bridge of a ship. There were six large colour monitors over the top of the console; two of them showed views aft, from port and starboard, so that even though the bridge had aft-facing windows, they could watch the state of the towed vessel without stirring from the big leather chairs. Another two monitors showed the engine room – the engineer was based on the bridge and rarely needed to go below.

The fifth monitor displayed a real-time view of the North Atlantic Ocean from a satellite hovering 20,000 miles overhead. And the sixth monitor was tuned to a VCR unit that was showing one of last April's Ajax games; De Wit had new tapes flown over every week in the season when he could.

But, for a change, their eyes were not fixed on the monitor showing the football but on the satellite view. It showed clearly the coast of Greenland to the right and the icy wastes of the Canadian north to the left. The line of the ice cap was clearly visible to the south; but the northern coast of Canada was now invisible under a cloud formation measuring over 1,000 miles from edge to edge.

The formation was almost perfectly circular. Around the edge the cloud was breaking up in speckles, but towards the centre it grew darker and darker, other than in the dead centre – now located somewhere over Labrador – where there was a tiny clear space. It was a big summer storm, brewed up in the collision of the hot air mass over the continental United States and the cold Atlantic air, sending the hot air racing skywards and pulling the colder air in underneath, setting up powerful winds and massive thunderstorms that had drenched the Great Lakes before travelling northwards where the jet stream – the ever-present current of air moving eastwards towards Europe – would nudge it out into the Atlantic where it would probably spend itself or, if it survived, would create yet another wet summer weekend in England.

'So, what do you think?' asked Bakker eventually.

De Wit sipped from the china coffee mug. 'Who knows, Martyn? Maybe it will run south of us. Maybe it will just die off.'

'And if it doesn't?'

'Fuck knows. I've never tried to tow a 60,000-ton battleship in a storm before. Neither have you. I guess we hang on and see what happens.'

'You don't want to warn our esteemed client?'

'Warn him? Why should I do that? He'll shit himself. We'll worry about it if it gets near us. Leave him be, otherwise.'

Neither man was worried about the *Zuider* in the possible storm. They'd been through hurricanes before now and the ship was built to take the worst that the oceans of the world could throw at it. And this storm was a pussycat by comparison with some storms they had seen. Radar readings taken by the satellite showed winds of more than 50 mph around the centre where it would be at its worst. To De Wit, and to Bakker, it was little more than a stiff breeze.

But 60,000 tons of dead weight behind them would create a different picture. The *Zuider* had ample power to keep pulling the hulk. The problem was the tow-lines, the biggest that De Wit had ever trailed. Their weight, plus that of the towed ship, was already substantial. The extra force of a storm could be enough to snap the cable, leaving the *Hindenburg* drifting in the wind. Then it would be next to impossible to reconnect a tow-line until the wind died down. In the same circumstances, the normal practice was to take the tow-lines off and then stand by the salvaged vessel until the storm spent itself before re-rigging the lines. That way, you stayed in control and – most importantly – you preserved your towing-lines. Once parted, they could not be repaired, and even the *Zuider* didn't carry enough heavy steel hawser to replace the lines that would be lost.

If the storm got bad, De Wit would have no choice. But he didn't relish having to tell Billy Tan that he was thinking about letting his precious battleship go.

*

Christian Bach had changed. Sam Lauder had come running back and breathlessly insisted that Bach *immediately* accompanied him to the studios. Bach could see he had his man on the line, and so now he could afford to relax. All he had brought with him were jeans and boots, so he calmly informed Lauder that he would have to wait until he had been out and done some shopping. Sam had no option but to park himself in the seedy hotel lobby and wait for Bach to return.

He was re-reading a three-week-old copy of *Time* with the cover missing when he suddenly became aware of somebody standing in front of him. He looked up into the face of a tall black man, slightly overweight.

'You're waiting for Christian, aren't you?'

Sam stood up. 'Why, yes. You know him?'

'Oh sure. Me and him, we go back years. Nice guy.'

'Yes, indeed.'

The black man settled his large frame in the seat next to Sam and lit a cigarette without offering Sam one.

'You know Christian well?'

'Oh, well enough, well enough.'

'So where you from?'

'Me? I'm from Newsworld.'

'Newsworld? You mean the TV station? Wow!'

Sam Lauder always enjoyed telling people who he was and what he did.

'That's the one.'

'And what's Newsworld doing with my good buddy Christian Bach? He rob a bank or something?' The black man laughed, sharing the joke.

'Oh, no, nothing like that. No, just a story we're following up.'

'A story? I hear you TV reporters are pretty shit-hot,

huh? Some big deal, I guess?'

'Well, I'm not sure I should be . . .'

'Hey, kiddo, don't worry about me. I ain't no reporter. You think that? Don't worry. I'm just a buddy of Christian's. It don't worry me, boy.'

Sam Lauder didn't know what to say. But he desperately wanted to say something.

'It's about the *Hindenburg*. You know, the ship his grandfather arrived on? You know we're covering the story?'

'No shit? The *Hindenburg*, huh?'

'That's right. We plan to make it a big thing. Otto Heine is already on the ship; he's the guy who sank it in the first place. We want to introduce them: Heine and Bach. On the ship. Great shot.'

'Yeah. Great shot. And Christian's going to do this, is he?'

'Oh, well, I hope so. Yes, I'm sure he will. I'm waiting for him to come back now. From some shopping.'

'Sounds terrific. Well, I gotta go. Nice talking to you.'

'OK. I'll tell Christian I ran into you.'

'Yeah, kid. Do that. Give him my best,' and the black man got up and calmly but quickly disappeared from the hotel. Sam didn't want to chase him to ask his name. He was sure Christian would know who it was.

*

Otto Heine had barely moved from the stern deck of the *Zuider*, leaning on a guard rail, his wrinkled hands now grey with cold, staring out across the 500 yards of water spanned by the four steel cables. The rusting *Hindenburg* had settled into a comfortable passage, its once-forbidding bulk following its tow ship meekly like a big dog out for a walk.

Heine did not see the ship even though he was looking directly at it. He was doing his best to see the gold instead – the fat, dull grey shells sitting like eggs in the magazine, still there, filled with pure gold looted from the Reich. In 1945, as far as he was concerned then, the gold was the government's gold. Now that he knew where it really had come from – looted by the Nazis from the crippled states of Europe – he somehow felt even more strongly that it was his to remove. It had never even belonged to those Nazi crooks after all. He kept trying to calculate what his deal with Tan would buy him: $20 million and no tax to pay.

But what Heine was really seeing was ghosts.

He could see on the distant deck those people from more than fifty years ago. Vogele, the young lad who had helped him with the mutiny; Bach, and Schiller of course, both long gone; the dreadful Rois and the fat body of Schnee oozing blood like a slug on the bridge floor. They were memories that had faded soon after he arrived in America; but now, ever since he first saw the *Hindenburg*, they had sprung back, complete and vivid, as though they really belonged to the ship and had been waiting all those years for him to return. As Heine leaned on the railing looking across the water at the battleship, they seemed to be leaning on the stern rail looking back at him. Not just them, either, but the whole crew of young, frightened, lost and lonely kids, cast adrift at the tail-end of a war that none of them wanted and none of them understood. He had never even wondered what had happened to them until now.

Would Captain Erich Bach and Schiller and all the rest of them enjoy the irony that Heine, the man who had stopped the original voyage, had come back after all this time to help them complete it?

Beneath his feet, the *Zuider's* engines gave out a steady, deep drone that was felt more than heard. The wake of the Dutch ship unrolled steadily behind them. A pair of curious gulls had taken up residence in the gentle slipstream. There had been a stillness about the sea and the air that was the same as he remembered when he left Greenland behind him. Now he was suddenly aware of a flickering breeze. He looked up. The sky overhead, instead of being streaked with ice-white clouds, now showed a heavier greyness in the west.

*

Bethe Fischer, seated in her comfortable office in Bonn, watched the interview with Otto Heine. She had leaned forward in her chair, arching her fingers against each other to make a steeple of her long, elegant hands, and stared at the screen over the top of her gold-rimmed glasses.

'Play it again,' she ordered, when the tape had finished. Her assistant dutifully rewound the cassette. Once more Otto Heine's humourless face answered DeAngelis's questions with a quiet, accented English.

> '*So, can you tell us exactly what happened to the ship?*'
> '*Oh, yes. There was some problem with the engines; I don't know what. They stopped and we had no power. We started to drift. Then the captain – Bach, I think his name was – ordered us to abandon ship. I was one of the last off, just as the ship was getting near to the ice.*'
> '*So it was definitely wrecked? Not scuttled? Not deliberately beached?*'
> '*Absolutely not. We had to get off and leave the ship to its fate. We were adrift, you see.*'

'Bullshit,' murmured Bethe Fischer in English.

'I beg your pardon?' responded the assistant. His grasp of English was not up to Fischer's.

'He's talking nonsense. The ship never started to drift. The engines were fine. Bach was turfed off, he knows that. So why's he telling this story?'

The assistant remained silent. He could add nothing.

Bethe Fischer sent him out of the room and, once the thick wooden door had closed almost silently behind him, she reached for the phone and dialled a long number. It rang for thirty seconds before a tired English voice answered it.

'Yes? Who's that?'

'Miss Beasley, it is Bethe Fischer, calling from Germany.'

'*What the hell do you want?*' shouted Lil. Like many of her generation, she assumed it would help her voice carry over the miles to Germany if she shouted.

'Miss Beasley, did you see that interview with Otto Heine? On board the *Hindenburg*?'

'Don't be bloody silly. I don't have a telly, do I?'

'Heine was on the ship. Your book said he was the leader of the mutiny, according to Schiller's account. Now fifty-five years later he suddenly turns up and claims the *Hindenburg* had lost power and Bach ordered them to abandon ship.'

'Total crap. You read my book.'

'I know that. Why would he tell them that?'

'Bloody obviously to let your Chinaman get his bloody boat out. Must have paid him. Or else he doesn't want to admit to the mutiny. Or probably both.'

'I suppose so.'

'Course it is. You're the bloody lawyer, woman.'

'Perhaps. But it doesn't sound right. I don't know why. Heine just didn't look like that sort of man.'

'According to Schiller, he shot a man and led a mutiny. What sort of person do you think he is?'

'Things were different in those days. People did

things they wouldn't normally have done. Circumstances. Heine just looks different, that's all.'

'Suit yourself. But he's lying through his teeth in any event.'

'You'd testify to that. I mean, if I needed you to?'

There was a snort from the other end of the phone. 'Only if you promise to hang the bastard.'

'Would you testify?'

'Why not?'

Fischer quietly put down the phone, then thought her plan through carefully. She had had some dealings with American courts before. Governments, even their own, were not liked by American judges; they tended to take the citizen's side. Foreign governments were liked even less, particularly the German government. Waking up a judge to demand an injunction would not really be a good idea, especially if used against an American citizen, and especially if the evidence was not rock solid.

Bethe Fischer also knew the power of the media in America. Most trials were over before they had begun. The arguments would be rehearsed in the press or, increasingly, on the TV for months ahead. No jury was immune – neither were most judges. The clever lawyers were those who decided to fight the cases in public before turning up at court.

She sent her assistant off to track down the telephone numbers. It took ten minutes to get the first call through.

'Miss DeAngelis, I'd like to talk to you about Otto Heine,' began Bethe Fischer.

18

Clear of the ice now, and with the eccentric Russian departed, the *Zuider* could make its way south and west at the best speed that De Wit judged safe. He had ordered revolutions for ten knots, and a rolling bow-wave cleaved away from the rounded stern of the *Hindenburg*, still following the Dutch ship faithfully through the warming seas.

The skies had already darkened. The storm was moving towards them, and they were moving to meet it. The faster De Wit went, the sooner they would be in the middle of it, and then through and out of it. He and Bakker had watched the satellite screen carefully. The wind-speed numbers had not changed dramatically. It would be uncomfortable, but neither of them could yet see much need to cast their charge adrift. They would have to take it slowly. At worst, they might have to merely maintain steerage way for perhaps six or seven hours to relieve the strain on the cables.

The long, slow Atlantic swell – with crests almost impossible to see, spread a quarter-mile apart – was still running, but the freshening breeze was rippling the smooth surface, and the clouded skies had turned the water from an ice-green to a dull grey. The

warmer air of the front turned to a light drizzle as it
met the colder air, and Bakker had turned on some of
the wipers on the bridge windows. They moved slowly
backwards and forwards across the misting glass.

The sea before them was still empty. The long coast
of Labrador was to their starboard, 300 miles away,
and it would be half a day or more before they started
to meet the traffic running to northern Europe and
Iceland up from the St Lawrence, mostly slow bulk
carriers heavy with wheat and lumber. Further south
they would begin to meet more traffic, the New York
tramps and cargo ships, high tankers returning in
ballast to Rotterdam; and further south still, the top-
heavy container ships running the east coast routes,
steel containers stacked seven and eight high on the
open decks, nothing more than one huge box of cargo
with a sharp bow welded on to one end and an engine
and rudder bolted on the back.

De Wit was in charge of an unwieldy vessel. He
couldn't stop, and he could barely manoeuvre. He had
already hoisted the 'vessel constrained in her ability to
manoeuvre' signal, but these days most crews keeping
a lazy watch on the bridges of nearing vessels would
have little idea what the flags actually meant, even if
they bothered to look at them.

*

Benjamin St James finished the greasy hamburger
and wiped his fingers. He dropped the sticky carton
into the bin at the side of his desk, then picked up the
file on Christian Bach once more. He had already read
about Bach's habits, noted by the FBI over the past few
years. He had always been graded 'suspicious' and for
some months, following several outrages by the survivalist groups with which he seemed to be in

sympathy, he had been watched closely. But apart from his unpleasant habits and opinions, he gave little evidence of being anything other than just a harmless loud-mouth, hence his status had month by month been downgraded to little more than 'interesting'.

But then Christian Bach had suddenly headed for New York. There was no reason to think anything other than that he just decided to take a trip, but he had hardly ever moved outside his home state and so it pushed him up the FBI lists a few more places.

Ben St James had been given the far from exciting job of finding out what this particular young man might be up to. Just routine. So Ben had wandered into the hotel lobby and been told by the clerk that no, Bach was out, but if he wanted to wait he could – and why not go and sit with the other guy who was also waiting for him?

Having returned from his brief conversation with Sam Lauder, Ben had pulled the whole file from the FBI's Washington HQ via the secure e-mail link. It had taken twenty minutes to print, and he had gone to get his hamburger while the printer rolled out the sheets of text.

As he read the file, what was puzzling Ben St James most was the *Hindenburg* story. There was only the briefest mention in the file, but no detail whatsoever. Now Bach had popped up out of the woodwork, ready to go on some high-profile TV show, to talk about something that the FBI had no information on. That alone made Ben worry. What was this little jerk up to? The guy was a high-class weirdo into the bargain. Bach was a loner, into guns, hated the government – in other words, almost the classic profile of the kind of psychopath who had bombed, shot and gassed their ways around the civilian centres of the West for the last ten years. Except that Bach had actually done none of those things. Yet.

Ben put down the file and lumbered to his feet. Time to go and see the boss. He pulled on his jacket and went down the corridor to where Max had his small office. Ben rapped on the glass door loudly.

'Yeah,' shouted a voice from inside.

Max was on the phone, and as Ben came in he cupped his hand round it and turned his back. Ben waited for a full five minutes until Max finished his call.

'Ben, what can I do for you?' he asked with a slightly harassed air.

Ben St James sat down without being asked and related the story of Christian Bach, or at least what he knew. Max nodded all the way through like a dog.

'So?' he asked finally, when Ben had finished. 'You got nothing, Ben. Supposition. Imagination. No evidence of any sort. He's not armed, is he?'

'Don't know, Max. But it sure as hell stinks to me.'

'Sure as hell stinks to me as well, Ben. Looks like you got no option, really.'

'Pull him in?'

'That's what I'd do.'

'He'll scream like hell.'

'Be polite to him.'

'He'll want lawyers, all that shit.'

'Don't violate his civil rights, then, Ben. Like I said, be nice to him.'

'You authorise this? For the record?'

Max looked up at the agent. 'Sent me a note. I'll sign it.'

And Ben St James left the office to go down to the echoing underground car park where he kept his Toyota.

*

Louise DeAngelis had scribbled down everything that
Bethe Fischer had said – and Bethe had said a lot about
Otto Heine. As far as DeAngelis was concerned, it was
pure gold. Ever since Zee Prebble, her editor in New
York, had called her with the idea of the Bach interview in the shadow of the guns, she had felt the
initiative starting to slip, and for Louise DeAngelis that
was not a happy state of affairs.

Bethe Fischer had given her four pages of hastily
scribbled notes. But right at the end of them were two
simple questions – did Otto Heine really organise a
mutiny on the ship, and what then happened to
Captain Erich Bach? If the German woman was right,
Heine was not the simple crewman, the nice old
guy, he claimed to be. And, as Bethe was at pains to
point out, it made Heine's previous claims to have
abandoned the ship highly suspect. What had *really*
happened?

It would make a great scene, a damn sight better
than Zee's idea of having the two of them – Heine and
Bach – meet under the shadow of the guns. It was the
kind of stuff the channel would love: confrontational,
exclusive, probing. It raised the story to a matter of
high politics and history and would give Louise
DeAngelis a gravitas that sometimes she felt she
needed.

It didn't really matter whether what Bethe Fischer
had said was true or not. As far as Louise DeAngelis
was concerned, truth had nothing to do with it. Just
standing there and asking the questions would be
enough. An old man; a German, to boot. And, Bethe
suggested, it would be more than interesting to ask
Otto Heine exactly how he had got into the country.

It was going to be difficult to play this one, thought DeAngelis, unless she kept it all secret. Billy Tan would go crazy. Heine was the man who made the operation legitimate. Throw doubt on his story and the whole thing began to get weak. But then, she thought, that too would make a pretty good scene. And Louise DeAngelis would be at the centre of it. Eat your heart out, Ted Turner.

Now she needed to get hold of Otto Heine for tonight's broadcast. She'd do it live, for the 6 pm bulletin, just to make sure the other stations could pick it up for the later newscasts, and to guarantee that the morning papers would be able to do full justice to the story. They'd even have time to get some stills.

She made her way up to the saloon just beneath the bridge, hoping to find Otto.

*

Christian Bach and Sam Lauder had decided to walk. It was only a few blocks down the street. The weather was nice, the heat was not too oppressive, and in any event Zee had still refused to send a limo. 'Get a fucking cab' was her reply to Sam's request.

Christian had managed to find himself just about the worst outfit imaginable for a TV interview: a loud yellow-and-red check jacket that would strobe furiously on camera, and underneath it an orange shirt that would make it impossible to balance the colour, thought Sam, taking pride in his professionalism. He was going to advise him against wearing that combination, but something about Bach made him feel nervous. What the hell. They could sort it out when they got there.

They had just turned the corner from the hotel. A dull red Toyota was cruising slowly behind them.

They turned to the right to cross the street, but the lights at the intersection stopped them from doing so. The Toyota stopped as well, even though the lights were green for the traffic.

Two van drivers and half a dozen cab drivers leaned on their horns and yelled out of their windows.

'You fucking blind? Move the fucking car, dummy,' shouted the van driver right behind Ben. Ben simply opened his door, raised a single finger to the driver and walked quickly out towards Christian. The van driver screamed some more, hauled his wheel round to pass the Toyota and accelerated past it, still yelling from the window. But Ben was too big to get out and argue with.

'Christian Bach? Ben St James, FBI. I'd like a talk with you,' said Ben, showing his ID and standing right in front of Bach, up close, forcing Bach to stand back a little and look up. The agent's size was impressive.

'What the fuck do you want?' asked Bach, taken aback.

'Like I said, I'd like a few words with you.'

'I can't. I'm on my way with this guy. To the TV place.'

'You're the guy who I spoke to in the hotel,' said Sam.

Christian Bach looked at Sam. What the hell was happening here?

'I won't need you for long. Get in the car. It's just routine. I mean, I can arrest you if you'd prefer,' growled Ben reasonably.

Bach scowled. The man was not going to go away. 'OK. Sam, I'll be late. Half an hour tops. Just you wait, you hear?'

'Sure, no problem,' replied Sam, not knowing quite what to do.

Bach got into the waiting Toyota. Ben climbed in next to him. The car pulled out suddenly. Ben waved his arm lazily out of the window and did a slow U-turn, ignoring yet more screams of rage from the drivers for whom a second's delay threatened to cause mass heart attacks. The Toyota sped back up the street, leaving Sam on the pavement being jostled by hurrying pedestrians, staring after it.

*

'Why? I have answered your questions. What more do you need?' asked Otto Heine testily. He didn't like the woman, and he didn't like the way the camera was shoved in his face and the bright lights were shone in his eyes and the way he was being treated like a performing circus animal.

'Oh, just a bit more background. Some of your recollections about the ship. That sort of thing. You're quite a personality back home, Mr Heine, you know that? People want to hear more about your story.'

Otto did not want to be a personality or to tell any more of his story. He wanted to go home without any fuss, collect Tan's cash and spend it on a luxurious retirement. The last thing he needed was other people poking into his business.

'No, I've done enough,' he replied. 'No more,' and he turned to leave.

Louise DeAngelis was desperate. 'Listen, you know the German government is trying to stop this thing, don't you?'

Heine stopped. He had heard about Billy Tan's legal problems. The idea that the German government was behind them suddenly filled him with fear. His past was not one that would have endeared him to the Germans, either then or now. And the image of Schnee's fat body expiring on the bridge still gave him nightmares, that one day they would catch up with him. It was more than fear that flashed through Heine; it was a sudden, heart-stopping terror. He had come so close. Would the bastards still take it away from him?

'It's impossible. This has nothing to do with them. They cannot stop it.'

'Oh, but they can. You see, if they can prove that the ship was scuttled, not wrecked, then the ship is still Germany's. I had one of their legal people call me, only this afternoon.'

'But the ship was wrecked. I have already said so,' Heine protested.

'But you need to say so *again*, don't you see? Some more detail would help. Otherwise they will make such a fuss in the courts that Tan will have to stop. Do you want that? It's up to you, really. You can stop it if you tell everyone exactly what happened again. I mean, you were the only one there, weren't you?'

Heine looked at her suspiciously. He didn't like her. Not at all. But she was right. Only he knew what had really happened. No one else could possibly know the truth.

'Very well,' he replied finally. 'Five minutes. No more. And that's all.' He didn't see what option he had. He would have to elaborate a little more on his story, that was all. It wouldn't be a problem.

'That's just great,' beamed DeAngelis. 'It's best done live. We have a slot coming up about two hours from now. We'll do it out on the deck with the old ship behind us. Looks as if it's going to rain. You'll need that sailor stuff on – maybe one of those cute hats? Can you manage that?'

Louse DeAngelis could see the image in her mind. A windswept deck, the old ship behind them and ancient Otto Heine, small and wiry, done up like a real sailor in a big jacket and hat. And then she too could dress the same way ... the salt wind blowing in her hair. She'd have to remember to put on waterproof make-up. Great shot.

Heine scowled. 'Very well. Two hours' time. And remember, just five minutes.'

'No problem, Otto. Can I call you Otto?'

But Otto Heine had turned his back and was already going.

*

The captain of the *Momo*, Gabriel Garcia, was hardly feeling the storm even though he was in the middle of it. His ship was a fully laden 210,000-ton dead-weight crude oil tanker that sat like a rock in the water, barely moving as the huge Atlantic waves rolled up to his stern and travelled along the length of his ship, taking nearly half a minute to complete the half-mile that lay between Garcia's high bridge and the blunt bow. The bigger waves broke over the gunwales as they travelled, sloshing green water lazily across the wide red deck. His tanks were full of crude oil from the Gulf of Mexico that was mostly destined for Rotterdam, but 20,000 tons were to be delivered to Reykjavik in Iceland along the way, and so Captain Garcia was running well north of his usual route that would have taken him through the Western Approaches and the English Channel.

Although it was not a route he knew well, he remained relaxed and unhurried. It lay well outside the normal shipping lanes and in this weather the local traffic would be shut up in port, safe and sound.

The coast of Labrador was well to his port, about 300 miles off, and he was pushing through the wind-blown sea on a north-easterly course with the wind behind him. The wind was gusting outside, but the bridge was silent and warm. The single engine, deep below, made only the gentlest hum, and the motion of the tanker in the sea was not even enough to upset Garcia's afternoon cup of coffee, served in a small china cup and saucer by an Indian steward in a white coat.

Garcia sat in his captain's swivel chair and leaned on the armrests to take another look at the radar screen. He was not one of those tanker captains who would switch on the autopilot, set a twenty-mile alarm zone on the radar and then go below. He was a responsible and conscientious skipper who ran a good ship, which was why he was trusted with one of the biggest vessels in his owner's fleet.

The screen was empty. Even the wave clutter had been tuned out, and the only sign that the set was actually working was the occasional haze of a distant heavy rain shower, flickering on like a coloured rash and then fading.

Garcia turned to stare out of the windows. This was the sort of trip he enjoyed. With two years to go before retirement, he liked voyages like this one: steady, peaceful and unexciting.

*

Christian Bach sat alone in the white-painted interview room that Ben St James had shown him into fifteen minutes ago, and then left him. 'Cooking' was the trade term.

He had been nervous at first, but now he was starting to get annoyed. He was on his way to stardom and then these people pulled him in. What for? What did they want?

In Christian Bach's mind, the role of the FBI was a clear one and, at least to him, perfectly logical. The government consisted of degenerate criminals, out to line their own pockets and to take away every honest citizen's freedom to do what they wanted in the privacy of their own towns. Withdrawing the freedom to own a gun – even if it was a high-powered machine gun that could punch through a concrete wall – was just one sign of what they were trying to do. There were the blacks and the Jews, put in positions of power. There were the drug dealers, let loose to get to the kids. As far as Christian Bach was concerned, the American people had their backs against the wall and needed to defend themselves against these men. It was the only honourable thing to be done.

These were not mere opinions, voiced when he had drunk too many beers. For Bach, they were deeply held views – in fact, they were not views at all, but an absolute, crystal-clear reality. And the FBI were nothing more than paid hoodlums, tasked with finding people like himself who were fighting for their rights and intimidating them. In his world, the FBI were the bad guys. And now they had him.

The door opened suddenly. Ben walked in, dragged out a chair and plumped himself behind the table facing Bach.

'So,' started the big black man, reading from the e-mail prints he had gathered together in a buff folder stamped *Top Secret*, just to look impressive. 'Christian Bach. That's you, am I right? Sure I am. Now, you wanna tell me just what the fuck are you doing here in New York? You belong in that shitty little hick town of yours with all your weirdo friends. What are you doing here in civilisation? You wanna tell me *that*?'

'Take a ride,' said Bach as aggressively as he dared.

'Take a ride, huh? It's you that's taking the ride, Bach.

Back to your fucking woods. We can live without your sort here, boy.'

'You can't do a thing.'

'Listen, boy, we're the fucking FBI. We can do what we want – particularly with creeps like you. Now, you going to tell me what you're doing here?'

Bach stayed silent. Ben St James watched him from across the table. His eyes fixed Bach's, and they stared at each other, unblinking, for a full ten, maybe twenty seconds. Then Ben St James burst out laughing.

'What's the problem?' asked Bach, unsettled.

St James kept laughing, still staring at Bach. Then his beaming smile vanished. He stood up suddenly, keeping his eyes fixed on Bach, walked around the table and bent down to thrust his face into the other man's, so that their noses almost touched.

Bach was taken aback. He shuffled back his chair, trying to escape. St James grabbed his shoulder firmly so that he couldn't move.

'I'll tell you what the problem is, Bach. You're here for some reason and I and the rest of the FBI just won't feel happy until we know what it is. Now, you can either tell me what you're doing here, or I'll make the rest of your very short stay in New York so goddamned uncomfortable that you'll wish you'd taken up my invitation anyway. So?'

Bach wriggled free of the grip and stood up.

'Jesus. You want to know what I'm doing here? I'll tell you. There's this ship. My grandfather came to this goddamned country on it and they killed him for it. Now they're dragging it out of the fucking ice and bringing it back. What I'm doing here is being interviewed by the fucking TV, is what I'm doing. They want *me*, understand? That's it, for God's sake. Now, you gonna let me get on or do I get my fucking lawyers on you?'

Ben St James looked at him. The kid was rattled, and probably telling the truth.

'You? On some TV show?'

'I swear to God. Newsworld. You fucking watch it and fucking see.'

'Christian Bach, get out of here. People like you should not be on TV. You shouldn't be alive. If I were you, boy, I'd get my ass out of New York by tonight. Now fuck off, and if I see you again I'll fucking kick five kinds of shit out of you.'

'Just let me out of here,' replied Bach sullenly.

In less than five minutes, Christian Bach found himself back out on the street. He'd beaten them again, he told himself, smiling. They had nothing on him.

He walked now, and twenty minutes later he arrived at the Newsworld office. He proudly went into reception and asked for Zee Prebble and Sam Lauder. The receptionist took his name and he sat down and waited.

The wait grew uncomfortably long. He had read the four magazines – or at least looked at the pictures – and he was getting bored. He went up to the receptionist.

'What's the problem? How long do I have to wait?' The girl looked up and asked him to sit down before making another, secretive call. A further five minutes passed, and then two stocky black security guards walked quickly into the area.

'Mr Bach?' asked one.

'Yeah. I been waiting for ages. What's the trouble?'

'You're to leave. Sorry. There's been a mistake,' said one.

'What do you mean?'

'He means get out, sonny. Now,' ordered the other one.

'I'm here for a fucking interview. Zee Prebble. Sam Lauder. You ask them.'

'We've been told to escort you off the premises. Do we call the police, or do you go?'

He looked at the two guards and at the receptionist. They were determined. Bach suddenly realised what had happened. That fat nigger at the FBI had spooked the station, that's what he'd goddam done: *Keep that Christian Bach off your programme. He's not one of us.* They worked together. The establishment, media bleeding hearts. They were probably queens as well.

'OK, I'm going. But you tell them from me that's not the last they've seen of me, no fucking way. You got that, nigger?' Angrily, Bach stormed from the building.

Still seething, he arrived back at his hotel and he went to the desk for his key.

'Sorry, Mr Bach. Here's your bill. Your luggage is there, by the door. We checked your card print and it's been declined. We need cash. Now.'

Jesus. They'd even got to the hotel people and the credit card outfits. He slammed some dollars on the desk without even looking at the bill and disappeared out of the door.

Christian Bach was on the streets of New York and he was starting to feel very, very angry.

*

Otto Heine was reluctantly wearing a bright orange waterproof jacket and a baseball cap with *Zuider* embroidered on the front. He flatly refused to put on the sou'wester that Louise DeAngelis offered him, so she was wearing it instead. She had spent several minutes examining herself carefully on the playback monitor, and whispered anxious questions to the cameraman.

Finally she was happy with the way she looked. She

checked her watch and glanced at the TV monitor,
which had been installed inside the saloon behind one
of the windows where they could see it out on the
rainswept deck. It showed the transmission from
Newsworld studio and would give DeAngelis her cue.
There were still several minutes to go.

The scene behind Heine was more perfect than
even Louise could have dared hope. The wind had
risen and storm-black clouds scudded across the sky,
throwing down sudden drenching showers. Apart
from looking good, the sound of the gusting wind
gave added drama, especially when the sound man at
DeAngelis's suggestion pulled away some of the 'fur'
that normally suppressed wind noise on his microphone. The seas had started to build up. The *Zuider*,
stabilisers notwithstanding, had developed enough
pitch and roll from the quartering seas to make the
horizon – as seen through the videocamera's view-
finder at any rate – pitch and roll alarmingly, even
though it felt nothing like as bad on the open deck.

And in the near distance – the cameraman could
make it look nearer and more forbidding by using a
long-focus setting on his lens – the great bulk of the
Hindenburg rolled gently in the seas. The ship was too
heavy to be moved much by the waves, but as she was
being hauled through the approaching seas stern-to,
they would smash against the blunt aft sections and
spray would burst high into the air before the wind
caught it and ripped it back across the old ship,
semi-obscuring the vessel.

Hollywood couldn't have made a better scene.

The Newsworld studio in New York had sent a time
code to the ship monitor, counting down for two
minutes. The cameraman heaved the big Sony on to
his shoulder and waited for the image to stabilise.

DeAngelis waited silently, her face unsmiling. Heine waited too, squinting against the bright white infill light that illuminated his face.

The sound man watched the monitor and gave her a five-second countdown with his fingers. As he closed his last finger in a fist, DeAngelis's face suddenly beamed a wide smile. She doesn't waste them, thought Heine.

'Good evening. This is Louise DeAngelis reporting live from the deck of the *Hindenburg*'s tow ship. As you can probably see and hear, we're caught in the middle of a fierce Atlantic storm. With me this evening is Herr Otto Heine, one of the original crew of the *Hindenburg* on its last fateful voyage. A few nights back, Otto gave us his account of what happened during those last days. But doubts still remain. Was the ship abandoned to its fate, as Billy Tan would have us believe, or did something altogether more sinister happen on that day fifty-five years ago? Only one man can answer these questions. Otto, you were there. Tell us about those last minutes.'

Otto Heine's heart started thumping. What the fuck was all this about? Why was she talking about 'something altogether more sinister'?

'I have told the story already. We had an engine failure; we were drifting. We were ordered to abandon the ship to its fate,' he replied, sullenly.

'And Bach? The captain? What happened to Captain Erich Bach, Otto?'

'As I said, I do not know. He was not on the boat I was on. I presume he was lost.'

'I see. Now, do you remember a man called Schiller? He was one of the officers.'

Schiller, the man who had left Heine to rot in the brig. He remembered Schiller. How in the name of God did this woman know about Schiller all of a sudden?

'I think so. Yes, I recall an officer called Schiller.'

'Did you know that Schiller was on the same boat as Bach, the captain? And that Schiller told a very different story, before he died?'

Heine stared at her. 'No, I did not know,' he said quietly.

Louise had him. She – and the viewers – could see the discomfort on his face, even in his body language. He was clearly hiding something. Great TV.

'According to Schiller, there was no engine failure, no abandonment. Schiller says that you, Otto Heine, led a mutiny on board the ship. You led the crew into a violent uprising and you even killed a man – Schnee. One of the petty officers. He says you then threw the captain off the ship, and he killed himself rather than face the shame of defeat. Is *that* what really happened, Herr Heine?'

Heine just stared. He could not find the words and the light was blinding him. DeAngelis was just a fuzzy shadow and he could not see her face at all.

'You have nothing to say, Herr Heine? Perhaps, then, I can ask you how you came to be in America? Is it true that you sneaked in across the Canadian border, just after the war? That you're really an illegal immigrant, and you've been living in New York all these years, hiding from the authorities?'

'I have told you what happened. We had to get off the ship. It was many years ago.'

'So how do you account for Schiller's story?'

'I have no idea. I have not heard this before today.'

'Is it true you had a criminal record in Hamburg? Before the war?'

Heine nearly spat. 'Many people were made criminals under the Nazis. Perhaps you had forgotten?'

But Bethe Fischer had found the old Hamburg

police records. There was an Otto Heine, whose age fitted, who had been prosecuted three times, all for minor theft, and had been jailed once. They were normal, civil crimes. She had given DeAngelis the details.

'But these crimes were not political. On 8th February 1939 you were fined for stealing some coats from a warehouse. On 19th October 1943 you were fined again for selling stolen cigarettes. In 1944 you were jailed for another theft. Is all that true?'

Where in the name of God had she got this from? 'Times were very difficult. People were starving. You had to make your own way in the world. It was war, you know. People forget what it was like. You never had those problems in America.'

'I see. So what really happened to the ship, Herr Heine? Didn't you scuttle it, after you'd mutinied and thrown the captain to his death?'

'It wasn't like that!'

'So you admit to the mutiny?'

'Listen. It was war. I lived in Hamburg, trying to make a living. The Nazis were killing people and the Americans were bombing us. I had to use my wits to stay alive. I was forced on to that ship at gunpoint, and I was beaten and abused and humiliated and locked up. Bach was a lunatic. You know what his mission was? He was sent to shell Washington. Your beloved capital city, Miss, was to be destroyed by the guns of the *Hindenburg*. It was revenge, nothing else. But Hitler killed himself. And you know what? Bach still wanted to carry on. He would have got us blown out of the water before we even got near Washington. Bach would die. I would die. The whole bunch of boys on that fucking ship would die. You know how that feels – you know what it's like when somebody is doing their best to kill you? Listen, Miss, it was simple. I either did something or they would kill me. It was forced on me. Sure, Bach killed himself. It was sad. He was crazy but an honourable man. I had to do it. I saved myself, I saved almost everybody else on that ship. And, fuck it, I think I probably saved Washington from getting the same treatment as you had been handing out to us Germans for years. That's what really happened. Do what the hell you like. It was the damned right thing, you know that?'

Louise almost went down on her knees to thank God. The man was passionate and didn't give a shit. He'd told the truth, and it was a better tale than anything she could have come up with. He was almost in tears, or was it just the wind and the rain? Who gave a fuck? It was brilliant TV, and Louise DeAngelis had done it.

Would he go any further? 'And what about the ship, Herr Heine? What really happened to the ship?' she asked softly, almost sympathetically. She knew her viewers would be feeling sorry for the old man after an outburst like that.

But Heine would have none of it. They had fitted a small microphone to his jacket. He tore it off and threw it to the wet deck, turned, and marched away.

Louise turned to the camera and put on her 'concerned and serious' face. 'Well, there you have heard one of the most dramatic stories of the high seas. Herr Otto Heine, the German mutineer, at last tells the real tale of those events fifty-five years ago. Who can tell the pressures and emotions raging on that night when Heine sent his captain to his death? And you heard tonight, for the first time, the story of what this huge battleship was really trying to do. We'll have to find out much more about these events, that's for sure.

For now, this is Louise DeAngelis, for Newsworld, live in the stormy North Atlantic Ocean.'

She held her concerned face until she could see the scene change on the monitor. Then she burst into a shriek of triumph and punched the air. The cameraman put down the big Sony.

'Way to go, Lou baby, way to go,' he grinned.

And then Billy Tan erupted from the door, shirtsleeved and oblivious to the wind and the rain, his face contorted into a red rage – and he was heading straight for Louise DeAngelis.

19

De Wit stared intently at the radar screen. Bakker, his first officer, had shown him a new blip on the screen two minutes ago, right at the edge of the set's range, where it had come and gone as the big scanner mounted high on the mast just detected its presence. But now the blip had stopped fading. There was no doubt about it: it was big, it was moving at around twelve knots and it was running on a course towards them, off De Wit's starboard bow about twenty degrees. Bakker had already punched up the range rings, which indicated the other vessel at thirty miles' distance, and the heading markers, which showed yellow dotted lines projecting forward the predicted course of the ships – Zuider's pointed directly 'upwards' on the screen, and the other ship's crossed from the right and intersected some eighteen miles ahead. According to the computer chip inside the radar set, the ships were on a collision course.

But at that range the computer that figured out the courses was often wrong. So De Wit was just quietly watching, waiting to see what would really happen. Every time the scanner swept over the other ship, it had moved along its course another few feet, and the computer updated its course prediction every five sweeps. The dotted yellow line indicating the other vessel's expected route swung across the screen like a pendulum at first, but now it had settled down and, apart from small changes, it was remaining stubbornly on an intersecting course.

De Wit was irritated more than worried. The other ship was clearly big – a tanker or bulk carrier of some sort – and they usually behaved as though they owned the seas, expecting everyone else to get out of their way because they were so big and difficult to shift. Most vessels were happy to oblige. Ships approaching each other were supposed to change course to pass port to port, and to make the course change big enough for the other ship to see it clearly. But this situation was slightly different. To pass port to port, this other ship would have to cross right over De Wit's course, and they were close enough to make that dangerous. The right thing to do was for De Wit to steer to port and the other vessel to change course to port as well, so that it passed to starboard. There was plenty of sea room.

But De Wit knew he would have to change course by at least twenty degrees to give them a safe clearance, which would bring him head-on to the seas. He had been taking them on the quarter, and the two ships had comfortably rolled with them. But on the bow, the ships would slam and jerk, putting a strain on the lines. De Wit wondered if he could get the other ship to make a bigger course correction so that he wouldn't have to do so.

He picked up the radio handset and asked the vessel to identify itself. The reply came quickly – the other master must have been aware of the situation as well.

'*Zuider*, good evening, sir. This is tanker *Momo* on

your bow. We have you on radar, but you are looking
very strange to us. You seem to be very long, over.'

'*Momo*, good evening to you as well. We are a
salvage tug, and we have an old battleship in tow and
we are currently showing our restricted flags. I take it
you are a VLCC?'

'That is correct. We are two hundred ten thousand
tons and laden.'

'I understand. It will be difficult for me to change
course by more than ten degrees. I propose to alter
course to port by that amount. I think it would be
easier for you to change course to port so that we pass
starboard to starboard. This I think will be easiest,'
suggested De Wit, aware that the etiquette of seaman-
ship did not allow for a direct request.

'Yes, I understand your suggestion. We go to port.'

De Wit found Garcia's accent difficult. 'No, I am
suggesting starboard.'

'Very well. Starboard. I will change course now, ten
degrees to starboard.'

The tanker Captain had totally misunderstood.
'*Momo*, I think we are getting confused,' tried De Wit
again. 'I suggest you make a turn to *your* port, repeat
port, your left-hand side. May I also request you turn
twenty degrees, repeat twenty degrees, as I am restricted
with my vessel. I will turn to port also, ten degrees.'

The hiss of the carrier wave was all that could be
heard for some moments. Garcia was thinking about
what De Wit had suggested. He shook his head. Why
was he suggesting a starboard-to-starboard manoeuvre
when the practice was clearly port to port?

'*Zuider, Momo*. I do not understand your last
message. Are you suggesting we do not pass port to
port, over?'

De Wit sighed. 'Yes sir, that is correct. I am towing a

very large ship and I am unable to manoeuvre very efficiently.'

There was another long pause. Then Garcia came back on the radio. 'Very well, I will change course,' and the hiss went dead.

De Wit was far from certain that *Momo* had any idea of what it should be doing. He had salvaged dozens of vessels before now, including the remains of several marine collisions. It was astonishing, but true, that two ships with hundreds of miles of sea room around them could run into each other, usually as a result of a simple misunderstanding about the other's intentions. He had always thought that the masters of such ships must be incompetent fools to allow such a thing to happen, but now he was starting to see just such a situation unravel for himself.

Still, he had some room and some time left. De Wit ordered his course changed; the *Zuider* started the turn to the left. De Wit also ordered the speed reduced to make sure that the strain on the cables was not too great.

The battleship was slower to react than the *Zuider*. The slowing speed let the cables slacken, just as De Wit wanted. But the dead weight of the old ship, suddenly released from the pull, was now free to move of its own accord, even if only for a moment or two. The wind was blowing on the port stern. High in the water, it presented a large area of windage. Just as the cable fell slack, a gust of wind gathered around the vessel and blew hard for a minute before dropping back. It was enough. The *Hindenburg*'s stern leaned slightly and started to swing round to starboard, away from the turn that De Wit had ordered.

De Wit didn't notice it. But Captain Gabriel Garcia – as De Wit had guessed, now confused as to the

Zuider's exact intentions – was very carefully watching the approaching blip on his radar to see exactly what he might be up to. The *Hindenburg*, being bigger than the tow ship, gave by far the biggest echo.

'Port, starboard, you should make up your mind,' he muttered under his breath. As he watched, the heading marker from the other ship swung clearly to starboard. Very well. You are going to starboard. We will pass port to port.

'Twenty degrees starboard,' ordered Garcia, looking up from the screen and out of the forward windows. But the squalls concealed anything that might be out there.

With its huge length and weight, the *Momo* was slow to respond to the helm. It took a full minute before the bow began to noticeably turn.

Back on the *Zuider*, De Wit was well into his own turn. Now the cables took up the strain again, and the old ship reluctantly started to follow where its master ordered it to go. The stern began to swing back round and took up the same heading as De Wit's.

Garcia didn't look at the screen. He was more interested in watching his own bow come round, making sure that the ship's motion in the seas was not going to be a problem. For five minutes he stood at his windows, looking out into the grey, spray-flecked wastes before him.

De Wit equally was concentrating only on the progress of his vessel and his tow. He was looking back now, across the aft deck, watching the cables lift clear of the water, watching his charge follow him around. Satisfied that the manoeuvre was completed without undue strain, he ordered his speed back up again. Then he went to check the radar.

'Oh shit!' he shouted. Bakker rushed over; he could

see the problem. The *Zuider* had turned to port but the *Momo*, instead of also turning away to port, had done the opposite and was coming round to its starboard. The yellow heading marker was still moving, and was cutting neatly through the *Zuider*'s projected path just five miles ahead. At the speeds both ships were moving, they would meet in under ten minutes. For ships of their size, slowness and unmanoeuvrability, it was moments away. He had to take action now.

De Wit had no option. Whatever happened to the *Hindenburg* would have to happen. 'Starboard, helm, starboard. Thirty degrees!' he ordered, shouting. He grabbed for the radio-telephone.

'*Momo, Momo*, this is *Zuider*. You are on a collision course, I repeat you are on a collision course. I have altered course to my starboard, I repeat to my starboard. You should take no action. Please confirm, over.'

But it was already too late. Garcia also had seen the danger. Like De Wit, he knew the distance between them was simply too little. Like De Wit, he knew he had to take avoiding action. He had already ordered his heading changed to port. Now both ships were turning inexorably towards each other at a closing speed of twenty-two knots.

There was a momentary silence on the radio, and then Garcia came on. '*Zuider*, we have problem. I too have changed course. I have ordered my engine full astern. We are very close.'

There was an inevitability that both captains recognised.

De Wit's course was now unchangeable, at least within the next few minutes. The big battleship was already straining at the leash. The *Momo* was equally committed. Whatever they did now, with helm or engine, was simply too late to affect the outcome.

De Wit stared with horror at the screen, looking at the dotted yellow lines that were shifting slightly but still intersecting neatly. They were now less than two miles apart. Where was the bastard? He peered through the forward windows. The squalls were slashing at the glass. What was that? A dim, squat shape emerged from the shower ahead. It was square, like a buoy in the water, but unmoving in the gusting wind. He seized his glasses. The shape resolved itself into the bow of the tanker; he could see the anchors jutting from the sides. He looked down at the forefoot. The bow wave was small; the bulbous bow would have thrown up a steep bow-wave if it was moving at speed. Garcia's order to run the engine astern was at least slowing the *Momo*, but it was clearly moving towards them.

De Wit put down the glasses. He now had just one chance.

'Bakker!' he shouted.

Bakker was at the other end of the long bridge. He ran.

'Let go the tow. Now! Cut the lines if you have to. Just lose the fucking thing. Get on with it.' Bakker needed no more telling. He disappeared from the bridge.

De Wit grabbed an internal handset. 'Engines? Listen. I want maximum speed in about two minutes. Fathers and sons, full ahead. Get them going and stand by,' and he slammed the handset down.

He looked again at the approaching *Momo*, now clearly visible. De Wit leaned on the alarm button: a manic siren yelled at high volume from every speaker on the ship. He looked from the aft windows to see Bakker shouting silently at crews who were starting to release the cables. All he could do was wait. He watched while the first cable was cast into the sea, then the second. He looked over his shoulder at the approaching tanker.

'Come on, you bastards. Come on for God's sake!' he shouted, even though no one could hear him.

They had the third cable off. De Wit didn't want to look over his shoulder now. The crew were working on the fourth cable.

He picked up the handset. 'Engines? Are you ready?'

They said they were. He looked at the struggling crew. No, I will not look at the other ship. He held the handset.

Suddenly everything slowed down. Although he wasn't looking at the other ship he could now feel it, looming just a few hundred yards away, moving towards them like a silent wall of steel. The crew were hammering at the latching mechanism of the capstan that held the cable. Something was stuck. Very calmly now, De Wit ordered the engines to go to full power. The vibration beneath his feet quickened, the ship began to haul forward. He could see the stuck cable suddenly lift from the water as it tensioned under the motion. Surprised, the crew stood away. Bakker looked over his shoulder, looked back, screamed something silently, and the crewmen turned and ran. The bow of the *Momo* suddenly moved into De Wit's vision, heading for the after end of his ship. But the four engines beneath him were whining now; huge bubbles of foam rose at the stern as the propellers thrashed at the water. As the tanker approached, the *Zuider* was starting to drive forward. Now the bows of the tanker were just yards away. The ship towered above them.

De Wit closed his eyes, waiting for the impact. But there was just a gentle shudder. He opened them to see the steel monster gliding past his stern, the gap widening. It had parted the foot-thick steel cable like a length of cotton yarn.

The *Zuider* had escaped. But the *Hindenburg* was now set free, and under the bidding of the waves and the wind was slowly turning its stern away from the ship that had dragged it reluctantly from its Arctic berth.

*

'Bitch!' shouted Tan. He had physically hauled Louise DeAngelis into the cabin. The cameraman was going to intervene, but Louise warned him off.

'Calm down, Billy, just calm down, OK?'

'Bitch!' was all he could say, his frustration welling over. He was sitting sprawled in a big chair, his black hair pasted by the rain to his round, red face. Louise was still standing.

'Billy, it was great TV. The ratings will have gone through the roof. Your fucking old ship will be more famous than you could ever imagine. What the fuck are you getting upset about? You couldn't buy publicity like this for love or money. Even your money, Billy.'

'You really don't understand, do you?'

'Billy, am I missing something here? I mean, that little Kraut is all over every TV in the country with your ship in the background and there's something I don't understand?'

'It's a legal problem, for Christ's sake. Your taking the piss out of Otto just now. The guy went on air to tell the world that it was a wreck, and now you're making out he's a liar. The Germans want to stop me and now you've given them enough to make a judge's hair stand on fucking end.'

'You mean if it was a wreck or not? But he never said a thing about it.'

'It doesn't matter. He was my big defence, but now he looks like a cheap hooker. Anyway, where'd you dig up this stuff?'

Louise DeAngelis suddenly realised exactly how Bethe Fischer had set her up; she'd done precisely what the German lawyer wanted. She stood there and looked at Tan.

'For fuck's sake, you were fed the stuff, weren't you?' he demanded, realising what had happened.

She had the grace to turn slightly pink.

'Who? The justice people, the Navy?'

'Sorry, Billy. It sounded like a good story. How was I supposed to know? It was the German lawyer, Fischer. She called the station from Bonn and they put her on to me.'

Billy Tan looked bleakly at her. He had no idea what to do next. He presumed Fischer's lawyers would already have got their act going. But Heine still owed him, if he wanted the money. Maybe he could get DeAngelis to do a follow-up interview where Otto Heine would say again that the ship was a wreck and ... there was an ear splitting shriek as the speaker in the cabin ripped out De Wit's alarm signal.

*

Freed of its tether, the great ship paused for a moment in the gusting wind and the rolling seas, as though it was deciding quite what to do with itself. But then the weather got to work, and inch by inch the stern swung away, the bow came round and like an exhausted whale she lay listlessly in the water, beam-on to the seas. The waves were now lumped hills of green water striped with foam that marched across an endless ocean. The huge weight of the *Hindenburg* – its massive sheets of armour-plate, its guns and its turrets and engine – was a mass of rust-streaked steel with the inertia of a barge of anchors. Beam-on to the wind, the stately waves at first simply broke against the side of the ship, bursting upwards into a cascade of white water that was grabbed by the wind and ripped across the streaming decks. The vessel hardly moved at first, but the rhythm of the waves was slow, and close to the natural rolling speed of the ship. Gradually the roll deepened as each wave burst against the sides.

The *Momo* was quickly disappearing, its round stern and high white superstructure receding into the ocean wastes and the swirling squalls. De Wit, watching from the high bridge, stared after it. Below, looking out from the saloon windows across the windswept aft deck, Billy Tan and Louise DeAngelis were also watching in silent awe as the tanker drew away to reveal the *Hindenburg* set free.

And Otto Heine, startled by the wailing of De Wit's alarm, had watched the whole scene unfold as well, braced in a corner of the superstructure against the wind, his face streaming with the wind and the rain, his fists clenched with fear as he watched his prize start to drift away.

There was a moment of silence throughout the ship. The years and the months and the weeks of work and waiting were destroyed. All any of them could do was stand and watch as the battleship, rolling and turning, moved steadily further away from them, surely now lost for the last time.

But Billy Tan's anger, only temporarily suspended, soon returned. Now he ignored Louise DeAngelis as he stormed up to the bridge. De Wit had also recovered his thoughts and was on the radio, with the tape recorder running, making it very clear to Captain

Gabriel Garcia that he felt his standards of navigation were slightly worse than they should be, just in case an inquiry was called. Tan burst through the door and marched up to De Wit. Had Tan not been a good foot shorter than De Wit, and had De Wit not been a good deal more physically imposing than Tan, Billy would have torn the handset from the captain. Instead, he stood in front of him with all the authority of the man who knew he was paying the bill and started yelling.

'Are you fucking crazy, De Wit? What the hell is happening? That's my ship out there and you've fucking lost it.'

De Wit looked down at him coldly and slowly replaced the handset. 'Mister Tan, it was an accident. We are lucky not to have been hit.'

'Fuck you, De Wit! I'm paying to get this ship back, not to run into tankers. For Christ's sake, didn't you see the damn thing coming?'

'Yes, I saw the ship coming. It was unavoidable,' replied the captain shortly, in no mood to explain the workings of the Collision Regulations and Garcia's failure to follow them with any logic.

Tan didn't see the look in De Wit's eyes and plunged on. 'So what about my fucking ship? I've got millions tied up in that heap of shit and no fucking Dutch tugboat skipper is gonna lose it for me. You got that?'

De Wit looked at Tan. His face was expressionless for a second and then suddenly the Dutchman's face creased into a wide smile that had no humour about it. 'Tan, you may be paying me but you are not paying me enough. All you've paid for so far is towing the wreck out, which is what I've done. You do not pay enough for the extra privilege of being rude to me. For another million dollars you may be rude to me; you may slap me around the face if you wish. But until that time, if you ever talk to me like that again I shall take you by the throat and drag you outside where I shall drop you into the sea.'

Tan opened his mouth to scream more abuse but he stopped, thinking better of it. De Wit was standing very close and looking very serious. Tan closed his mouth, scowled and then walked away towards the bridge door, breathing hard. He gripped the latch that would slide the door back, but then he stopped and turned. His face was less red now and his breathing was slower. Tan was not a stupid man; his temper had got the better of him, but now it was back under control. His emotions had stopped running him and his brain had taken over once more. And now a simple thought had occurred to him.

'Captain,' he began in a matter-of-fact voice as though nothing had happened, 'you know the law of salvage, don't you?'

Of course De Wit knew the law of salvage; it had been his living since he was a boy. He probably knew more about salvage law than most lawyers would ever know. He just raised his eyebrows by way of an answer.

Tan walked slowly back on to the bridge. 'You know the problems we had with the battleship? Why we had to close off the valves?'

'I was there, Mr Tan. Don't worry. Your secret is still safe.'

'That's not what I was driving at, Captain. The point is, that stupid bitch TV woman nearly screwed the thing up. Maybe you didn't see the broadcast. She made out the old Kraut guy to be a liar. In other words, the courts could have a go at our story – that the ship was a proper wreck, I mean.'

'So?'

'So? Well, you're the expert. What's the ship *now*?'

'Legally? It's abandoned.'

'Not scuttled. Abandoned. Therefore?'

'Therefore, Mr Tan, available for salvage.' De Wit suddenly understood. 'I see what you mean. You are right. Whatever happened to the ship before, it is now clearly abandoned. No doubt about it.'

'Exactly. All we have to do now is get it back again. Then it's mine, legal and above-board. Doesn't matter what happened before. They can't do a thing. Right?'

But De Wit sadly shook his head. 'Legally you're right, but you do not have a hope in hell in this weather. Look outside. There's a storm going on out there, Mr Tan. To reattach the cables I would need a crew of half a dozen men on the ship. In this weather it would be suicide; they wouldn't do it.'

'Fly them on. You've got a chopper.'

'Too much wind. I couldn't get the crew to do it, not in this shit. It's madness.'

'What the fuck do we do? Just wait?'

'That's exactly what we do. We stay near the ship, follow it, and when the weather eases we get the crew on.'

'How long will that be?'

'I have no idea. Two days. Four days. Maybe longer.'

'And in the meantime those bastards go to court and get me thrown off? Not a chance, Captain, not a fucking chance.'

'Listen to me, Mr Tan. That ship will drift as an abandoned wreck for as long as it needs to. The only thing that brings it legally back into our hands is if we can get somebody on board to claim it as a wreck. And the chances of doing that are zero.'

Tan stopped and thought for a second. 'Getting someone on board? Not getting a tow-line on? Just *someone*?'

'Legally it would be ours. But they'd have to be mad to do it. Nobody's that stupid on board my ship, Tan.'

'They don't have to be stupid, Captain. Just desperate.' Billy Tan turned and left the bridge to find Otto Heine.

*

The helicopter pilot – a small, dark Italian called Rico Mascali – was used to flying hazardous missions, deck-to-deck, usually in the sort of weather that made boat operations difficult if not impossible. That was why he worked on board De Wit's ship. But even he flatly refused Tan's request.

'Look at the damn wind. I'm not flying in that. It's not safe.' According to the manual, flying the heli-copter in winds above thirty-five knots was not recom-mended; and above forty-five knots was forbidden. The anemometer read-out on the bridge was flickering between fifty and sixty knots most of the time, and every now and then would gust to sixty-five. It was the very height of the storm, and the wind had increased since the near miss with the *Momo*.

'Captain, I said I will do it. It doesn't frighten me; not at my age.' Otto Heine looked determined to go through with it. De Wit wondered what in the name of heaven Tan had said to him to make him do this, but he kept his thoughts to himself. It seemed irrelevant.

'You heard. Heine is game,' said Tan.

'Let him fly the chopper then. I'm not,' replied Mascali flatly.

'How much?' asked Billy.

'How much what?' asked the Italian.

'Name your price. You get it if you come back. Your family gets it if you don't. How much?'

'You kidding me?'

'One million? Will that do it?'

Mascali looked at De Wit. 'Boss, is this guy kidding me or what?'

'I doubt it,' confirmed the Dutchman gloomily.

'Show me the money.'

Tan pulled out a chequebook and quickly scribbled a cheque for $1 million. Mascali took it doubtfully.

'It's good. Tell him, Captain,' said Tan.

'Sure, it's good,' replied De Wit.

'What the hell? We're all gonna die anyway. Old man, get yourself ready. Immersion suit, the works. Shit,' he said again, clutching the cheque in disbelief as he wandered off to get the machine ready.

De Wit was not going to let Tan off that lightly. 'You sign disclaimers before you go, Rico. Also for you, Tan, indemnities. For the helicopter. That's another half a million. You're some kind of crazy bastards, you know that?'

But Billy Tan just smiled.

*

Outside, Mascali, clad in a bright orange immersion suit that would automatically inflate if they ditched and protect him from hypothermia for twelve hours – or so the label claimed – climbed into the helicopter to start it up. The machine was already shaking in the wind, tethered firmly on to the deck, the roof of the hanger having slid silently away. The rain rattled on the perspex windows.

He couldn't hear a thing. He had already strapped on the black helmet and was talking to Parrish, the trainee who had been hanging around the chopper ever since he got on the ship. Parrish was Mascali's ground crew.

While Mascali started up the turbine, Heine – also clad in an immersion suit – was told to wait. Mascali just felt better starting the machine on his own. He turned on the electrics, turned on the fuel systems, didn't bother with the navigation electronics, glanced briefly at the hydraulics, which looked OK, and then turned on the autostart for the turbine. Deafened by the headphones, he watched the jet pipe temperature gauge suddenly move as the engine lit, and then saw the revs start to climb.

He waited a full two minutes. Everything looked normal. Rico Mascali switched off the helmet microphone, crossed himself and shouted three Hail Marys as loudly as he could.

He switched the mike on again. One million dollars, he kept telling himself. One million dollars!

'Parrish, get the old man on board. Tell De Wit I want the ship into the wind as soon as he can.'

The flimsy door was opened and Mascali felt the lash of wind and rain, even through the suit and the helmet, as Otto Heine climbed slowly into the seat. Mascali had to lean over to help him buckle on the harness. He dropped another helmet over Otto's pale face and connected up the microphone lead.

'You OK? You ready?' shouted Mascali.

Otto simply nodded. Mascali could see the way the old man was gripping the side of the seat; he was frightened to death. But then, so was Mascali himself.

'Parrish, you listen good. I give it full power. Get someone on the other restraint. When it's tight, release the clip. It's easy. You understand? And keep your fucking head down. You got that?'

'I got it,' replied Parrish. The youngster collared another crew member and showed him what to do. The wind around the helicopter was dropping quickly.

De Wit had turned the ship bow-on to the wind, so the helicopter deck was now sheltered by the super-structure. Mascali's only problem now was the rise and fall of the deck underneath him.

As the deck was rising, Mascali opened the throttle and pulled up the collective lever. The blades slashed violently through the still air and the machine pulled up against the two restraining cables.

Just as the deck reached the top of its rise, Mascali yelled at Parrish to loose the clips. Parrish signalled frantically at the other crewman. Both clips fell with a crash to the deck. The helicopter was free ... it leapt into the air.

Mascali knew what was going to happen, but even he was unprepared for the force of it. As soon as the machine cleared the shelter of the superstructure the wind struck it like a giant hand. It threw the helicopter violently forward and flicked it round so that it was facing the bow, and the wind. Mascali swore loudly in Italian. Otto Heine tightened his grip on his seat, his fingers tearing into the plastic covering.

Mascali opened the throttle even more to gain some altitude, and hauled the machine around to try to ride the sudden gusts. The whole thing shook and shuddered violently, and bobbed up and down like a cork in the water. Mascali could hear Heine muttering what he supposed was a prayer, but it was in German and he couldn't understand a word.

The rotors above were whipping the air in a panic. Mascali had the throttle to its limits.

'Fly baby, fly ...' he groaned, closing his eyes as the helicopter lurched downwards. Nothing happened. He opened them again; he had climbed 100 feet and was still climbing.

'How about that? You see that? How you feeling, old

man?' Mascali yelled cheerfully as he watched the heaving seas roll on beneath him. But not a word came from Heine. His face was hidden by the tinted visor of the helmet; behind it he had his eyes closed and screwed up in sheer terror.

Now that he had some altitude, Mascali could get some control over his aircraft. The *Hindenburg* was some five miles away, and the Italian hauled the machine round to drive it more or less in the right direction. The wind was with him, and he closed the gap in minutes. As he arrived near the rolling grey monster, he tried to turn into the wind to maintain a hover.

'Shit, old man, this is not gonna be easy, you want to know that?' he shouted. Heine kept his eyes closed and his grip tight as the helicopter wobbled and shook in the wind.

The aircraft had a small winch just outside the passenger-side door. Mascali's idea had been simply to drop Heine on the deck from the winch, hovering twenty feet above the ship, and then fly back. It was clear now that he didn't stand a chance. The deck was heaving through more than twenty feet and the gusting wind just added to the problem. He would smash Heine into the deck if he tried it.

'Listen. Forget the winch. I'm going down to the deck. Unbuckle your straps and hold on. Get ready to jump out.'

Heine opened a terrified eye, glanced at the pilot without looking down and unbuckled the seat harness.

'Here we go. Hold on to your fucking ass!' Mascali waited until the ship was finishing its roll and then closed the throttle down and dropped the collective lever. He had chosen the aft deck, where the missing guns created a large, clear space.

The deck started to roll again, coming up to meet the helicopter. The helicopter in turn descended, badly, and moments later one connected with the other with a sickening crash that collapsed the flimsy skids that acted as the chopper's undercarriage.

'Get out, get out!' screamed Mascali. Heine needed no prompting. The moment the aircraft connected with the deck he heaved open the door and dived, headfirst, on to the deck. Heine was not as young as he thought he was. He landed on one arm and there was an audible crack as a pain like a red-hot axe cleaved through his shoulder. He screamed and cursed but still rolled away.

As he came to rest, he caught sight of Mascali through the open door of the helicopter. The Italian was concentrating on something, but the collapsed skids of the helicopter meant that on the drenched decks the machine's belly had no grip. It was sliding away from Heine. Then the roll stopped and paused; the helicopter hesitated for a second. The opposite roll started. At first the machine didn't move, but as the angle of the deck increased it suddenly began to slide in the other direction. It gathered speed as with a tearing sound it scraped past Heine and ploughed into the guard rails. Mascali seemed to give Heine one last look as it paused on the edge and then, rotors still beating the air, toppled slowly over the side. Mascali and his helicopter disappeared. In the screaming wind nothing could be heard.

Heine knelt like a dog, on all fours, pain washing in waves over his whole body. He was alone on the streaming deck of the rolling ship. Once again, after fifty-five years, Otto Heine was back in reluctant command of the *Hindenburg*.

20

Christian Bach, still in the new yellow-and-red check jacket and orange shirt he had bought for his cancelled TV appearance, was sitting in Don's Bar in the basement of a brownstone building on the lower West Side just on the border between run-down and respectable. He had drunk six beers and the alcohol had warmed up his anger. He had spent a night and a day simply walking and sitting. In the sitting sessions, he had turned the insults he had endured around and around in his mind where they fed each other until they became like physical assaults. When the anger became too much to bear he would walk furiously, striding across parks and pavements, where his scowling face and curious clothing made even hardened New Yorkers stare at him.

Bach had not shaved or washed and his long hair was damp and stringy from his exertions. He had kept looking over his shoulder for the bastards from the FBI. He was sure he was being followed, and it would have made him angrier still if he had realised he was not. Ben St James hadn't bothered; he'd kept him off the TV and he'd had him thrown out of town. What more harm could Bach possibly do?

He shook a cigarette from a packet and lit it with his Zippo. 'You got cable on that thing?' he asked the black girl behind the bar, nodding his head in the direction of the TV set suspended from the low ceiling. She hadn't liked the look of Bach when he walked in an hour ago, and was going to throw him out; he looked like a vagrant. But he seemed to have plenty of cash and, apart from drinking more than was good for him – which was not unusual in Don's Bar – he had stayed peaceful enough, even if he was muttering soundlessly to himself at times.

'Yeah. We got cable,' she replied.

'Gimme Newsworld,' was all he said. She liked him even less. But there were only five other people in the bar and nobody was watching the TV anyway. She found the remote and flicked the channels until the Newsworld logo came up on the corner of the screen.

'Turn the fucker up,' he growled. She turned up the volume a single notch, just enough to keep him quiet. The station was broadcasting the closing Wall Street report and a shirt-sleeved young man in glasses was talking earnestly about futures.

Bach looked at it for a second, then turned away. He pushed his glass forward. 'Gimme a beer,' he ordered.

'I think you've had enough,' said the girl.

He looked at her. 'Gimme another fucking beer, for Christ's sake,' he said, and he gripped his glass as though he was about to pick it up and throw it.

The girl took the glass and filled it with another beer. It wasn't worth the argument. Don himself would be here in half an hour and he could deal with him.

Bach remained silent, drinking his beer, as the TV finished the Wall Street report. There were a handful of commercials; then there was the studio announcer, with a huge red-and-black swastika in the back-ground, looking earnest.

'The latest twist in the extraordinary saga of the rescue of the *Hindenburg* took place just a few hours ago. Here's Louise DeAngelis, on board the rescue ship, with some dramatic footage. Louise?'

Christian Bach swung round on his stool to watch as the features of Louise DeAngelis filled the screen, clad in waterproofs, her blonde hair only slightly ruffled by the wind. She told the story of the near-collision with the *Momo*, showed some tape of the event. And then she showed the last flight of the helicopter, including a jerky, distant shot of the machine descending towards the deck of the battleship and then vanishing in the spray and the wind.

'And no sign of the helicopter pilot?'

'None whatsoever, Bill. The weather out here is appalling as you can see. The captain on this ship has told me it's impossible to even launch a boat in these conditions, so he's keeping alongside the wreck. There doesn't seem to be much hope, Bill.'

'So the *Hindenburg* is finally going to end up as a tourist attraction?'

'Looks like it, Bill. A fortunate outcome of this sad disaster – fortunate for Mr Billy Tan anyway – is that we have now heard that the German government has called a halt to a legal action. As you'll remember, they were claiming that the ship was not abandoned but legally left in the ice – *scuttled*, the sea dogs call it, Bill. But now they've got someone on board, that challenge has disappeared. This ship really is salvage.'

'We can expect to see the ship very soon, then, Louise?'

'If they can get the towlines back on, that's right, Bill. No doubt about it now. The weather is promising to ease in the next couple of days, so I think you can expect to see a German battleship coming into Chesapeake Bay by the end of the week if all goes well.'

Her face was set in the concerned but hopeful expression she had been practising as the image faded and returned to the studio. 'Now the latest on the congressional ...' Christian Bach turned away. Once again the thoughts were churning through his head. It was his ship as much as anyone else's. He should have been there, telling his story. But he was being ignored, cut out. They were trying to shut him up, keep him quiet. Those bastards in Washington. They didn't want the truth to come out. They tried to kill our family, they're trying to kill me, they're trying to kill every honest American.

He picked up his glass once more. It was still half full of yellow beer. Turning back to the television, he hurled the glass at the TV set with all the force he could find. His aim was perfect. The glass smashed into the screen and with a sound like a cork coming out of a bottle the screen burst into a mist of glass splinters and beer. The rest of the set fizzled with sparks and then died.

'That's my fucking ship, you hear?' shouted Bach. He looked around at the silent and frightened faces. The bar girl was backing away.

Bach spat on the floor and walked across the bar, his feet crunching through the shattered glass. He pushed the door open with both hands and disappeared into the evening.

*

De Wit was wrong. The storm didn't last four days. After twenty-four hours the wind was dying and the heaving seas had lost their foam-streaked violence and settled into glassy swells. He looked out across the water towards the *Hindenburg*. The ship was rolling still, but more slowly, in a calm and stately way. With the wind and rain dropped, De Wit was now considering getting some men on to the ship. They had not heard from Heine, who had taken a VHF radio but had not used it. They had spotted him – or at least, his bright orange suit – crawling into shelter just after the helicopter had gone overboard, and that was the last they knew.

With the helicopter gone, De Wit had no option but to wait until he could bring a boat alongside the ship. His biggest problem would be getting his men up the steep sides of the vessel. For that operation, it would have been handy to have Heine helping them, letting down a ladder or taking a line. But if they couldn't rely on that they'd have to get grappling hooks up, and for that to work De Wit needed a calmer sea than the one he was looking at.

He consulted Bakker. It was late now. They would wait out the night and in the morning they would make their first attempt.

*

For perhaps the first time in his life, Christian Bach's paranoia was founded on fact. He decided not to use the airport to catch a flight south to Washington, since he thought the FBI would be watching. They were. His description had been circulated and the near-invisible agents who wandered around near the gates – especially the Washington flights – would have had no difficulty in spotting him.

When he had stormed out of the bar, his anger was flaming, but after more walking his mind had calmed. He was not, he told himself, going to put up with this. He was not going to let them win. The world owed Christian Bach more. He was damn well not going to retreat back home with his tail between his legs and give that FBI nigger something to smirk about.

After two hours, he finally reached his decision. It was now time to do something. He didn't know quite what, but he knew it was time for action.

First, he had to get down to where that ship would be coming in. Chesapeake Bay, said the TV station. He could make a plan on the way. His temper had turned into a calmer, deadlier resolve, and he was starting to think things through in a more rational way.

He checked into a cheap hotel for the night. The FBI hadn't got to this one at least, and having paid cash in advance he let himself into a dingy room with noisy air-conditioning. He cleaned himself up, and first thing in the morning bought himself a change of clothes: jeans and a shirt. He decided to wait out the rest of the day, and in the evening he found the nearest Avis. It took just twenty minutes to get himself a dark blue Ford, and soon he had joined the evening rush-hour traffic heading south through the Lincoln Tunnel.

*

That same morning, as Bach was getting up, De Wit looked out across the sea. The wind overnight had all but died away, and the seas were now down to little more than a metre. The great battleship was riding them steadily with barely any movement other than a slow tilting from side to side. There was still no sign of Heine. It was time to go.

On the leeward side of the *Zuider* a small hydraulic arm plucked a six-metre rigid inflatable boat from the deck, swung it out over the water and lowered it carefully to the sea. Bakker, clad in a black wetsuit and bright orange lifejacket, with three other crew members similarly dressed, waddled down fixed steel steps near the stern of the ship and arranged themselves inside the RIB. Once settled, they loosed the straps from the lifting arm and it returned to the deck to swing out once more, this time dropping a net containing equipment, which Bakker and his crew quickly stowed. The RIB was ready.

They started the single Suzuki 70 hp outboard, dropped the line, and with a buzz curled away from the lee side of the *Zuider*, bow high in the air. Once they cleared the shelter of the ship, the modest chop made the RIB jump and a cascade of spray plumed from the craft. At thirty knots it took Bakker four minutes to complete the trip from the *Zuider* to the steel walls of the *Hindenburg*, half a mile away.

He drove the RIB down the length of the ship, then rounded the stern and started up the other side where the shelter of the massive vessel left a calm patch of sea. He slowed down, looking upwards at the guard rails to find the best place to get the grapple fixed. Just forward of where the superstructure started, the rusted rails looked strong enough to support a man.

Bakker stopped the engine and brought the RIB to a halt alongside the ship, but standing off about twenty feet. One of his crewmen already had the grapple in his hand with a hank of line. He paused, then heaved the grappling hook high into the air towards the railing. The steel hook looped through the air with the line snaking behind it, but it missed the railing and clanged on to the top of the hull before falling with a small splash into the water. The crewmen reeled it all back in, carefully gathering the line in. He threw once more; again it missed. He went through the process of reeling it in again, and then gathered himself for another throw.

'Erik, just get the fucking thing on, will you?' muttered Bakker. The crewman cast the hook upwards into the air once more. Seeming to travel more slowly than before, it sailed calmly over the railing and landed on the deck. The crewman smiled and slowly dragged the hook back. It caught the railing and wedged itself securely into place.

Now Bakker motored tight in to the side of the ship. The crewman ran the line through a mountaineer's shackle that would allow the line to pass through one way only, and would lock if he started to fall. He began to haul himself hand over hand up the line, bouncing against the hull with his feet. Every six feet he stopped to rest. The shackle locked and he could hang there, swinging with the gentle movement of the ship. He finally made the top, reached out to grip the rail and swung himself inboard, breathing hard.

He had to pause to get his breath back. After half a minute he hauled up the line and loosed the grapple. Then he took the rope ladder off his back, secured it to a cleat on the deck and let it down. Bakker reversed his craft to the hanging ladder, secured it with a line and then led his remaining crew up the sheer steel wall.

'You guys, call De Wit and start getting the lines on. We go from the bow. I'll try and find that stupid German. Get on with it,' he panted. He was not as fit as he had thought.

As the three crewmen hurried forward with the equipment, Bakker crossed the deck to the twisted guard rails marking where Mascali and his helicopter had slid overboard. Where was Heine? There was a door nearby, half open. Bakker walked quickly towards it. It was dark inside. He flicked on the Maglite and the sharp white light illuminated the rusting, dripping interior.

'Herr Heine? Herr Heine?' he called. His voice echoed through the silent dark interior. There was no reply.

He went back on to the deck and walked further

down. Coming to another half-open door, he stepped inside and called for Otto, but again there was nothing but silence. Where in the name of hell had the old man gone?

Bakker looked inside another four doors but found no sign of Heine. By now he had worked his way well forward of the ship and was standing just below the steps leading up to the bridge. He could see his crew forward and walked down to see how they were getting on. They already had one steel hawser in place and were hauling in another line that was connected to the next cable, using the portable winch they had brought. It was backbreaking work and Bakker stayed to help; he could resume his search after they got the lines secure. They finally brought the dripping line on board and Bakker, sweating in his wetsuit, stood up to wipe his dripping face.

Then he saw it: a flash of bright orange up high, out of the corner of his eye, up at the bridge window. He looked directly at it and it disappeared.

He left the crew to the task of securing the line, ran back across the foredeck and climbed quickly up the ladders. The steel rails were rusting and the wooden steps were split and slippery. He made the last flight and hauled himself up them. Now he was standing on the wing bridge.

'Herr Heine?' he called, but this time softly. The bridge door was closed. He pulled it open. There was a musty, damp smell as he went inside.

Heine was leaning against the aft bulkhead, his eyes closed, one arm folded stiffly across the chest being supported by the other one.

'Herr Heine? Is that you?'

Heine opened his eyes and looked blearily at Bakker, but he gave no reply.

Bakker went up to him. 'Are you hurt?'

'Just my arm. I'm sorry about the helicopter pilot.'

Bakker shrugged. Mascali's family would be rich, at least. Maybe they had got the better end of the deal – Mascali was rarely at home with his wife and daughter.

'Sit down. I'll take a look at it.'

There was a chair on the bridge that was once covered with leather, but it had rotted away and only the wooden frame was left. Heine allowed himself to be seated while Bakker started to pull away the immersion suit. It took him ten minutes to see that Heine had probably broken his collarbone. The old man was covered with black bruises into the bargain. Bakker did what he could and tied the arm into a sling. It obviously hurt like hell, but Heine seemed unconcerned.

'That's the best I can do. Now, we'll get you back to the ship and see to you properly. We have a boat. Do you think you can make it?'

'No.'

'I'll help. Don't worry.'

'No. I mean, I can make it. But I don't want to. I stay here.'

'You can't,' replied Bakker, surprised.

Heine just shook his head. He was not going to move, not now. The ghosts were all round him. Schiller and Rois and Schnee and Bruller and Vogele and the rest of them. And Bach – especially Bach, with his crew-cut and his sharp face and his big ears, and his duty still to be done. They were standing and watching him, waiting for his orders. He, Otto Heine, press-ganged in Hamburg, leader of the mutiny, American alien, now once more commanding the ship. He had never wanted it. But the ghosts were telling him to do it. You owe us, Heine. You got us here. Now finish the job. And there was still the gold, sitting in the turret and in the magazine. It had nearly slipped Heine's grasp for the second time and he wasn't going to let it go again.

'Leave me here. Bring me some food and water. I stay here until we reach America,' said Heine in a voice that brooked no discussion. And so for the last stage of the *Hindenburg's* interrupted voyage, Otto Heine remained steadfastly at his haunted station watched over by the stern, proud figure of *Kapitan sur See* Erich Bach, who was trying to say something to Otto though no words ever came from his mouth.

*

For the final stage of their journey the weather had decided to be kind to them. The storm moved quickly away to the north and west and the sun came out. They had not realised how far south they had travelled, and the sun was hot when it emerged from behind the last line of charcoal-grey clouds. The skies turned a deep blue and the ocean had fallen back to a long, slow, lazy swell.

The crew of the *Zuider* quickly took advantage of the weather, the way seamen do on a ship that has been cold and wet and swaying for days on end. The wide aft deck of the salvage craft looked like the deck of a cruise liner as almost everyone stripped off to the waist and lazed in the sun. Louise DeAngelis arrived after a few hours wearing an improbably brief bikini that consisted of three small triangles of white silk held together with string; but even she noticed the awed silence on the deck and, after half an hour of uncomfortable sunbathing, she eventually retired wrapped in a towel, and returned an hour later in shorts and a T-shirt. Even that was impressive, but at least the crew were capable of speaking once more.

The only people who missed the sight were Bakker, Tan and a small crew.

Tan had demanded that they get someone on to the battleship to do something about the guns. He was going to make his entrance in a huge glare of publicity – DeAngelis's newscasts had ensured that – and he wanted the ship to look menacing and impressive. The rust he could live with; it gave the ship a historical authenticity. But the huge guns in the forward turrets drooped 'like limp fucking pricks' according to Tan, and gave the ship a sad and dejected appearance. This was not the evil German battleship that Tan wanted, and he demanded that somebody went over to fix them.

Bakker and an engineer had taken a look at them. The hydraulic system that elevated the guns was still sound, though the seals were perished and the fluid had long ago drained out. But it could be fixed. They had already installed a big generator set when the ship was still aground in Greenland to provide power for the crews who had pumped out the vessel. That allowed them to work on the systems and get them back into running order. The mechanism was superbly engineered, mostly in brass and stainless steel and copper, so the rust that grimed and clogged the other parts of the ship had little effect inside the turret.

Bakker's people oiled and polished and soon the turret started to come back to life. Some parts had to be replaced, taken back to the workshop on board *Zuider*, stripped and repaired and got working once more. Hydraulic pipes and seals were simpler. *Zuider* kept a stock on board for its own complex systems, and what didn't fit was easily modified.

They already had turret Anton working. The guns would lift and drop and the turret, powered by the generator, had light inside. All it wouldn't do was traverse; the turret looked fine pointing forward, and they could fix that once they got to the anchorage. The long, drooping guns were now standing proud once more. While the sun shone, they worked on Bruno.

De Wit had recovered his tow 250 miles east of Milne Bank where the North Atlantic Drift had pushed the battleship. He had had nearly 1,600 miles to haul his prize to Chesapeake Bay, and in the calmer weather he had maintained a steady twelve knots. The journey to the entrance had taken a little over five days in total, and as the afternoon sun sank and a cool ocean breeze forced the crew back inside from their sunbathing, De Wit was already working out the procedures for the entrance to the bay early the next morning.

Chesapeake Bay is the largest bay on the Atlantic Coast of North America: 170 miles long from its entrance to the Susquehanna River in its upper reaches, it is less of a bay and more of a small inland sea. The state of Virginia occupies most of the eastern side, and Maryland takes the head and western side. The bay carries shipping to the ports of Norfolk, Newport, Baltimore and, via the Potomac River, Washington itself.

Some of the most famous names in American history are based around the bay: West Point, home of the academy that has trained generations of military men; Williamsburg and Yorktown, scene of battles for independence; the Naval Yards at Norfolk; the Naval Academy at Annapolis; Patuxent River, home of Navy aviation and training ground for the earlier astronauts.

Hitler could have chosen nowhere that gave him such a concentration of targets for his last mad gamble. Washington itself – the Capitol and the White House – was just twenty-two miles from the upper reaches of the bay towards Baltimore, where deep-draught ships regularly run.

The range of the big guns was twenty-five miles, and had the battleship stood any real chance of running past the defences situated all around the bay – and given the element of surprise, it might well have got close – the very heart of the nation would have lain within its range.

But what might have happened more than fifty-five years ago was the last thing on De Wit's mind. At the moment, the bureaucracy of entry was uppermost. Tan had already arranged his anchorage, just south of Annapolis, but De Wit would have to take on a pilot at the entrance and see if he could avoid a quarantine inspection that would mean taking his huge tow into Hampton Roads, a far from easy manoeuvre and one he would want to avoid.

The pilot vessel would be moored just north of Cape Henry, the southern edge of the entrance. Then the final leg would begin. De Wit and Bakker worked through their charts carefully, getting everything ready for the final approach. Tan and DeAngelis had already warned the media – even now they were gathering on the Chesapeake Bay bridge to gain the best views of the huge battleship passing through.

Just as dawn was breaking, the *Zuider* and the *Hindenburg* would work their way towards the entrance and the pilot station and should, if their calculations were correct, pass the bridge by nine in the morning.

De Wit hated this part of any trip. At sea, even a

hurricane didn't worry the Dutchman. But, for some reason, docking and manoeuvring in close quarters always filled him with dread. The worst he could do was dent his ship, and it was probably one of the safest parts of any voyage. But perhaps he disliked the idea of being so close to land. He checked his charts and notes, then checked them again, and finally, at nearly midnight, he retired to his cabin and fell into a fitful sleep.

*

Christian Bach had rested overnight just outside Washington and caught up with the latest news of the ship, conveniently provided by the Newsworld channel who were still making a fuss of the story. He had driven carefully from New York, so as to avoid the attention of traffic patrols, and had found a small motel. Having slept much of the morning, during the afternoon he drove further on, about fifty miles south of Washington towards Richmond, where he found a small gun shop in a town whose name he couldn't even find on the map.

He bought a Smith and Wesson .38 and a box of shells, paid cash, and found another motel for the night. According to the TV, the ship would be passing through the Bay Bridge the next morning but one, and Christian Bach would have ample time to drive down to Norfolk, on the southern edge of the entrance to the bay, and try to figure out a way to maybe get himself on to the ship. At least he wanted to see the damn thing.

The next morning he continued his drive. He made Norfolk mid-morning and then drove on towards the coast, finally stopping at the resort of Virginia Beach, not far from Cape Henry, where De Wit was expecting to take on his pilot.

He parked the car and walked down towards the

seafront, where the land was low and there was a clear view out to sea. Several large vessels – a tanker and two top-heavy Japanese container ships – were steaming slowly towards the bay. What the hell was his next move? Finally, hunger drove him into a small diner on the southern edge of town, where he sat at a greasy counter and ordered a burger and fries.

The diner was nearly empty but for a short, stubby man in overalls, also sitting at the counter.

'You live round here?' ventured Bach.

'Sure do,' muttered the man without turning round. 'Navy?'

The man laughed. 'Gimme a break. Fishing. Oysters. You like oysters?'

'Yeah,' replied Bach, who had never tried one.

'Can't stand them. Gimme burger any time. You from someplace else?'

'Yeah. West.'

'Figures. You down to see the ship come in? The German battleship?'

Bach went cold. 'Maybe.'

The man laughed again. 'Hey, don't look so worried. The place is full of people like you. Ain't nothing to get embarrassed about. Sure gonna be a sight.'

'Tomorrow morning, it's supposed to be coming in.'

'You got it. Listen, I'm taking a bunch of people out in my boat to look-see. You wanna come? Twenty bucks a head?'

Bach thought about it. 'How many in your boat?'

'Ten. Why?'

'Tell you what. Give you three hundred bucks for the whole boat. Just me. Can't stand crowds.'

'You serious?'

Bach produced three $100 bills and gave them to the fisherman. 'Sure. You wanna do it?'

'Fine by me,' replied the fisherman, pocketing the notes. 'Five at the fish dock. You can't miss it. Boat's called *Paddler*. I'm Harris. Don't be late.'

'I won't be,' said Bach.

*

At five-thirty De Wit was up and on the bridge. The low coastline was invisible in an early morning haze, but the radar clearly picked out Cape Henry lighthouse. It was time to get the show on the road.

'Virginia pilots, this is motor vessel *Zuider* out of Rotterdam, vessel in tow, inbound, ETA your position one hour, over,' he called on the VHF. He hoped they would be awake.

They had been awake for a good hour since. The arrival of the battleship had been about the biggest thing in those parts for years.

'*Zuider*, Virginia pilots. We have you on radar. Maintain your course and speed, please, sir. We will embark port side.'

The black boat with its yellow funnel hastily slipped its mooring three-quarters of a mile north of Cape Henry and motored through the flat, calm sea to meet the incoming ship.

*

'What's that?' asked Christian Bach. He was watching the black pilot vessel through glasses as it cut through the water. The mist that hung over the sea made the sea itself invisible, and the wake that curled away from the pilot boat made strange lines in the nothingness like soft creases in white paper.

'Pilots,' said Harris, the fisherman, from the comfort of his wheelhouse. Like all Harris's charter passengers, Bach had to stay outside.

Bach knew nothing of ships or the sea. 'Pilots? What for?'

'Pilots. To take the ship up the bay. Gotta have 'em. Regulations.'

'The ship shows them the way?'

Harris shook his head. 'The pilot gets on the ship.'

'How?' asked Bach, taking a sudden interest.

'They put a fucking ladder down, for Christ's sake.'

Bach nodded. They put a ladder down, that's how you got from a small boat up on to a larger one. Now he understood. He moved his glasses to follow the pilot boat, but it soon became hazier and hazier until it vanished.

'So where's the battleship?'

'Four, five miles out. That's usually where the pilots pick them up. It'll come through this shit soon.'

'Can we go out towards it?'

'Sure. You're paying.' Harris opened the throttle and turned the boat's head towards the east. He had no radar and no way of seeing through the murk but he knew the mist would vanish soon, and he knew these waters like he knew his own backyard. *Paddler* ran at twenty knots flat out; in ten minutes the squat, fat shape of *Zuider* loomed out of the calm mist, looking as though it was suspended in the air.

They motored on. Suddenly, towering over the tow ship, the top of the massive superstructure of the German battleship floated above the *Zuider*.

'Look at that mother,' murmured Harris. Even at this distance the ship was awesome, far more so than the TV pictures made it out to be. But Bach was silent. He was looking at the *Hindenburg* through his glasses: a spectre emerging from the mists of the war. It was why his family was in America, poor and harassed, instead of being wealthy and respectable in Germany.

The ship was his enemy and his friend; it had taken Erich Bach, his grandfather, to his death, but now was returning to bring his grandson, Christian, a new life. Somehow, he had to get on that ship. He knew he would be just another sightseer if he remained where he was; the FBI had seen to that. He had to get back to the centre of the stage.

They had beaten the pilot vessel. Only now was it coming up alongside the *Zuider* to land the pilot, and De Wit had dropped a gangway down to a few feet above the sea to let the pilot board comfortably. This was happening on the port side.

'Run us down the other side. I want a closer look,' demanded Bach.

Harris slowed *Paddler* down and closed in to the other side. They passed *Zuider* and a few crewmen leaned over to look; they were expecting sightseers. They motored, much slower now, about 100 yards off the approaching *Hindenburg*. As it came closer, the scale of the ship seemed to double and then double again. Bakker had succeeded with the guns; all four of them stood firmly outwards. Tan was right. The ship, for all its rust, now had a menacing air.

The crumpled bow was clearly visible. A gentle ripple spread from the stem into water that was wrinkled by the wake of the tow ship. Behind the bow followed an almost endless steel wall, disappearing into the distance. It was so vast that it was the water that seemed to moving past a fixed structure, like a quayside, rather than a ship moving at all.

Harris now pushed the throttle back to idle ahead, so that the small boat made barely a couple of knots into the water. The grey walls towered above them as the huge ship glided silently past. There was a soft hiss from the water.

'Big mother, ain't she?' called Harris admiringly from his cabin.

But Bach stood there silently, watching the sides of the ship as it crept past them. Then he saw it: Bakker and his crew, now all on the *Zuider*, had left a rope-and-wood ladder secured down the side of the vessel to give them easy access for their comings and goings.

'Take me to that ladder,' ordered Bach.

Harris looked out through his window. 'What for?'

'Just take me to the fucking ladder, OK?'

'Listen, fella, I don't know what you're planning but you can't get on that ship. You know that?'

'I don't give a shit. Now take me to that ladder.'

'Maybe we better turn for home. You seen the ship; that was the deal.' Harris opened the throttle and wound his wheel to port to take them away from the *Hindenburg*. The boat pushed its nose into the air as it gathered speed.

'Turn this fucker back,' shouted Bach over the racket of the engine.

'You heard me. That's the trip over. I'll give some money back if you want.' Harris didn't like the stranger at all. There was something frightening about him now.

Bach walked into the hallowed space of the cabin. 'Listen, you turn this thing back to that ship and drop me at the ladder. You know what this is?' Bach was holding the Smith and Wesson.

Harris's eyes widened in sheer terror. 'Listen, fella, no problem, OK?'

'Just get me there.'

Harris, his hands visibly shaking, slowed down the boat and turned the wheel to bring them round in a full circle so that once more they faced the slowly oncoming ship. He steered towards the side and watched the ladder approach. As it drew level he opened the throttle once more, circled his boat quickly and drew up level with the steps. He pulled back the throttle until he matched the speed of the battleship and was soon alongside the ladder.

'Tie us up. I ain't jumping,' ordered Bach. Harris moved in as close as he could and then leaned over the gunwale to catch the ladder. He tied a line to it, but his hands were still shaking and he fumbled until he finally made it secure.

'Don't tell anyone, you got me?'

'Sure. No problem,' replied Harris, terrified.

Bach looked at Harris, who was standing by the gunwale holding on to the ladder for him. He was a small man, middle-aged and overweight. Bach climbed on to the gunwale and gripped the ladder; he was about a foot above Harris when he brought the butt of the revolver down hard on the fisherman's head. There was a loud noise, like a sigh, and Harris collapsed as though his legs had been taken away from him. But when he hit the deck he rolled and started trying to struggle to his feet. Bach jumped down. He crashed the butt on to the back of Harris's head once, and then again. Blood suddenly spurted from the fisherman's head, but he fell back to the deck and lay still. Bach was breathing hard. He thought about trying to heave the man overboard; but when he bent down to pull on Harris's arm, he realised the weight would be too much to shift over the side. He went into the cabin and looked around. He turned the wheel to the right as far as it would go and then pushed the throttle right open. The boat started shaking as the engine howled but, held by the line, it stayed put.

Bach ran from the cabin, jumped up on to the gunwale and then on to the ladder, where he reached back and pulled clumsily at the bowline that Harris had used to secure it. The rope was ripped from his hands as the boat careered away, heading first for the open water and then straightening up as the force of the water pushed the rudder back to midships.

Bach watched the *Paddler* curl away and then hauled himself up the ladder. It was further than he thought, but finally he pulled himself on to the deck.

It was deserted and silent, since almost everyone had gone back on board the tow ship while they negotiated the last few miles. Bach looked across the expanse of deck, bigger than it should have been because the aft turrets had never been fitted.

Finally, he had made it. Christian Bach was now treading the very spot that his grandfather had trod half a century earlier. He smiled to himself, for the first time in days. His world was coming right again.

And as he stood on that open deck, the idea that had been lurking at the back of his mind – the idea that had really driven him all along but had, even just a few days ago, seemed so improbable as to be not worth thinking about – suddenly threw itself into the forefront of his mind as though a spotlight had been shone on it.

Captain Erich Bach had set out on a mission to shell Washington. Now his grandson, Christian, would show those degenerates in the White House what he was made of. He could now finish the job that his grandfather had started.

21

De Wit watched nervously as the pilot carefully took them towards one of the gaps in the Chesapeake Bay Bridge where the road disappeared downwards into a tunnel. The artificial islands were about a mile apart but the buoys marking the channel were tighter in, giving a quarter-mile-wide gap. For a vessel of their size this was narrow, and the incoming tide was running behind them and shifting their tow. But the pilot looked relaxed enough.

Tan was also watching carefully from De Wit's bridge. They had come this far and now he was within a few dozen miles of his final anchorage. He had already spent millions and didn't want it screwed up at this stage.

But he watched with satisfaction, as well. The low bridge in the distance was packed with unmoving traffic, since what looked to him like half of Washington had turned out to see the entry of the ship. Louise DeAngelis was still helping things along nicely: right now, as they approached the bridge, she was doing a live broadcast from the aft deck of the *Zuider*.

The ship and its tow made slow progress. The pilot

wanted to ease his unwieldy charge through the gap carefully. It would not have been the first time that a ship had missed the gap and taken a chunk of the fragile-looking trestle bridge away. But the weather was good and the *Zuider* was powerful enough to haul the old wreck with no trouble.

The Dutch ship passed through the gap easily. Then the *Hindenburg* followed, all 823 feet of it, progressing steadily between the two low islands.

There was a low moaning sound rolling across the water, like distant cattle, quickly increasing in volume. Tan and De Wit looked out of the port bridge door in the direction where the sound was coming from. There was a Navy anchorage over by Little Creek, and a handful of grey US Navy warships were greeting the arrival of the old battleship, sounding off their horns in a long cascade of sound. Tan smiled. Just what he wanted. He hoped the woman was getting this on tape.

De Wit answered the greeting with three short blasts on his own horn. Other ships anchored nearby in Hampton Roads and The Tidewater joined in. Soon the still water was echoing with the sounds of several dozen ships. It was like the mating calls of whales in the lonely ocean.

The *Hindenburg* cleared the islands and they moved steadily along the marked channel. Now the small boats started to join them – cabin cruisers, RIBS, jet-skis and small yachts running on their engines. They gathered not around the *Zuider* but around the battleship, a tiny armada at the battered, rusting prow of the *Hindenburg*. The pilot looked back at them from the wing bridge. It was an unseamanlike mess and he hoped to heaven they would stay clear, because even if he ran one down he wouldn't feel a thing.

They had been allowed past Hampton Roads and

the quarantine formalities. The port officials agreed with De Wit's suggestion that towing the wreck into the confined waters would not be good for anyone's health; he would clear the formalities once anchored.

They pushed north past the York River channel and followed the buoys up towards the York Spit channel – narrow but deep, and clearly marked. The sun had broken through the morning mist and was shining brilliantly across the water. The armada had grown, too. A Coastguard vessel had joined them, well aft of the battleship, just to make sure that the sightseers didn't all drown themselves in the melée.

After several miles the narrow channel suddenly opened out. They were passing the Rappahannock River entrance to port, with Fredericksburg nearly 100 miles away at the head of the river. From here the passage was easier, with deep water all around them.

There was little other major traffic to worry about. It was still early; and the authorities had asked most large vessels to stay at their berths or to delay their entrance while the battleship was towed slowly up the bay. But a German freighter out of Hamburg, coming down from Baltimore, said it had a tight schedule to meet, and it passed the *Hindenburg* heading south towards the York River channel. Its ensign was flying at half mast as it passed the ship, and it gave no greeting, moving past the noisy armada with a disapproving silence.

They continued their slow progress northwards. The bay itself was wider here, nearly ten miles across, and the coastlines to each side were low and marshy so that it looked even wider. They steamed through the middle of the bay for another ten miles before a line of buoys led away to the north-west and the bay itself seemed to widen to the horizon. This was the

entrance to the next great river, the Potomac, the
border between Virginia and Maryland and navigable
all the way up to Washington, ninety-five miles away.
The mouth of the river was nearly six miles across and
the grey water moved slowly with the tide across low
mudflats.

The pilot now directed the helmsman to move
slowly towards the western side of the bay where the
water ran deepest. There was still more than fifty feet
of water under the keel.

By now the sun was blazing hot. It had taken them
nearly six hours to reach this point and the armada
was beginning to disperse in the heat, thinking about
lunch. They still had another five or six hours to go
before they reached the anchorage.

Two helicopters had turned up and were hovering
on each side, chartered by the TV stations who wanted
their own coverage of the event. Newsworld's ratings
had shot through the roof in the last week as it docu-
mented the arrival of the battleship, and the big networks wanted in on the story. On the aft deck, Louise
DeAngelis was working harder than ever. She had
already had a call on her mobile from NBC – and would
she like to join them for lunch once the ship landed?

Attended by its admirers, the rusting pride of the
German Navy sailed serenely onwards.

*

Bach was working his way towards the bow of the
ship on the inside, keeping himself well out of sight of
the helicopters that were following them. He had
thought to bring a small flashlight with him, lifted
from Harris's boat, and he had found a long companionway that seemed to run the length of the vessel. Now
he moved carefully along it.

The interior of the ship had an acrid, damp smell. The bulkheads had once been painted, but over the years the paint had flaked away and the raw steel underneath was crusted with damp rust. In places he saw words that had been stencilled on the bulkhead. He knew no German, but the words were stencilled in traditional German black-letter. With a shock he saw one notice that had an eagle gripping a swastika in its claws, and the unmistakable 'Heil Hitler!' stencilled underneath. This really was an old German battle-ship, Bach thought. It had become all the more real now.

He had reached about halfway down the ship, according to his reckoning, when the utilitarian doors – oval shaped, with screw-down locking nuts on some of them – suddenly gave way to a line of wooden doors. The wood was spongy and rotten when he touched it; they were nearly disintegrating. Across the middle rail of each door was carved a German word. Bach recognised only one: *'Kapitan'*.

When he pushed carefully against the fragile door, it squealed against the hinge. He shone his flashlight inside, expecting a rich, panelled suite, but instead it was just a sparse, cold room. He shone the torch around the walls. There was a portrait of an old German in a uniform, with a big moustache, unfamiliar to Bach. On the floor, with the glass long since gone, was a print of someone he did recognise – Adolf Hitler. The pictures were both covered with large brown spots.

There was a small desk to one side. It was empty, but on the floor lay a pile of rotting paper. He pushed the mushy heap around with his foot and uncovered a book bound in brown leather. He picked it up and saw it was a notebook, the pages covered in neat, tiny black handwriting. Unable to understand a word of it, he dropped it back to the floor.

Near the desk was a run of bookshelves. On the bottom shelf was an old wind-up gramophone, and an ancient 78 was still sitting on the turntable. Bach picked it up. 'Beethoven' he recognised, but the rest of it was meaningless.

There was a bunk, but the mattress had turned into a set of rusting springs; and there was a cupboard with the door hanging open, but nothing inside other than a small heap of metal buttons on the floor, and a dark green bottle. There was no label on it and Bach couldn't tell what it had contained.

This was grandfather Bach's cabin, where the old man had spent his last days. Christian Bach felt no emotion as he looked around the place. He had never known the man, just heard the stories. In some ways he blamed the captain. Why didn't you do better for me? What happened to all the money you were supposed to have? The musty room was just a wreck. He left the cabin and tried to close the door behind him, but it was stuck. What the hell ...

Christian Bach continued along the gloomy, dank passageway towards the front of the ship.

*

They were past the Potomac entrance now, clearing Point Lookout and making their way slowly towards Point No Point and its octagonal lighthouse. The pilot was taking them towards the starboard side of the channel where the water ran deepest. For another ten miles the featureless lowlands on each side slid gently past.

Point No Point receded behind them, and the ruins of Cedar Point lighthouse and the entrance to

Patuxent River came into view on the port side. Just inside the river mouth was the Naval Air Station where some of the earliest astronauts had trained as test pilots in the 1950s and 1960s. Another small group of boats was waiting for them and, as the armada that had joined them from the Potomac turned for home, the new acolytes took their place.

The coast was rising now. A few low, wooded hills started to emerge in the distance.

Past the Patuxent River entrance, they carried on northwards past Cove Point and a group of five offshore platforms. Herring Bay was the next landmark, some twenty-five miles further up the channel. The slow beat of the *Zuider*'s engines marked each passing mile with a dull regularity; the ship had settled in the heat to a steady routine. The pilot watched the passing of the buoys, which every few miles marked the deep water. He had made this run countless times before, guiding everything from Panamanian freezer ships to Russian tankers carefully through the waters. He had never had charge of an old battleship before, and certainly not one that had attracted so much attention, but by now the novelty had worn off. He yawned slightly and ordered the helmsman to a slightly changed course as the buoys slipped past on the starboard side.

De Wit was leaning over the railings on the port wing bridge, watching the coastline glide slowly past them. For him, the voyage was nearly over. He would soon collect a substantial heap of cash from Billy Tan. Anybody other than De Wit would be looking forward to spending it. As a good Dutchman, he was looking forward to putting it into his pension fund.

Only Billy Tan was still excited. They were drawing nearer and nearer to their final destination, just off Bay

Ridge a few miles outside Annapolis. It was the ideal spot. With its naval traditions, Annapolis would provide the perfect backdrop for the battleship. The naval anchorage was a couple of miles north of the position and would create an excellent atmosphere for the hundreds of thousands of visitors which Billy was confident of getting. The water was sheltered; and given the huge size of the ship, it would be clearly visible from the busy William P. Lane Jr. Memorial Bridge, spanning the upper reaches of Chesapeake Bay just five miles north of the final resting place of the *Hindenburg*.

It had cost him a lot of money, both legally and illegally, to secure the place. A certain Maryland senator would be forever grateful to him.

It was early evening before Herring Bay was astern and the white tower of Thomas Point Shoal lay clear ahead of them. They had to round Thomas Point, and sheltered behind that was their waiting anchorage. It was the last few miles, and Billy Tan had several bottles of Dom Perignon already chilling in ice buckets, ready to celebrate the homecoming of this extraordinary ship.

*

Otto Heine had remained stubbornly on the bridge of the *Hindenburg* throughout the closing stages of the voyage. When they took on the pilot at the approach to the bay, De Wit had asked him if he wanted a doctor. The old man just shook his head firmly and made it clear that he wanted to stay where he was. Bakker was sent in to rig up a sling that supported his arm and stopped it moving too much, and he left him with a large bottle of Distalgesic from the medicine chest, which kept the pain at bay.

It would have to do. Having finally got back on to

the ship, the last thing he intended to do was leave it. Or his gold.

Heine watched the coastline slip slowly by. Fifty-five years ago he had watched a curiously similar coastline – the low banks of the Elbe – also slide by as the ship had started out on its maiden voyage.

Now he could see the shoreline of the bay for himself, he shook his head to think of the idea for the ship's original mission. Bach must have been a fool ever to think he could get away with sailing through here and shelling Washington. There was not a hope in hell that he could have done so. The huge naval bases they had already passed – full of ships now and surely packed with them in the last war – would have sunk them in minutes, and even if they did get past them, the bay was just too big for them to simply charge up and fire the guns. If they weren't sunk, they would have grounded. From his vantage position he had watched the low mudflats on each side, almost invisible, stretching into the bay. Unless you knew the waters you would have no chance.

He had made himself comfortable on the bridge. Although what was once the command centre of the huge ship was now a rusting, stained room, Bakker had found a chair for Heine and he made himself comfortable, sleeping now and then but still in his way standing guard over his ship and his treasure.

The sun and the heat had dried out the bridge. The musty smell had vanished, and a peaceful afternoon light dappled the bridge floor. Heine had taken one of his pills half an hour ago, and now that the throbbing pain had subsided the heat was making him sleepy. As he settled into the chair, his eyes began to close and the warm, peaceful breeze drifted quietly through the open door.

He woke with a start and he looked around. What was the noise he had suddenly heard?

He looked ahead. There was a white, six-sided light-house on their left-hand side, about half a mile away; the Dutch ship had turned and was now pulling them across the channel instead of straight up it, and it felt as though it was slowing down. What had made the noise? He could see nothing. He settled down again and decided he had probably been dreaming.

But then, there it was again: a creaking sound from somewhere outside, and coming closer. The creaking stopped and then he heard footsteps, clearly, climbing the ladder that led up to the bridge. It was probably Bakker, or one of the Dutchman's crew, coming to check on him again. De Wit had never been comfortable leaving him on board on his own. Heine was irritated. Why can't they just leave me be?

With some difficulty he pulled himself to his feet. His shoulder was free of pain other than a dull throb. He walked slowly to the edge of the bridge, to the doorway. There was nobody in sight, but he could still clearly hear the footsteps coming up from somewhere just below.

'Who's that?' he called out, loudly.

The footsteps stopped. There was a sudden, suspicious silence.

'Who's there? Is that you, Bakker?'

There was no reply, no sound of any sort, just a sudden fading scream from a gull in the distance. Heine began to feel nervous.

Since he was six, he had lived a life that varied between the mildly dishonest and the outright criminal, and even during his years in New York he had always lived on the edge of legality. His fear of the knock on the door was not a paranoia, but common sense.

There were too many people who would like a little private conversation with Otto Heine.

He had grown to be watchful. And now every sense in his body told him to be more careful than he had ever been in his life. He had thought he was alone on this ship. Now someone else was here and they had decided to stop, and stay silent, the moment he shouted at them. This was not a friendly visit, and Heine started to move accordingly, as he always had done, by looking for somewhere to hide.

At the back of the bridge was the chart room, and a door – still on its hinges – concealed it from view. Very slowly, and as quietly as he could, he moved into the room, opening the door and praying the rusting hinges would stay silent, which they did. He pulled the door closed behind him, but left a small crack open to give him a view.

His heart was pounding and now his shoulder started to flare up as he waited for a minute, then two.

And then the footsteps started again, this time very, very softly and slowly.

Whoever it was had resumed their progress, but they were creeping now, and Heine could hear the soft creak of the steps as one by one they came up towards the bridge. Through the crack in the door he saw a shadow rise outside the bridge, which resolved itself into the shape of a man. Then the doorway filled with the figure as he came on to the bridge itself.

The light was behind him and it was impossible to see his face. But it definitely wasn't Bakker. Too thin.

The figure looked around and then walked to the other side of the bridge and turned. Now the light was on his face and Otto Heine could see him clearly. He had never seen him before, but even so there was something vaguely familiar about him. He was a young man, of ordinary height, and he had a thin, pale face with deep blue eyes and large ears.

He would have been a pleasant-looking young man except for the look on that face – a hunted, anxious expression that gave his eyes a wildness and his mouth a bitter, unhappy expression. He was sweating too; his face had a sickly shine that made him look sinister.

Heine breathed as slowly as he could, trying to calm himself down.

Once the intruder saw that the bridge was empty, he would surely go away. Heine's VHF radio lay on the chair, together with a chart that Bakker had left so Heine could follow their progress. He would call for help when he could. But the intruder showed no signs of moving. Instead he was looking around the bridge. He went to the chair, picked up the radio and the chart, and slipped them inside his jacket. He looked out from the forward windows, across the huge guns and the tow-lines curving away towards the *Zuider*.

Heine almost stopped breathing. The man was now directly opposite him.

Suddenly the figure turned and pointed a gun straight at Heine, concealed as he was behind the door.

'Come out. Now,' commanded the figure.

Heine paused, and then slowly pushed the door open. He stood where he was.

'Who the fuck are you?' asked the figure.

'Otto Heine.'

'Otto Heine, huh? The old German guy. You were on this ship, weren't you? I mean, when it was in the war?'

'Yes.'

'Well, don't that beat everything! You know what, you would have known my dear old grandfather. Erich Bach was his name. He was the captain of this thing. You knew him?'

God in heaven, thought Heine. The captain. His grandson. Standing there, pointing a gun at him, looking as though he would use it. Fifty-five years later, Otto Heine was facing another Bach on the bridge of the *Hindenburg*.

*

The anchorage was a small bay between Thomas Point Shoal and Tolly Point, well off the main channel but still in water that was deep enough to keep the ship afloat at low tide. They arrived by seven in the evening, and the sun was starting to sink over distant Washington.

They would have to drop the anchors of the *Zuider* and then simply let the battleship swing to anchor with them until the morning, when the task of securing the ship would start. The tide was weak that night, the wind non-existent and forecast to remain so.

The pilot brought the *Zuider* into the inflowing tide, bow facing south now, and De Wit ordered both anchors released. With a crash they plummeted into the murky water and plunged fifty feet into the soft mud of the bottom. Huge links of chain thundered out of the lockers. De Wit ordered slow astern as the anchors dropped, and the ship moved gently aft, taking up the strain on the chains and anchors. In the tide, the *Hindenburg* drifted back as well, keeping the tow-lines firm. After ten minutes De Wit was sure that the anchors had caught, and he ordered 'Finished with engines'. The distant vibration of the big diesels soon died away and a calm settled over the ship.

They now had to shorten the tow-lines. These were attached to massive capstans on the aft deck, each one powered by a separate engine, and for half an hour they slowly turned to wind the cable on board and bring the battleship closer. When the ship was within 100 yards of the *Zuider*, the capstans were stopped. Operations were finished, at least for the night.

The *Hindenburg* had been brought home from the ice, across stormy seas, up the Chesapeake Bay and was now in its final resting place. By next spring, once Billy Tan's restoration teams had finished, it would become one of the greatest tourist attractions of all time. Billy was delighted. At last it was time to open the champagne.

Louise DeAngelis was planning a final broadcast from the aft deck of the *Zuider*, with the dramatic backdrop of the bow of the *Hindenburg* and its massive guns still standing proudly from the turrets. Then she could get off this damn ship first thing the next morning and see the network chiefs who were by now falling over themselves to talk to her. She wanted a shot of Billy, champagne in hand, toasting the old ship. It would be the perfect end to the story.

*

'Listen, old man, and you won't get hurt. You know how to get to those guns?' asked Bach.

Heine nodded. What did he want with the guns? Did he know about the gold in the magazine below the turret?

'Take me down there, OK? Just keep your head low when we go outside and stay out of sight of that other ship. You got that? Don't fuck about with me, either. I can blow the head off a fucking chicken at fifty yards if you don't believe me,' Bach said, waving the gun at him.

'I believe you. No problem.'

'You make sure you do. Now get going.'

Heine led Bach down the bridge steps and then forward across the deck. He was making for turret

Anton, the foremost of the two turrets. Being lower down, at deck height, it was easier to get to. And, most importantly, his golden shells were in the magazine below Bruno, not Anton. To Heine's pleased surprise, Bach didn't appear to notice or to mind; he didn't seem to know about the gold after all. It was a mystery what he was after, but for now, thank God, Otto Heine's gold was safe.

They reached the rear of the turret, where a short ladder lead up to an armoured door. On the deck nearby was the generator set which Bakker's team had used to provide the power to get the mechanisms running again. The thick cable snaked up to the door and disappeared inside it.

Heine climbed up the short ladder with some difficulty, holding on to the rusted steel railing with one arm. He reached the top and, balancing on the narrow step, he pulled open the door.

Bach came up behind him. 'In,' he ordered.

Heine stepped inside. Bach had his flashlight and switched it on. Bakker's team had done a good job. To get the hydraulics functioning they had had to run through the whole system, fixing perished seals, so that not only did the gun elevation mechanism operate but all the other hydraulically powered systems worked as well. They had cleaned and polished as they went, and even rigged up some internal lighting inside bulkhead fittings hung from projections inside the turret.

The turret interior was dominated by the two huge breech doors of the guns, like bank vault doors. Machined from stainless steel, they had grooves cut all around them, like screws; once these were shut into the breech and turned, they would lock into the back of the barrel to stand up to the force of the cordite charge igniting.

The doors were suspended on massive hinges. The rest of the space was crowded out with the equipment required to move the shells and propellant charges from the shell-handling room immediately below the turret into the breech.

'How do these lights work?' asked Bach.

'The generator. Outside.'

Christian Bach looked at the scene in the dim yellow beam of his flashlight. He knew nothing about ships, but he knew a lot about guns. This was just an oversized rifle, he thought. The workings of the whole system were obvious, the longer he stood and looked.

'Where's the ammo?' he asked.

'The shells? Below us. And the charges. In bags, in the magazine.' What the hell did he want to know that for?

'How do I get there?'

'Not from here. There's another door.'

Bach motioned Heine out of the turret and followed him. Heine showed him the access door to the shell-handling room and the magazine.

'OK, old man. You stay here. Turn around.' From somewhere, Bach had found some line. He wrapped it round Heine's one good hand and then tied it firmly to his legs, leaving just enough line to allow him to stand but not sufficient to move. Then he tied him to the turret steps.

Heine couldn't do a thing. Bach was gone for what felt like half an hour but was probably much less. He came back breathing hard and sweating.

'OK, old man,' he said as he untied Heine's ankles, 'you just walk ahead, up those steps, back where I found you.' He pushed Heine towards the bridge, up the steps, and finally back into his chair. There Bach set to work on him once more and tied him up, deftly and firmly. Bach then simply vanished, walking off the bridge. Heine noticed that the anxious look on his face had disappeared; he looked happier now.

Minutes passed, then Heine heard the generator start up from below. It was well muffled and made little sound.

A nagging thought had been creeping into Heine's mind, but he had kept pushing it out. Now it forced its way in again. What in the name of God was Bach doing? Why was he here? Why the interest in the guns? Why had he started the generator? The answer that Heine's brain kept shouting at him was so improbable that he pushed it back deep inside himself yet again.

He found himself alone. Whatever Bach was up to, Heine now had an opportunity to escape. He pulled his legs against the knots, but they were firmly tied. His good arm was secured to the chair.

He thought it out for a moment. His other arm was still in its sling; Bach had left it free, presuming it was useless. Heine had only one chance; he would have to use this arm, and he would have to twist it in such a way ... it didn't hurt at first, and he could get his fingers to within an inch of the knot. He closed his eyes, took a deep breath and lunged. It was like a sword being sliced into his shoulder, and he gasped and had to stop.

He took another breath and then made another lunge. This time he grasped the knot, but again the pain won and he had to let his arm go. But now the pain didn't stop; he'd done something to the fracture. Fuck it! He willed his arm across again, gripped the knot and slowly untied it. The pain came in waves and sweat began to run from his face. He started swearing in German, softly, lest Bach hear him, but he kept his arm pulled across his body until finally he had untied the knot and freed his arm.

He rested for a moment, breathing hard, his shirt sticking to his back and drops of sweat creeping down his forehead.

The note of the generator changed, speeding up. Bach had switched something on, putting a load on the engine.

Heine was free. Carefully he stood up from the chair, but immediately had to sit down again. His legs were like jelly and wouldn't support him. He paused again and looked around for the VHF radio that Bakker had left him. It was missing; Bach had taken it.

He took several more deep breaths and tried again to stand. His knees still quivered, but now his legs held him as he went to the forward bridge windows and looked out. They were very close to the coast. It looked as though they had stopped. The *Zuider* was nearer now than it was before.

Heine couldn't see much of turret Anton other than the very top and the guns. Bruno, standing much higher, obscured most of the view. Bach must be inside the foremost turret, doing something – God knows what.

Heine was free, but he had no intention of escaping from the ship. Bach had frightened the life out of him but that made him all the more determined to stay.

He had risked his life for that gold twice already. He had waited fifty-five years. Now he was not going to run from this stinking rust-bucket just because some lunatic had frightened the shit out of him.

And what in the name of heaven was Bach up to anyway? What was he doing on this ship if it wasn't for the gold? There was no other explanation. He *must* know about it. He must have heard some story from his grandfather. It had to be: otherwise it was simply too much of a coincidence.

Heine was not going to let him have it, not now. He found the Distalgesic tablets and took three, then started to make his way down the bridge steps towards the turrets.

*

Bach had lived with guns all his life. Born with a natural gift for machines and inanimate objects, he had loved tinkering with an old tractor at the age of four – or he had when his pa wasn't yelling at him to get inside. Once the generator was running and he had power inside the turret, it took him less than half an hour to get the hang of how the whole of the big gun's systems operated. Bakker's crews had done their jobs well. The hydraulics were running, the electrics re-wired and by-passed to give light. The guns moved up, and down, although he ran them for only the briefest of moments to avoid attracting attention from outside. The breech door and the shell ram worked. But how did the turret traverse? He had found what looked like a big electric motor linked via a cog to the toothed annular ring, but it looked way beyond repair.

And the shell lift didn't look very hopeful either. Its electric motor had long since corroded. Bach made his way down to the magazine several decks below the turret and found the cordite bags still intact as well as the shells. The shells in the magazine would be impossible to move up to the turret, but the cordite bags were manageable with much sweating and shoving. He went up to the shell-handling room, immediately below the turret. There were a dozen shells stored there; he saw the hooks in the noses and realised they would need fuses. After some searching he found the armoured locker where the fuses were kept. They were grey steel tubes, about the size of a beer bottle, machined with the screw thread to fit in the nose of the shell when the lifting hook was removed.

Inside the handling room, although there was a lift there was also a block and tackle hanging down through an opening, covered with an armoured anti-flash hatch. He pushed the hatch open and found it led upwards into the turret. He grinned. The old German bastards had wanted the ship to fight to the end. When the power gave up, they could still haul the shells up to the gun. There must be a way of hand-cranking the turret round, as well. They wouldn't leave the gun with no means of aiming as long as it could still shoot.

Bach went back up the turret and looked out through the door. The sun was setting and the evening was starting to draw in. It was time to get to work.

*

Louise DeAngelis was finishing off her hair. She wanted to look good for this, her last broadcast. The people she was meeting for lunch the next day were sure to be watching.

The cameraman was still adjusting his lights. He wanted Billy Tan well lit, but he wanted to be able to see the big battleship in the background as well, and as the light faded he kept having to adjust his whole set-up. He would have preferred to do it in the daylight, but the slot wasn't until nine. He would have just enough light.

Billy Tan was also dressing for the part. He was wearing a shiny suit and a narrow leather tie, but on his head he now sported a baseball cap emblazoned with a German eagle and the word *Hindenburg* across it. He would waste no opportunity to give his project as much publicity as possible. He had even calmed down about Louise DeAngelis's pointed questions over the legality and, indeed, morality, of the rescue. After all, it had made a much bigger story. He was ready for any questions she wanted to ask.

It was ten to nine. The ship had anchored and the mooring lights were on. They had fixed flashing lights on the battleship and a small RIB was ambling around the vessel, patrolling the waters and making sure no unauthorised visitors tried to get on board, such was the interest it had already created.

DeAngelis had finished her hair and was studying herself in the monitor.

'I look sick. Give me some colour,' she ordered. The cameraman adjusted the colour balance to warm up her features.

'Better,' she said, and looked at her watch.

*

He didn't need to be accurate. Close would do. He had Heine's chart of the bay to guide him. He knew what his current position was, therefore moving the turret to the required bearing was straightforward. He had already discovered the crank handle and established that it worked. Luckily for him, the ship was lying with its bow facing 320 degrees – there was a large compass inside the turret – and the required bearing was 300, just 20 degrees round to his left. The elevation was more difficult. He had measured off the distance at 24½ miles. He knew it was close to the maximum range of the guns, therefore the elevation would need to be high, and the cordite charges would have to be the maximum. This much Bach understood. But what the exact elevation would be was an entirely different question. He'd just have to try trial and error.

He reckoned he could get off a few shots before they knew what was happening. He would then simply swim back to shore under cover of darkness in the panic, and make good his escape. He was a good swimmer, and covering the mile or so back to the shoreline gave him no problems. They would have no idea who it was. He would sort out the old man on his way out. Maybe they'd pin the blame on him? It was the perfect act of terrorism. They wouldn't know what had hit them.

He had already manhandled bags of cordite up to the turret. The silk bags that held the charge were delicate after all the years in the Arctic. The silk was specially treated to withstand life at sea and had held together remarkably well, but it needed to be handled carefully and moving the charges took a long time.

He had used the block and tackle to bring up a shell, and it was resting on the cradle in front of the open breech door. He had replaced the lifting hook with a fuse – God knows which one – but even if the shell didn't actually explode it didn't really matter. He pulled down the lever, and the ram hissed and pushed the shell into the breech. The cordite bags were next. Finally, Bach closed the breech door. It hissed and turned through almost a full quarter-turn, locking itself in place against the blast.

All that remained now was to aim the gun. And then fire it.

*

Billy Tan stood in the white glare of the light. Louise DeAngelis watched the monitor showing her the New York studio, and in her earpiece she heard the count-down.

'Five ... four ... three ... two ... cue!'

'Good evening. This is Louise DeAngelis in the Chesapeake Bay, and behind me you can see the massive bulk of the *Hindenburg*, the ship that was towed out of the ice by *this* man ... Billy Tan. Billy, looking back at this ship, how do you feel now?'

Billy did as she had told him and looked back at the ship. 'Well, Miss DeAngelis, obviously I'm feeling absolutely delighted to have ...' he faltered for a second '... delighted to ...' and now he stopped altogether. He was looking at the battleship. Slowly but unmistakably, the forward turret was swinging round.

'Billy?' asked Louise anxiously. This was not going well.

'Sorry. Just a minute. De Wit? Where the fuck's the captain?' he shouted.

'I'm sorry, ladies and gentlemen, we seem to have a bit of a problem here,' said a flustered Louise to the camera. Billy Tan had disappeared, running across the deck, trying to find De Wit.

The cameraman, lacking an interviewee, focused on the battleship. He too had seen the turret move and zoomed in so that the turret and the two 15-inch guns filled the frame.

But now the turret stopped moving. Instead, the guns were slowly lifting into the darkening sky.

DeAngelis had to hoof it. 'Well, here you can see the big guns of the old battleship, and look at that, they're moving round.'

The guns stopped and Tan's voice could be heard in the distance. There was silence now. She could think of no more to say.

The light came first. It wasn't a flash, more like a very fast-burning light, deep red to start with and then growing quickly before erupting into a brilliant orange bloom of flame, surrounded by black and purple smoke. While Louise and half of America watched, a small black object streaked from the mouth of the gun, clearly visible in the light. The sound and blast wave came half a second later. As DeAngelis and the cameraman were hurled across the deck by the shock, and the last image that the world saw was from the camera flying through the air before landing on the deck and dying.

Through the evening gloom, arching high over Annapolis, a single high-explosive 15-inch shell whined through the sky on its way towards Washington and, hoped Christian Bach, the White House.

22

Otto Heine was behind turret Anton when Bach pulled the firing lever and the gun blasted its shell out into the evening gloom.

The turret probably saved him. It shielded him from the blast wave and, even though he was knocked to the ground, the shock passed him over and the effects of the flash – which otherwise would have burned him to a crisp – simply singed his hair.

He picked himself up and shook his head. First one Bach tried to kill him, and now this one, his grandson, was shooting at the Americans – in about five minutes flat this ship would be blown out of the water, and Otto Heine's gold would either be vaporised or buried so deep in the mud that he'd never find it. The fear had gone. He was angry now.

There was a distant, rumbling sound, like thunder. The shell had landed somewhere to the west of them. God knows what damage it had done.

Heine looked around. There was no sign yet of any reaction to the shot, but it could not be long in coming.

He climbed the ladder leading to the door of the turret, now firmly closed. The pain in his shoulder was forgotten. Either the pills had worked or Heine's brain had decided to ignore the screaming nerves. He gripped the lever handle, pushed it down and opened the door as quietly as he could. A sudden, stinging smell assaulted him. The burnt cordite had filled the turret; giant fans, powered by electric motors, were designed to remove the stench, but these motors too had long ago failed and the inside was reeking. The electric lights were still on, but there was a mist that made it difficult to see.

There was a choking cough coming from inside. For all his experience with guns, Christian Bach had expected nothing quite like this. The mechanism worked perfectly. The recoil of the gun against massive shock absorbers drove itself backwards into the turret, and engaged an automatic latch which opened the breech door, speeding up the loading process. The fans would have taken the gas out. But now, once the door opened, it billowed back into the turret as though it was on fire. His eyes streaming, Christian Bach was half-blinded by the smoke. He was half-deaf as well. The original turret crew would have worn ear-protectors, and the sound of the gun going off left him with a shrill ringing in his ears.

Bach was hanging on to a short section of railing, uncertain what to do next. He neither saw nor heard Heine come into the turret, but just leaned there, gasping. He knew he had to get the next shot off quickly, and was hoping he would recover his breath.

Heine saw that his man was incapacitated. And that in the heat of the turret, he had taken his jacket off. His gun had been in his jacket ... where was the jacket? A quick glance around the turret. Nothing. Must be down in the shell-handling room. The access was back outside. Heine quickly retreated and now, almost running, got to the room below the turret. The lights were on. There was Bach's jacket hanging, with a studied casualness, over a shell. Heine picked it up. It was heavy on one side and he found the gun, an enormous lump of polished steel, and threw the jacket down. He headed outside again and reached the turret door, to find Bach standing there, wiping his eyes with his sleeve, in the clearer air.

Bach took one look at the old man, gun in hand, and quickly realised what was happening. He tried to push back into the turret and close the door, but it was stiff and Heine, with surprising strength, pushed his way in again. Bach was backing away; Heine levelled the gun.

Bach stood and watched him, half with fear and half with contempt. But Heine no longer cared. Decades of anger welled up in his soul. Here was a man whose family seemed out to kill him.

'Bach, what in the name of God are you *doing*?' asked Heine softly, pointing the gun at Bach's nose. The weapon quivered slightly.

Bach shrugged. 'Showing them,' he said simply, after a long pause.

'Showing them? Who?'

'Who? Listen, old man, it would take too long to explain.'

'I asked a question.'

'Sure. Those people. Washington. You wouldn't believe it. I know things about them, things they try to hide. Don't believe what you read in the papers, old man. They deserve it.'

'Shooting at them with this?' asked Heine, finding Bach's explanation difficult.

'Sure. Anything. This is just one hell of a way of doing it. You know what, they nearly killed my mother and pa. My grandpa, the guy you sailed with, he was rich, you know that? In Germany, I mean. Estates, castles, all kind of shit. He was a famous captain. The Russians took the estates and the Americans took the money. My money. Then they wanted rid of us. Me too. You know they arrested me in New York last week? I tell you, old man, these people don't want me making a fuss.'

'Bach, your grandfather was not a famous captain. He was a simple man who was chosen for an impossible job and was lied to and cheated. He was crazy, like you are. He wanted to kill everyone. Duty, he called it. He was a fool, but at least he died honourably. He would have beaten you, Bach, for behaving like this.'

'He was a great captain,' insisted Bach sullenly.

'Well, you sure as hell don't take after him. What do you think's going to happen next? You're surrounded by warships and fuck knows what else. They'll blow us out of the water in ten minutes' time.'

'Listen, you're a German. Like me. This is our revenge, don't you understand? Now it's your chance to get even. I could have got another few shots off. It's too late. We go overboard, swim to shore in the dark. No one will find us. I'll help you,' pleaded Bach.

'They'll blow the ship up,' said Heine, still thinking about the gold. All he had ever wanted was the gold.

'We've got time, if we go now,' smiled Bach, advancing towards Heine.

'Stay there. Don't move an inch. You wouldn't be the first person I've killed on this ship. You understand?'

Bach froze. He knew more than most what a bullet from a .38 would do to him. The old man's aim didn't need to be good.

Heine now knew what he had to do. He had, he thought, about five or ten minutes, not a second longer, before the might of the US military turned up.

'Listen to me, Bach. Walk past me very slowly and out of the turret. Keep your hands on your head.'

Was Heine letting him go, letting him escape? Bach shuffled past him and made his way to the turret steps. Heine let him hold on with one hand and then insisted his hands went back on his head again. Directed by Heine, an increasingly puzzled Bach arrived at the door to turret Bruno and went inside. Heine switched the lights on.

'You know where the main magazine is?' asked Heine, but it wasn't really a question.

Bach nodded, looking worried and confused now.

'OK, I've got a job for you.'

*

The shell, spinning rapidly, rose quickly through the night sky, leaving a trail of condensation in the humid air that was unseen. Within seconds it reached an altitude of three miles, then its trajectory flattened out and started curving back down towards earth. Bach's guess on the gun's elevation was close. The shell was now travelling faster than the speed of sound and so it arrived just outside the centre of Washington in silence. It raced down to the ground, plunging itself into the wooded acres of the National Arboretum, six miles from the White House. At over 2,000 mph, the two tons of steel and high-explosive drove itself into one of the small roads just south of New York Avenue.

Bach had fitted a delayed-action fuse, although he didn't know it. This was a slow-burning fuse that allowed the shell to penetrate the opposing ship's armour and reach the innards before exploding, thus creating the maximum damage. The shell smashed into the thin concrete paving and, some twenty feet underground, the fuse detonated the explosive inside the shell. A dome of earth and concrete bulged up and then the centre erupted, spewing upwards into the air into a huge cascade of debris, taking with it a single car, which it smashed and threw across the nearby freeway before slowly falling back to the ground, leaving a crater forty feet across, gently smoking.

The sound of the explosion echoed across the park, across the city, and rumbled as far as the White House where the windows rattled.

'What the hell was that?' asked the Chief of Naval Operations, Admiral Jack Marshall, putting down his glass of Bourbon and looking across the table at the shirtsleeved President whom he was about to relieve of $100 on a nice hand of poker. The CNO was walking over to the window to see what was happening when a phone rang. It was the red one.

*

Bach was sweating so much that he had to stop to wipe his eyes every few minutes. Heine had directed him down to the main magazine and ordered him to take six wooden boxes up to the deck. Each box didn't weigh very much, but they weighed enough, and running up and down flights of ladders as fast as he could manage was more exercise than Bach had had in years. But Heine promised him that once he'd got the boxes, they would get off the *Hindenburg*, together.

Bach knew that Heine was right. It was only a matter of time before they would be under attack. He had to get off the ship . . . but not together. Heine's body would be found on board in the morning, and they would blame the shelling of Washington on a crazy old German who wanted his final act of revenge. No point in letting him drown on the swim back; they might not find the body. This way, there was somebody to point the finger at and no one would be looking for Christian Bach.

He dumped the last box on the deck, breathing hard.

'OK, now can we get off the ship?' he panted.

'Wrap them in this,' ordered Heine, pushing a bright orange object towards Bach with his foot, still pointing the gun at him. While Bach had been labouring with the boxes of shells, Heine had retrieved De Wit's flotation suit from the bridge. The shells would float easily in the garment.

Bach hastily wrapped the six boxes – each the size of a cereal pack – inside the suit and secured it by tying the arms and legs to each other to make a crude parcel.

'Now, push it to the railing,' ordered Heine. Bach was pushing the package along when a distant but rapidly approaching sound came through the night sky, a *whump-whump-whump* which Heine hadn't heard before. But Bach had.

'Helicopters! Coming this way,' shouted Bach. The noise grew quickly. He couldn't see the machines, but he could see the flashing red navigation lights, and suddenly four brilliant shafts of light, like stilts, were tottering towards them.

Heine couldn't help himself and looked up at where Bach was pointing. Bach needed no more opportunity. He grabbed Heine's hand, wrenched the gun from his grip and pushed the old man to the deck. He couldn't shoot him, not if he wanted to get away with all of this.

The lights were coming rapidly closer.

'Get up!' screamed Bach. Heine scrambled to his feet. 'Get inside, quick,' shouted the younger man again, waving the gun at an open door leading to the interior of the ship. Get out of sight of the helicopters, thought Bach.

Heine stumbled over the deck and reached the doorway, climbing over the sill and stepping inside the darkness. Bach followed. The old man stumbled, but Bach caught him. The thumping of the helicopters grew louder and louder until they throbbed almost overhead, the noise deafening both of them. The lights flickered about the deck, looking for something or somebody.

One of the helicopters detached itself from the group, approached low over the forward section of the deck and started to hover. Bach knew they were about to land marines; he'd seen it on training exercises he'd attended when he tried to join the National Guard, until they threw him out as an undesirable. Time was running out. He found the flashlight he had used before, lit up the interior of the rusting hulk and pushed Heine deeper into the ship. He wanted to find the long companionway that led back to the stern sections. This would allow his escape – after he'd disposed of Heine.

They went down the corridor and turned a corner. 'Stop!' ordered Bach.

Heine knew exactly what Bach had in mind. He had not lived for so long and come through so much without realising the dangers he now posed to him, but his instincts for self-preservation were strong. Bach saw an old man, hurt and in pain. Heine knew he had to do something quickly to save himself.

Heine stopped as ordered and turned to face Bach, who shone the flashlight on his victim.

'Your grandfather – Erich, his name was. His cabin is on this ship,' started Heine.

'I know. I found it,' replied Bach, advancing on the old man.

'So you found the gold?' asked Heine in a panic, desperate to stop the young man from executing him then and there.

'Gold? What gold?' asked Bach, stopping.

Heine breathed again. 'The gold in his cabin. That's what this is all about. Me. Tan. This old hulk. You didn't believe the stories, did you? You were right about Erich. He was rich. His money was on the ship, probably in the cabin. Millions of dollars' worth; everything he had.'

'You're lying.'

'Up to you. Do you really think somebody like Billy Tan would spend all that money just for a wreck? Use your sense, man.'

Bach stayed still. The noise of the helicopter could be heard outside as he looked back at the door.

'Hurry, for God's sake. I know where it is,' urged Heine.

Did he have the time? The captain's cabin was half-way down the central companionway, the way he meant to go to escape anyway. Why not?

'Hurry, old man,' he said, and pushed Heine once more. Otto Heine needed no prompting. He knew the way. Bach shone his flashlight and Heine went ahead, dodging confidently around the corners and down ladders until they reached the long, musty passageway that led through the spine of the ship.

*

It had been a long time since the CNO had taken direct control of an operation, but this was an extraordinary event and he felt justified in running it from the White House, in person. More to the point, he was enjoying every moment of it.

Immediately after the explosion, he ordered the President to take cover, but before the man even had time to put his jacket on a posse of secret-service men burst in and hustled him away anyway.

Marshall set up the room as his command post. His first step was to call the commander at Washington Navy Yard at his home. He was shaken at being spoken to by the big boss himself, without warning, at that time of night. But the commander had watched events on the TV and knew what had happened. In that, at least, he knew more than the CNO.

'You mean that old ship is shelling us?' asked Marshall, incredulous.

'That's right, sir. Saw it for myself on the TV just now. Opened up like you never saw in your life.'

'Commander?' said Marshall in his sternest voice. He never asked the commander his name.

'Yes, sir?'

'You just get out there and sink that mother before it does anything else, you hear that?'

'Yes, sir. No problem,' and he pushed down the button on the phone to cut off the call without replacing the handset. Then he called Annapolis and within ten minutes helicopters were winding up their engines, filled with confused marines who were wondering what the hell was happening. They were trying to get some naval craft running as well. A small *Perry* class frigate, USS *Clark*, was moored about a mile from the site of the *Hindenburg*, and frantic messages were being passed to the captain to start engines and investigate.

But De Wit and his crew, recovering from the sudden shock of the blast of the guns, had only one thought in mind, and that was to get away from the big ship as fast as they could.

They had cut through the lines and were starting engines and hauling in the anchor chains. Tan was screaming at De Wit about losing his precious ship, but all De Wit growled at him was that he was welcome to swim to the bastard and climb on it if he really wanted it that badly.

The weak tide was starting to ebb now and the *Hindenburg*, cut off from its tow ship, was starting to gently drift with the tide, southwards, like a bloated carcase.

*

Heine and Christian Bach reached the captain's cabin. His grandson's flashlight illuminated the rotting door, left half-open. The same damp smell came from inside, reeking through the darkness.

'It's in here. I'll show you,' insisted Heine.

'Go in, old man, go in.' As he did so, there were two distant explosions. The marines had tossed grenades into the turrets, just to make them safe.

Heine went in first; Bach was behind. 'Where is it?' demanded Bach.

'There. Behind the desk. Under the floor.'

What harm could Heine do? He was old, for God's sake. Bach went round behind the desk, placed the flashlight on the top, and kneeled down to look for the gold.

Heine seized his chance. He grabbed the flashlight and dashed from the room, leaving Bach in total darkness.

Now the old man ran with surprising speed, heading down the long companionway, and once he could see a turning he remembered he switched the flashlight off and slowed to a walk – feeling his way along the corridor, touching the rusting, weeping bulkheads, making his way through a darkness that was silent and profound – until Bach's angry and frightened voice screamed through the blackness.

'Heine! *Heine*!' he yelled.

But Heine kept the flashlight off. He didn't want Bach to know where he was going. He felt his way along until suddenly the bulkhead disappeared; he had reached the turning he knew was there.

A sudden explosion boomed down the companion-way. Bach had fired the gun into the blackness, down to where he thought Heine was. The bullet stuck a bulkhead and whined off in a ricochet, sounding like an angry wasp. But Heine had vanished around the corner. He knew where he was going now.

There was only one way to get rid of Bach and stop the bastards blowing his ship and his gold to splinters.

But Christian Bach was far from done. The old man had fooled him, but he would get him one way or another. He had to. Heine could identify him; he had to make sure that he was silenced. He wasn't going to leave it to chance, hoping he would get killed when they attacked the ship. Besides, he was angry that Heine had fooled him so easily. Gold, for God's sake! He would show Otto Heine that Christian Bach was not to be taken for a ride.

When he groped for his Zippo and flicked it, the wavering blue flame lit up the mess in the cabin. There was a chair, just legs and a back and no upholstery. Bach grabbed the chair and swung it against the wall, and one leg came away in his hand. He pulled off his shirt and tore it quickly into rough strips, then wrapped them around the chair leg. When he needed light, he would use it as a torch.

He stepped back into the corridor and started his slow pursuit of Heine, blowing out the flame every few feet and proceeding in darkness until he was unsure of the way, then lighting it once again for a brief moment to get his bearings.

With the revolver in his other hand he headed after Heine.

*

Imperceptibly the huge ship turned as the tide coaxed it southwards. The bow was drifting out towards the centre of the channel. The water here was deeper than at the edge, and so the tide was stronger. As the bow caught the faster tide, so it was pulled further and further out. Where previously the water under the keel was shallow, now it rapidly shelved downwards to seventy and eighty feet, and as more and more of the ship drifted into the deep channel, it started to slowly gain extra way.

To the north, off Greenbury Point, opposite Annapolis, the USS *Clark* had got its twin gas turbines running and was casting off from a mooring buoy. Captain Martin Colling nervously watched his young crew rushing to get the ship ready. This was his first command; he had been appointed yesterday and had never even sailed in the *Clark* before. What was making him even more nervous was that his orders had come from the CNO himself, Admiral Marshall, and had been communicated to him just three minutes ago by telephone. 'Sort that bastard out' seemed vague as an order, but judging from the tone of his voice the CNO meant it. Every word. Colling's hand was still shaking slightly.

*

Heine was working his way down a series of ladders. He kept the flashlight on now. He had left Bach far behind and he couldn't hear anyone following. The ladders were rusted and weak, and some of the treads bent and broke under his footsteps. He had descended six deck levels already and counted the landings one by one as he moved down deeper into the bowels of the ship. Fifty-five years ago, he and another man – what was his name, Ecke? – had been down here on exactly the same mission.

He knew what he was looking for. Somewhere in the bilges, on the bottom-most part of the ship, were two big valves, closed by wheels, that opened directly to the sea.

But Bach could hear Heine's distant footsteps, and the flashlight, although hidden round corners, shed a dim, eerie glow from far away that showed where Heine was going. He was trying to catch up, but the darkness meant that he needed to flick his lighter on every few steps to avoid falling over some obstruction. He followed the distant glow to the ladders and then, as quickly as he could, made his way down them. The old man was moving at a surprising speed.

The step treads ended, and now Bach could see Heine's flashlight wavering in the distance down the end of a long companionway. He couldn't use his lighter now in case he gave himself away. As he trod gingerly along the deck, he could feel water under his feet, and in some places the steel felt soft and spongy. The distant flashlight still wobbled as Heine continued on his mission.

Bach lifted the gun and aimed to one side of the light where he assumed the old man must be. But the aim was difficult; if he missed, he would just give himself away. He lowered the gun and carried quietly on.

Now Heine had reached the valves. There was a pair of them, about two yards apart, straddling the centre line of the ship. The casings were still unrusted, cast from manganese bronze, but the hand-wheels were red and crusty with corrosion.

Heine had to put the flashlight down somewhere. He needed the light, but with one arm still almost useless he also needed his hands free. He looked around and saw some drums standing twenty feet away. Heine positioned the flashlight on top of the drums so that it pointed at the valves and then set to work.

He gripped a wheel with his good hand and pushed as hard as he could. The wheel creaked, gave a millimetre and then stuck fast. It had sat in the Arctic for fifty-five years and was not going to move with just a gentle heave, even though De Wit's crew had secretly closed them just weeks back. It needed something better; something stuck between the spokes that would provide leverage. Heine started looking around.

In the distance, Bach had gained on the light, which was now thirty, perhaps forty feet away. And after waving around, it was now still. Heine must be resting. There was the light; the old man was to one side of it. His injured arm was his left, so he was probably holding the light in the right hand. Bach carefully lined up the gun to the left of the light.

Christian Bach could drop a deer at over 100 yards with a rifle, nine times out of ten. This was no problem. He squeezed the trigger. The noise of the gun in the cavernous bilges was strangely muted, but the echo repeated the shot seven or eight times. The flashlight hurtled into the air and tumbled to the deck with a muffled splash. It landed in the deep pool of stagnant water and instantly went out.

Bach smiled to himself. Got the bastard! Maybe they'd never find him down here, but at least he was probably no longer alive to tell the tale. It didn't matter if he'd killed him or not. Heine would die soon enough. Now it was time to get out.

He flicked the Zippo and set light to the torch of rags wrapped round the chair-leg. The material smouldered and burned badly, but it provided just enough light to see by as Bach started retracing his way back through the pools of water on the deck. The place looked different with the dim light and going in the opposite direction as he made his way hesitantly back to where he thought the ladder steps were.

Heine had found his lever – a length of thick steel rod that had lain neglected on the deck – when Bach's shot rang out and knocked over the empty drum, spilling the flashlight to the floor. He crouched, silently, while he watched Bach's distant lighter flicker with a blue flame and then smelt the tang of burning fabric as he lit his makeshift torch. Heine watched the dim light slowly make its way back towards the steps they had both come down.

Bach must have thought he had shot him. Very well. He could continue with his task. Even though it was dark, Heine knew where he was. The dark was so deep that he could almost see the valve and its wheel clearly, his imagination not distracted by any reality. Silently he wedged the lever into the wheel and started pulling and pushing, back and forth, trying to free the rusted wheel and valve mechanism.

It seemed as though it was welded into place. He pushed and pulled with his one good arm until the muscles in his shoulder felt as though they would split. His hand was burning with the friction. He paused for a moment, swore silently but violently, thought again about the gold, took a deep breath and heaved on the lever.

This time the wheel moved. It groaned, and in the darkness it sounded like a scream. Heine froze and waited, but there was no reaction from Bach. He pushed again and the wheel moved, stiffly at first but easier and silently now. He followed the wheel round and after one full turn he could hear the water gurgling through. He made another circle. The gurgle was a flow now, then after two more turns it was gushing into the bilge. The water was curiously warm, much warmer than the clamminess inside the ship, and as it lapped at his ankles it felt quite pleasant.

The next valve was just a few feet away. In the darkness he managed to find it, and started to repeat the operation. In the distance the dim, dark red light suddenly stopped.

Bach had heard the water but assumed, at first, that it was just the water outside the hull. Then it grew louder and louder. He looked back but saw nothing. It didn't matter. It was time to go. But where were those damn ladder steps, for God's sake? The light from his torch illuminated only the few feet in front of him. As he looked down, the red light was reflected in water. It seemed to be getting deeper.

The darkness was beginning to feel oppressive. It folded around him like thick curtains. Where *were* the steps? He was no longer absolutely sure that he was even going in the right direction. And where was that water coming from? He started to hurry now. A sense of panic began to rise. The steps – they were surely over this way … and suddenly, with a shock that cascaded like molten iron in his stomach, he realised that the water really was rising. He had been slopping in it before. Now he was paddling, and it was up to his ankles.

Heine, holding on to the valve, kept his bearings. He watched with grim amusement as the dim light started to move to one side instead of moving away. Bach didn't know the ship; he was getting lost.

But Otto Heine was no stranger to the ship, even if

Bach was. The sea was now flowing in and, although it was impenetrably black, Heine made his way forward, feeling a line of rivets on the deck, through the rising water, as a guide to keep him straight. He knew there was another set of steps about fifty feet away, and he was making his way confidently towards them.

The seawater gushing through the open valves was roaring in at the rate of thousands of gallons a minute. The valves had been designed to let in as much water, as quickly as possible, in the event of the ship needing to be scuttled. The designer had done his job well. Nearly a foot of water now covered the rusting bilge plating.

The panic in Christian Bach was rising just as fast. He was beginning to wade now. There was nothing around him, nothing that he could see. No ladders, no walls, just an endless darkness and the rising water. The light from his torch reached out into the gloom but found nothing other than the water to reflect from. He was alone in a giant cavern.

He started to take smaller steps; he wanted to run, but he was afraid of what was in front of him. Perhaps he should turn? He started back on himself, managed two steps and then tripped on a welded seam on the plating. He crashed into the water, and the torch guttered out. As he pushed himself to his hands and knees, the sound of rushing water was getting stronger. There was a hole in the ship. He was sinking in the darkness!

Heine had reached the steps and was already out of the water when he heard the distant splash and Bach's muttered swearing. The light had disappeared.

'Bach, can you hear me?' he asked softly.

A long pause. 'Heine?'

'Yes. It's me, Otto Heine. I'm going now, Christian Bach. This ship killed your grandfather, which was sad, and now it will kill you. Say your prayers, Bach. Say your prayers.'

'Fuck you, Heine. Where are you?' came the distant, frightened voice. It boomed in the darkness.

'Going, Bach. I'm the last voice you'll hear. If there is a heaven and you see your grandfather, tell him one thing,' shouted Heine.

'You can't leave me!' Bach shouted back.

'Tell him this, Christian. Tell him that you managed to do the one thing that he never achieved – or the rest of the whole German Navy put together. You shelled Washington. He has at least one thing to be pleased with in his grandson.'

'For God's sake, Heine,' and now Bach's voice was rising into a scream. But Heine was gone, pulling himself up the steps.

Bach got to his feet. Where was his lighter? He fumbled in his pocket and found it, opened it and flicked the wheel desperately. But it was too wet. The water was reaching his knees.

'Heine? *Heine?*'

Otto Heine could hear the shouting as he moved steadily up the ladder, and it receded into the distance. Then there was a loud crack. Moments later the ship started to lean to one side. One of the bottom plates, almost rotten, had finally collapsed under the inrushing water, and millions more gallons of water began to flow in through the gash, making the great battleship start to list as it drifted southwards.

A wall of water hit Bach. He surfaced and struck out, flailing with his arms and trying to swim, but the rush of water pushed him back and he turned over and over in it. The darkness was forgotten now. There was no air. He couldn't breathe. He thrashed the water with his arms and his legs, but the air wasn't there.

And suddenly there was silence. The darkness lifted. A bright light and a pleasant warmth surrounded Christian Bach. He stopped feeling frightened. He smiled to himself and leaned back in the water, relaxed now, letting the drift take him where it would.

*

Colling, on board USS *Clark*, was powering at twenty-six knots towards the flashing white and red light of Thomas Point Shoal, hoping to God almighty that if there were any fishing boats out there they would have the sense to get out of his way, because sure as hell he wouldn't be able to see them and avoid them even if he had one of his men watching the close-range radar like a hawk. His mission, direct from the CNO, was still ringing in his ears, and the orange blob of the *Hindenburg*, drifting at three knots in the tide, was showing on the screen at just a mile and a half away.

Catching it would not be a problem. What he was going to do about it, it seemed to Martin Colling, was an altogether different matter.

'Searchlights. Everything on,' he ordered.

'Searchlights aye,' called a voice from the back of the small and crowded bridge. In quick succession, pencils of yellow lights poked into the darkness towards the flashing navigation lights of the four helicopters that were keeping pace with the ship. They wobbled for a second or two and found the grey colossus out in the channel, more or less beam-on to the tide, 823 feet of rusting steel drifting implacably down the bay.

Colling had an open line to the CNO in the White House already established.

'Visual, sir,' he reported, nervously.

'How close, Colling?' Marshall demanded.

'Mile and closing fast.'

'Right. We're taking the marines off now. Wait until the choppers are clear. Then shoot.'

'I beg your pardon, sir?'

'Shoot, Colling. Sink the thing. We must stop whoever is on that ship, and we have to stop the ship before it starts wrecking half of Chesapeake. You understand? What have you got on that ship of yours?'

'Harpoons, sir. And torpedoes. And a seventy-six millimetre and a Vulcan.'

'Get the missiles ready, Colling. They'll stop her.'

'Yes, sir,' replied Colling, and ordered the crews to get the Harpoon missiles ready. The covers were stripped off and the fire control systems started to acquire the target, which was not difficult. Colling ordered his engines to idle. He was near enough to be able to throw the missiles at the huge battleship if he wanted to.

The helicopters were moving away now, apart from one, which looked as though it was hovering over the aft deck, but then it too started to climb and leave the ship behind. Now the vessel was clear, and with the *Clark* almost stopped the range was well over a mile now.

'Fire control ready, sir.'

'Thank you,' replied Colling calmly. He'd trained for this a hundred times. 'Fire!' he ordered.

A moment later the missile launcher on the foredeck burst into light and a Harpoon streaked from it, racing like tracer toward the floodlit *Hindenburg*. It took three seconds to cover the distance. There was a brilliant flash as the missile struck the side of the ship and then the explosion, crackling, rolled over the water. It was a direct hit, about a dozen feet above the waterline.

The smoke drifted away. Colling picked up his glasses and looked for the damage.

'Motherfucker!' he exclaimed.

There was a black stain on the side of the ship, but no other sign of damage. The solid armour-plated sides, bolted to the ship in the Hamburg yards half a century ago, were thick enough to keep out 15-inch shells. High-explosive missiles had little impact on the armour belt.

'Fire control, make ready,' he ordered. He'd fire every Harpoon he had if he needed to. The CNO was waiting.

*

The bilges of the huge ship were now filled with thousands of tons of water, and the vessel began to sit deeper in the channel. The tide continued to drag her along. Most of the water was collecting towards the after end of the *Hindenburg*, and the rudder was starting to scrape along the mud in the shallower edges of the channel. This began to drag the aft end of the ship around; the bow was still being pulled by the tide. The combination of forces acting on a ship weakened by age, by rust, and by being dragged half-way across the Atlantic Ocean, was enough. The bottom plating, already strained, started to rip apart. The warm waters of Chesapeake Bay now flooded into the ship. The rudder stuck in the mud and the stern sections began to bed themselves in as well. The huge ship stopped, paused for a second and then decided it had had enough.

*

'Wait,' ordered Colling, as the fire control officer reported the Harpoon ready. 'Look at that,' he said.

On the bridge, the eight officers gathered and watched the awesome sight.

The *Hindenburg* was giving up of her own accord. The bow had swung round, but now the ship was listing, slowly at first but gathering pace. It was rolling away from Colling, the high superstructure tipping over towards the water as the bottom of the ship rolled upwards.

The roll gathered momentum. Like a huge whale lazily turning to sun itself, the ship showed more and more of its ripped and torn belly, streaked with rust and weed, shining in the glare of the searchlights. It paused for a moment, leaning at forty-five degrees, waited, and then tipped over into the water in its last dying gasp before coming to rest on its side, its days finally done.

A great wave, six feet high, was spreading out from the stricken ship. It hit the *Clark* on the bow and the frigate jerked upwards. The men on the bridge had been silent, watching the massive battleship in its death throes. Now they suddenly seemed to wake up. A tinny voice was yelling from the handset. Colling picked it up.

'Damn it, Colling, what the hell's happened?' demanded Marshall.

'Mission completed, sir. The *Hindenburg*'s finished.'

'Well done, Colling,' said Marshall, enthusiastically.

But Colling didn't say a word.

EPILOGUE

KENT ISLAND,
EASTERN CHESAPEAKE BAY

The low and wooded shoreline was silent and dark. To the north, out over the water, lights were blazing and helicopters thumping. The noise was muted by the distance and by the emptiness.

Driftwood, lengths of old coloured rope, cans and plastic bottles and tangles of nylon netting bobbed in the scum at the very edge of the water as it crept slowly up over the black mud that lined the bay.

The old man was breathing slowly, lying on his stomach, his face turned to one side so that his mouth was just clear of the water. The air was cool and a gentle breeze moved the overhanging branches into a rustling shiver. He was still gripping the length of wood that had supported him as the current drifted him down from the middle of the bay and deposited him gently at the water's edge.

He lay there for another ten minutes and then, carefully, supporting himself on one arm, he pushed himself painfully to a kneeling position and looked around. A yard away, on the water itself, a plump orange mass was slowly twisting around in the breeze. He slowly lifted his legs. The mud was sticky but firm enough, and he finally got to standing position. Water streamed from his clothing. He paused to gain breath and then, taking slow and careful steps, he reached the plump parcel and took hold of it with one hand. His other arm lay motionless at his side.

He dragged the parcel from the water and pulled it on to the mud. It was heavy, and left a trough as he dragged it inch by inch across the flats. He was struggling, and it took a full five minutes before he reached the firmer ground above the waterline.

Well inside the trees now, he sat down with a sigh and slowly untied the parcel. Carefully, one by one, he unwrapped the small, fat shells from the flotation suit and laid them down on the grass. He sat there looking at them, a hunched and lonely figure in the darkness.

Otto Heine had finally brought his treasure home.

THE IRON MAN

John Watson

The *Stalin*: the largest, fastest and most heavily armed
battleship in the world is making its maiden voyage – half a
century after it was built.

Why?

The men who have requisitioned it know why – but they're
not telling the crew. Captain Yakov Zof thinks he knows
why. Like many others betrayed by the collapse of the
Soviet Union, he is turning, against his will, to crime.

Two defenceless ships in the Pacific soon know why.

Then the alarm bells start ringing in the nerve centres of
Britain and America. The *Stalin* is not just committing the
most audacious act of piracy ever seen on the high seas.
It is embarking on something altogether more sinister.
Something that will test the might of their high-tech
weaponry, will pit sophistication against sheer brute force
– and lead to the last great battle between the dinosaurs
of the sea . . .

ISBN 0 7515 2147 7

REQUIEM FOR A
GLASS HEART

David Lindsey

Irina Ismaylov kills men and women and she kills at the
behest of Sergei Krupatin, the Russian crime lord who
exerts a monstrous hold over her.

FBI special agent Cate Cuevas, still in mourning, has just
learned of a devastating betrayal by her slain husband.
Wounded and shaken, she is plunged into the most
dangerous assignment of her career. The leaders of three
great international crime organisations are to meet in
Houston. The implications are stunning, and horrendous.
But the FBI has a chance to stop this unholy alliance, if
Cate Cuevas can infiltrate the Russian contingent – and if
she can get out alive.

When Cate and Irina meet, they are drawn to each other
strangely and powerfully. And as Cate and Irina fight to
survive amidst the intricate and deadly stratagems of men
of violence, their relationship becomes an ever-more-
intimate dance of sexual attraction and murderous intent.

'No recent thriller has so clearly pointed up that in
criminal and law enforcement hierarchies, a woman is still
expected to do her most useful work in bed – a profoundly
affecting portrait'
Publishers Weekly

ISBN 0 7515 1852 2

STATE OF MIND

John Katzenbach

A pulse-pounding ride of non-stop action and
psychological suspense . . .

A professor of abnormal psychology, Jeffrey Clayton
struggles with a dark past. Twenty-five years before, Jeffrey
and his mother and sister fled his tyrannical father – a man
who was later suspected in the heinous murder of a young
student. Though never charged, he committed suicide. Or
so it seemed. Jeffrey's mother and his sister, Susan, have
since concealed themselves in the remote tangled swamps
of Florida's Upper Keys. But someone has sent Susan a
cryptic note that carries a terrifying message: I have
found you.

'Katzenbach has a sure way with suspense and there are
moments of genuine horror'
Crime Time

'Smart, American serial killer thriller, dedicated to the
atmosphere of pursuit and fear . . . This is Thomas Harris
land, Stephen King country'
New Law Journal

'Very clever with real characters and an excellent plot'
Publishing News

ISBN 0 7515 2319 4

FINAL JEOPARDY

Linda Fairstein

'An authoritative and scary view from one who has battled
evil and locked it away'
Patricia Cornwell

The days of Assistant D.A. Alexandra Cooper often start
off badly, but she's never faced the morning by reading her
own obituary before.

It doesn't take long to sort out why it was printed: a
woman's body with her face blown away, left in a car
rented in Coop's name in the driveway of her weekend
home. But it isn't so easy to work out why her lodger – an
acclaimed Hollywood star – was murdered, or to be sure
that the killer had found the right victim.

As Coop's job is to send rapists to jail there are plenty of
suspects who might be seeking revenge, and whoever it is
needs to be found before her obituary gets reprinted.

'Has the impact of early Cornwell'
Time Out

'Gripping'
Sunday Express

'*Final Jeopardy* has it in spades ... engaging characters, an
intelligent story full of twists'
Marcel Berlins

ISBN 0 7515 1502 7

Other bestselling Warner titles available by mail: